3

MW00380804

WASTES

TEARS

THE NORTHERN
GRASSLANDS

*URGHUD

BLACK RIVER

THE SWEET
SEA

DRAGON'S
BEARD

THE
WATER ROAD

THE BAY of
DRAGONS

THE INFINITE

*THE IMPERIAL CITY

RIVER

THE AZURE STRAIT

THE AZURE ISLES

THE AZURE SEA

JINGXI

KASONG *

MOUNT ZANHEI

•CHANGXI

ZANHEI*

SISTERS

THE
MORNING
REALMS

THE EAGLE
of THE NORTH

THE DRAGON
of THE EAST

THE UNICORN
of THE WEST

THE LION
of THE SOUTH

Guardians of Dawn

ZHARA

ALSO BY
S. JAE-JONES

Wintersong

Shadowsong

GUARDIANS OF DAWN

ZHARA

S. JAE-JONES

WEDNESDAY BOOKS
NEW YORK

First published in the United States by Wednesday Books,
an imprint of St. Martin's Publishing Group

GUARDIANS OF DAWN: ZHARA. Copyright © 2023 by S. Jae-Jones.
All rights reserved. Printed in the United States of America.
For information, address St. Martin's Publishing Group,
120 Broadway, New York, NY 10271.

www.wednesdaybooks.com

Designed by Devan Norman
Endpaper map illustration by Rhys Davies
Sunburst illustrations © Diana Kovach / Shutterstock.com

The Library of Congress Cataloging-in-Publication Data
is available upon request.

ISBN 978-1-250-19142-7 (hardcover)
ISBN 978-1-250-19144-1 (ebook)

Our books may be purchased in bulk for promotional, educational, or
business use. Please contact your local bookseller or
the Macmillan Corporate and Premium Sales Department at
1-800-221-7945, extension 5442, or by email at
MacmillanSpecialMarkets@macmillan.com.

First Edition: 2023

10 9 8 7 6 5 4 3 2 1

FOR ALL THE BESTIES WHO
READ FANFICTION PRINTOUTS
IN THE BATHTUB INSTEAD OF
DOING THEIR MATH HOMEWORK

A NOTE ON THE USE OF LANGUAGE IN
GUARDIANS OF DAWN: ZHARA

When I first published *Wintersong,* I had a reader ask me why I had chosen to set my debut novel in eighteenth-century Bavaria instead of an Asian country. Back then, I had a glib answer for everything, and I believe I said something to the effect that I wouldn't have written about classical music if it hadn't been for my Asian mother putting me through piano lessons when I was four. Yet the true answer to this reader's question was that I hadn't yet developed the skills to navigate how to convey cultural norms in English—and to a Western audience—without resorting to clunky exposition or alienating a reader unfamiliar with Asian social context or philosophy. There is always a fine line to walk between letting my audience figure things out for themselves and holding their hands, and I elected for the former in *Guardians of Dawn: Zhara.*

When writing a fantasy world not inspired by a Western country, I always run into the problem of translation. Do I use the word *hanfu* or *hanbok* or *kimono,* or elect to use *robe* instead? Would a word like *boudoir* make sense when the idea of the French language doesn't even exist? The land of the Morning Realms is inspired by East Asia, and while there is no one-to-one direct correlation between existing cultures and languages, the one thing I tried to carry over from languages like Chinese and Korean was the fact that there is no gendered third-person pronoun. As such, all characters are referred to with the ungendered third-person pronoun "they" until they explicitly gender themselves.

The use of pronouns like "she" and "he" thereafter are merely used for clarification. Similarly, I tried to preserve levels of formality in speech by avoiding the use of the second-person pronoun "you" until the character is granted explicit permission to address someone directly.

In the end, I made choices with the text and I stand by them. As a child of the Korean diaspora, I am constantly navigating what I know, what I should know, what I think I know, and what I think I should know when it comes to exploring and writing about my cultural roots. If my choices are lost in translation, then I hope you'll grant me a little grace and understanding.

Summer, fall, winter, spring

Guardians rise and justice sings

When Tiyok stirs to life again

Darkness falls and chaos reigns

Fire, wood, wind, and water

Join together to prevent a slaughter

Summer, fall, winter, spring

Guardians rise and justice sings

—TRADITIONAL CHILDREN'S SONG
IN THE MORNING REALMS

PART ONE

THE THOUSAND—CHARACTER CLASSIC

And in the 2,647th year of the Mugung Dynasty, the emperor—being afflicted by magic—was cursed by the Immortals and transformed into an abomination. The Gommun Kang, known throughout the Morning Realms as the Warlord, rode down from the north with his Golden Horde and put all magicians—suspected and otherwise—to the sword in order to rid the land of a blight. The tools of the magician were also put to the pyre— the brush, the inkstone, and the seal—and any citizen with knowledge of the Language of Flowers was burned alongside the books of magic. Every year thereafter, the Gommun Emperor decreed there be a purge of every city, every town, every village, and every province, so that the embers of magic might never again grow into the wildfire of abomination.

—From *Annals of the Great Bear*

1

THE RENT WAS DUE, RODENTS HAD GOTTEN into the rice, and Zhara had just dumped a bag of salt into the custard filling.

"Mother of Demons!" she swore, trying in vain to scoop the excess out of the mixing bowl with her fingers. Bits of beaten egg and flour spattered an open book propped up on the counter and Zhara yelped, frantically wiping at the mess with her sleeve. "No, no, no, no, no, no," she moaned, dabbing at the stains. "Master Cao is going to kill me."

On the pantry shelves above her, a small, scruffy ginger cat gave an amused snort from his perch.

"Hush, Sajah," Zhara said irritably, struggling to get the page to lie flat. Over the years, the little bookseller down in the Pits had allowed Zhara to borrow as many titles from him as she liked, providing she returned them all in perfect condition. "*The Maiden Who Was Loved by Death*," she said mournfully, smoothing down the cover. "And the next volume comes out today."

The Maiden Who Was Loved by Death was the most popular romance serial in the Morning Realms—so popular that Master Cao and his scriveners could scarcely keep up with demand each time an installment was released. There were only so many copies a person could write out by hand, so each little paperback volume was worth a premium. One Zhara could not afford.

Prrrrt, said the cat, the tiny bell about his neck jingling as he jumped from his perch to nose at the coin purse tied at her waist.

"I know, I know." Zhara weighed the purse in her palm. Their coffers were rather empty of late, with every spare coin going to the astrologer, the aesthetician, the dressmaker, and the matchmaker in the hopes of securing a good marriage for her little sister, Suzhan. Nearly all the wages Zhara earned as an apothecary's assistant disappeared into their ever-growing pile of debts, but every month she managed to save a few coins for herself and her small but growing collection of secondhand romance novels. Just enough for a harmless little treat every now and again.

Not enough to make her stepmother suspicious.

Zhara counted the coins, glancing at her threadbare slippers beside the kitchen threshold. She desperately needed a new pair, but she figured she could fix the stitching herself and pay Master Cao back. A new book cost more than two pairs of shoes from the cobbler down by the docks. Reading was a luxury, and one she could not often afford.

Miaow, Sajah said, batting at the bowl of salted custard filling.

"Blast." Zhara winced. "The custard buns." She had hoped she could tempt Suzhan into eating something—anything—before meeting her future husband at the matchmaker's later that morning. Nerves dwindled her sister's appetite to nothing, and Suzhan needed all the strength she could get.

They needed all the strength Suzhan could get.

"Maybe it's salvageable." Zhara dipped a finger into the mixture for a quick taste. She gagged. "Never mind." She choked.

Niang, said the cat, primly washing his whiskers.

Zhara cast a desperate eye over the paltry contents of their pantry. It was too early for the shops to open, and all they had left were two shriveled onions, a bunch of dried hot peppers, a vase of cooking oil, a jar of fermented black-bean paste, and a leaking crock of soy sauce. While Zhara was well acquainted with the alchemy of stretching one meal into two or three or five, even her creativity had limits. "I can work magic," she muttered. "Not miracles. Although . . ." She trailed off, looking to the wooden plaque on the wall above the stove. It bore the name *Jin Zhanlong.*

Miaow, Sajah cautioned.

A faint glow glimmered where Zhara's skin met the smooth curve of the bowl. She could hear her father's warning voice at the back of her mind. *Be good, little magpie girl. Be good, and be true.*

"Small magic, baba," she said to Jin Zhanlong's death tablet. "Too small to be of any notice."

Miaow, Sajah said again, but Zhara ignored him, closing her eyes and finding the light inside. She had always imagined her magic as a steady flame within her, and the world around her as her kitchen. Elements were ingredients to be played with, like dough beneath her fingers. Zhara held her breath and concentrated, applying her magic to the mixture in her hands like heat to a pot of water.

A sudden, bright burst of light nearly startled her into dropping the bowl, but Zhara managed to catch it and set it gently on the counter. Dipping her finger into the mixture once more, she took a tentative lick.

Sweet.

"Well," she murmured with a satisfied smile. "Maybe I can work a little miracle every once in a while."

The cat sniffed.

"Yah," Zhara protested. "Considering I have no idea how magic even works, I think that was pretty impressive." She finished making the custard buns, tempering the beaten eggs, milk, sugar, and rice starch over the stove. "Like cooking without a recipe!"

There had been recipes—spell books—in the Morning Realms once, but they—like her father, like every other magician in the land— had been destroyed in the purges following the Just War. It was not only rare to be a magician; it was dangerous. Not only because someone might turn her over to the Falconer for treason, but because of the harm she could accidentally cause with her power.

Had accidentally caused.

Once the custard had thickened, Zhara took the pot off the heat and reached for the ball of dough she had set aside earlier, dividing it into palm-sized balls and rolling them out into thin discs. Sajah butted her arm with his head, purring suggestively.

"Not for you," she said, adding a dollop of custard in the center of each disc. "We can barely feed ourselves, let alone a stray."

The cat scowled and gave a spiteful swipe at her knuckles.

"Aiyo!" she hissed. With a deft twist of her fingers, Zhara sealed the buns shut and set them in a steamer basket. "At least *you* have somewhere else to go." Cats were sacred to Zanhei's guardian beast, the Lion of the South, and it was unlucky to turn one away. "Unlike the rest of us," she said quietly, studying her father's death tablet.

"Sajah's not a stray, nene," said a voice behind her. "He's part of the family."

Zhara turned to find her stepsister standing at the kitchen threshold. "Suzhan!" she said, leaping forward to take the girl's hand. "I didn't hear you come down."

"I left my cane upstairs," Suzhan said wryly. "I didn't want to wake Mama with the tapping." Her eyes wavered. "You know how she gets after a late night at the tavern."

Zhara did know. The two of them had woken up with the bruises to show for it often enough. "You're up early, mimi," she said instead, fetching the low stool from the corner and setting it down before her sister. "Dawn's not for an hour yet."

"Couldn't sleep. Too nervous." Suzhan felt for the seat and missed, knocking over the stack of paperbacks by Zhara's bedside. "What's this?"

"N-nothing," Zhara said quickly, shoving the books beneath her pallet. "Just some notes for Teacher Hu."

Her sister gave a little smirk as she settled onto the stool. "You mean *The Girl Whose Lover Died*, nene?"

"*The Maiden Who Was Loved by Death*," Zhara corrected, a trifle defensively. "I mean," she said, panicking a little, "I d-don't know what you're t-talking about."

Suzhan laughed. "You're a terrible liar," she said. "Your tongue betrays you whenever you try."

A flush of shame heated Zhara's cheeks. "Don't tell Madame," she said, stacking the books back into a neat little pile. "Please."

Suzhan looked hurt. "I wouldn't tell Mama," she said. "You know I wouldn't."

Zhara's gaze fell to the constellation of fading welts on her sister's calves and shins, twins to the welts on her own legs. "I know," she said softly, but secrets were hard to keep in the face of the Second Wife's capricious cruelty. Zhara cleared her throat and opened the steamer basket to check on the custard buns. "Anyway," she said, "I've made breakfast. Are you hungry?"

Suzhan shook her head. "I'm not sure I can eat anything," she said, rubbing her hands over her belly. "My stomach's all tangled up in knots."

"You should try to have a bite anyway," Zhara urged. "Bad luck starting a new venture on an empty stomach, lah?"

"True." Suzhan wrapped her arms tighter about her middle. "It's just that I can't stop thinking about what would happen if Lord Chan decides not to go through with the marriage."

Several other offers for Suzhan's hand had fallen through before. "I'm sure it will be fine," Zhara said with a confidence she did not quite feel.

"Will it?" Suzhan raised her gaze to her sister's face, pupils flickering across Zhara's features as though trying to find purchase. "What if Lord Chan meets me and decides I'm"—she gestured toward her eyes—"damaged goods?"

Shame swept over Zhara like wildfire. Her little sister had always been nearsighted, but no spectacles—no matter how strong—could improve the dimness of her vision. Not anymore. Not after what Zhara had done. Magic lit her hands with a faint glow, as though the memory of her mistake still lingered in her skin. "Th-that's not your fault, mimi," she said, hiding her hands behind her back. "You're not flawed."

Suzhan's lips thinned. "That's not what the others said."

Even though her sister couldn't see her expression, Zhara still looked away. "Lord Chan knows about your blindness and still wishes to marry you," she said quietly, taking the steamer basket off the heat and setting the buns on a plate to cool. "Surely you can take comfort in that."

"Can I?" Suzhan nervously picked at her lower lip, her eyes twitching back and forth even faster than before. "What sort of man settles for a girl like me, especially a man so rich and powerful?"

Zhara cringed, hearing the echo of her stepmother's acid judgment in her sister's tone. "A good man," she said, wanting her words to be true. "A kind man."

"Do you truly believe that?" Suzhan sounded skeptical.

"Of course I do." Zhara brought the plate of custard buns to her sister. "Here, mimi. Your favorite."

Suzhan sniffed appreciatively. "Ooh, nene," she said, face brightening. "Custard buns?"

"Yes." Zhara smiled. "Eat up."

Her sister needed no further encouragement. Suzhan picked up the first bun and took an enormous bite, closing her eyes to savor the taste before immediately devouring the rest. The first was gone in three bites, and the next disappeared even faster. "These are amazing," she said through squirrel cheeks.

It warmed Zhara's heart to watch her sister eat with such gusto. "Slow down, mimi," she laughed. "You'll give yourself the hiccoughs."

Suzhan paused halfway through chewing. "Oh," she said, swallowing and setting down her half-eaten custard bun. "Maybe I shouldn't finish them then."

"What?" Zhara was startled. "Why?"

Suzhan hunched her shoulders. "Mama says I should be mindful of what I eat," she said, her voice scarcely audible. "No man wants an oafish giant of a wife."

Sudden, sweeping indignation stoked the furnace at Zhara's core. "You are neither oafish nor a giant," she said fiercely. If anything, her sister was far too thin, her bony wrists and ankles on painful display beneath the hems of her too-short clothes. At thirteen, Suzhan was growing faster than a bamboo shoot during monsoon season and suffered terribly from both muscle and hunger pangs. "You're just tall, mimi," she said.

"Yes, well." Suzhan picked at her lip again. "She also says no man wants to marry a girl twice his height."

"Bog rubbish," Zhara scoffed. "Madame is tall and she's been married. Twice."

"Yes, but Mama is beautiful," Suzhan said glumly. "And I'm— well, I'm not." As the plain daughter of a pretty mother, Suzhan was painfully and acutely aware of her less than perfect appearance. The Second Wife had once been considered one of the Five Great Southern

Beauties in her youth, praised by painters and poets alike for the symmetry of her face.

Zhara took in several deep breaths to calm the rage—the magic—within her. Her palms itched with power, and the desire to just *do* something with her gift was overwhelming. What was the point in having magical abilities if she could do nothing to help those she loved? Then she remembered the last time she had tried to help Suzhan with her power. It had not turned out well.

"Yah," Suzhan said suddenly, squinting in Zhara's direction. "What's that light over there?"

Looking down, Zhara saw that her hands were bathed in a rosy luminescence. That light—that glow—was one of the few signs of her magic she could not hide. "Oh," she said, tucking them into her apron. "Probably the rising sun. I should probably get to work soon."

"But the drums haven't sounded the daybreak hour yet." Suzhan frowned, her unfocused eyes fixed on the muffled glimmer in Zhara's pocket. "Are you sure?"

"I'm sure." Sweat broke out along Zhara's hairline, although the late-spring morning was still pleasant and cool. "Eat up, mimi," she said, pressing a custard bun against her sister's lips. "I've got to go."

"But I—aiyo!" Suzhan snapped her head back in surprise. A glowing red mark lingered on the edge of her bottom lip, almost like a burn, where Zhara's fingers had brushed her skin. "Something stung me!"

For one heart-stopping moment, Zhara thought she had done it again, that she had somehow hurt her sister, but the burn on Suzhan's lip soon faded away. "Oh," she said, hastily setting the custard bun back on the plate. That sting—her magic touch—was the other sign she could not hide. "M-maybe you should w-wait until the others cool before eating the rest."

Her sister narrowed her eyes. "Your tongue betrays you again, nene. Is something the matter?"

Just then, a persistent drumming sounded from the city watchtowers, signaling the daybreak hour. "I'm s-sorry, mimi," she said hurriedly. "I h-have to go. You'll be all right getting upstairs on your own?"

"Yes." Suzhan tilted her head. "Are you sure you're all right?"

"Of course," she said, wrangling her words into obedience. "I'll see you tonight, lah?" Zhara stuffed her copy of *The Maiden Who Was Loved by Death* into her work satchel and slung it over her shoulder. "Good luck, mimi. Eat up."

She could feel her sister's worried, unseeing gaze on her back as she hurried across the courtyard. "There aren't enough custard buns in the world for all the luck *we'll* need," Suzhan murmured. "Is there, Sajah?"

The cat did not reply.

Zhara was practically to the courtyard gate when the sharp, nearly acrid tang of cheap osmanthus perfume assailed her nose.

"Child," came a disembodied voice from the corner. "A moment, if you please."

Whirling around, she caught sight of the Second Wife lounging beneath the wisteria tree, an elegant but threadbare robe draped about her willowy frame. Zhara's stepmother was never awake at this hour; like the night-blooming cereus, the Second Wife was withered and wilted by dawn, having come into her full brilliance the evening before in the taverns and teahouses of Zanhei City. Fear suddenly drenched Zhara's body with cold dread.

"Of c-course, M-madame," she said with a bow, clutching her satchel to her chest. "How m-may I best s-serve Madame?"

The Second Wife leaned against the courtyard wall, arms crossed, expression unreadable. "I don't want anything from you," she said. The reek of stale rice wine lingered in the early-morning haze. "I'm here to issue a warning."

"A w-warning?"

The Second Wife drew close, studying her stepdaughter's appearance with narrowed eyes. At this distance, Zhara could see her stepmother's bloodshot gaze and the vessels about her nose and cheeks, bursting in a drunkard's flush. "Beware," the Second Wife said, blowing a boozy breath in Zhara's face, "they say that Kestrels have flocked to Zanhei."

An entirely different sort of terror washed over her. "The W-w-warlord's peacek-k-keepers?" she asked. In an instant Zhara was ten years old again, hiding at the bottom of her stepmother's clothes chest while the Kestrels dragged her father away. "Wh-why?"

It was a long moment before the Second Wife replied. "There are rumors," she said quietly, "of monsters in the marsh."

"Monsters?"

Her stepmother's expression hardened, etching lines of age and worry deeper into her face. "Abominations."

Zhara went still. She had been but a baby when the Just War began, but she was old enough to remember the stories of magicians transforming into monsters—hideous, uncanny, unnatural creatures that scarred the mind and devoured the flesh. Old enough to remember the slurs that had trailed her parents as they fled from town to town, two steps ahead of the Warlord's horde. Magicians were an affront to reason. Anathemas. Abominations. Bile rose in Zhara's mouth, bitter like ghosts at the back of her throat.

"A Kestrel's eyes are sharp," the Second Wife said softly, lightly tapping the back of Zhara's wrist with her fan. The telltale glow of magic was still visible in the early morning light. "So be careful."

She had taken much harsher strikes to the wrist before, yet an unexpected prickle of tears stung Zhara's lashes at the uncharacteristic concern in her stepmother's voice.

"I will, Madame," she breathed, pulling her sleeves down over her hands.

The Second Wife flicked open her fan and waved it desultorily before her face. "It's a dangerous world out there, Jin Zhara," she said. "Remember what your father told you, lah?"

"Be good, and be true," Zhara whispered.

"Yes." Her stepmother smiled, but it was as warm as the winter sun. "Be good, lest you forget who has protected you all these years."

It was the Second Wife who had hidden Zhara from the Warlord's peacekeepers the day they took Jin Zhanlong away, tucking the little girl beneath layers and layers of robes and gowns until the danger had passed. Zhara's stepmother was the only one who knew of her magic, the only one who kept her secret, the only one who kept her safe.

"I will never forget," Zhara said with a bow. "I am indebted to Madame in more ways than one. My gratitude knows no bounds."

"Excellent." The Second Wife slapped the fan shut with a crisp *snap!* "Don't be late tonight," she said, tightening her robe about her slim figure. "I'm in the mood to celebrate my daughter's betrothal with something delicious for dinner. I'm thinking"—she pursed her full lips—"braised beef short ribs, Azurean style. What do you think, Jin Zhara?"

Zhara swallowed. "Beef is expensive, Madame," she said. "But would steamed pork spare ribs suffice?"

The Second Wife narrowed her eyes, her gaze flitting to the book poking out from Zhara's satchel. "If we must," she said coolly. "Although I must say I'm rather disappointed." The Second Wife's tone was neutral, neither cruel nor casual, and it was this state of uncertainty that made Zhara the most anxious.

"I—I will see what I can do," Zhara stammered. She thought of the mixture she had transformed from salty into sweet not even an hour before, and her magic flared in response. Her stepmother glanced down at her hands, and Zhara curled her fingers into fists to hide their light.

"There's a good girl." The Second Wife's eyes glittered. "I shall look forward to celebrating tonight. I do so enjoy your cooking, child."

Zhara cringed. "I t-try my b-best, Madame." She lowered her gaze and bowed.

For a long moment, the Second Wife said nothing, and Zhara could feel the stinging intensity of her stepmother's gaze on the back of her neck like a sunburn. The moment stretched taut between them, growing more unbearable by the instant before the tension was broken by the Second Wife yawning in exhaustion.

"Well, be off," she said dismissively, turning to head upstairs to her sleeping quarters. "I trust you won't let me down." The Second Wife paused and glanced over her shoulder. "After all, you are a good girl." Casual malice laced her words. "Aren't you, Jin Zhara?"

2

THE SKIES HAD ONLY JUST BEGUN TO thin from gray to pink, but Lotus Bridge was already crowded with foot traffic as Zhara made her way down from the city to the Pits. There was an unusually large number of people teeming about, and Zhara wondered if there wasn't some sort of festival going on. A significant population of peoples from beyond the Shining Sea lived in the marshy lowlands just outside Zanhei—Buri, Malang, Cham, Tuong—and all celebrated their own gods and holidays in the Morning Realms. She wouldn't be surprised if this festival was for one of their minor deities.

Officially, the name of the settlement across the Great Canal from the city was Zanhei Port, but for as long as anyone could remember, it had been called the Pits. Far older than the walled city across the water, the Pits had first been settled centuries before by traders and migrants from every corner of the empire and beyond. They brought their cuisines, clothes, and customs to the Infinite River delta and established the heart of trade in the southern provinces. At the center of the myriad waterways stood the Temple of the Immortals, surrounded on all sides by the oldest covered market in the empire, where both Master Cao's bookshop and Teacher Hu's apothecary were located.

"Hoi, miss!" shouted the shopkeepers and stevedores as she passed. "Stop and have a bite of breakfast with us!"

The tantalizing smells of sizzling red chiles, tarragon, garlic, red pepper, cumin, coriander, tamarind, fresh basil, and lemongrass filled the air as vendors set up their portable grills and braziers in their boats along the canals crisscrossing the covered market. Each floating restaurant boasted its own particular specialty—broad, flat egg noodles sautéed in black-bean sauce, steamed fish wrapped in banana leaves, crab and river shrimp stew served over rice—dishes from every culture.

"Another time," she called back regretfully. Today, as every other day, her pockets were as empty as her stomach.

Still, looking cost nothing. As she drew closer to the heart of the covered market, Zhara stopped before Master Cao's bookshop to stare longingly at the tables in front, stacked high with brand-new paper-backs. The latest volume of *The Maiden Who Was Loved by Death*. A large crowd was already gathered before the still-shuttered doors, and Zhara found herself jostled about by the press of pedestrians.

"Yah!" she yelped as a tall student in black-and-white university robes carelessly stepped on her shoe. Zhara felt the last of the stitching holding her soles together give way. So much for holding out on buying a new pair. "Watch where you're putting those enormous feet of yours, learned one."

The student turned and gave her an awkward, belated bow, tripping a little over said enormous feet. "Pardon, pardon, a thousand pardons." The reek of stale sweat and rice wine wafted from their robes, and Zhara wondered if they weren't a little drunk. University students of-ten came to the Pits to avail themselves of the many pleasures in Flower Town before stumbling back home by dawn. "I just didn't expect so many people to be at the bookshop today."

"Are you also here for *The Maiden Who Was Loved by Death*?" Zhara asked with some surprise. She didn't think university students were keen on light romance novels.

"The what?" The student's eyes kept darting to a pair of northerners several yards away, conspicuous in their knee-length woolen tunics and leather boots, which were too heavy for the humid southern spring.

"*The Maiden Who* . . ." Zhara trailed off when the student met her gaze, suddenly struck by how good-looking they were. Chiseled cheeks and pouting lips were framed by an angular jaw, while large, round, puppyish eyes were anchored by a strong nose ever so slightly too big for their face.

"The maiden who what?" The student stared quizzically at her.

Zhara coughed, feeling giggles rise up like bubbles in her throat. Oh no. The Good-Looking Giggles. She resisted the urge to clap her hands over her mouth. "The next volume of *The Maiden Who Was Loved by Death*," she managed.

"What's that?" the student asked.

"Only the most popular romance serial being written at the moment," said an excited voice over Zhara's shoulder. The student startled when Madame Hong, the mussel-monger, appeared at their elbow with her copy of the previous installment of *The Maiden Who Was Loved by Death* pressed to her ample bosom. "They say Master Cao and his scriveners were up all night making copies, but there are only three hundred to be had."

"So few?" Zhara asked in dismay. "There were four hundred and fifty available last time."

"Yes, but I heard several of his scriveners disappeared last night."

"Disappeared?" the student asked. "Where would they go?" Their gaze flickered back to the northerners over and over, their hand going to a small pendant on a ribbon at their throat. The northerners wore their hair in the steppe fashion, with the sides shaved and the rest worn in a long horsetail braided with beads and feathers. Twin long-bladed knives were strapped crossways on each of their backs, causing the hairs to rise at the back of Zhara's neck. Only nobles and the Warlord's peacekeepers were allowed to carry blades throughout the Morning Realms.

"Who knows?" Madame Hong shrugged. "None of his scriveners ever lasted long anyway. More likely they quit because of hand cramps or something." She rolled her eyes. "If you ask me, that little bookseller is doing this on purpose, just so he can drive up the price."

"I doubt that, auntie." Zhara laughed. "Bookselling isn't seasonal; its supply doesn't come and go like the tides."

"Well, that makes more sense than the other rumor I've heard." The mussel-monger grinned.

"Which is what?" the student asked, fiddling with the pendant about their neck. It was small and round with a hole in the center, like a coin.

The fishwife dropped her voice so the student had to lean in close. "That the bookseller is running some sort of illegal smuggling operation in the basement of his bookshop."

Zhara shook her head. "There aren't any basements in the marsh, auntie."

"That's just what I've heard," Madame Hong protested. "Scriveners go missing all the time, in and out of that shop, and the man is chronically understaffed. What other conclusions am I supposed to draw?"

"Understaffed, eh?" Zhara asked. "Do you think Master Cao is looking to hire someone new? I could use the extra wages."

"Don't lie." The mussel-monger slapped her good-naturedly on the arm. "You just want to read what happens to Little Flame and her supernatural lover before the rest of us. I'm on to you, child."

"It would be the only way I could afford to read the next installment now." Zhara sighed, thinking of the stained copy stuffed in her satchel. "Unless you'll let me borrow yours, auntie." She twinkled at the fishwife. "Please?"

"Get on with you," the mussel-monger said, playfully shoving her away. "I know how you treat your books. Scorch marks and soot everywhere from falling asleep reading before the hearth."

Zhara stumbled over her broken shoe and straight into a broad, barreled chest. One of the northerners, short and stout. "Pardon, pardon, a thousand pard—" The words froze in her throat.

A white swath of silk, onto which a pattern of black wings had been embroidered, banded around the northerner's left arm. The Warlord's Golden Horde was comprised of the north's most elite warriors organized into five wings—the Red, the White, the Blue, the Green, and the Yellow—each focused on a different branch of military strategy and weaponry. But there was also an unofficial sixth wing, the Black, that served as the Warlord's eyes and ears throughout the empire.

The rest of the realm called them Kestrels.

"Did you see where the student you were speaking to went?" the stout northerner asked in their flat northern accent.

"The s-s-student?" Zhara whirled around, both relieved and surprised that she was not the target of the Warlord's peacekeepers. She found the student crouched down low among a few hopeful readers in line at Master Cao's bookshop, trying their best to disguise their most distinguishing feature—their height. Their eyes met hers, and Zhara carefully looked away. "N-n-no, I have not," she said. "My apo-pologies to Their Excellency."

The Kestrel grunted, giving her and Madame Hong a long, hard stare before moving away.

"Where black wings flock together, black hearts will be found," the fishwife murmured. "A bad omen." She glanced in the direction of the Temple of Immortals, its towering, multitiered red gate visible for yards around. "It's happening again, isn't it?" The mussel-monger traced something over her heart with the tip of her finger, a shape Zhara did not recognize.

"What's happening again, auntie?"

But Madame Hong did not reply.

It was several moments before Zhara was able to clear the crowd around Master Cao's bookshop and make her way to the apothecary shop. She was going to be unforgivably late, not that Teacher Hu ever noticed. Sometimes she wondered why the old herbalist had even hired her, since there wasn't much work to do for the apothecary at all. Most of the time, Zhara sat behind the counter and read romance novels while Teacher Hu came and went from her own shop.

"Li Ami and her father are long gone," said Master Cao's voice from a darkened alleyway. "The girl hasn't worked in my shop for the past six months."

To her surprise, Zhara found the good-looking student on their hands and knees before the diminutive bookseller, forehead pressed to the dirty ground in supplication.

"Then could you—Master Cao—could Master Cao at least tell me where they went?" The student sat back on their heels, hand going to the pendant about their throat.

"No." The bookseller's answer was uncharacteristically curt. "I can't."

"Can't, or won't?"

Master Cao did not respond.

"If the bookseller can't tell me where Li Er-Shuan and his daughter have gone," the student said, snatching the pendant from their throat and pressing it into Master Cao's palm in desperation, "then can he tell me where I might find the Guardians of Dawn?"

At that precise moment, the bookseller caught Zhara's gaze and stiffened. She ducked behind a pillar, feeling terrible for eavesdropping. It was none of her business, although she couldn't help being curious. The Guardians of Dawn were a fairy tale, legendary elemental figures and companions of the Sunburst Warrior, who defeated Tiyok, Mother of Ten Thousand Demons, by sealing her in a realm far beneath the earth.

"Ah," said Master Cao. "I see. And why are you seeking the Guardians of Dawn?"

"I—I have a little brother," they said in a halting, hesitant voice. "A little brother with . . . gifts."

Something about the way the student said *gifts* caught Zhara's ear. She peered around the pillar, curious despite herself.

Master Cao studied the pendant in his palm before returning it to the student. "Then I have a book that might be of some interest to you."

"A book?" The student was confused. "What sort of book?"

"A primer," Master Cao said. "Full of a secret language and secret codes. Codes that, when properly deciphered, might lead you to what you are searching for."

"A map?" the student said hopefully.

The bookseller cast another glance in Zhara's direction. "Be careful," he said in a low voice. "For the walls have ears."

"Eh?" The student looked over their shoulder and caught Zhara's eye.

Feeling guilty, Zhara immediately made herself scarce and headed toward the apothecary. As she made her way through the covered market, she discovered there was a much larger Kestrel presence in the Pits than she had realized. Around every other corner, brown-and-white tufted feathers fluttered, noticeable among the smoothed-down topknots or bare heads of the southerners. Something jangled lightly above her head. An unusual reddish bird of prey with a bell around its neck looked down at her from its perch on a nearby shop roof, its fierce golden gaze piercing and sharp. A crawling sensation tickled between her shoulder blades and she couldn't help feeling as though she were being followed. Out of the corner of her eye, there was the persistent flap and flutter of fabric disappearing from view. Zhara picked up her pace and ran—

—straight into a very broad, very firm chest. Her satchel went flying as she stumbled to the ground, scattering the contents everywhere.

"Pardon, pardon, a thousand pardons!" It was the tall, good-looking university student, crawling on all fours to help gather her things. "But I had to cut you off before I lost you."

Suddenly she realized the color of their school robes matched the flutter of fabric that had chased her throughout the covered market. "That was you?" she asked, half flattered and half annoyed by their attention. "Why were you following me?"

"Because I had something I wanted to give you," the student said earnestly, reaching to undo their waistband.

"Hold—hold a moment," Zhara said. "I'm not that sort of girl, learned one. At least"—she winked—"not before someone buys me a meal."

"Eh?" A wrinkle of confusion creased their dark brows before smoothing away into an expression of abashed embarrassment. "Oh no, no, no, no, I'm not that sort of boy either." He laughed nervously, his cheeks flushing pink. The student pulled a slim paperback out from his sash and presented it to Zhara with a bow. "Here."

She frowned. "What's this?"

"A copy of that really popular romance book," the student said. "*The Damsel Who Married a Demon.*"

It was a moment before Zhara realized he meant *The Maiden Who Was Loved by Death.* She was taken aback. "Why—why would you give me this?"

The student blinked. "Because . . . because you wanted it?" When Zhara didn't immediately accept his gift, he continued on uncertainly. "You said . . . you said the only way you could afford to read what happened next was if you worked for Master Cao." He dropped his hands. "Do you—do you not like it?"

She could feel the Good-Looking Giggles tickle the back of her tongue, pressing at her lips, but swallowed them back down. "I . . . do . . ." she managed. "Th-thank you."

The student smiled so brightly at her that Zhara choked. Dimples. He had dimples. Why did he have to have dimples? She started giggling uncontrollably and turned away to avoid meeting his eyes.

"Hoy!" A Kestrel stood some distance away, brandishing one of their long knives menacingly in her direction. "You there! What's that you have in your hands?"

Alarm flared through Zhara's body, stoking the furnace of power at her core. Oh no. No. She tugged at her sleeves to hide the telltale magic glow of her hands, feeling the seams of her too-tight tunic tear with the strain across her shoulders and chest. She cast about frantically for some avenue of escape, wondering whether she should run or feign innocence.

"It's just a romance novel, Excellency," the student said. He held the slim paperback before the Kestrel's gaze. "See?"

The peacekeeper narrowed their eyes. "*The Thousand-Character Classic,*" they read aloud. "Doesn't sound like a romance title to me." They turned to Zhara and cocked their head, gaze fixed on the faint glow emanating through her shirtsleeves. "Why don't you show me your hands——"

A jingle and piercing shriek rent the air as the large reddish bird Zhara had seen earlier dove at the Kestrel, its claws raking their face before circling back up to the nearest roof. It fixed her with its golden glare as though telling to her to run.

"Come on!" the student shouted, grabbing her wrist. "Let's go!"

She didn't need to be told twice, limping along as fast as her unraveling shoe would allow. The passersby and vendors screamed and threw themselves to the side as they barreled past.

"We need"—the student panted—"to hide!"

Ahead, a small ginger cat sat in the middle of the street and stared Zhara down as they approached before darting into a narrow gap between buildings at the very last second. She chanced a look over her shoulder; the Kestrel was some distance behind them, staggering back and forth, wiping blood from their eyes. "This way!" she gasped, throwing herself into the space where the cat had disappeared.

It was barely wide enough for the student's shoulders. The two of them somehow managed to wedge themselves in facing each other.

Zhara and the student stood with their backs pressed against opposite walls, legs entwined, chests barely touching as they breathed, shallow and fast. She held herself rigid and closed her eyes, trying her best not to rest her weight against the student. This close, the reek of rice wine wafting from his robes was overpowering, but to her surprise, beneath it all, his skin smelled like jasmine and ylang-ylang soap.

Oh no.

The Giggles.

Zhara shifted, and her legs accidentally brushed against his. The student gave a soft yelp of surprise before clamping his lips shut.

Beyond their hiding space, the *clink-clink* of Kestrel boots drew ever closer. Her fear increased with every step . . . along with her magic. Zhara sucked in a sharp breath, straining to create as much space between herself and the student as possible. If her skin met his, if he got burned by her power—

"Who's there?" The Kestrel's voice came from just beyond their hiding space.

The student clapped a hand over her mouth. Zhara's eyes went wide as her magic surged, but despite the touch of bare skin against bare skin, he did not seem to be affected. Her pulse stuttered and skipped with more than excitement as she held her breath. There was the metallic *shing!* of blades being drawn just outside the alleyway.

"What's going on here?"

Thinking quickly, Zhara wrapped her hands around the back of the student's neck and pulled his face down to hers, angling their heads so the two of them would appear as a pair of trysting lovers in the midst of a clandestine assignation. The student squeaked, half in protest, half in eagerness, his hands flapping uselessly about her head before settling on the wall behind her.

The Kestrel made a disgusted noise. "Lovebirds," they muttered. "Get a room, you two."

Zhara could feel the pounding of the student's heart against her own rib cage, swift and erratic and in time with her own. It wasn't until the *clink-clink* of the Kestrel's boots had faded away entirely that the ersatz lovebirds allowed themselves to relax.

"Ahem, er, ah, er, thanks," the student stammered, sliding sideways out of the alleyway. "That was some, uh, quick thinking." A bright red flush covered his face and neck, glowing nearly as bright as the magic in her veins.

Zhara cleared her throat. "You're welcome," she said thickly, trying in vain to contain her giggles.

The student coughed. "Anyway," he said, reaching back into his sash. "Before we were so rudely interrupted"—he pulled out a slightly battered paperback—"I believe I was in the middle of giving you a present."

She laughed as she accepted the book from his hands. "This isn't *Tales from the Downy Delta,* is it?" she teased. "I won't get arrested by the Warlord's peacekeepers for having this in my possession, will I?"

The student blinked in confusion. "Is that poetry?"

Zhara bit the inside of her cheek. "Pornography."

"What?" He jerked his head up in confusion, round eyes made even rounder with panic. "I wouldn't—I've never—I mean, I don't—"

She chuckled. "You're awfully innocent for someone who smells like they slept in a winery."

"I don't drink," the student protested. Then he discreetly brought his sleeve to his nose, sniffed, and winced. "I'm allergic to alcohol."

Zhara took in his stained robes with a skeptical eye. "Truly?"

"Truly!" the student said eagerly. "All the men in my family turn this mortifying shade of plum red the instant any bit of liquor passes our lips, so I abstain for vanity's sake. And health," he added as an afterthought. "But mostly vanity."

"Oh?" Zhara pressed close, trying not to laugh as the student suddenly scurried backward. "Because you're awfully red right now, Master Plum Blossom."

The student splayed his hands on the wall behind him and coughed. "Well, ahem, that is"—he cleared his throat—"that is entirely due to your intoxicating presence and nothing to do with alcohol, I assure you." He tried a flirtatious wink on Zhara, which was an abject failure, but his effort made her smile nonetheless. If he weren't so devastatingly handsome, she would have called him cute.

"Is that so?" She looked up at Master Plum Blossom through her lashes and he choked, pulling at the collar of his robes. "Then it seems I'm even more potent than either rice wine or brandy." She grinned, and he tripped over the hem of his robes.

"I meant to do that," he announced, brushing himself down. "Just, uh, light-headed, is all."

"Maybe you really are drunk after all, Master Plum Blossom," Zhara said, lightly tapping his chest with her finger. "Stop by Teacher Hu's apothecary and I promise I can find a cure for whatever ails you. Well, except your innocence, I suppose," she added mischievously. "You'll have to go to the blossoms of Flower Town for that."

The student turned even redder than before. "I—"

Drums from the city watchtowers across the river began sounding the early-daylight hour.

"Mother of Demons," he swore. "I'm late." He turned to Zhara and bowed, dimpling at her one last time. "Farewell, Mistress Brandy. Thanks again for saving my life."

It wasn't until he was gone that Zhara realized she was again, holding the wrong book in her hand.

"Oh, Master Plum Blossom." She smoothed her hand over the slightly battered cover of *The Thousand-Character Classic*. It looked like one of those poorly printed pamphlets of pornographic poetry passed from student to student at Zanhei University. "A tawdry book of bawdy poetry, is it?"

Zhara opened the book, then immediately shut it and shoved it down the front of her tunic with shaking hands.

The pages had been covered in a language she could not read but recognized all too well. Glyphs, logographs, carefully crafted characters—the Language of Flowers. Zhara now understood why Master Plum Blossom had not wanted the book to fall into the Kestrel's possession. *The Thousand-Character Classic* was not a book of poetry.

It was a book of magic.

HAN HATED THE SMELL OF ALCOHOL.

Especially as he didn't drink.

But he could have used a stiff one just then, trapped in a storm drain with his hindquarters sticking out. And in the women's quarters no less. "I—don't—understand—how—this—happened," Han grunted, straining to back himself out of the channel. "I could have sworn the passage was bigger last time."

Although he supposed he *had* grown since the last time he tried this passage as a little boy. His shoulders especially, which were wedged in the opening, too broad to fit. "All this working out, and this is where it gets me," Han muttered. "Stuck in a storm drain until I'm discovered by the Chancellor." He paused. "Or die." He wasn't sure which was worse.

Han raised his eyes toward the heavens. "All right, I've learned my lesson," he called. "Vanity is a fruitless pursuit. Now, if you would please send someone to get me out of here, I promise to stop working so hard on my impressive physique."

Silence. Han sighed. According to his Uncle Li, the former court astrologer, the Royal Heir had been born under the mansion of the Second Immortal, who governed sudden changes, strange ideas, and twisted luck. Said Immortal was probably up in the heavens right now, having a good laugh at his current predicament. Han wriggled his hips experimentally, wondering if he could shimmy himself back out the way he came.

"All this hard work and no one around to admire the view," he complained.

"I wouldn't say that, Your Grace," came a light, amused voice from behind him. "In fact, there is someone admiring the view right now."

Han banged his head against the top of the grate. "Xu?"

"The one and only." Han could only imagine the gleeful grin on his best friend's immaculately painted face. "The answer to the Royal Heir's prayers."

"Great. Now, would you please get me out of here before someone fetches my father, or worse—yours." Xu's father was the Chancellor and regent of Zanhei while Prince Wonhu was in mourning.

Han's father had been in mourning for the past six years.

"The Royal Heir will allow me to place my hands upon his august personage?" his friend gasped in mock horror. "Whatever will his father say? Whatever will *my* father say?"

"Xu, I order you to put your hands upon my august and appealing ass and get me out of this storm drain before the Chancellor shows up and beats it to a pulp."

"Fine." They grabbed Han's ankles and braced themself. "On the count of three?"

"Three," Han agreed. "One, two, three—"

With a mighty tug and a tearing sound, Han was wrenched free. Xu cried out as the back of Han's head met their nose, sending them both crashing to the ground with an audible *snap!* Xu lay sprawled out across the courtyard cobblestones, moaning theatrically with one sleeve pulled over their eyes.

"Oh no," they said, sounding muffled. "I think it's broken."

"What's broken?" Han demanded. "Are you hurt?"

Xu reached under their back to pull out their fan, broken in two and hanging together by a thread. "It was Wulin silk too," they lamented.

Han rolled his eyes. "You have *five* Wulin silk fans, you vain peacock," he said as he helped them to their feet. He glanced around at the Hall of Earthly Delights to see if anyone had heard the ruckus. The courtyard was empty, filled with the sleepy murmurs of handmaidens and palace attendants getting ready for the day.

"Yes, well, now I only have *four* Wulin silk fans," Xu pouted. "Four is an inauspicious number." They brushed off their robes, straightening their shoulders and their expression. "So," they said carefully. "Would His Grace like to explain what he is doing in the courtyard of the women's quarters, and"—they sniffed—"why he smells as though he slept in the gutter all night?"

Han gave his best friend what he hoped was his best disarming smile. He had learned long ago just how effective his dimples could be on the fairer sex, and Xu was the fairest of them all. "Nothing. Just tripped during one of my morning laps around the palace grounds." He jogged in place to demonstrate.

Unfortunately, Xu was also the sharpest of them all. "Now, His Grace wouldn't have done something so stupid as to sneak outside the palace without me, would he?" they asked, crossing their arms expectantly. "And then try to sneak back in through the Hall of Earthly Delights lest someone recognize him at the front gate?"

Han hung his head. "Yes," he mumbled shamefacedly. The sharp, sour stink of someone else's sweat wafted upward as he lifted his arms in acknowledgment.

Xu pinched their nose with a grimace. "What happened to His Grace's clothes?"

"These? I borrowed them from a sleeping student in the university district."

"His Grace did *what?*" they said in a horrified voice. "Why?"

"So no one would recognize me," Han said proudly. "Don't worry, I left the student my own robes in exchange. A fair trade, wouldn't you say?"

Xu looked as though they couldn't decide whether to laugh or cry. "His Grace is aware that no one knows what he looks like, yes? Officially, the Royal Heir has never left palace walls."

Han blinked. "Oh. I forgot."

His best friend palmed their face. "Sometimes," they murmured, "I despair of getting my prince to his majority alive."

"Don't worry," Han said cheerfully. "We only have six more months before I turn eighteen."

Xu shook their head. "If His Grace wanted a premature tour of the pleasures of Flower Town, he could have simply asked me to play chaperone." They narrowed their eyes. "But that's not why he left the palace, is it?"

"No," Han admitted.

Xu sighed. "This is about Li Er-Shuan and the Guardians of Dawn, isn't it?"

Han fingered the pendant he wore on a string about his neck. "Yes."

It was a long while before Xu spoke. "Oh, Han," they said softly.

He turned his face away. It was the pity more than the dropped honorifics that hurt Han most. "I'm so close, Xu," he said. "I'm so close I can taste it."

"It's been six years, my prince," his best friend reminded him gently. "Six years is a long time to be searching for something that may or may not exist."

Six years since Han's mother was dragged before the Warlord's executioner to be burned at the stake in the courtyard of the very palace in which he lived. Six years since she had made him promise he would keep his brother safe at all costs. Six years since the Royal Consort pressed a coin in his hand and told him to find the Guardians of Dawn, a secret society dedicated to magician liberation to which his mother and his Uncle Li had belonged.

"The Guardians of Dawn *does* exist," Han insisted, holding his necklace out to his friend. "Master Cao recognized my mother's pendant." At first glance, the pendant looked like any other coin, but with a round hole instead of a square one in the middle. Ringed on each face was a pattern of circular flames in a sunburst motif instead of the bear claws issued by the Warlord's imperial mint.

Xu looked skeptical. "Who's Master Cao?"

"A bookseller down in the Pits." Han reached into his waistband for his copy of *The Thousand-Character Classic*. "My cousin Ami used to work at his shop before she and Uncle Li disappeared. The bookseller knew something about the Guardians." He handed the book to Xu. "He gave me this book." Han bit his lip. "He said it was a"—he frowned—"primer for a secret language and secret codes."

His best friend frowned. "*The Maiden Who Was Loved by Death?*" they asked in confusion.

"Eh?" Han snatched the book back from his friend and flipped it open to the first page. He read, *"Once there was a little girl who played her music for a little boy in the wood*—oh no. Oh no, oh no, oh no." He raised panicked eyes to Xu. "Mistress Brandy!"

They arched an immaculately penciled brow. "Mistress Brandy?"

But a startled scream and the sound of shattering porcelain pierced the air before he could answer. A handmaiden making the rounds had spotted Han in the bushes with Xu. "Intruders!" she gasped. "Men in the Hall of Earthly Delights!"

"Excuse me," Xu said irritably, hands on hips. "Who are you calling a man?"

Han did not bother to listen to the handmaiden's reply. He shoved *The Maiden Who Was Loved by Death* back into his sash and raced toward Paramour's Escape, the old myrtle tree growing in the southwest corner of the women's quarters. Somewhere in the distance, a gong began to sound the alarm. Ahead, he could see he was not the only or even the first intruder in the Hall of Earthly Delights to flee the gong that morning. Several sheepish guardians and a handful of smug scullery rats emerged from rooms and private residences, all racing toward the poor, spindly, and long-suffering myrtle tree. Already a small, skinny youth was scaling its beleaguered branches, while a stocky off-duty guard waited behind them.

"Forget this," Han muttered. "I can't believe there's a *line* for an escape."

He scanned the walls of the courtyard, the tops of which were just barely out of reach. If he got a good enough running start, he might just be able to grasp the ledge and haul himself over without having to climb Paramour's Escape himself. Behind him, the shouts of the Royal Guard grew louder.

"Moment of truth," he told himself, rolling up his sleeves. "All that working out can't have been for nothing."

Backing up several paces, he took off at a sprint for the wall and leaped. The top of the wall was wider than he thought, and his fingers scrabbled for purchase. But Han managed to hold on long enough to get a solid foothold on the textured brick wall and hauled himself onto the top, lurching forward bit by bit on his stomach. He swung his leg over in an ungainly fashion and fell flat on his back on the other side.

Han closed his eyes, allowing himself a moment to catch his breath.

"Well, well, well," said a silken voice. "What have we here?"

Han opened his eyes. The shadow of a spread-winged hat fell over him as the whisper of green silk robes embroidered with cranes brushed his arm. A pale green jade pendant dangled from a red-beaded string above his face, carved into the smiling face of a wide-mouthed frog topped with a laughing monkey. The seal of the regent. Only one palace official carried such a seal.

The Chancellor.

"Good morning, Your Eminence," Han said, and closed his eyes once more.

"The Hall of Earthly Delights?" Prince Wonhu thundered from his throne upon the dais. "What were you thinking?"

Han knelt before his father in the middle of the Hall of Heavenly Wisdom in the appropriate and proper pose of regret, after the Chancellor unceremoniously dragged him in by the scruff of his neck. It was a pose in which he often found himself, although rarely with an entire audience of cabinet ministers in attendance. Two scribes sat behind the royal dais with brushes and inkwells at the ready, partially obscured by a gauzy screen. Han didn't know whether to be offended or flattered that his misdeeds were to be recorded for the annals of his father's reign.

"You have sullied a sacred sphere!" Prince Wonhu paced back and forth before his throne, his face turning the same shade as his oversized scarlet court robes. Han's father had never been an especially big man, but he seemed smaller than ever these days as grief and poor health hollowed out his bones. "A man! In the women's quarters! Have you no shame?"

Han kept his forehead pressed to the floor in abject apology. On the platform beneath his father stood the Chancellor, his wet, bulging eyes looking down upon the Royal Heir with his customary blank, placid gaze. As the regent of Zanhei, the Chancellor oversaw the mundane governance of the province during Prince Wonhu's period of mourning. Not even the Royal Heir could claim rank over the regent——or at least, not until Han reached his majority at age eighteen. Six more months, he told himself. Only six more months.

"Was it an assignation?" Prince Wonhu demanded. "Speak!"

Han sputtered as he lifted his head. "An ass-assignation?"

"Dalliance," his father supplied. "Affair. Tryst. Illicit rendezvous." He fixed Han with a steely expression. "Do you require a dictionary, my son?"

A cough rose from somewhere within the ministerial ranks.

"No, no," Han said quickly, ears burning. "I know what it means. It's just that I never, well, it didn't occur to me that . . ." He trailed off.

Another cough from the ranks, and this time it sounded suspiciously like the word *virgin*.

"You will not address me so informally," Prince Wonhu said sternly. "In this Hall, we are a prince and his heir, not father and son."

"We're barely that either," Han muttered. "Not since Mama died."

A hush fell over the assembly room. Six years ago, the Royal Consort had been executed by the Falconer for treason, for the crime of conspiring with magicians. Both her name and any mention of her person was forbidden, and the floorboards creaked as a ripple of discomfort ran through the sea of ministerial green. The Royal Consort's death was the reason Prince Wonhu had abdicated his throne, and the reason he had abdicated all the responsibilities of fatherhood, naming the Chancellor as regent.

"If I may, my liege," the Chancellor interjected smoothly from his seat at the foot of the dais. "Perhaps a neutral party can be of assistance."

Han snorted. His father's regent was about as neutral as the Azure Isles to the east—surreptitiously stirring up trouble whenever possible. Only six more months, he reminded himself. Six more months.

Prince Wonhu nodded. "Go on."

The Chancellor bowed. "His Highness is most gracious." Straightening, he turned to address the assembled ministers. "Now, what is to be done about the Royal Heir? What lessons can we impart to this wayward young man so that he may grow in wisdom and maturity?"

A rustle rose within the ranks as the ministers stirred and sniggered. Han wished he could get to his feet and look them all in the eye—after all, these were men he had known his whole life—but he could not rise unless given permission by either his father or the Chancellor.

"Confinement?" *That must be Official Deng,* Han thought, judging by the meekness of the tone. The twitchy, rabbity Minister of Taxation.

"We've tried that. Several times." Han couldn't place this minister's voice. "The infamous Monkey Prince always wriggles his way out of house arrest. What about manual labor? The marshes outside the city are in constant need of draining while we finish building those wells and fountains."

"Gentlemen," said a deep, melodious voice. The Minister of Culture, Official Quan. "Is it not the measure of a man to reflect on his wrongdoings and spiritually grow from the shame? Let the Royal Heir write a few lines of apology and read it aloud for the assembly to hear."

"Poetry? Is that a punishment for the Royal Heir or for the rest of us?"

Snickers burst throughout the Hall of Heavenly Wisdom. Han pouted. His poetry wasn't *that* bad.

"I have an idea."

Everyone's heads swiveled to the back of the Hall of Heavenly Wisdom where General Hong stood in the corner, conspicuous in his lack of court dress. Although he was technically the Minister of War, General Hong eschewed all symbols of his office, preferring utility to etiquette. It was rumored he was never out of his armor, and even went to the baths dressed in full battle gear.

"I say we send the Royal Heir to one of my military outposts in the western reaches," the general said. "A few months serving with my soldiers and the imperial army against the resistance would do wonders for his attitude."

"Resistance?" Prince Wonhu stirred on his dais. "What resistance?"

"It's not much . . . yet," the Minister of War said quietly. "My scouts say the clans and tribes out there are flying the banner of the Four-Winged Dragon."

There was a sharp, collective intake of breath in the Hall of Heavenly Wisdom. Han racked his brain, trying to remember the significance of the Four-Winged Dragon. Xu would know; they actually paid attention during their history lessons.

"That standard hasn't been seen since the end of the Just War!" Official Quan exclaimed.

"Yes," General Hong said in a heavy voice. "The battle flag of the deposed Mugung Dynasty. Magician sympathizers."

Magician sympathizers. Han went still, resisting the urge to clutch his mother's sunburst pendant. The Guardians of Dawn *were* out there. They had to be. If he could just find them, he could keep his little brother safe.

Promise me, little lemur, his mother had said before she died. Before she was murdered. *Promise me you'll protect Anyang.*

"Are you saying, General," Prince Wonhu said softly, "that you would send my son to the western front to quell a potential insurrection?"

Arguments broke out among the ministers as each argued for and against the different proposals for punishments. Han rocked back and forth on the ground, trying to get the blood circulating in his legs again. A position of abject apology was hard on the knees.

After a moment, the Chancellor spoke again. "My friends!" he called, clapping his hands. "I thank everyone for their suggestions. Now, if I may offer up my own solution." He turned to Prince Wonhu, who inclined his head. "I have decided to propose . . . a proposal."

A few of the ministers scratched their heads beneath their spread-winged hats. "Go on, Your Eminence," said Official Deng.

A soft smile spread across the Chancellor's too-wide lips. "The Royal Heir was caught trespassing in the Hall of Earthly Delights," he said. "But is it not natural for boys to be curious, to wish to sample the very earthly delights from which they are forbidden?"

"Oh ho ho," said the Minister of Culture. "I see where His Eminence is headed, and let me be the first to say *good luck.*"

"What?" Han asked, unable to restrain himself. "What are we talking about?"

"Marriage." The Chancellor's eyes glittered. "They say marriage makes men out of boys."

"Then His Eminence must be a man many times over," murmured

one of the lower-level bureaucrats. "Since I hear congratulations are to be offered soon for the fourth time."

Han studied the Chancellor's face, wondering what his wives had found so attractive about him that he was so much-married. Lord Chan wasn't an old man, but having married and buried three wives in the past decade seemed rather excessive. Xu's mother died when they were born, and each successive stepmother had been closer and closer to them in age.

"We've been trying to marry the Royal Heir off for years," said the Minister of Culture. "No one wants him. There was that offer from House Durumi. And House Haitun. All withdrawn with no explanation once the girl arrived for a visit."

Han allowed himself a small smile of satisfaction. It had not been easy finding out each potential bride's particular distastes and dislikes, but he had made sure Xu seeded each lie about the Royal Heir well in the taverns and teahouses of Zanhei. The girl from House Durumi was sensitive to smells, so he pretended to have bad digestion and even worse breath. The girl from House Haitun was said to be vain, so Xu spread the rumor that the Royal Heir had too little chin and too much ear as well as stubborn hairs sprouting from his nose that he refused to trim.

"I am well aware of the Royal Heir's defects as a romantic prospect," the Chancellor said, reaching into his sleeve and pulling out a scroll. "But we have received an offer for His Grace's hand, and this time, I don't think we can refuse. Nor would we want to."

Han's smile slid off his face. He suspected this betrothal offer was not a spontaneous suggestion, but a plot long in the making, judging by the Chancellor's smug expression. The regent had been waiting for the perfect opportunity to announce it, he realized. A cold, sinking feeling settled in Han's stomach.

Prince Wonhu sat up straighter on his throne. "Who is it from?"

The Chancellor bowed. "If I may, Your Highness," he said as he unrolled the scroll. Han's father gave him a tired nod. "We have been honored with an offer of marriage from Princess Yulana, First Daughter of the Gommun Kang, Emperor of the Morning Realms, and"—a triumphant smile split his slimy lips—"the Warlord's most beloved grandchild."

4

THE HOLLOW CHIMES RANG ABOVE TEACHER HU'S booth as Zhara entered the apothecary. "Sorry I'm late, auntie," she panted as she rushed inside. "I—"

To her surprise, the herbalist was not alone. Meng Grandmother, one of the matriarchs of the Buri people, sat on a stool across the counter from Teacher Hu, gnarled hands curled atop her rattan cane. The Buri didn't often venture into Zanhei proper, preferring to stay in their floating villages in the marsh, but Meng Grandmother was accompanied by two younger members of her clan—a parent and child, by the looks of their matching red-beaded bracelets.

"I don't understand," Teacher Hu was saying. The apothecary was a short, wiry woman in her middle years, with iron-gray hair pulled back into a severe low bun. "Are you saying there *aren't* any crowned fern fiddleheads or that your people *won't* go up to Mount Zanhei to look for them?"

"Both," Meng Grandmother said, the beads dangling from her patterned blue headdress clacking together in frustration. Her clan made their living foraging for herbs and other edibles on the slopes of the volcano upriver and had done business with Teacher Hu since before Zhara had been hired. "I'm telling you, it's no longer safe up there for my people. Bad air. Bad energy. Bad ki. The mountain is awake, and it is angry."

Zhara began cleaning up the booth, quietly clearing away half-finished cups of tea and the half-eaten remains of past meals. Teacher Hu might have been the most brilliant herbalist in the southern provinces, but fastidiousness was not one of her virtues.

"Awake?" The apothecary frowned, removing her spectacles and letting them dangle from a string of topaz beads about her neck. "As in . . . active?"

"I mean *awake,*" Meng Grandmother said irritably. "I know you city dwellers revere your Immortals and their mansions of Reason, but the world is bigger than reason and logic and order. Don't you remember what happened during the Year Without Summer?"

Zhara organized the loose sheafs of paper and notebooks scattered about as inconspicuously as she could, sorting and putting away the various ingredients into cabinet drawers. She discovered a stool beneath a stack of old prescriptions and offered the seat to the pair standing behind Meng Grandmother. The adult flinched and shied away, eyes wide and wary.

"Despite my looks, I wasn't alive a millennium ago, so no," the apothecary said in a dry voice. "But according to the annals of history, the Year Without Summer was the last time Mount Zanhei erupted, covering the Morning Realms in a cloud of ash so thick it blotted out the sun, plunging the earth into never-ending winter."

The Buri matriarch shook her head, sending the beads on her headdress twirling about her face. "Our people have other stories."

Teacher Hu lifted her brows. "Such as?"

"Tiyok," the child beside Meng Grandmother whispered.

The adult gripped the child's shoulders. "Don't swear; it isn't polite," they murmured.

"Forgive these two for speaking out of turn," the Buri matriarch said wryly. "This is my granddaughter, Dieu, and her son, Thanh."

Dieu tightened her arms about her son. "Apologize to Teacher Hu for the foul language, Thanh."

Zhara gave the boy an encouraging smile. "Did you mean the Mother of Ten Thousand Demons?" she asked in a kindly voice, but his mother pulled him away. "Who was defeated by the Sunburst Warrior and the Guardians of Dawn?"

Thanh flicked his gaze at her and Zhara was taken aback. There was an unnerving emptiness in his eyes—not the blank-eyed look of a disinterested child, but a mesmerizing void. His hollowness scratched at Zhara, and her magic stirred, uneasy and uncomfortable. She had a creeping sensation of being watched by someone unseen, as though another consciousness stared out from the depths of the little boy's dark, dark eyes.

"This is my assistant, Jin Zhara," Teacher Hu said, returning the introductions.

"She's a smart one, your assistant." Meng Grandmother tapped her cane at Zhara's feet approvingly. "She knows the old stories."

But everyone knew the legend of the Sunburst Warrior and the Guardians of Dawn. It was the founding myth of the Morning Realms, and the favorite fairy tale of every traveling troupe of players from the western reaches to the Azure Isles. Just this past summer, Zhara had seen the Bangtan Brothers stage a performance of it in the Pits; people couldn't stop raving about it for weeks afterward.

Then she thought of that strange scene she had witnessed between Master Plum Blossom and Master Cao outside the bookshop. *Tell me where I might find the Guardians of Dawn.*

"I'm not sure what the Mother of Ten Thousand Demons has to do with . . . anything," Teacher Hu said, crossing her arms. "The fact of the matter is, I still need crowned fern fiddleheads for my tinctures, and they only grow on the slopes of that volcano."

"Didn't you hear what I said?" Meng Grandmother said in an exasperated voice. "There are none to be had. Plants wither and die, fish rot in the streams, and the animals and birds fall silent up on Mount Zanhei."

The apothecary tapped her chin thoughtfully. "Some sort of blight, perhaps?"

"I suppose," the old woman said grudgingly. "If you want to think of things that way. Yes," she nodded, the beads on her headdress swinging back and forth. "A blight that corrupts the ki of everything it touches— plants, animals, people."

"People?" Teacher Hu said in surprise. "What do you mean by that?"

Behind the Buri matriarch, Dieu shifted nervously on her feet, worrying the red bead at her wrist. "Grandmother," she said in a low, pleading voice. "Don't."

But the old woman ignored her. "Our loved ones disappear in the caves surrounding Mount Zanhei," she said, "and those who come back"—she glanced warily at her great-grandson—"come back changed."

"Changed?" The apothecary raised her brows. "How so?"

For a brief moment Meng Grandmother seemed troubled, then she beckoned for Thanh to come forward. "Come here, boy," she said. "I want the apothecary to have a look at you."

"But I'm not a healer," Teacher Hu protested. "I'm an herbalist."

"You're the only city dweller I know with a sound head on her shoulders," the old woman retorted. "Come, boy."

The apothecary fumbled for her spectacles and placed them on the end of her nose. "What am I looking for?" she asked, coming around the counter to examine the child.

Meng Grandmother hesitated. "He is one of the changed," she said in a low voice. "Thanh was always a cheerful child," she said sadly. "Eyes bright, easy to laugh, easy to cry. And now . . ."

Dieu choked back a sob.

"What happened?" Teacher Hu gently held the boy's wrist, taking his pulse beneath her fingers.

The Buri matriarch twisted her cane round and round in her hand like a drill. "We're not sure. Of the five children that went out to play in the marsh that day, only three returned. Only Thanh is able to speak, but he won't tell us anything."

"The marsh?" the apothecary asked. "Not Mount Zanhei."

"No, but it's the same sickness as the others who came back from the mountain," Meng Grandmother said. "The same . . . corruption of the spirit."

"What of the other children?" Teacher Hu gently coaxed Thanh's mouth open to peer at his tongue. The boy was obedient enough, but his actions were lifeless, stiff, like a puppet manipulated by an unseen hand. "The ones who returned?"

"Also changed, also . . . corrupted," Meng Grandmother said in a grim voice. "It is as though they are the walking dead, eyes hollow and minds empty."

Dieu buried her face in her hands, shoulders shaking as she sobbed. Awkward silence fell over the apothecary as the young woman wailed—Meng Grandmother and Teacher Hu discomfited, Thanh indifferent.

Zhara cleared her throat. "Would the—would the lady like some tea?"

After a moment, Dieu sniffed and nodded.

"Could it be," Teacher Hu murmured as she examined the boy, "the old blight?" Struck by a sudden thought, she scrabbled for something on the counter. "Zhara," she said irritably. "Where is my notebook? And why must you always be moving things around where I can't find them?"

"Sorry, auntie, sorry!" Zhara set down the tea she was preparing and retrieved the notebook from its place on the desk.

"And the missing?" the apothecary continued, scribbling down her observations. "Any idea where they might have gone?"

"None." The Buri matriarch sagged in her seat, suddenly looking very old and very frail. "That's why I was hoping you could treat Thanh somehow, so he could tell us where they have gone."

Teacher Hu closed her notebook, a furrow of concern etched between her brows. "I'm not sure what I can tell you, Meng Grandmother," she said. "He has no fever and his throat is clear. His pulse is a bit sluggish for someone his age, but nothing out of the ordinary." The apothecary got to her feet and removed her spectacles. "Physically, there is nothing wrong with the child."

"Of course there's nothing wrong with him," Dieu burst out, leaping to her feet. "Nothing! He is a perfectly ordinary boy." Her eyes shifted left, then right. "He is!"

"I never said he wasn't," Teacher Hu said in a mild voice. "Unless . . . there is something you haven't told me, young lady."

"No, no," Dieu said quickly. "We have nothing to hide." But she couldn't meet the apothecary's eyes as she spoke, continually worrying the red bead at her wrist. Zhara narrowed her eyes, studying the young mother closely as she poured cups of tea.

"Hmm," Teacher Hu said, returning the boy to his mother's arms. "I don't think I can treat Thanh. His low mood may be due to some sort of blockage in the boy's meridian. I can refer you to an acupuncturist, if you'd like."

"I don't think the boy can be cured by the Sixth Immortal's arts," Meng Grandmother muttered. "It's a matter of magic, not medicine."

"Grandmother!" Dieu cried.

Crash!

The teapot shattered as it struck the floor. "Pardon, pardon, a thousand pardons!" Zhara said, hands trembling as she gathered the pieces.

"Have a care, Meng Grandmother," Teacher Hu said in a low voice. "The Falconer has his eyes and ears everywhere throughout the city."

"Would you turn me over to the Warlord's justice then?" the old woman scoffed.

The apothecary shook her head. "Of course not," she said heavily. "You know better than anyone what little love I bear the Kestrels."

Zhara paused. She had never heard her mentor express an opinion on magic before—positive, negative, or otherwise. Fetching the broom from behind the counter, she slowly swept the broken shards, listening closely. Hopefully.

Meng Grandmother closed her eyes. "The world is out of balance," she said. "And when the balance between Order and Chaos is gone, demons start roaming the land."

Dieu gasped and tightened her arms around Thanh. "Demons?" The boy was beginning to grow restless.

"Surely not," Teacher Hu said skeptically. "Abominations haven't been seen in the Morning Realms since the end of the Just War."

"It's only a matter of time," the Buri matriarch said ominously. "The risk of possession remains as long as there are magicians to turn into monsters."

The broom in Zhara's hands flickered, and for the briefest moment, she found herself holding a rusted blade. She nearly dropped it in surprise when it flickered again, turning back into a broom. She set it aside and shoved her hands into her sleeves.

"But not all magicians turn into abominations, yes?" Dieu asked anxiously. In her arms, Thanh protested his mother's smothering and wriggled out of her grasp. "Some of them . . . get better?"

Teacher Hu and Meng Grandmother exchanged looks. "There is

no cure for possession," the apothecary said. "If there had been, we wouldn't have gone to war."

"Of course there is a cure," the old matriarch retorted. "It's in all the old stories. They say that in the war against Tiyok, the Guardian of Fire transformed all the monsters of the land back into magicians."

"Oh, Meng Grandmother." The the herbalist sighed. She tossed her notes carelessly on the counter and rubbed her eyes. "There is magic, and then there is myth."

Silence fell over the booth, the only sounds being the soft scratching sound of Thanh playing with something on the ground. With a start, Zhara realized it was a small blade that the apothecary used to shave down dried roots and herbs. She quickly went to his side and tried to pry the knife from his grasp.

"No, no," she said gently. "This isn't a toy." Thanh bared his teeth at her and wrapped his hand around hers in an attempt to reclaim his prize.

The world went white.

Alarm raced along the ki pathways of Zhara's body at his touch, but it was not fear that set her magic alight; it was recognition. A sudden sense of familiarity flooded her bones, a rush of feeling that was both intimate and intimidating. The sensation of the boy's hand against hers was a language she knew in a foreign land, a friend among strangers. She knew that touch, and would know it forever.

Thanh was a magician.

The boy was a magician, but there was something terribly wrong with him. His touch was rotten. His touch was poisoned. It was as though his soul was not part of the threads that connected the world, for there was no sense of anything living within him. Instead, something foreign, something inhuman held on to her hand as the corruption slowly spread from his soul to hers.

Her magic rallied.

A wave of power surged through her hands and into the boy's body, lighting the ki pathways along his meridian. It was as though she could see the lines of energy flow along his arms and legs and back. What should have been bright, illuminated power was blighted, diseased, corrupted. Thanh hissed with pain as her magic burned through the darkness, and he wrenched himself away before collapsing, eyes rolling to the back of his head.

"Thanh!" Dieu cried, throwing herself on her convulsing son. She glared up at Zhara. "What did you do to him?"

"N-nothing!" Zhara stumbled back, a cold sweat breaking out along her hairline. "I didn't do anything!" The memory of Suzhan twitching and moaning in the same way all those years ago returned to her. Zhara covered her mouth with her hands, choking back a sob. Had she damaged the boy with her magic as well?

"Shhh, shhh," the apothecary soothed, kneeling beside Dieu. "Let the child breathe." Teacher Hu gently untangled Dieu's arms from about Thanh's neck and supported his head upon her legs. Presently, his limbs stopped jerking, and the stiffness of his muscles eased. "He has a fever now," the herbalist said with a frown. She placed the back of her hand against his forehead. "That's likely what caused the fit."

Dieu turned to Zhara. "She did something to him," she said, pointing an accusing finger. "She's a monster!"

Zhara cringed, thinking of her sister's sightless eyes. "I—I'm sorry," she said, stepping forward helplessly. "I don't know what happened—"

"Stay away from him!" Dieu gathered up the now-sleeping Thanh and tried to carry him on her back. "Help me, Grandmother," she said to the Buri matriarch.

The old woman leaned heavily on her cane as she heaved herself to her feet. "I suppose we must be going now," she said regretfully.

Teacher Hu opened and closed several cabinet drawers, pulling out various herbs and powders and folding them up in paper. "Here," she said, handing them to Meng Grandmother. "For the boy's fever. And for you," she said to Dieu, hesitating before reaching into the small pouch of coins she carried at her waist. "Take this." She held up a small bronze coin with a circular hole in the center. "If you or your son need help, show this token to Master Cao here in the city."

Dieu's mouth tightened. After a moment, she accepted the pendant with a bow.

Thanh stirred on his mother's back, meeting Zhara's gaze as they left, his eyes no longer blank and empty. Instead a strange expression crossed his face, his features now animated by an intelligence that had not been there before, something far older and far less human than the little boy he seemed to be.

There are rumors of monsters in the marsh.

The hairs stood up on the back of Zhara's neck.

5

NIGHT HAD FALLEN, HIS BROTHER WAS MISSING, and Han was in desperate need of the next installment of *The Maiden Who Was Loved by Death*.

"I can't believe that's how it ends!" he yelled, throwing the slim little paperback across his room.

After his disastrous audience with his father and the Chancellor, Han had been unceremoniously escorted back to his quarters and confined there with no visitors and nothing to do. Although he wasn't much for reading, he decided to give this *Damsel Who Married a Demon* or whatever a try, just to pass the time. Several hours later, he had finished the entire thing in one sitting and was in agony over the fate of Little Flame now that she had agreed to be the Death Lord's bride in exchange for her sister's life. He desperately wanted to talk about the cliffhanger with someone, but the guards posted outside his door were utterly uninterested in having a conversation consisting of sentences longer than two syllables.

With nothing else to preoccupy his time or his mind, Han got to his feet and began doing squat exercises beside his bed, trying his best to sweat out the anxiety crowding his thoughts. He supposed he could try to work on his latest poem, but he had lost interest in the subject— push-ups—last week and was unmotivated to finish it. On the other hand, he had had an idea for an acrostic syllable poem for Mistress Brandy he could try to write . . .

"Miss," he muttered, feeling the burn in his thighs. "Miss . . . mistress . . . mistake . . . ugh!"

Han flopped onto the floor and lay on his back, staring up at the ceiling. It was nearing midnight and he still had no word from Xu as to his little brother's whereabouts. Anyang's most recent nursemaid had only resigned the day before, and already his little brother was causing trouble.

The matter of Anyang's nursemaids was a puzzle neither he nor Xu knew how to solve. They had gone through six in the past month alone, the longest lasting one full week before running out of the Second Heir's quarters in terror. She babbled about floating vases, strange sounds, and mysterious stains, believing the palace haunted. Han said nothing to discourage the assumption, and paid the woman a hefty sum before sending her on her way.

To those who knew him well, Anyang was a sweet little boy, full of affection and hungry for love. But to those who did not, the Second Heir was an erratic, fickle child, prone to strange and destructive outbursts. The tantrums were unmanageable, the nursemaids claimed before they resigned. The child was possessed.

That was rather closer to the truth than was comfortable.

Han flopped onto his bed, buried his face in the cushions, and screamed.

Sometimes the weight of his responsibilities was unbearable, crushing his ribs beneath a mountain of dread. He tried not to think about it much; in fact, he tried not to think too much at all. Thinking led to worrying, which led to panicking, and the last thing Anyang needed was his big brother losing his head. With their mother dead and their father lost to grief, Han was the only person left who could protect him from the Warlord's justice.

Rolling over, he threw an arm over his eyes. The hour was late, and he ought to sleep, but he couldn't get the look of triumph on the Chancellor's face out of his mind. For years, he had played a game of cat and mouse with his father's regent, evading all the matrimonial traps and pitfalls laid for him, but Han knew Princess Yulana was one snare he was not going to be able to wriggle out of so easily. As the granddaughter of the Gommun Emperor, Princess Yulana was a match too politically powerful to turn down. And as the granddaughter of the man who waged war against magicians, she was also the most dangerous one to accept.

Scritch, scritch, scritch.

Han sat up with a frown. A mouse? A rat?

Scritch, scritch, scritch. "Gogo?" A small voice came from his window. "Let me in!"

He bolted to his feet and opened the latch. "Anyang?" Looking down, he saw his little brother crouched just beneath the windowsill, hiding from the guards patrolling the palace grounds outside. "What are you doing here? And where have you been?"

"Gogo," Anyang whispered. "I don't—I don't know." He lifted a panic-stricken face to his brother, holding up his hands for Han to see. The palms glowed faintly in the dark, as though his bones and blood were made of fire.

Alarm galvanized Han's limbs. He leaned out his window and grabbed his brother beneath the shoulders, hauling the little boy up into his room before slamming the shutters closed. "What happened?" he demanded. "Are you hurt?"

Anyang shook his head. "I think—" He gulped. "I think I might have had a bad dream."

Han blinked. "A bad dream?" he asked incredulously. His little brother was covered in dirt from head to toe, his royal robes muddied and torn as though he had gotten into some sort of scuffle. He ran his hands lightly over Anyang's body, but the boy didn't seem to be injured in any way. "Are you sure?"

"I think so," his brother said, voice shaking. "Because the frog demon was there."

Ever since the Royal Consort's death, Anyang suffered from night terrors. His dreams were filled with monsters and other horrifying creatures, but the worst figure of all was one he called the frog demon. The frog demon was a recurring figure in the boy's nightmares, a fearsome creature made of absence and emptiness that could only be kept at bay by Han's presence or a candle left burning all night. Han had learned over the course of many sleepless nights that the monster's appearance was changeable—sometimes it was a frog, sometimes it was a terrifying creature with snakes for fur and a scorpion's tail. No matter what form it took, his little brother's nightmarish haunt always wanted the same thing: to take his magic and consume it.

"*There?*" Han furrowed his brows. "Where were you?"

It was a moment before Anyang replied. "The meditation gardens."

"Is that where you've been hiding all day?" Worry turned Han's voice shrill. "What were you doing there?"

Anyang studied his feet. "Playing with Yao."

"Yao? Who's Yao?"

"A kitchen servant," he said. "And . . . my friend."

"Your friend?" Fear drenched Han's bones in ice. "Didi . . . you didn't." He wrapped numb fingers around his brother's arms. "Please tell me you didn't tell this boy about—about . . ."

"My magic?"

Han flinched.

"I did."

"Anyang!"

"But only because he's a magician too!" the boy said defensively.

Han staggered back. "What?" he breathed. A strange mixture of curiosity, relief, elation, and dread stirred in his chest. Could this kitchen boy and his parents be part of the Guardians of Dawn? Or know where the Guardians could be found? And why hadn't his little brother said anything to him about this before? "How—how did you know . . ." *that you could trust him?* he wanted to finish.

Anyang shrugged. "I just knew." He held out his little glowing hand to Han, who took it in his own. "He feels like you, gogo," the boy said softly. "Safe."

"Does anyone else know?" Han asked. "About Yao, I mean." He plucked at the few strands of hair sprouting from his chin. "His parents?" he added hopefully. Someone he could talk to—talk with—commiserate with.

Anyang frowned, his lower lip pushed out in thought. "I don't know."

"Then maybe I could talk to Yao," Han said desperately. "Could you arrange a meeting?"

Anyang blinked rapidly several times, tears spilling over and leaving muddy trails down his cheeks. "Oh, gogo," he said in a trembling voice. "I don't think so."

"You could tell him I'm safe—"

The boy shook his head. "He's gone, gogo. He's gone, and it's all my fault!"

Han went still as all his anxiety returned in a rush. "What do you mean *gone*?" he said tightly. "What happened?"

"Yao and I had been playing tag all day in the meditation gardens when I got tired and decided to take a nap," Anyang said with a sniffle. "Yao was supposed to stand guard in case someone went to go fetch the Chancellor and I got into trouble for skipping out on my lessons."

Despite the dread filling his lungs, Han could feel the edges of fond nostalgia threatening to curl his lips into a smile. He and Xu had gotten into very similar antics when they were young.

"I dreamed of the frog demon." Anyang wrapped his arms about himself, rocking slightly, back and forth. "It was . . . bad."

"How so?" Han asked softly.

"Usually, when I dream of the frog demon, he sits beside me and asks me to give him my magic. When I say no, he tries to grab my magic through my chest and pulls. It hurts," Anyang said, pressing a filthy hand to his chest. "It always hurts."

Han said nothing. The piercing screams that woke the palace up in the mornings were a testament to his brother's nightly pain.

"But this time," Anyang went on, "the frog demon told me that he . . . he couldn't wait any longer. So he—he—" His voice broke and he began sobbing in earnest. "He cracked my ribs open and tried to crawl inside."

Han didn't know which hurt more—the sight of his brother's tears or the fact that he could do nothing about them. He fell to his knees and pulled Anyang into his embrace, feeling protective yet awkward at once.

"I screamed and screamed, and then"—Anyang hiccoughed—"then Yao pulled the frog demon off me."

Han drew back to look at his brother's face. "In your dream?"

Anyang frowned in confusion. "I—I'm not sure," he said with some surprise. "When the frog demon saw him, he hissed and said Yao would have to do for now. The two of them disappeared, and when I opened my eyes, it was dark and Yao was gone."

"Gone?"

Anyang nodded, running his hand across his eyes. "I think . . . I think the frog demon took him." His face was a mess of tears, snot, and mud as he lifted it to meet his brother's gaze. "And it's all my fault!"

It was likely this kitchen boy had simply returned home, but Han held his tongue. "Tomorrow," he said instead. "We'll look for your friend tomorrow."

Anyang relaxed. "Thank you, gogo," he said. "He's a boy my age, with a large, purplish birthmark here." He pointed to his collarbone, then an enormous yawn threatened to split his head in two. "Can I stay with you tonight?"

Han gave him a crooked smile. "All right, didi," he said gently. "But first let's get you cleaned up."

He helped his little brother out of his soiled clothes, washing down his hands and face with a dampened rag before handing him a clean nightshirt to wear. The two of them then climbed into Han's platform bed, Anyang snuggling in the crook where Han's arm met his shoulder. He shifted, trying not to disturb his little brother. Summer came early to the southern provinces, and the nights had already grown uncomfortably warm. Han ran hot as it was.

"Move over," the little boy grumbled. "I'm gonna fall off."

Han obliged, inching backward to allow him more room.

"More," Anyang said petulantly. "You're too big, gogo."

"And whose bed is this?" Han complained.

He could feel his brother's lips curve into a smile against his shoulder. "This is nice," Anyang murmured sleepily. "It's like when Mama was alive and we used to sleep in her bed."

"You remember that?" Anyang had only been four years old when their mother died.

The boy nodded. "Sometimes I sneak into her old residence and sleep in her bed."

"Really? Why?"

He shrugged. "It's a good place to hide."

Han supposed that was true. After his wife's death, Prince Wonhu had ordered Elegant Tranquility to be locked up and the windows covered, condemning the building to disrepair and decay. His father had abandoned their mother's memory, just as he had abandoned his sons.

"You're not scared, didi?" he asked softly.

"Of what?" Anyang asked drowsily. His lashes fluttered as his lids drooped shut.

Han pulled the sunburst pendant from beneath his shirt and studied it. "Ghosts," he said quietly.

He himself had not set foot inside Elegant Tranquility since the Royal Consort's execution. The hallways and corridors were haunted with too many memories. In the good ones he was sitting at his mother's feet as she taught one son poetry and the other son spells. Anyang would have only been three years old or so—too young to do much with the ink and brush but make a mess—but Han recalled how his mother would wrap her hand around Anyang's chubby fists and write, channeling her magic to create floating ink bubbles, fluttering paper fireflies, or simply make the wind chimes outside dance and sing.

There was only one bad memory.

The day the Kestrels had come for the Royal Consort to drag her from her beautiful, elegant quarters and condemn her as a traitor, a monster, and a magician before a crowd. The Chancellor had made the Royal Heir and his brother stand beside their father and watch as their mother was put to the pyre, made to keep their eyes open and teeth clenched as her screams of agony rang out over Zanhei. Han had had to be strong for Anyang, to keep a brave face for his little brother since they had no one. Ever since her death, Han and his brother had become orphans, their mother lost to flames, their father to grief.

Promise me, little lemur. Promise me you'll protect Anyang.

He looked to his little brother slumbering peacefully by his side. He tightened his arms around Anyang, and for a moment, the weight of that small, sleeping body soothed the endless rattle of concerns and fears within him. As long as Anyang was still safe and still alive, he had a reason to keep fighting.

Because he was so very, very tired.

Every year, every day, every hour that passed, the burden of carrying his brother's secret weighed heavier and heavier upon his soul. He had Xu to share the burden, but Xu was the Chancellor's eldest and only child. Han's best friend's position in the palace was, in many ways, just as precarious as Anyang's—walking the masculine and feminine realms of court life, defiantly both and neither at once. They were all treading water, struggling to stay afloat, stay alive. Han desperately needed help.

He studied the sunburst pattern engraved on the face of the pendant in his hand. The etched motif had faded to nearly nothing from the number of times he had worried the coin between his fingers. The Guardians of Dawn. A secret society of magicians and their sympathizers. Perhaps he was chasing a fairy tale, just like Xu had said.

But the Guardians *were* real. He had held the proof of it in his hands.

Han sighed and let his hand drop, glancing at the copy of *The Maiden Who Was Loved by Death* lying on the floor where he had tossed it. He wondered if Mistress Brandy had discovered yet that their books had been switched. He hoped not. If she figured out the significance of *The Thousand-Character Classic* . . . well. He hoped not.

"Oh, Mama," he murmured. "I made you a promise and I'm keeping it the best I can." Han tucked the token back under his nightshirt. "But it's so very hard."

At his words, Anyang stirred. "Gogo?" he asked, his voice hoarse.

"Sorry, didi," Han said softly. "Go back to sleep."

His little brother nodded and turned over. But after several moments, he flopped back and stared Han in the face. "I can't," Anyang complained, restlessly kicking at the bed linens. "I'm not tired anymore."

Han rolled over and buried his face into a cushion and groaned. "I can't do this anymore, didi," he mumbled into the pillow. He lifted his head. "Go back to sleep or go back to your own residence."

"No!" Anyang clung to his arm. "I'll be good, I promise. Just . . . maybe you can tell me a story?"

The first thing that came to Han's mind was *The Maiden Who Was Loved by Death,* which—while entertaining—was probably not something a ten-year-old boy would want to hear as a bedtime story. "How about a lullaby instead?" he suggested.

His brother shrugged. "Whatever you want."

Han cleared his throat. "*Summer, fall, winter, spring,*" he sang gently. "*Guardians rise and justice sings.*"

Anyang closed his eyes as his breathing began to slow.

"*When Tiyok stirs to life again,*" he went on, his voice growing thick with approaching slumber. "*Darkness falls and chaos reigns.*"

Soft snores arose from his brother's side of the bed.

"*Fire, wood, wind, and water, join together to prevent a slaughter.*" Han closed his own eyes, letting the last lines of the song drift into the night air.

> *Summer, fall, winter, spring*
> *Guardians rise and justice sings*

6

THE MEETING WITH LORD CHAN HAD NOT gone well.

The first sign was her sister weeping in the corner, her left eye swollen with more than tears.

The second sign was the Second Wife sitting stony-faced at the low table in the middle of the room with hands folded like a magistrate waiting to pass judgment.

The third—and most dangerous—sign was the open bottles of rice wine before her.

"Where have you been, Jin Zhara?" The Second Wife's voice was calm, cool, quiet, but lightning flashes of temper flickered deep within her eyes, a distant warning.

"Pardon, pardon, a thousand pardons." Zhara brought the large dinner tray through the doorway, laden with bowls of freshly steamed rice and the Azurean-style braised beef short ribs. She had swallowed her pride and asked for an advance on her wages from Teacher Hu at day's end in order to afford the expensive cut, and even then, the dish was more taro root and radish than meat. The short ribs had taken longer than anticipated to prepare, but Zhara was proud of the feast she had made. Yet as she laid the dishes out before her stepmother in that stale, sour room, the food looked more fit for a funeral.

Zhara bowed and retreated, steeling herself for the Second Wife's reprimand.

But it did not come. "Stay," her stepmother said, gesturing toward the seat before her. "Eat."

Zhara quickly glanced at Suzhan, then at the table. There were only two place settings, and neither was meant for her. "M-madame?"

"I feel as though we never get to talk much," the Second Wife continued silkily. "Do we, Jin Zhara?" She narrowed her eyes. "Sit."

Zhara obeyed with another bow and kneeled down on the shabby mat on the other side of the table. She kept her hands folded in her lap as the Second Wife picked up her chopsticks and took a bite of beef.

"Delicious." The Second Wife delicately dabbed at the corner of her mouth with a napkin. "What a skilled cook you are, child."

Zhara flinched. All she had ever wanted was to be worthy of her stepmother's approval. Acceptance. Affection. But the Second Wife's praise came laced with poison and Zhara braced herself for the coming pain. "I—I live to serve, Madame," she whispered.

"What a good girl." Her stepmother cracked a smile, but its edges were sharp. "You will make some lucky man a wonderful wife one day." Her eyes slid toward her daughter cringing in the corner. "What do you think, my treasure?"

The words cut deep, but it was the sickly sweet tone that sliced to the bone. Heat rushed to Zhara's cheeks as she struggled to keep her eyes down, to keep her hands to herself, to keep herself from doing anything that might set off her stepmother. Magic prickled her palms and she surreptitiously rubbed them against the fabric of her trousers beneath the table.

"Well?" The Second Wife's smile did not waver. "Why aren't you answering, my darling? Or are you dumb as well as blind?"

Suzhan took several small, strangled gulps. "Yes, Mama," she said thickly.

"Yes, what?"

Zhara held her breath as her sister lifted her head, eyes flickering sightlessly back and forth at the scene before her. "Yes," she said, quietly but clearly, "I think nene would make someone a wonderful wife someday."

"Hmmm." The Second Wife returned to eating, unsatisfied with her daughter's response but unable to find fault with it. "You," she said irritably, pointing her chopsticks at Zhara. "Why aren't you eating?"

Zhara picked up her own utensils with alacrity, forcing down several small mouthfuls of rice that stuck in her throat. Many nights she had gone to bed with a belly as hollow as a drum, but tonight she thought she might have preferred the hunger.

"So, tell me, Jin Zhara," the Second Wife said pleasantly, her consonants blurred and slurred with wine. "What would you say are the most important qualities in a wife?"

Dangerous waters. Zhara knew she would have to chart her course carefully. "D-diligence, d-duty, and d-dedication to the family, Madame," she said.

The Second Wife studied her through red-rimmed eyes. "And what would d-d-dedication to the family entail, Jin Zhara?" she sneered.

Suzhan gave a soft hiccough of despair from her corner. Zhara kept her eyes on her bowl of rice.

"Would it, for instance, entail ob-obedience to your elders?" her stepmother asked in a hard voice.

Zhara swallowed. "Yes, Madame," she said cautiously.

"Even if what they ask of you is not to your"—the Second Wife's lip curled with disdain—"liking?"

Suzhan sobbed even louder. Zhara set down her chopsticks and closed her eyes. "Yes, Madame."

"Because they know better?"

"Yes, M-madame."

"I can't hear you, Jin Zhara."

Zhara looked helplessly to her younger sister. "Yes, Madame," she repeated in a clearer voice.

"Good." The Second Wife's eyes grew small and mean. "Now, you are a good girl, Jin Zhara. You would do anything to help your family, lah? Especially if our fortunes depended on it?"

Zhara nodded, unable to speak.

"And if you had already made a promise?" her stepmother went on. "Would you break it just because the whole of the situation wasn't to your liking?"

Dread dragged Zhara's stomach down to the depths. She glanced at the purpling bruise swelling on her sister's cheek and understood that Suzhan had refused her suitor. She closed her eyes.

"Answer me." The Second Wife's voice was sharp.

"N-no, Madame." Zhara wanted nothing more than to vanish through the floorboards back to her kitchen, to hide among the soot and ashes of her hearth rather than to endure what was to come next—to be forced to become complicit in her sister's agony.

"Of course, we all have our burdens to bear." The Second Wife poured a teacup full of rice wine and slid it across the table to her stepdaughter. "We've carried the fortunes of this family on our backs for a long while, haven't we, Jin Zhara?" She held up her cup of wine. "Drink," she demanded.

Zhara quickly picked up her cup and met her stepmother's toast, watching as the Second Wife swallowed down the alcohol in a single shot. She turned away and pressed her lips tightly together as she touched the rim of her cup to her mouth, pretending to take a sip.

"It's not too much to ask my daughter—my own flesh and blood—to share in that burden with us, is it?" The Second Wife kept her eyes focused on Zhara and not Suzhan. "Is it . . . children?"

Children. Zhara's heart skipped and stuttered, hope and self-hatred fluttering about her rib cage in equal measure. She kept her gaze on the still-full cup of wine in her hands. "N-no, Madame," she said softly.

Suzhan whimpered her own assent from the corner.

"Good." The Second Wife poured herself some more rice wine and tipped the bottle over Zhara's cup. "Why aren't you drinking?" Her lips thinned into a malicious smile. "Come, come, child. Down it goes!"

Zhara's stomach turned. She had never drunk alcohol before, but she was intimately acquainted with the sweet-sour stench of stale sick from the times she had to clean up after her stepmother's nights out. Magic rose along with the bile in her throat, warming and softening the porcelain cup between her fingers. Zhara quickly tossed back its contents and swallowed the wine down with the magic.

Not wine. Water. Zhara coughed in surprise as she set down the empty cup, her palms tingling. She resisted the urge to examine her hands and folded them back under the table.

"They say the first sip is the roughest," the Second Wife said in a consoling voice, pouring her stepdaughter another drink. "Unfortunately, the taste doesn't get any smoother with time, but everything else around you does." She cackled, and her manner was suddenly loose, friendly, and warm as she leaned across the table with a convivial smile. "Drink up," she repeated. The Second Wife refilled Zhara's cup with the last of the liquor, shaking out the droplets with a frown.

Zhara wrapped her hands around her own cup but her magic seemed to have retreated. The first sip was indeed rough, the wine more fire than water as it slid down her throat. She coughed and dabbed at the tears streaming down her cheeks, trying her best not to gag. Hunger tumbled with the liquor in her gut, and she felt rather ill.

"You're not eating." Zhara looked up to find her stepmother studying her with a small smile, her red-rimmed eyes glassy and mean.

"I—I'm not hungry, Madame."

"No? I'm not either. A pity then"—the Second Wife gestured to the spread before her—"that all this should go to waste."

Suzhan lifted her head. Zhara could see the ghosts of starvation that waited in the shadows beneath her cheeks and along the sharp points of her collarbone. "Madame," she began uncertainly. "There's no need—"

"The food won't keep." The Second Wife picked up the dish and walked it to the window overlooking the street below. "We might as well throw it out." She met her stepdaughter's gaze, a malicious smirk lingering about her lips.

"No, wait!" Zhara scurried to her feet. "I—I—" She caught Suzhan's pleading expression, the subtle shake of her sister's head. It would be worse for the two of them if Zhara intervened, if she begged on her sister's behalf. She knew it, and she hated it. Zhara bowed her head and returned to her seat. "I'm sorry, Madame."

The Second Wife watched the silent exchange between her daughters, a smirk spreading across her face. "Hungrier than you thought, Jin Zhara?" she asked sweetly. She brought the plate back to the table and set it down before her stepdaughter. "Eat up." The Second Wife slid the chopsticks over. "Go on. We don't mind, do we, Suzhan?" She glanced over at her own daughter in the corner. "Do we, my treasure?"

Suzhan choked back her tears. "No, Mama," she said, her words clotted with hunger. Beneath the swollen bruise on her cheek, she barely had enough flesh to fill out the bones of her face. "Go on, nene," she said in a thin, pinched voice. "I'm fine. Honest."

Zhara slowly picked up her utensils and picked at the ribs. The cold, callous smile never left the Second Wife's face as she ate bite after reluctant bite, the meat oily and tasting of guilt as it slid all the way down.

It was well past midnight before the soft *tap-tap-tap* of Suzhan's cane coming down the stairs woke Zhara from slumber.

"Nene?"

At the sound of Suzhan's voice, Zhara immediately sat straight up on her pallet before the hearth, coughing as she waved away a cloud of cinders. She had fallen asleep before the fire while trying to make sense of *The Thousand-Character Classic*. The book of magic lay open on her pillow next to a sleeping Sajah, its pages smudged with ash and drool. "Mimi?" she croaked, throwing her arms about her sister as she got to her feet.

Suzhan flinched and hissed with pain.

"Did I hurt you?" Zhara asked anxiously, gently touching the bruise on her sister's cheek. "Did Madame . . . ?" She didn't finish the sentence.

"I'm fine," Suzhan said, brushing off her sister's hand. "You just surprised me is all."

With some reluctance, Zhara retreated to the hearth and lit a taper, bringing it over to the stove to start the fire again and reheat the congee she had thrown together from the dinner's leftovers. "You must be starving," she said, rolling out a small, round folding table from the corner. She set down a bowl of congee before her sister. "I know it's not much," she said apologetically.

"It's better than nothing," Suzhan said quietly. "Thank you, nene." She scooped herself a large mouthful then winced as the motion pulled at the swelling on her cheek.

Zhara wet a rag and pressed it against the bruise. "This looks bad, mimi," she said, hissing in sympathetic pain. In the firelight, the bruise was an enormous spiderweb that covered one side of Suzhan's face, the purpling cheek mottled black and red.

"I've had worse."

They both had. The long-healed scars on Zhara's back and legs throbbed in time to the bunching muscles of Suzhan's cheek as she chewed and swallowed, chewed and swallowed. Zhara held her tongue, letting Suzhan finish her meal in peace. She would speak when she was ready.

Suzhan finished the last of the congee with a loud slurp and set the bowl down on the table with a satisfied smack of her lips. "That was delicious, nene," she said. "Thank you."

A meal scrounged from the sad remains of better feasts. "I know it wasn't what you wanted, mimi," she said regretfully.

"What I want doesn't matter," Suzhan said bitterly. "It never has. Nobody cares what I want." Her shoulders dropped, and she suddenly looked old, far older than her thirteen years, the flesh of her face collapsing into the hollows of her bones. "I suppose you want to know what happened today."

Zhara cleared the dishes and put the folding table away. "Only if you want to tell me," she said, taking the pot of congee off the burner ring.

"I know—I know I've disappointed everyone," Suzhan quavered. There was a jingle by the bed as Sajah shook himself awake, coming to comfort the girl by rubbing himself against her legs. "Lord Chan was—is—our last and only chance to save us from debt bondage." Suzhan picked up the cat and buried her face in his fur. "Or worse."

Zhara scrubbed the dishes without another word. Her entire life with the Second Wife was one of indentured servitude, but with a bond debt she could never hope to repay. But Suzhan was right; life could get much worse than this. Magic warmed her hands, casting a soft light in the dark kitchen.

"I was so scared to meet him," Suzhan whispered. "I was scared that my husband would be cruel or harsh or unkind. I found out when we got to the Peony Garden teahouse that I was to be his fourth bride."

"Fourth?" Zhara was startled.

Her sister nodded. "While Mama and the matchmaker were finalizing matters in the other room, I overheard the servers talking about Lord Chan." Her lips twisted. "Sometimes people think if the blind can't see, then the blind can't hear anything either," she said wryly. "So they'll be indiscreet."

Zhara was almost afraid to ask. "What did they say?"

"That each of my three predecessors had died under mysterious circumstances."

All the hairs stood up on the back of Zhara's neck. Sajah snapped up his head to gaze at Suzhan with concern, the tip of his tail flicking back and forth with worry. "Mysterious . . . circumstances?"

Suzhan nervously picked at the fur on top of Sajah's head, who hissed and scowled with displeasure but made no effort to move from her untender ministrations. "I was too afraid to ask," she said in a voice so small that Zhara had to strain to hear her words. "Do you know what they called him?" She laughed darkly. "The Black Widower."

Zhara flinched. "I'm sure there's a perfectly reasonable explanation—"

"For the untimely death of three different wives?" Suzhan said scornfully. "Lord Chan is either extremely unlucky or extremely careless." She turned her dim gaze to the flickering fire. "If it had been the former, I would have said yes. Heavens know we need the money," she said. "But the moment I met my future husband, I knew it was the latter."

"How so?"

It was a long while before Suzhan replied. "It is one thing to be cruel or unkind," she said softly. "But it is another thing altogether to be empty."

"Empty?" Zhara frowned. "What do you mean?"

Her sister stared into the darkness. "Devoid of feeling," she said at last. "Soulless." She worried the edge of a fingernail, the tip bitten to the quick. "There are some," Suzhan said, "who are dead even as they breathe."

Zhara didn't know how to respond. There were no words of comfort she could offer her sister, no hope, no encouragement. Magic flickered in her veins, distant lightning before a storm. "We should get you back upstairs," she murmured. "Before Madame discovers you're gone."

"Mama's dead drunk," Suzhan said flatly. "Not even the return of Tiyok and the Ten Thousand Demons could wake her right now." She reached out, hands grasping for her sister's arm. "Let me stay here tonight, nene," she pleaded. "She won't even know I was gone."

Zhara knew that as the older sibling, she ought to be the responsible one, to make sure Suzhan made it upstairs to her own bed before the Second Wife discovered her daughter missing. But the sight of her sister's unshed tears melted Zhara's resolve, and she shook her head with a sigh.

"All right," she said. "But as long as you go back before dawn."

"I promise," Suzhan said eagerly, climbing into her sister's bed. "Eh?" She pulled out a slightly rumpled paperback from beneath her. "What's this?"

The Thousand-Character Classic. Zhara quickly plucked the book of magic out of her sister's hands and shoved it under her pillow. "N-nothing," she said. "Just a romance novel."

Suzhan chuckled. "Did you get your hands on the latest volume of *The Girl Whose Lover Died?*"

"What?" Zhara blinked in confusion.

"I'm only teasing, nene," her sister said. "I know it's *The Maiden Who Was Loved by Death.*"

Master Plum Blossom's face rushed before her mind's eye, and the Good-Looking Giggles returned. "Oh." She laughed, realizing her encounter with him had been only hours ago. "No, I didn't I'm afraid."

"Too bad." Suzhan snuggled deeper into the pallet with Sajah curled up in her arms. "I know you were in agony over the last cliffhanger." She yawned. "Maybe you could read some to me."

Zhara slid *The Thousand-Character Classic* farther beneath her pillow. "It's too dark to read now, mimi."

"Oh." Suzhan blinked. "Sometimes I forget. No matter." She smiled and closed her eyes. "Sing me a lullaby, nene," she said, her words slowing and softening with encroaching sleep.

"You know I can't sing." Zhara lay down beside her sister. "Besides, you're the musical one, mimi." Back when her father was alive and they had money to spare, Suzhan had taken zither lessons. The tutor had even called her extraordinarily gifted and had recommended the girl for the academy at Jingxi. But that dream, like so many others, had disappeared down the debt abyss.

"Music isn't only about the notes," Suzhan said. "It's about the feeling." Her fingers plucked at invisible strings, the memory of songs she had once played still lingering in her hands. "Sing, nene. Or if you won't sing, then tell me a story."

Zhara snuggled closer despite the heat of the fire at her back. Sajah removed himself from Suzhan's embrace and curled up at their feet, his deep, thrumming purr sending a comforting rumble through their bones. "I only know love stories, and you hate romances."

"Doesn't matter," Suzhan mumbled. "I just like the sound of your voice." She yawned. "Tell me again of the magpie lovers."

Drowsiness draped its heavy wings over Zhara's eyes and weighed down her lips, her teeth, her tongue. "Long, long ago," she began, "before Reason and Order governed the land, a fairy prince fell in love with a woodcutter's daughter."

Her sister fell asleep long before Zhara even reached the climax, when the gods unleashed the River of Stars across the blanket of night to separate the two ill-fated lovers forever. Only on the Night of the Sevens, when the magpie star appears between their constellations and creates a bridge across the heavenly river, are the fairy prince and the woodcutter's daughter reunited, and the land rejoices in romance. The tale of the magpie lovers held a special place in Zhara's heart; she had been born on the Night of the Sevens, and her father had called her his little magpie girl—the star born of the impossible love between a magician and a girl from beyond the Shining Sea.

And like the fairy tale, her parents' romance had ended in tragedy.

Despite her exhaustion, sleep felt like a distant shore she could not reach. Fatigue dragged down the last of Zhara's emotional defenses, drowning her in the aftermath of the terror and anxiety she had carried within her all day. The Kestrels, the little magician boy, abominations, Suzhan's marriage, the looming threat of debt bondage . . . each and every worry hit her again and again like an incoming tide, each wave higher than the last. Not even her sister's presence at her side nor Sajah's weight at her feet could soothe the rising panic within, and Zhara turned over and over, restless and agitated.

Her fingers brushed against the copy of *The Thousand-Character Classic* beneath her pillow.

An over-large nose, adorable dimples, and enormous doe eyes rose up in Zhara's mind, and she found herself giggling uncontrollably again. Suzhan stirred sleepily beside her, and she clapped her hand over her mouth, trying in vain to contain her laughter.

Master Plum Blossom. She recalled the jasmine and ylang ylang—soap smell of his skin as they were pressed together in the alleyway, the pulse of his heart beating against her chest as they waited for the Kestrels to pass. Until now, she had not allowed herself to dwell on their encounter in the covered market, waiting to savor that memory like a piece of dragon's-beard candy she had saved for a treat.

For the first time all day, Zhara allowed herself to unwrap the feeling contained around the boy she had met in the marketplace. An emotion both exciting and tender, exhilarating and terrifying at the same time. Warmth kindled about her heart, a glow that enveloped her body and skin like magic. It felt like magic. It felt like . . .

Hope.

The reason Master Plum Blossom hadn't wanted the Kestrels to find him in possession of *The Thousand-Character Classic* was because it was a book of magic. Master Cao had given a book of magic to Master Plum Blossom. The reason the bookseller gave him a book of magic was because his little brother had . . . gifts.

Gifts.

Zhara sat up in her bed.

Master Plum Blossom's little brother was a magician. If his little brother was a magician, then it meant Master Plum Blossom was . . .

Safe.

"Nene," Suzhan mumbled. "Is everything all right?"

Zhara settled back down beneath the covers. "Yes, mimi," she said softly. "Everything is going to be all right."

As the tides of anxiety began to ebb, drowsiness came in instead. Hope filled the low places of her soul like a well. For the first time in a long while, Zhara found herself looking forward to the morrow instead of dreading the dawn.

7

MAGICIANS, ZHARA DECIDED, WERE AN OBSTINATELY OBTUSE group of people.

"*The heavens were black, the earth yellow,*" she read aloud, running her finger over the first line of *The Thousand-Character Classic* and trying to decipher its meaning for the thousandth time. "*The universe vast and limitless.*"

Teacher Hu had left early again on one of her mysterious errands, leaving Zhara to run the apothecary until closing. Usually she would have taken this opportunity to catch up on one of her many romance serials, but she had spent the afternoon trying to make sense of *The Thousand-Character Classic* instead.

As far as she could tell, *The Thousand-Character Classic* was some sort of primer on the Language of Flowers, the system of writing magicians used to record their history and their spells. What she *couldn't* make sense of was the language itself. Magicians didn't appear to use an alphabet; in fact, each word seemed to be represented by a single logograph comprised of a complex series of lines and strokes. If that were the case, then a magician would have to know at least a couple hundred characters to write out a single thought—several thousand if they wanted to write out more than a mere handful of spells.

"What an incredibly inefficient way of doing magic," Zhara grumbled as she thumbed through the pages. She only had a few hazy memories of her father actively casting spells; her earliest years were spent in a rural farming village leagues outside Zanhei, where her father had been the only magician for miles. To her, magic was the shuffle of feet on the platform outside their door. The ringing of chimes that heralded a visitor. The low murmurs and requests for rain, a good harvest, remedies for everything from a fever to a broken heart. The exchange of goods or money. Her father's hands opening an enameled rosewood box. Inside, nestled on silk, a lavender quartz pendant carved with a sunburst pattern, a violet inkstone, and a brush. The tools of a magician.

Those tools were gone now, charred to ash like her father's remains.

Zhara traced the first four characters of *The Thousand-Character Classic* onto Teacher Hu's countertop, imagining magic pouring like ink from her fingertips. "Heaven, earth, black, yellow," she said, then gasped in shock when glowing rose-gold letters left trails of light on the wooden surface. Pulse pounding with excitement, she held her breath as the light faded.

Nothing happened.

Feeling sheepish, Zhara studied her hands, wondering what she had done wrong. Lines of fire still crisscrossed her palms, but the magic lingered beneath her skin. She thought of the brush and inkstone that had hung from her father's belt as he went about his commissions, and considered the strange glyphs and characters on the pages before her. She had never needed the medium of writing to perform magic before; for her, magic seemed to be a matter of will, not writing. But perhaps learning how to write the Language of Flowers would help her channel and control her power. Zhara rubbed her palms together, thinking of Suzhan, the custard she had turned from salty to sweet, and the rice wine she had transformed into water. Flames blossomed in her hands like a bouquet of flowers, bright and beautiful.

The chimes above Teacher Hu's booth jangled.

Zhara clapped her hands together in panic, smothering the flames and giving a nervous bow. "Welcome, customer, welcome— Oh, Meng Grandmother," she said, somewhat relieved. "Teacher Hu didn't say the Buri were coming in today."

"Where's the herbalist?" the Buri matriarch asked brusquely. She stomped into the apothecary shop, unaccompanied. The Buri rarely traveled into the city alone, and a person of Meng Grandmother's status would almost certainly *never* go anywhere without a member of her family escorting her.

"Unfortunately, Teacher Hu has left for the day," Zhara said, rushing to the old woman's side. "But perhaps I can be of assistance?"

"I don't want you," Meng Grandmother snapped, impatiently brushing her off. "I need Teacher Hu."

Zhara flinched and brought the back of her hands to her forehead and bowed deep from the waist. "Beg pardon," she whispered. "I did not mean to offend Meng Grandmother."

"Oh, get over yourself, child." Zhara lifted her head in surprise as the Buri matriarch shook her head with a sigh. "I don't mean to growl at you, it's just"—she wrung her gnarled hands atop her cane—"Thanh and Dieu have gone missing, and it's all that meddling herbalist's fault."

The magician boy and his mother. Zhara absentmindedly rubbed at her arms, trying to rid herself of the remembered sensation of Thanh's twisted ki—sticky, rotted, *wrong*. "They've gone missing?"

Meng Grandmother nodded. "No one's seen them in nearly a week." She wrung her hands over the top of her rattan cane, worrying the polished wood over and over again beneath her fingers. "I thought—I had hoped . . . that the apothecary might know where they had gone."

Zhara shook her head. "I'm sorry," she said regretfully. "I haven't seen either Thanh or Dieu since the last time they were here in the shop."

At her words, the Buri matriarch seemed to collapse about herself, and Zhara hurried to fetch her a seat before the old woman crumpled to the floor. Her dark complexion was ashen beneath the beads of her midnight-blue headdress, the skin about her eyes sagging and swollen with fear. "That fool girl," Meng Grandmother muttered to herself. "What has she done to my great-grandson now?"

"Teacher Hu?" Zhara was confused.

"Dieu," the old woman said furiously. "She was always a flighty one, she. Twitchy and nervous, like a rabbit. And now she and the boy have run off, straight into the claws of the nearest Kestrel. I ought to—" Meng Grandmother abruptly turned her head, beads clacking as she dashed angry tears from her cheeks. "I ought to have taught her better," she finished softly.

Zhara didn't know what to say. Any words of comfort would be insufficient and insincere in the face of the Buri matriarch's fear and grief, and the touch of her hand seemed too intimate and impertinent all at once. She would have offered the old woman some tea, but had forgotten to replace the broken teapot. "Wouldn't we have heard if the Kestrels made any arrests?" she asked tentatively.

"True," Meng Grandmother said darkly. "The last time the Falconer's peacekeepers swept through the south, they left burning bodies in their wake."

Zhara winced, remembering the purge pyres in the marshy fields outside city walls, the smoke, the screams, the smell. "Then perhaps Thanh and his mother have simply run away," she said in what she hoped was a reassuring tone of voice.

"And gone where?" The old woman drummed the tip of her cane against the floor, a nervous *rat-a-tat-tat*. "And for what reason? I suppose it's too much to hope that my foolish granddaughter had the wits to actually find those blasted rebels calling themselves the Guardians of Dawn."

At first Zhara didn't think she had heard the old woman correctly. "The Guardians of Dawn?" she asked. "As in . . . the elemental companions of the Sunburst Warrior? The Guardians of Fire, Wood, Wind, and Water?"

The Buri matriarch gave a derisive snort. "At least you seem to have a good head on your shoulders," she said. "I suppose you don't lend credence to these rumors of a secret magical resistance organization either."

All the hair stood up along Zhara's arms as her magic leaped to the surface of her skin. "A secret magical resistance organization?" she asked, trying her best to keep the excitement out of her voice. Suddenly Master Plum Blossom's plea to Master Cao made sense. *Then can he tell me where I might find the Guardians of Dawn?* She stifled a gasp when she realized that if *The Thousand-Character Classic* had come from Master Cao, then the little bookseller must know something of magic himself. "N-no, I haven't heard anything about them."

Meng Grandmother narrowed her eyes in suspicion as she reached into the collar of her dress and pulled out a pendant strung on a piece of twine. Taking it off, she thrust the necklace into Zhara's hands. "Do you know anything about this?" she demanded.

Zhara examined the pendant. "What is this?" At first glance it appeared to be a coin with a circular hole instead of the customary square, stamped with a sunburst pattern on the face. "Some sort of token?"

"How should I know?" Meng Grandmother said irritably. "Your Teacher Hu gave it to my impressionable granddaughter when we were last here. Told her to go find a seller of dirty magazines or something." She made a sound of disgust deep at the back of her throat. "And here I thought your apothecary was one of the reasonable ones," she grumbled. "So much for that."

Zhara studied the pendant again. The sunburst pattern was familiar, and she had definitely seen it before, but she could not place where. For some reason, the image of her father's hands opening his enameled rosewood box returned to her over and over again, but that box had been covered with images of magpies and spotted deer, not the sun.

Then she remembered.

The lavender quartz seal that had proclaimed Jin Zhanlong as an imperial magician of the previous dynasty. The sunburst was a symbol of the Mugungs, the family that had been deposed when the Warlord took the Sunburst Throne.

She sucked in a sharp breath as her magic roared within her, the furnace of power fueled by realization. The pendant in her fingers flickered from bronze to bone. Startled, she dropped the token and it landed on the floor with a dull *clack!* When Zhara picked it up again, she saw what had been a metal coin was now an ivory button. Sweat beaded along her hairline as she tried desperately to change the pendant back without the Buri matriarch noticing.

"C-could the Guardians of D-dawn be real?" Zhara whispered. Her magic flickered and wavered beneath her, buffeted about by the winds of anticipation and not a little fear. In her palm, she could feel the token changing back and forth between bronze and bone, bronze and bone. The possibility that there were other magicians alive in the

Morning Realms, that there may be those who had managed to escape the Warlord's purges after the Just War, made Zhara feel . . . hope.

For a moment, she thought Meng Grandmother would scoff and dismiss her question outright as wishful thinking. After all, the notion of a secret society of rebel magicians was ludicrous. But the Buri matriarch pursed her lips thoughtfully, her faded eyes soft and pitying as she studied the light that emanated from Zhara's hands.

"If the Guardians of Dawn are real," the old woman said, "then I'd say they're shit at what they're supposed to do."

"Which is what?" Zhara asked.

Meng Grandmother held her gaze. "Protect those in need," she said softly. "And get that usurping northerner off the Sunburst Throne."

Zhara clapped a hand over her mouth. "That's treason, Meng Grandmother."

The old woman shrugged. "And maybe that's what the world needs now. For my great-grandson's sake." She reached out her weathered, withered hand and rested it on Zhara's arm. Zhara flinched, but just as with Master Plum Blossom, her magic did not seem to sting or burn the Buri matriarch. "And yours."

Zhara turned her hand over. The pendant lay in her palm, solid bronze once more.

"Keep it," Meng Grandmother said, closing Zhara's fingers over the token again. Her smile was warm, but her eyes were sad. "Who knows? Maybe you'll have a chance to use it and find out if the Guardians actually exist."

"But what about Thanh? And Dieu? Won't they need it? What if they come back?"

The old woman shook her head, the beads of her headdress clacking mournfully about her face. "Wherever my granddaughter and great-grandson have gone," she murmured, "I'm afraid they're beyond our help."

8

UNFORTUNATELY, THE ROYAL PORTRAIT ARTIST WAS GOOD.
Very good.

Too good.

Han stared morosely at the ink painting of his face and hated how accurately Master Kong had managed to capture not just his features, but the ki that animated them. The face that stared back at him from the silk scroll was strong-jawed and willful, with large, intense eyes, a prominent nose, and a good-natured expression. Looking at the portrait was like staring into his mother's and father's faces all at once. His mother's eyes and mouth were framed by his father's nose and jaw, both familiar and foreign to him at the same time. He was handsome, Han realized with some surprise and not a little pride. Of course, he had always known he was considered good-looking, but he had always assumed his attractiveness was mostly due to his royal title, not his actual looks. For the first time, Han wondered if this was how other people saw him, as a collection of features arranged in a pleasing manner.

He wondered if this was how Mistress Brandy had seen him.

"Extraordinary," said Xu, getting up from their perch on the couch to examine the painting more closely. "Master Kong certainly is a genius with the brush. The likeness is uncanny; no one will fail to recognize His Grace in the streets now."

Han glared at his best friend, who flicked their fan open to deflect his scowl.

"Ooh, look, my prince," Xu continued. "Master Kong has even managed to capture His Grace's angry dimples."

Said angry dimples deepened as Han tightened his jaw. "Very impressive," he said stiffly.

"I hope His Grace is pleased with the result," the artist said nervously, cleaning his brushes with a soft cloth. His assistants bustled about, clearing away dirty bowls of ink and water. "Prince Wonhu decreed that his son be portrayed in the most flattering and accurate manner."

Han smiled, but it was more grimace than grin. "You're too skilled, Master Kong," he said through clenched teeth. "Truly."

The artist looked relieved. "His Grace is too kind," he said with a bow. "I would be most grateful if the Royal Heir would convey his commendation of my work to the Chancellor."

Han sighed as he watched Master Kong and his assistants carefully put his portrait away. "How long before the betrothal announcement goes out?" As per Zanhei tradition, his father had commissioned Han's portrait to be painted and disseminated throughout the city along with the announcement of his engagement to Princess Yulana. *How long before my days of anonymity are over?* he wanted to ask, but held his tongue. No one knew what the Royal Heir looked like because the Royal Heir had never left the palace in an official capacity. But soon, a change of clothes would no longer suffice as a disguise whenever Han wanted to leave the palace in an *un*official capacity.

If he would ever leave the palace again in an unofficial capacity.

"It will be a few days before my assistants can produce enough copies to distribute throughout the city," Master Kong replied. "But they shall be ready before Princess Yulana's arrival next week, never fear, my prince."

Han and Xu exchanged startled glances. "What?" he asked. "So soon?"

A journey from the northern capital of Urghud down to Zanhei took at least two months—longer during the upcoming monsoon season. Unless Princess Yulana and her entourage traveled on magical steeds, there was no way his future bride could arrive in Zanhei so quickly . . . unless this marriage had been arranged far more in advance than he had been led to believe.

"Yes, Your Grace," Master Kong said, eyes flitting from Han's angry dimples to his furrowed brow. "Princess Yulana is to arrive in time for the Night of the Sevens, where I believe His Eminence the Chancellor intends to formally introduce her to the citizens of Zanhei at the masquerade ball."

The Night of the Sevens was Zanhei's most famous festival, and travelers from throughout the Morning Realms flooded the southern capital in order to witness the week-long celebration of the magpie lovers. There were street fairs, wish lanterns, dancing, and celebrating, all of which culminated in a masquerade ball and a fireworks display at the palace. It was Han's favorite holiday—former favorite holiday now, it seemed.

"How romantic," Xu cooed, clapping their hands excitedly. Then, seeing Han's thunderous expression, they quickly began ushering Master Kong and his assistants toward the door. "Anyway," they said in a bright voice. "Exquisite work, as always, Master Kong. Immaculate. Marvelous. Absolutely meritorious. Many thanks for your time and talent." Xu succeeded in efficiently bustling the artist and his assistants out of the Royal Heir's residence just before Han's temper tempest struck.

"Mother of Demons!" Han burst out, pulling and tearing at the myriad strings and buttons of his princely attire. The stiff, starched collar of his royal-blue robes cut into his neck, and he wanted nothing more than to rip off the trappings of his title and fling them all into the sun. "I've been set up."

Xu let out a long-suffering sigh as they shut the enormous wooden doors firmly behind Master Kong. "As the heir to Zanhei's throne, His Grace has always known his marriage would be one of politics, not personal preference," they reminded him gently.

"I know," Han growled, struggling with one of the many knots holding his entire ensemble together. "But I could have found out sooner." He frowned as he picked at the string, which only seemed to make the tangle worse.

"I think my father has learned by now that His Grace is on a need-to-know basis with regard to marriage proposals," Xu said mildly. "Considering how his other betrothals ended."

Han grunted in frustration and grabbed at the layers of silk surrounding him, attempting to simply pull all seven layers of his royal regalia over his head. "Get me out of these," he barked. "Before I tear them off."

"As my prince commands," Xu purred. Their nimble fingers made short work of the several hundred fastenings on Han's attire. "I thought he would never ask."

He knew his best friend was trying to tease him out of his bad mood, but Han was in a pit of despair so deep there was no digging himself out. A profound sense of powerlessness settled over him as he thought of his predicament—and Anyang's. Princess Yulana was the Warlord's granddaughter. The Warlord had gone to war to rid the land of magicians. The Second Heir was a magician. And if the Warlord's granddaughter found out . . .

Han grabbed his headpiece and tossed it across the room, kicking at the puddled robes about his feet for good measure.

"Your Grace," Xu said softly.

It was the sorrow, not censure, in his best friend's voice that made Han pick up his discarded things and lay them out on his bed. He supposed he could call in the valets waiting just outside his door to handle his regalia and put it all away with the respect and care that said items deserved, but having worn his royal face for the past several days, he just wanted to take off that mask and just be Han for a moment. A seventeen-year-old boy about to be married off against his will to the granddaughter of the very person who could destroy everything he had ever loved.

He sat down on his bed and buried his head in his hands. "What am I going to do?" The sunburst coin slipped out from beneath the collar of his undershirt and dangled beneath his nose. He reached up to fiddle with the pendant, feeling its familiar shape press grooves into the palm of his hand. "Is there some way to . . . call this betrothal off?"

"I don't think so," said Xu regretfully. "The entire Morning Realms would think His Grace mad for refusing the hand of the emperor's granddaughter . . . mad or worse."

"What could be worse than madness—oh." *Magic. Of course.* "So you're saying that if I refuse to marry Princess Yulana, I'm essentially giving us away?" Han pinched the bridge of his nose to stave off the headache brewing there. "I hate this. Why couldn't we just say it was a matter of . . . incompatibility?"

"His Grace has always known his marriage would be a matter of politics, not—"

"—personal preference," Han finished. He sighed. "I know." Unbidden, the image of Mistress Brandy returned to him, or rather, the memory of her laugh as she teased him about his blushing cheeks. Although he would never admit it to anyone, he imagined her face whenever he read about the heroine in *The Maiden Who Was Loved by Death,* and himself as the dark, handsome, mysterious hero. As next in line to the throne of Zanhei, Han had never given much thought to romance—his parents had been in love, and that love had mattered little in the end. In the end, his father had still seen his beloved perish by fire and done nothing to save her. But for the first time in his life, Han wondered what it would be like to be married to someone he . . . liked. Someone he wanted to see again. And again. And again. And get to know better and better, more and more.

"We could always try to get the princess to call off the engagement herself," Xu suggested. "It's worked several times before."

Han snorted. "If she's heard all the unflattering rumors about me and *still* agreed to this marriage, then she's either spineless or more strong-willed than we thought." He frowned. "I'm not sure which is worse."

Xu sighed as they carefully began smoothing the creases out of Han's royal regalia. "Well, short of sending an assassin after Princess Yulana— which I do not recommend, by the by, hiring killers is a bureaucratic *nightmare*—perhaps the easier course of action would indeed be to find the Guardians of Dawn to see if anything could be done about the Second Heir's . . . fits."

Han shot his best friend a sharp look. "How do you know that about hiring assassins?"

They didn't reply and continued to neatly fold the royal robes, a little smile playing about their lips.

"Well, if you have any suggestions about where to start looking, I'm all ears," Han said.

Xu shook their head. "I'm not sure where to start looking for the Guardians of Dawn, but I believe we can start with something easier and more to His Grace's liking."

Han sat up straighter on his bed. "What is it?"

They walked to the wardrobe containing his undergarments and rooted about the bottom before pulling out a well-read paperback. "I propose an exchange."

"Yah!" Han started forward. "How did you find that?"

"Oh, please," Xu said disdainfully. "I've known His Grace since we were both babes in our mothers' arms, and I know he—like every other boy his age—has absolutely no imagination when it comes to hiding that which he does not want to be found. Although," they grinned, "I admit this is the first time I've seen a boy hide a romance novel and not *Tales from the Downy Delta*."

Han snatched *The Maiden Who Was Loved by Death* out of Xu's hands. "It's not *just* a romance novel," he said, somewhat defensively. "It's a story about selfish and selfless love."

"*And* stolen kisses under the moonlight." Xu fluttered both their fan and their eyelashes at once. "We can't forget that."

"They haven't even kissed yet," Han muttered, then scowled. "But that's not important." He crossed his arms with a pout. "You said I would like your plan."

"Yes," Xu said simply. "Because it involves sneaking out of the palace in disguise and seeing"—their eyes twinkled knowingly—"Mistress Brandy again."

Han slipped from his seat in excitement. "Mistress Brandy?" he squeaked, before clearing his throat and regaining his composure. "What for?"

"For her copy of *The Thousand-Character Classic,* of course."

He felt an unexpected pang at the loss of his beloved romance novel before he realized that he could probably buy another copy. And all the other installments in the series. And anything else the author, Jae Hyun, might have written. Han's spirits lifted right back up before falling again. "You're presuming she still has it," he said. "And that she hasn't—I don't know—turned it over to the Kestrels or something."

"I doubt that, my prince," Xu said. "If His Grace's mystery lady turned a book of magic over to the Warlord's peacekeepers, we would have heard about it by now. The news of someone still producing books of magic isn't some trivial matter to be brushed aside. No," they said. "It's far more likely that she's held on to or destroyed it."

"And what if she's destroyed it?"

Xu shrugged. "Then she's destroyed it. But at least we'll know she's still trustworthy."

Understanding dawned on Han's face. "Because she didn't betray us to the Warlord's justice."

They inclined their head. "Just so, my prince."

Han's spirits lifted again. "All right," he said eagerly. "When do we leave?"

Xu furrowed their brows. "As soon as we can figure out a way to get His Grace out of the palace without being recognized. Those royal portraits will be disseminated throughout the city in a few days, and it'll be too late by then."

Han glanced at the copy of *The Maiden Who Was Loved by Death* in his best friend's hand. "About that disguise . . . I might have an idea myself."

9

I**N THE DAYS FOLLOWING MENG GRANDMOTHER'S VISIT** to the apothecary, Zhara didn't have much chance to ask Teacher Hu about the Guardians of Dawn, nor was she sure how she would broach the subject if she did. But if the apothecary were indeed involved in a secret, magical resistance organization, then that could explain her mysterious and unpredictable absences from work. Zhara felt rather sheepish for never once bothering to ask about Teacher Hu's odd hours, but she had respected the herbalist's privacy because the herbalist had respected hers. It was Teacher Hu's discretion, more than the wages, that had convinced Zhara to accept the job. Discretion wasn't as good as protection, but it was enough to survive on.

Be good, the Second Wife had said, *lest you forget who has protected you all these years.*

For as long as Zhara could remember, her stepmother had kept her safe from the Warlord's justice. In the months after Jin Zhanlong's death, the Second Wife had testified before the Falconer that she had had no knowledge of her second husband's magic, and that his young daughter, Jin Zhara, had died with her mother during the Just War. As far as city records were concerned, Jin Zhara was dead. Jin Zhara had died so Jin Zhara could live.

She never knew why her stepmother had saved her life. She had never dared to ask, unsure of whether or not she wanted to know the answer. The Second Wife had not known, when the Kestrels came to drag Jin Zhanlong away, that the little girl she had hidden in her clothes chest was also a magician. Not then. It wasn't until Zhara had accidentally set the tea roses in the garden on fire that her stepmother discovered just what she had brought into her home. Back when they had a home with a garden. Before the debt collectors came.

The Second Wife could have turned her stepdaughter over to the Warlord's justice then. The head Kestrel, also known as the Falconer, had not yet disbanded the tribunals overseeing the trials and sentencing of accused magicians, and there were at least one or two people being brought before them every week or so. Some of them had even been children younger than Zhara, all consigned to die by fire. But the Second Wife never gave her up, never betrayed her.

And for that, Zhara could never repay her. As much as Zhara respected and admired Teacher Hu, who had given her a job in the apothecary when she had nowhere else to go, the herbalist could never live up to that sort of trust.

Drums sounded the sundown hour. Another day, another evening alone in the shop. But Zhara didn't mind; she loved closing up shop. Afterward, she would allow herself to wander through the covered market and look at the beautiful and expensive wares on display for the upcoming Night of the Sevens festival, imagining what she would wear if she were ever invited to the masquerade ball at the palace.

Imagining herself dancing with Master Plum Blossom on the most romantic night of the year.

It was silly, she knew, daydreaming about a boy whose name she didn't actually know, but dresses were expensive and dreams were free.

She paused before a booth to admire a pair of white satin slippers on display. The intricate glass beading on the toes caught the setting sun and sparkled like starlight on water, and the sides were embroidered with a design of the palest pink and yellow water lilies. The insides were lined with plush red velvet and Zhara could only imagine what such luxury would feel like beneath her feet. It would feel like walking on clouds. She looked down at her own shoes, where her littlest toe was beginning to peek through the threadbare canvas, and sighed.

"You touch it, you buy it," came a voice from inside the shop. A grumpy, sleepy-eyed merchant emerged from the shadows. "Otherwise, be off with you."

"How much?" she asked. She knew she couldn't afford them, but she didn't care.

The merchant took in her shabby tunic and trousers, the oft-repaired seams of her shoulders and sleeves, and the ragged, unfinished hems of her too-short pants. Zhara squirmed, self-conscious of how the fabric bunched and stretched across her chest and armpits ever since she had grown curves.

"Too much for the likes of you," the merchant said with a sniff. "Now be gone."

Zhara flushed and made an abrupt about-face, hurrying away as though she could outpace the shame that nipped at her heels. She left the luxury-goods sector and found herself in the religious district, where a large crowd was gathered in the commons outside the Temple of the Immortals. Someone in the purple-red tunic and feathered hat of the royal crier stood on the proclaiming platform, flanked by a pair of Kestrels. They held a small brass gong aloft, ringing it with a mallet to bring everyone to the square.

"A pronouncement, a pronouncement, a royal proclamation!" the crier called out. "Gather around and heed the words of our sovereign, Prince Wonhu!"

Terror gripped Zhara's neck, and she wondered if she were about to witness the first arrest of a magician since the Kestrels arrived in town. Her hands immediately went to the copy of *The Thousand-Character Classic* tucked into the back of her sash, her eyes darting back and forth for the nearest escape.

The royal crier pulled a scroll from their sash with a flourish. "*Cit-izens of Zanhei,*" they said, reading aloud in a sonorous voice. "*Let it hereby be known that the House of Wonhu has been honored with an offer of a marriage alliance with the Gommun Kang, the clan of the Great Bear of the North, from which our esteemed and august emperor is descended, may his reign last for ten thousand years.*"

A murmur of surprise went through the audience. Zhara paused, wanting to find out more despite the presence of the Kestrels on the platform. She knew she shouldn't stay too long, but Zanhei's royal family had not made any sort of pronouncement since the Royal

Consort's execution. Prince Wonhu had not been seen or heard from in six years, leaving the regency of his throne to the Chancellor.

"*Therefore,*" the crier went on, "*Prince Wonhu decrees that the city prepare itself for the arrival of Princess Yulana, the Warlord's beloved granddaughter. Let the streets be swept, the walls be cleaned, and the doorways and windows be decorated to celebrate this joyous news.*" They rolled the scroll back up with great ceremony, waiting for cheers.

Scattered applause arose from the crowd, half-hearted and not a little apprehensive. The Kestrels stared straight ahead, their faces impassive, but the crier looked disappointed. "Come, come," they urged. "Let's hear it for this momentous occasion!" They brought their hand to their ear, and the audience obliged with a less than enthusiastic cheer.

"Who does the crier think they are?" muttered an onlooker beside Zhara, a tall youth in a pointed hat. "The Bangtan Brothers?"

The crier pulled another scroll from their belt, looking a little wilted. "I have a portrait of the Royal Heir!" they shouted.

The prospect of laying eyes on the face of their future sovereign did energize the crowd. "Give it here!" someone called. "Let us have a look at the face that frightened off a thousand maidens!"

"I heard he's missing teeth!" another yelled.

"I heard his breath always stinks of onions!"

"I heard he never washes his feet!"

"I heard that he never changes his undergarments!"

Raucous laughter rose from the audience as they exchanged the various unflattering stories of Zanhei's Royal Heir they had heard bandied about in Flower Town. The crier looked flustered, then defensively held the scroll out before them. The crowd pushed forward eagerly, pressing Zhara from all sides. She craned her neck and stood on tiptoe, hoping to catch a glimpse over the heads of everyone in front of her, but she was too short.

"Wah," someone said disbelievingly. "The Royal Heir is actually quite handsome!"

The youth standing next to Zhara snorted. "Any royal portrait artist knows to exaggerate a prince's good features and minimize the less flattering ones."

Zhara laughed and caught the eye of the youth, who gave her a side-long grin. The stranger was dressed rather heavily for the weather in a dark blue, woolen, knee-length top, trousers with rainbow-striped cuffs, leather boots, and that whimsical pointed hat, but even more unusual than the hat were the wisps of ruddy hair peeking out from beneath the brim. She had never seen anyone in the Morning Realms with tresses the color of blood before.

"The Royal Heir is handsome enough," said another person dismissively. "But he has nothing on the Bangtan Brothers, especially the one who plays all the romantic leads."

Zhara jumped up and down, struggling for a look at the Royal Heir's portrait. Curiosity consumed her, and she was dying to know how the prince compared to the image of a royal hero from her romance novels.

"Shall I describe the Royal Heir to you, little lemming?" Zhara glanced at the youth in the pointed hat, who was studying her with interest. They spoke with the flat, informal accent of the northern steppes, oddly charming amid the more musical tones of the south. "I'd give you a boost up, but where I come from, it's considered rude to lay hands on a lady before you've become better acquainted." The redhead gave her a flirtatious wink, and Zhara noted a light sprinkling of rosy freckles across their tanned cheeks and the bridge of their nose.

Oh no. The Good-Looking Giggles rose in Zhara's throat, threatening to choke her. "It's fine." She coughed, feeling her face flame with embarrassment. "I'll get a closer look once the crowd is gone."

But the crowd didn't appear as though it would dissipate any time soon; in fact, more and more people were joining the throng. Sweat beaded through the back of Zhara's tunic from the press of humanity and humidity, but the northern stranger beside her seemed strangely unaffected by the heat.

Or the people.

Or . . . their surroundings at all.

Someone bumped into Zhara from behind, sending her tumbling toward the ground. She threw her hands out on instinct, grabbing the red-haired stranger's wrist to prevent herself from falling.

Recognition rang a gong deep within her. Startled, Zhara and the youth stared at each other, wordless shock passing between them like conversation.

"You . . ." Zhara breathed. Beneath her hands, she could feel the redhead's magic, both familiar and foreign at once. She was reminded of when Thanh had taken her hand in Teacher Hu's apothecary shop, when she sensed the lines of power flowing along the boy's meridian lines. But this youth was different; there was no flesh, no veins, no body to contain their magic; they *were* magic—an entire manifestation.

"You can—you can feel me?" the redhead asked, eyes wide with both fear and hope. "But—but . . . I'm not even there!"

"There?" Zhara looked at her fingers wrapped around the stranger's wrist. "Don't you mean . . . here?" With a gasp she realized she couldn't feel the stranger's pulse . . . that she could see *through* the body, ever so faintly, to the ground. Zhara looked up at the stranger's face. The outlines of their features were ever so slightly blurred, the edges indistinct and transparent. "What are you?" she whispered. "Are you a ghost?"

"No." The not-ghost tried to break her grip and narrowed their eyes. "Who are *you*?" they demanded. "What sort of magician are *you*?"

The word *magician* muffled the crowd around them in a blanket of silence. On the platform beside the royal crier, the Kestrels turned their heads in Zhara and the redhead's direction.

"Gommun's claws," the stranger muttered. "They've spotted me."

Soft yelps and gasps of protest rippled through the throng as the Warlord's peacekeepers waded their way toward the source of consternation. Magic surged through Zhara's hands, but instead of scalding the redhead, it only seemed to solidify their presence.

"Let me go," the redhead hissed. "Let me go or you'll get us both in trouble." They glanced desperately over Zhara's head at the tufted brown-and-white feathers fluttering toward them.

With effort, Zhara unclenched her hands and tore herself away from the not-ghost. In that instant, the redhead vanished to cries of surprise.

"Abomination!"

In the distance, more cries—this time of pain—as the Kestrels shoved people aside to get to where the redhead had been.

Where Zhara was standing.

She had to run.

Zhara turned and elbowed her way toward the canals, but the mass of bodies before her was too much. Throwing caution to the wind, she laid her hands on the nearest person, who yelped as her magic seared their skin.

"Abomination!"

No time to think, no time to regret. Hands upon backs upon shoulders upon elbows, Zhara swam through the crowd as fast as she could, not daring to look back, not daring to breathe.

She had stayed too long.

And she was going to get caught.

10

THE SHADOWS WERE LONG, BUT ZHARA'S TIME had grown short.
Indigo chased lavender chased gold across the western sky as
the sun slipped beneath the horizon. Zhara hurried down the covered
market streets toward Lotus Bridge, desperate to make it behind city
walls before the watchtower drums sounded the sundown hour. Once
the gates to Zanhei were closed, the only way into the city was with
cash or an official pass, neither of which Zhara possessed. The Second
Wife would be sure to punish her if she wasn't home in time to make
dinner.

But she had greater concerns on her heels.

In the wake of the confusion and chaos caused by the appearance
and disappearance of the redheaded not-ghost, Zhara had managed to
lose herself in the swell and press of the crowd. For once she was grateful for her dull appearance and drab attire—the faded colors of her
threadbare tunic and trousers blended into the dust-colored walls of
the buildings in the Pits. But all around her, Kestrels were still on the
hunt for a rogue magician, hovering and circling the streets of the covered market like massive, black-winged raptors, keen eyes ever alert
for signs of magic.

Which Zhara was trying her best to keep hidden.

A small but persistent glow seeped out from between the fingers
of her clenched fists, a glow that was growing brighter as the shadows
grew darker. Zhara gave a nervous glance at the deepening twilight
around her. Overhead, a large and unusual bird was circling, its crimson feathers stained purple by the oncoming night. It was said that
sunlight revealed many secrets, but it was darkness that would betray

hers. Zhara kept to the emptied and quiet streets of the covered market as she made her way toward Lotus Bridge, her progress agonizingly slow for the detours and doubling back she had to do in order to avoid others.

Boom, boom, boom, boom!

The watchtower drums sounded the nightfall hour.

Throwing caution to the wind, Zhara picked up her pace, tripping a bit over her unraveling slipper. To her surprise and dismay, a pool of people puddled at the entrance to Lotus Bridge, the flow of traffic out of the Pits and into Zanhei slowed by a bottleneck.

"What's going on here?" a voice cried. "Let us in!"

"Give me your hand," came another voice, vowels flattened by a distinctive northern accent. "No one enters the city before we've taken their hand."

Zhara stiffened. A pair of Kestrels stood guard at the entrance to Lotus Bridge, their tufted hairstyles visible over the heads of the crowd. Frustrated by the hunt, they had gone and laid a trap before the city walls instead. Her eyes darted about the crowd, then down to the canals. Black-and-white gondolas drifted down the waterway from Lotus Lock to Flower Town at all hours of the night, ferrying passengers to the pleasure district. Perhaps she could make her way down to the docks and find another way home.

"But why?" said another voice in exasperation. "We're all human, look at us! No scales, no fur, no fangs. We can't be magicians; we're not monsters!"

"Yeah!" A chorus of agreement arose from the crowd. "Why waste your time with clean, upstanding citizens? Go down to the marsh and find those abominations among the muck dwellers there!"

Muck dwellers. The Buri, the Malang, the Cham, the Tuong, and even some of Zhara's mother's people from the southern archipelago populated the marshes upriver. Immigrants. Refugees. The poor, the unskilled, the unwanted. She tugged uselessly at the hems of her too-short sleeves, as though she could cover up her own sun-darkened and work-roughened skin.

"An abomination can easily hide among humans," another Kestrel replied, "by deceiving the eyes of the righteous with beauty. Only by touch"—they lifted a bare hand high above the heads of the crowd—"can we know a magician as evil."

"By touch?" someone else called. "How?"

"Their skin," the Kestrel said solemnly, "burns."

Zhara chanced a glance at her hands. Fire limned the cracks of her palms, and she quickly clasped them back together to extinguish their light.

"Wah." Beside her, a tall, well-dressed person in green brocade gave a sharp gasp. "What's that?"

One by one, nearby heads turned to stare. "What? Did they see something? Someone?"

Zhara slowly began backing away, willing her magic to subside, to dissipate, to vanish, but felt her control over her power slipping instead.

"Them." The well-dressed person in green brocade pointed an accusatory finger at Zhara. "Their skin—"

A shrill scream rent the air as a scarlet shape cut through the crowd, scattering everyone with several flaps of its enormous wings. The ruddy bird with the bell about its neck. It fixed its familiar, golden gaze upon Zhara and shrieked as though shouting at her to run.

She obeyed.

Cries of confusion erupted behind her as chaos descended. Zhara darted left and right, keeping her traitorous hands close to her body, not daring to even hold them out for balance as she ran, fearful of an accidental touch giving her away. Ahead, the bird dove back and forth, directing her down one alleyway and then another before disappearing from view. She dared not look back to see if anyone followed her, caring only that each footfall took her farther and farther from danger.

Panting, Zhara stumbled down an abandoned street. Behind her, the sounds of the crowd were muffled, distant, but the slap-splash of her slippers through puddles of slightly fetid river water echoed loudly against empty walls. She took a moment to catch her breath and regain her bearings.

A dead end.

Night had not yet fallen completely, but the shadows were thick in this part of the Pits. No lights shone in the windows of the buildings overlooking the street, and the stars above were hidden by a haze of late spring humidity. She recognized nothing in this part of town and had no way of knowing how to get back out. Zhara was lost; even her magic had deserted her, leaving everything cold and dark.

A chitter. A squeak. A rustle. A whisper.

Zhara.

Her blood ran cold. At the far end of the street, a pair of eyes glinted, lit by a phantom light she could not see. In that instant, she could sense another's presence, another's breath thickening the air between them.

She wasn't alone.

"Wh-who's there?" She thought of the redheaded not-ghost and wondered if they hadn't followed her somehow. "Show yourself!"

Zhara jumped as something small and furry ran over the top of her foot. Rats. Just rats. Her heart skittered and stuttered with both relief and disgust, her skin crawling as she realized this dead end must be teeming with them—piles of discarded fish heads, rotting vegetables, and other bits of decaying rubbish were scattered around her, the air rank with refuse and another curiously sharp, almost sweet smell. Reining in her panic, she reasoned she must be by the eateries along the canals leading toward the pleasure district. The city gates were closed, but perhaps she could somehow make her way to Lotus Lock and find some way back.

"One step at a time," she murmured. "One step at a time." The eyes at the other end of the street were gone. "You're just imagining things."

Zhara.

The whispering of the rats seemed to grow louder as she passed. "Ignore it," she ordered herself. "You're overwrought is all, Jin Zhara."

That sickly sweet scent was growing stronger with each step. She brought her hand up to her nose, but nothing could stop the stink; the smell of spoilage was not in her physical senses somehow, but beyond them.

Help . . . me . . .

Startled, Zhara tripped and went sprawling headfirst into a puddle of slimy river water. This time, she didn't think she had imagined a voice speaking to her, pleading for her help. "Wh-who's there?" she called out in a quavering voice.

There was the tinkling of a tiny bell, and then a pair of glowing golden eyes suddenly materialized before her. *Niang.*

"Sajah?" Zhara said incredulously.

Niang, the ginger cat replied. He nuzzled her head reassuringly before cuffing her ears with his paw. *Niang,* he commanded.

"Aiyo!" she protested. "What was that for?"

"Zhara . . ."

This time, the voice was right beside her. Zhara startled to her feet with her back against the wall. A disheveled head with hollow, haunted eyes peeked out from behind a rubbish barrel, and a small, brown, wiry body emerged, filthy and stinking of the gutter. A child, she realized. A child wearing the stained and tattered remains of what was once a blue-and-white-patterned cloth. A pattern she recognized as belonging to the Meng clan.

"Thanh?" she breathed. She remembered the Buri matriarch bursting into Teacher Hu's apothecary that afternoon, terrified that her granddaughter and great-grandson had been taken by Kestrels. "Is that you?"

The boy nodded. "Help me," he whispered. His voice was thin, reedy, as though he were pushing his words through with tremendous effort. "Please."

Relief made Zhara go boneless. "I will," she said, extending a hand to the child. "Let's get you home safe. Your grandmother has been worried sick about you." She knelt before him, trying to assess his state of well-being in the dark. "What happened? Where is your mother?"

Thanh worried the red bead on his bracelet, his sunken eyes staring straight ahead into nothing. "Mama," he said hoarsely. "Mama. Mama."

Her heart sank. The boy was clearly traumatized and needed more help than she could give. Had he been abducted by the Warlord's peacekeepers? Had he managed to escape? Holding out her arms, Zhara moved to take Thanh in her arms when a flash of ginger streaked past, scratching and spitting and shrieking in fear.

"Sajah!" Zhara cried, trying to grab the frantic, flailing, furious cat.

Thanh hissed in pain, snatching back his arm to cradle it in the other.

"Are you hurt?" Zhara managed to drag Sajah away before he could inflict further damage. "Let me see—"

"No!" The force of the child's voice took her aback. "Mama," Thanh croaked. "I want my mama."

Dieu. "I know," Zhara said, throat tightening. "I'm sorry." She crept closer, slowly, smoothly, not wanting to scare the boy away. "I'm not your mother. But I'm someone who can help. Come on, let me take you to—"

"No!" Thanh's outburst was more forceful this time. "They took her away." Even in the darkness, Zhara could see the whites ringing the pupils of his eyes. "The Kestrels."

All the hair at the back of Zhara's neck stood on end. "Where, Thanh?" she whispered, not knowing if the boy would be able to answer. "Do you know where the Kestrels took your mother?"

The boy hunched his shuddering shoulders, wrapping his skinny arms about himself as though trying to hold his own body still. A sudden calm fell over him, and his arms and legs drooped as he slid to the ground. "To where the Mother of Demons sleeps," he murmured. "Waiting to enter the world."

Zhara frowned. Thanh's voice had not sounded like that of a young boy's—it was deeper, flatter, and oddly formal. Dread crept up her throat as she recalled the sensation of another intelligence peering out from the depths of his gaze. "What does th-that m-mean?"

The boy did not answer. Instead, his eyes rolled back into his head as his limbs seized up. With a cry, Zhara leaped to her feet, wanting to turn and run. But she couldn't. She shouldn't. He was only a child and he had asked for her help; she couldn't abandon him.

Out of nowhere, Sajah leaped atop the boy, yowling and hissing and spitting. Thanh cried out, convulsing and twitching, clawing and pawing at the air as he tussled with the cat. Thanh grabbed Sajah by his tail and hurled him against the wall with all his might. An explosion of rats skittered from behind the barrels, swarming and rushing toward Thanh as though to smother him with their squiggly, wriggling bodies. Zhara could hear their nipping, gnashing teeth, the rip and tear of flesh, and felt sick.

"Thanh!" She reached through the mass of rodents to grab the boy's shoulder.

Magic blazed through her body as she touched him, and that sense of rot, of decay, of filth and corruption returned. Immediately, Thanh's convulsing ceased and he opened his eyes with a knowing smile. Zhara staggered back. Where before he had seemed haunted and hollow, now he was full and . . . famished. An inhuman intelligence stared at her out of those dark eyes, and the boy's features moved and slid over the bones of his face as though someone else was trying on Thanh's skin for size.

"Guardian of Fire," the boy said, licking his lips. But it was not the boy; his voice was doubled, as though another deeper voice puppeted his throat, teeth, and tongue. "There you are. I recognize your touch."

Zhara slowly moved away. "Thanh?"

The boy chuckled, but his laugh belonged to an entity far older than a child of ten. It made all the hairs on the back of her neck stand on end, and she tripped in her haste to leave, to get out of that dank, narrow alleyway, to escape. A tiny bell sounded as Sajah roused himself and returned to Zhara's side. He suddenly seemed much bigger than he had been before, his fur standing on end and crackling with lightning.

"Guardian of Fire," Thanh said again. "Have you returned to this world along with my master?"

"I don't understand what you're talking about," Zhara said helplessly. "Who is your master? Who is the Guardian of Fire?"

"You will find out soon enough." The thing wearing Thanh's face grinned. "Little Guardian girl. How little she knows."

The boy's hand shot out and snatched up a passing rat, snapping its spine. All at once the other rats collapsed and went still, as though their necks had been broken as well. Zhara recoiled. Thanh gave her a cool glance, and there was no emotion or expression in his gaze. An emptiness mirrored by the rat's glassy, unseeing eyes, but accompanied by that creepy, inhuman grin.

She should have run. She should have screamed. She should have cried for help.

But she did none of those things as Thanh raised the dead rodent and cradled it to his chest. The action was that of a small child clutching a cherished toy close for comfort, and Zhara hesitated. Whatever—whomever—else he was, Thanh was also only a child. A magician child, a monstrous child . . . just like her. She couldn't abandon him. She couldn't throw him to the Warlord's hunting birds. Meng Grandmother would never forgive her.

She would never forgive herself.

"Thanh," she said, mouth dry. "Thanh, please—"

But the child said nothing, merely stroking the rat's lifeless body in his hands. The creature began twitching and dancing, as though stung by a million biting flies. A sucking sound, as though the air around them were being drawn in by a breath, filled Zhara's ears and made them pop. The rat squeaked and Thanh dropped the creature on its back. It jerked and flopped, its movements stiff and unnatural as if it were being manipulated by an unseen hand. It managed to flip itself onto its belly and began crawling—lurching—toward Zhara's feet. The thing was still very much dead, its eyes still vacant, its broken body bent and twisted in terrible ways.

"What—" Zhara croaked. "How—"

With a cry, the boy convulsed and contorted in pain. Joints snapped and ligaments popped as Thanh writhed on the ground. His skin bubbled and blistered, the knobs of his spine stretching, growing, elongating into spikes. The blisters on his arms and back turned into pustules, into eyes, into tiny black holes that dotted the landscape of his skin like the underside of a lotus pod. The boy's jaw unhinged and lengthened, teeth jutting forward as his mouth split open. His nostrils became slits, sliding up his face to the middle of his forehead as the eyes bulged out and slid down. When Thanh turned to face her, the grotesque parody of a grin stretched his mouth impossibly wide to reveal row upon row upon row of sharp, needlepoint teeth.

Zhara was rooted to the ground in fear. She understood now why the Warlord had been so terrified of her kind, why the empire had gone to war over the matter of magic, why the Kestrels still roamed the land in search of magicians.

For while the creature standing before her might have been a magician, he was no longer human.

He was an abomination.

11

IN HINDSIGHT, DONNING THE GARB OF A priestess of Do hadn't been one of Han's better ideas.

"That disguise," said Xu, "is *ridiculous.*"

Unfortunately, Han couldn't disagree. The identity-obscuring white robes, broad-brimmed hat, and floor-length black veils had seemed like the perfect way to sneak unnoticed about town while lounging in the cool recesses of the palace, but out in the sweltering swamp of a southern spring, he wanted nothing more than to rip the entire ensemble off his head.

"I don't care," Han said stubbornly, trying hard not to trip over the hem of his robes. Humidity clung to the myriad layers of silk and chiffon, weighing the fabric down so that it tangled about his arms and legs. "At least no one will notice me like this." He glanced out of the corner of his eye at yet *another* poster announcing his betrothal to Princess Yulana pasted on a wall. Master Kong's apprentices had been quite diligent in making enough copies of his portrait to disseminate throughout the city, although with varying degrees of accuracy. This one didn't even have his angry dimples.

"Recognize His Grace? Probably not," Xu conceded. "But I would hardly call this"—they pointedly looked Han's lumbering and labored appearance up and down—"unnoticeable."

Alas, his best friend had a point. An audible hush trailed in their wake, with several people giving them confused or fearful glances as they passed. Priestesses of Do were not often seen outside their mountain retreats save for two occasions—to help usher life into the world and to oversee the passing of souls from it. To many, the sight of their long, flowing white robes and face-covering veils was a bad omen, as they were often around to ease the dying of the very old or the gravely ill. Although their hands were said to be skilled in the arts of healing, there were even more rumors that they were equally adept in the arts of killing.

Or at least that was what Han had read in *The Maiden Who Was Loved by Death,* anyway.

"Well, you didn't offer a better suggestion at the time, so we're stuck with death nun, I'm afraid," he said irritably. "I can't risk going barefaced anymore, not after, well . . . you know." He gestured to a different betrothal announcement. This portrait seemed more nose than face, and Han fingered the bridge of his own nose, suddenly insecure about its size.

"I did offer a better suggestion, my prince," Xu replied, with only the barest hint of a sigh. They had foregone their usual makeup and accessories and had dressed themself in the fashion of a nobleman—a long, slim-fitting tunic over loose trousers and boots, belted just above the hips, with their hair smoothed back into a simple high bun—elegant, yet inconspicuous. Xu being Xu, of course, had managed to add their own inimitable touch of style with a scarlet headband tied about their forehead, a dangling string of beads topped with a peacock feather hanging from their belt, and the barest hint of carmine on their lips. "I suggested I find the girl myself and spare His Grace"—they twirled their fan in Han's direction—"all *this.*"

"I had to come with you," Han protested. "I'm the one who knows what she looks like."

The corners of Xu's lips turned up ever so slightly. "Which is?"

"Pretty." The word slipped out before Han could catch it. Despite the stifling heat beneath his costume, he was suddenly very glad of the face-obscuring veil that hid his blush.

"Pretty?" His best friend flicked open their fan and fluttered it excitedly. "Ooh, and here I thought His Grace was terrified of women."

"I'm not terrified of women!" he squeaked, then coughed. "Some of them are just . . . a lot." Han thought of the court ladies and their handmaidens and how their faces transformed from pleasant to predatory in his presence, their hunger for his status disguised behind elegant makeup and expensive fans. Agility, both physical and mental, was required when evading matrimonial traps. "Besides," he said, "the search went faster because I came along."

Xu eyed the sun balanced on the edge of the horizon. It wouldn't be long before the watchtowers would sound the sundown hour and the closing of the city gates. "Did it, my prince?" they asked mildly. "We've searched practically every apothecary from the palace to the Pits because he couldn't remember the name of the shop where she worked. Or," they said, leaning in with a sly smile, "did His Grace insist on coming because he wanted to set eyes on Mistress Brandy once more?" They wrinkled their nose and waved their hand before their face. "Phew, is that *sandalwood*?"

"Why, does it smell bad?" Han asked anxiously. He lifted the collar of his robe for a whiff. A bit sweaty, perhaps, especially beneath the sweltering veil, but he didn't think he stank.

Xu pursed their lips in distaste. "Sandalwood is not as appealing a cologne as boys think it is, my prince, especially in the vast amounts they apply to themselves."

"I was told girls liked it," Han said defensively.

"Really." Xu crossed their arms. "Who said that?"

Han mumbled an answer.

"What was that?"

"I read it in *The Maiden Who Was Loved by Death*," he said, fidgeting with the sunburst pendant at his neck. "The hero smells of sandalwood and winter bonfires, and the heroine loves it, even if she can't admit she loves *him*."

Xu groaned. "I can't believe I'm about to say this but . . . His Grace shouldn't believe everything he reads in books." They tilted their head, straining to look past the gauzy, black priestess veil to the expression on Han's face. "Hold a moment," they said with delight. "Am I to understand that His Grace has doused himself in sandalwood perfume . . . just to impress *a girl*?" They pressed their hands to their chest and gave a theatrical sniff. "My little prince . . . all grown up and becoming a man." Xu wiped away an imaginary tear. "I don't know whether to be encouraged or heartbroken!"

Han did not deign to answer, lengthening his strides and trying to outpace his discomfort. Growing up, he had never given much thought to romance or attraction; as a prince, who he loved mattered less than who his wife was—her bloodline, her status, her wealth. Of course, being the Royal Heir had never stopped anyone from pursuing less "official" relationships before, and Han was certain he had several unknown relatives scattered throughout the southern provinces due to his ancestors' numerous indiscretions. But that sort of relationship had never interested him much either, nor did it interest him now. Yet whenever he thought of Mistress Brandy, a strange, tingling sort of warmth seemed to settle somewhere around his stomach.

Indeed, his stomach kept giving little flips of excitement any time he passed a smallish, feminine person with deeply tan skin and wavy hair, even if his eyes insisted none of them were her. They were all too old, too thin, too tall, too young, and while many of them were quite lovely, none of them made his breath catch the way Mistress Brandy had when he saw her standing outside the bookseller's stall for the first time. Her dark eyes had shone like polished jet, bright and intense, as she stared hungrily at the stacks of paperbacks piled on the tables before her, as though she could devour them with her gaze alone. Her face had been so alive to him in all her yearning, and for the first time in his life, Han understood what it meant to *desire*. To want. He had never known what it was to want; he had only ever known what it was *not* to want. To want was to *live,* and until that moment, he had not realized he was merely surviving.

So he bought her the copy of *The Maiden Who Was Loved by Death*. He had wanted to give her what *she* had wanted, to make her . . . happy. Vivid. Her vividness made Han feel more alive himself, as though he were doing more than surviving; he was thriving.

A distant drumming filled the air. The sundown hour. The last of the shoppers had disappeared, and now only the stragglers and shopkeepers closing up their stalls remained.

"My prince," Xu said regretfully, "we should probably head back. Getting past the city guard after the gates are closed will be even harder than getting out of the palace, even with His Grace's disguise."

They were right, of course, but Han couldn't help wanting to linger, to keep searching for Mistress Brandy. Partially because he didn't want to return to the palace, to the world of impending marriages and increasingly magical little brothers, but mostly because he wanted to hold on to this feeling of excited expectation. For the first time in a long time, he felt as though he could look forward to the future instead of fending off the present. There was a bubble of lightness in his chest that expanded whenever he thought of Mistress Brandy. It felt warm. Nice. It felt like . . . hope.

Or perhaps that was hunger. The vendors along the canals between the covered market and the pleasure district were setting up their skiffs and stalls in anticipation of the dinner rush, and the smells of greasy, fried foods permeated the air.

"Ai-yah, what is this?" Xu grumbled. Ahead a rather large crowd was gathered, blocking every street in several directions. They rose on tiptoe, craning their neck in an attempt to see what was going on. "It looks as though something—someone—is blocking Lotus Bridge."

"Then let's get something to eat before we return," Han suggested. "The palace kitchens will be closed by the time we get back anyway."

"What about curfew?" Xu asked.

Han eyed the lanterns lighting the waters that separated the covered market from the pleasure district. "Plenty of people come in and out of the city after dark," he said, pointing to the black-and-white gondolas ferrying patrons from Zanhei to Flower Town. "We can catch a ride with them, can't we?"

Xu raised their brows. "Am I hearing this correctly? My dear, sweet, innocent prince is suggesting we spend the night in the arms of the myriad blossoms of Flower Town?"

Han sputtered. "What? N-no." He glanced at the line of ferries making their way toward the teahouses and taverns downriver, all headed in the same direction. "I thought . . ." He trailed off when he realized that no water taxis were headed in the opposite direction, back into the city.

With a rising sense of panic, he understood that once someone entered Flower Town, there was no leaving Flower Town until morning.

His best friend shook their head. "The eateries along the canal should be opening up now," they said, patting their shoulder. "Come on; I know of a place that serves the best spicy braised prawn in all of Zanhei."

Buoyed and distracted by the prospect of delicious seafood, Xu led them down to the docks where a string of canal-side restaurants lined the streets across the waters from the pleasure district. But as they drew near, they found the establishments dark, their shutters closed, their tables empty.

"Strange," Xu murmured. "Things should be open by now." They drew close to one of the restaurants and peered through the slats. "Rats," they muttered.

"Tell me about it," Han grumbled, rubbing his stomach. "I'm starving."

"No. *Rats*."

Xu raised their fan with a trembling hand, pointing at an odd, rippling mass in the distance. A soft susurrus of scratches and squeaks could faintly be heard, growing louder with each passing moment. Han squinted, trying to make sense of what he was hearing and seeing.

Xu was right.

There were rats.

Many, many, many rats.

"Augh!" Han jumped back and pressed himself against the restaurant as the tide of rodents flowed toward them. To his horror, he could see that some of the rats were not exactly in the best of health—some were missing limbs, chunks of flesh, and even entire heads as they twitched and lurched forward in stiff and unnatural ways. Hundreds of beady red eyes gleamed at him, thousands of bared white teeth shining in the moonlight as they inched closer. And closer. There was no end in sight.

"My prince!" Xu shouted from the roof. "Up here!"

Han paused for the briefest moment, weighing which was scarier—the height or the rats. Then the scaly, fleshy worm tails of the rat kings began wrapping themselves about his shins and ankles, and he leaped up after his best friend, cringing when he accidentally crushed one underfoot. The meaty squish and crunch of broken rodent bodies made his stomach churn. Well, at least he was no longer hungry.

"What . . . is that?" Xu asked weakly, looking down the street.

A limping, lurching, lumbering figure was making its way toward them. It was getting too dim to make out much, but Han didn't think it was human. All the hairs rose along his neck as his mind struggled to reconcile what he knew to be true with what he was seeing.

A monster.

12

DRIPPING FANGS. GLOWING EYES. LIMBS AND FINGERS and claws where they shouldn't be. Hide full of holes into the abyss, tiny pinpricks across its still all-too-human skin. Flies. Bugs. Disease. Mold. The horror was unspeakable and Han did not know where to look. Beside him, Xu moaned and covered their face with their fan.

The monster turned its face? head? eyes? at the sound, the slits on its head widening as it drew in a deep breath. Xu moaned again as the horror sniffed and lumbered toward them. Han pushed his best friend farther up the roof, tearing off his hat, veil and robes.

"Go!" he yelled at Xu. "I'll hold it off!"

"Are you out of your mind?" they yelled back, dropping all pretense of courteous speech. "You may have an appealing physique, my prince, but you're not fit for this!"

They might have had a point; he worked out for aesthetics rather than function. Han scrambled for some sort of weapon, any weapon, settling for a loose roof tile beneath his feet. It was heavier than he expected, but not nearly as heavy as he needed, considering the size of the monster advancing upon them. As the beast lurched forward, he threw the tile as hard as he could against what he hoped was the creature's head. His aim was true, and the tile landed with a solid *thunk!* squarely between the two horrifying holes he thought might have been eyes. It was hard to tell. There were so many of them. Holes, that is.

Slowly, surely, like corpses sinking in a bog, the broken bits of the tile were absorbed by the monster's skin. As it swallowed the ceramic and glaze and grout, oily black bubbles popped up in each piece's wake.

Each bubble blinked several times and Han realized that they were more eyes. He wanted to throw up. He wrenched another tile from the roof and readied to throw it again when a voice cried out:

"Thanh!"

Both the monster and Han turned to see the source of this new voice. "Mistress Brandy?" he gasped. He really was born under the Second Immortal's star. After an entire day of searching, he happened to find her again at *this* exact moment. With a monster. Possibly about to lose their lives.

"*That's* Mistress Brandy?" Behind him Xu raised their eyes to the heavens. "Tendi's twisted luck indeed, my prince."

"Thanh!" the girl called again to the monster. "Please! You can fight this!"

"Is it just me," Xu muttered, "or is she *glowing*?"

Han rubbed his eyes. Dusk had fully fallen now, and in the deepening twilight, Mistress Brandy's skin seemed lit by the rays of an unseen sun. Han stared at her, transfixed. She glowed like the edge of a candle flame, a halo of light surrounding her like one of the celestial maidens in the fairy tales his mother used to read to him.

The beast snuffled and pawed the ground with its enormous claws, leaving deep grooves in the cobblestones. For an instant, something akin to regret or desperation appeared in its myriad eyes, and Han shuddered with revulsion at the humanity of it.

Then the monster lowered its head and prepared to charge.

"Come on, Xu!" Han cried, ignoring his fear of heights and leaping from the roof. "We have to help her!"

"What makes you think I'm the sort of person who runs *toward* danger instead of away from it?" they demanded.

Han grabbed a chair from one of the street-side eateries, a flimsy construction made of hardened bamboo, and raced toward Mistress Brandy, throwing himself between her and the creature. He swung the chair at the creature's dorsal slits. The legs bent, bounced, then broke on impact. The creature shook its . . . head . . . thing, as though shooing away a fly, and roared. It reared back, claws lengthening. Mistress

Brandy jumped back, crying out as she stumbled. Han reached down and hauled her to her feet.

"Go!" he cried as she limped away. "I'll distract it!"

He dodged the monster's swipes left, then right, grateful for all the time he had spent on his agility drills. Wooden beams splintered behind him as the creature's claws dragged through buildings and storefront awnings. Shards and stone exploded in every direction, and Han ducked to avoid being impaled. He tripped over a protruding beam and tumbled to the ground. He scrambled to his feet, then doubled over from the screaming pain in his middle.

Boom! Something shattered above him and Han covered his head as rubble rained down. The abomination roared and he curled himself into a ball, closing his eyes and waiting for the end. At least it would be a sensational end. Dying by monster was memorable.

But the killing blow never fell. Instead, there was a fierce yowling sound as a small ginger cat came flying out of nowhere to slash the monster's multiple eyes with its claws. The creature cringed and howled with pain, swatting the little feline out of the way.

"Sajah?" Mistress Brandy ran toward the cat lying on the cobblestones and knelt beside it. "Sajah!" Distracted by the cat, she didn't notice the beast advancing behind her, picking up speed.

Han leaped to his feet, wincing as a stabbing pain shot through his ribs. He had to do something. Anything. He noticed a large beam before him on the ground, sharpened at both ends, and picked it up. Hefting it over his shoulder like a javelin, he widened his stance and leaned his weight on his back foot. "Yah!" he shouted. "Get away from her!" Lifting his makeshift javelin behind his head, he hurled it at the creature with all his might.

It glanced harmlessly off its side.

Well, now he knew to add spear-throwing to his exercise routine. If he ever got to do his exercise routine again. Nevertheless, the projectile had its desired effect and the beast raised its head to look at him, away from Mistress Brandy. He pumped his fist with triumph before he realized he hadn't planned on his gambit working.

He backed slowly away as the creature lowered its head and prepared to rush him.

There was a high-pitched yell over his shoulder that grew louder and louder as a slim figure barreled past him and launched itself onto the monster's neck, clambering over its shoulders and onto its back.

"Run, my prince, run!" cried Xu as they stabbed the tines of their fan into each of the creature's eyes.

Han needed no further urging. Ignoring the pain in his side, he made use of his long legs and ran for shelter as the beast thrashed and roared in agony. Xu hung on for dear life, blinding the monster as best they could before it bucked them off, sending them crashing into Han.

"Thanh!" At the far end of the street, Mistress Brandy rose unsteadily to her feet. "Leave them alone!"

And then, with a gesture of her hands, the world erupted in flames.

Han backed away from the sudden, scorching heat, as did the creature. When his vision cleared, he saw that Mistress Brandy was no longer just glowing—she was *on fire*. No, not on fire—made *of* fire. She was an ethereal being of light and flame, a girl-shaped wildfire clinging to the monster's arm as its skin blistered beneath her touch. "I'm sorry," she sobbed. "I'm so, so sorry!"

Screaming through the agony, the creature shook her off and she went tumbling several yards away. The light crackled and dimmed as Mistress Brandy transformed back and forth, from girl to flame, girl to flame, struggling to maintain consciousness. The monster focused its multiple eyes on the girl and lurched in her direction, tearing through buildings and bits of rubble as it barreled toward her.

Han desperately cast about for some way to slow the abomination down, to trap it. A little ways away, a teetering stone pillar was resting precariously against a fallen awning. Large. Heavy. Perhaps even heavy enough to stop a monster.

"Mistress Brandy!" he called. "That way!" He pointed to the fallen awning and mimed the pillar crashing down. He ran toward the broken beams and scaled the nearby roof to brace himself against the stone column, trying not to look down. "Xu, help me!"

With effort, Mistress Brandy forced herself awake, saw what Han intended, and crawled out of the way.

Xu clambered up on the roof beside him and together, the two of them threw their weight against the pillar, pushing, shoving, hoping, praying.

"Now!" Mistress Brandy screamed. "Now!"

With one last herculean effort, Han and Xu gave everything they had.

Slowly, all too slowly, the pillar began moving.

"Come on," Han said through gritted teeth.

He grabbed Xu's hand and jumped back as the column gave way. Time seemed to grind to a halt as they watched the abomination inch closer and closer and the pillar fall faster and faster until—

Slam!

The building on which he and his best friend stood collapsed, and they tumbled down to the ground. Just past the rubble, there was an enormous explosion, and a plume of debris shot into the air, sending clouds of dust everywhere. Han covered his mouth and nose with the sleeve of his undergarment, choking as the dirt blew into his eyes. Between coughs, he strained to listen for the abomination's heavy snuffling. There was a gurgle—a groan—a long, rattling sigh—and then . . .

The brightest burst of light imaginable.

Followed by silence.

It was an age before Han and Xu managed to stir themselves and pick their way out of the building's ruins and into the street.

"Is it dead?" Xu croaked.

Han wiped at his streaming eyes, trying in vain to blink them clear. Dust and smoke hung like fog in the air around them, the moon casting strange, otherworldly shadows. His ears still rang from the crash and bang of battle, but he thought the street was quiet.

"I . . . I think so?" he said hoarsely.

"Good." Xu materialized beside him like a ghost, covered in white from head to toe. "Is Mistress Brandy all right?"

Somewhere in the distance, Han thought he could hear the jingle of a bell. He shook his head, trying to clear the ringing in his ears.

"I don't know." He wanted nothing more than to fall to the ground, feeling suddenly boneless as every ache and scratch and injury made itself known. He rubbed at his arm and found it sticky. Blood. There was a deep cut along his forearm. "Let's go look."

They gingerly made their way toward the pillar. The ash and smoke made it hard to see, blotting out the light of the rising moon. But as they drew near the site of the fallen column, the creature was gone.

"Where did it go?" Xu said in astonishment. There was no body, no sound, nothing but a gentle jingling that echoed off the broken buildings.

"Is that . . . a bell?" Xu asked.

"Not sure." Han picked his way laboriously through the wreckage, limping as he methodically searched the rubble for any sign of Mistress Brandy. "But I think it's coming from over there." He pointed toward the other end of the street, following the sound as it grew louder and louder.

With a groan, Xu heaved themself after him. Suddenly, two embers winked into existence before them. Han gave a high-pitched shriek and stumbled backward over a piece of broken cobblestone.

"What is it?" Xu demanded. "Is it the monster?"

The embers blinked, and then a small ginger cat materialized out of the haze, pawing insistently at his feet. It was the same one that had attacked the creature with its claws, and the source of the jingle was the bell it wore on a ribbon about its neck. "No, it's just a cat," Han said, feeling foolish. The feline tilted its head at him, baring its teeth in what felt like a mocking laugh. "Yes, yes, very good, you were brave," he said. "Now go away." He was allergic.

The cat sniffed, then turned to face Xu.

"Why hullo, little lion," they said, reaching down to scratch it behind the ears. "Where did you come from?" The creature purred, curling itself about Xu's legs.

Han huffed irritably. "Leave it; it's just another one of the thousands of strays in Zanhei begging for food." He brushed himself off as he got to his feet. The streets were silent, empty of any sound or presence. "Come on, we've got to find Mistress Brandy and see if she's all right."

"You wouldn't happen to know where to find Mistress Brandy, would you, handsome?" Xu cooed, stroking the cat's ragged fur and ringing the bell at its neck. "You probably know these streets better than anyone."

"It's a cat, not a dog," Han said flatly. "It wouldn't help us even if it could understand you."

The creature turned to face him with a baleful glare. It looked adoringly up at Xu, then with one last nuzzle of their fingers, darted away into the haze.

"See?" Han sneezed. "Contemptible little demon." He sneezed again.

After a moment, the cat reappeared. It stared at them, tail lashing impatiently, before turning around and disappearing into the shadows. Then it reappeared with a scowl.

"I think it wants us to follow it," Xu said uncertainly.

The cat nodded.

Han blinked. "Did that cat just . . . nod at us?"

It gave him an exasperated look, then turned its uncommonly knowing gaze on Xu.

"Well," they said with equanimity. "With everything else I've witnessed today, an unusually intelligent cat is downright mundane." The feline nodded again, and Xu began to follow it into the mist. "Come, my prince. This is as good a plan as any."

They let the cat lead the way through piles of rock and rubble, and presently they came upon a small figure crumpled on the ground.

"Mistress Brandy!" Han scrambled over bits of broken timber and brick to get to her side. But when he drew near, he saw it wasn't Mistress Brandy at all; it was a small child, about ten years old. They lay on their side in the middle of a crater of destruction, appearing for all the world to be asleep. Their hands, lightly curled into fists, twitched faintly with dreams, while the steady rise and fall of their chest reassured Han the child wasn't dead. Slowly, gently, he gathered the child in his arms, and the heavy flop of their limbs reminded him of Anyang when he used to carry his brother to bed after night terrors had chased him into Han's quarters.

"My prince!" Xu's voice rang out. "Over here!"

He followed the sound of his best friend's voice to find them kneeling over the limp figure of a girl on the ground with the cat beside them. A cold drop of fear settled into his stomach, spreading like ice through his veins. "Is that . . ."

"She's alive," said Xu. "But I can't tell how seriously she's hurt." They looked up at Han and frowned. "Who's that His Grace has in his arms?"

"I don't know." He looked down at the child, who was beginning to stir and murmur. "But they need a healer."

"I believe I can help with that."

Han and Xu whirled around, squinting through the haze for the source of the voice. An owlish gleam appeared to their right as moonlight caught the edges of a pair of spectacles. A dumpy silhouette could be seen through the shifting clouds of dust before the glasses winked out of sight as their owner stepped forward.

"My name is Teacher Hu," said the bespectacled figure. "And the Guardians of Dawn are here to help you."

PART TWO

THE GUARDIANS OF DAWN

13

THE FIRST THING ZHARA NOTICED WHEN SHE awoke was the smell. Musty, damp, and somehow vaguely mushroom-like, as though she were lying at the bottom of a well.

The second thing she noticed was something warm and furry by her side, which jingled as it shifted and moved.

And the third thing she noticed was her splitting headache.

Guardian of Fire . . .

With a groan she opened her eyes to complete darkness. She started, panicking a little about where she was, whether she was injured, or even whether or not she was dead.

"Shhh, shhh," came a soothing voice. A callused hand rested against her forehead, smelling vaguely of camphor and cinnamon. A familiar scent, and one she immediately recognized: Teacher Hu's. A calm settled into Zhara's bones, and she let herself go limp as a wet cloth was removed from her eyes. A pair of spectacles on a string of topaz beads dangled before her face as her surroundings came into focus. "You shouldn't exert yourself."

"Auntie?" she croaked. Her voice was hoarse, rusty from disuse. Something fuzzy nuzzled her fingers, and she glanced down to find a small ginger cat snuggled at her hip. "Sajah?" The cat miaowed in greeting. "How—"

"Shhhh," the apothecary said again, rewetting the washcloth in a bowl of fresh, cool water on the ground beside her. "Take it easy. You've been through quite an ordeal."

Zhara blinked, her mind desperately trying to fill in the blanks of the past several minutes?—hours?—days?—as she took in her surroundings. "Where am I?"

"With the Guardians of Dawn." Teacher Hu tried to place the damp washcloth on Zhara's forehead. "Safe. For now, at least."

"The . . . Guardians of Dawn?" Her head swam as she groggily tried to piece together meaning from words she understood but did not comprehend. Elemental warriors. Meng Grandmother. Secret societies. "Who . . . what . . ." Groaning, she sat up and a bolt of pain shot through her temples as she tried to rally her wayward thoughts into some semblance of order.

"Stay still," Teacher Hu ordered, pushing her back down. "Fortunately you don't appear to have sustained any major physical injuries, but your magical energy has taken quite a beating, and it will take some time to regain your strength."

The Guardians of Dawn, the Buri matriarch had said, giving her a token with a sunburst etched into it. A whispered conversation in the alleyway between Master Plum Blossom and the bookseller. An eldritch voice hissing *Guardian of Fire, there you are* . . . "The Guardians of Dawn!" Zhara shouted.

"Yes, I just said that," Teacher Hu said, a trifle impatiently. "Now calm down, child, and let yourself recover."

Despite the apothecary's protests, Zhara sat up to better take in her surroundings. "What is this place?" She was in a small, windowless room made of packed dirt. The source of the musty smell seemed to be the bookshelves in the corner, stacked with waterlogged and molding texts of indeterminate provenance. A bundle of dirty rags lay heaped in the opposite corner atop a narrow pallet stuffed with what appeared to be horsehair.

"The basement of Master Cao's bookshop," Teacher Hu said. "The others are upstairs."

So Madame Hong the mussel-monger was right; Master Cao really did have a basement. Zhara would have laughed if her head didn't hurt so much. "The others?" she asked instead. "Who are the others?"

"The two youths we found with you. There was a slender, well-dressed one and a tall, good-looking one with dimples."

Fragments of the preceding events started to return to Zhara. She recalled seeing someone on a roof, hurling projectiles at . . . but her memory wavered, leaving the image blurry in her mind. "Master Plum Blossom?"

"That would be the dimpled one, I presume. He kept asking after you." Teacher Hu gave up trying to persuade Zhara to lie back down and moved to the bundle of rags on the other side of the room. "I didn't know you had a beau, child."

Zhara flushed. "He's not my beau, auntie. He's . . ." She trailed off, realizing that—despite his outsized presence in her daydreams—she knew next to nothing about Master Plum Blossom. She didn't even know his real name. "A stranger," she said. "A very kind stranger." She thought of his smile as he offered her a copy of *The Maiden Who Was Loved by Death,* a smile that had asked for nothing but her own in return.

"I don't know too many people who would risk their lives to save a complete stranger's," Teacher Hu remarked. "This young man must be very kind indeed. You should marry him." The herbalist soaked two clean strips of linen in the bowl of water and laid them on the bundle of rags. Zhara startled. Teacher Hu was not attending to a pile of dirty laundry, but a child.

A Buri child.

Guardian of Fire . . . there you are . . . I recognize your touch . . .

The hazy images in her mind came into sharp focus—dripping, slavering jaws above her head, blistered skin, and myriad oily eyes where a scared little boy had been. Flames all around them, around her, within her, the furnace of her magic becoming a blazing conflagration she could not control.

"Thanh!" she gasped, jostling Sajah awake. With effort, Zhara dragged herself out of her own pallet to crawl to the child's side. "Is he all right?" She recalled the blinding flash of light emanating from her hands when she touched him, and the image of Suzhan's sightless eyes resurfaced in her mind. "He's . . . unharmed?"

Teacher Hu nodded. "Asleep for the moment," she said. "Perfectly healthy, as far as I can tell, physically and magically. He's just exhausted."

Slowly, hesitantly, Zhara placed her hand on Thanh's cheek. Instantly, that sense of kinship that went deeper than blood or bone awoke within her, the knowledge that they were both magicians. But this time his magic was faint and clean—the meridian lines of power flowing throughout his body clear of any darkness or corruption. No sense of rot or infection or poison. The boy stirred, but did not wake.

"It's gone," she murmured.

The apothecary watched her curiously. "What's gone?"

Zhara removed her hand from Thanh's cheek and sat back on her heels. "There was a . . . blight . . . on his magic," she said, stumbling over the words. She knew so little of the workings or history or even the vocabulary of magic, that she was helpless to explain or even describe what happened. "I first felt it when he and Meng Grandmother came into the shop," she continued slowly. "When he took my hand." She rubbed her palms against her leg and Sajah nipped at her fingers. "I didn't know then that magicians could sense each other that way. By touch, I mean."

Teacher Hu smiled. "It's the chaos in our blood that calls to each other."

"*Our* blood?" Zhara studied her mentor with narrowed eyes. "Are you a magician too, auntie?" She didn't know whether to feel hurt or thrilled by the revelation.

"Alas, no." The apothecary's smile turned sorrowful. "But my brother was. He and I shared that chaos in our blood, but I lack the ability to manipulate the void." She snorted. "I'm what he called an anti-magician."

"An anti-magician?" Zhara was lost.

Teacher Hu held her hand out for Zhara to take. She slid her palm into the herbalist's and gasped when that marrow-deep sense of recognition rose between them. "Do you feel that?" the apothecary asked. "That resonance between us, like two strings singing together on a zither?"

Suzhan could have explained what that meant, but Zhara had no clue. Yet when she allowed herself to relax, to consider the sensation that flowed between her and the herbalist, she realized that her magic was echoed and amplified by Teacher Hu's touch. "Yes," she said with some surprise.

"That is the void." The apothecary withdrew her hand and the feeling faded. "The space between matter, the chaos between order, the place of potential."

Zhara had never thought of her magic as an *absence* or the *space between* things before. Whenever she considered her own gifts, she imagined them as a force outside herself, or perhaps a force *in addition* to herself. A furnace, not a void. Perhaps this was why all her attempts at casting spells had been so unpredictable and chaotic. Perhaps she had simply misunderstood and misapplied the underlying principles. "That's magic?"

"Well," Teacher Hu hedged. "Magic is not a thing in itself so much as it is something magicians *do*. Magic is action. Magic is change. Like water freezing into ice, wood burning into ash, earth melting into metal. The void is what magicians manipulate to create that change." The apothecary looked down at her hands. "I can't create that change, nor can I be affected by it."

"What does that mean?"

The herbalist smiled. "It means I can't do magic, nor does magic work on me. Hence *anti-magician*. Most anti-magicians come from magical families, you see." Her expression grew grim. "Perhaps that's why there are so many of us in the Guardians of Dawn," she said darkly. "Since so many of us lost our loved ones to the Warlord's justice."

The wound was still raw. "Who have you lost?" Zhara asked softly.

Teacher Hu's lips twisted, dry and humorless. "My brother," she said. "We lived in Fanwe, a tiny village in Jingxi province that no longer exists. Our family had always specialized in healing, and my brother spent most of his life studying healing spells." Teacher Hu's gaze went distant, her expression soft. "We worked together, blending both medical and magical practices together in treating our patients." Her mouth thinned, her eyes hard. "Then came the war. Then the purges." She turned her head away from Zhara. "It was the Guardians of Dawn who helped me escape to Zanhei when the Kestrels took my brother away."

The names and places were different, but the story was the same as Zhara's own. "I'm sorry, auntie," she whispered. "The Kestrels took my father away when I was ten years old."

The herbalist's gaze was full of terrible compassion. "I know."

"You know?" Grief and shock tightened their grip about Zhara's throat. "What do you mean *you know*? How—when—"

Teacher Hu looked away. "Your mother and father were the ones to help me escape," she said quietly. "They had also been in the Guardians of Dawn."

Zhara could no longer feel the tips of her fingers or nose. She felt as though her soul had come untethered, leaving nothing but numbness behind.

"After Jin Zhanlong died I tried to take you in," Teacher Hu went on. She moved to check the coals of a nearby brazier. "But by then that wicked stepmother of yours had her claws in you." The apothecary screwed her face in distaste as she poured water from a drinking jug into a pot and set it atop the brazier for tea. "And I was bound by oath not to reveal the existence of the Guardians of Dawn except to those in need."

"The Second Wife is not wicked," Zhara said automatically. "She isn't!" she insisted at Teacher Hu's disbelieving expression. "She was there when I was in need," Zhara whispered. "She protected me from the Warlord's justice."

Teacher Hu was unconvinced. "The Guardians of Dawn could have protected you. We could protect you now," she said, rummaging through various cabinet drawers for tea. "We could find a place of refuge for you, as we have for so many others."

Zhara shook her head. "I owe the Second Wife my life."

"You don't owe that woman anything," the apothecary said severely.

But didn't she? *Be good, and be true.* A good girl would never forget the debts she owed, or the wrongs she needed to address. Suzhan's sightless eyes and bruised cheekbone returned to her. "I can't leave, auntie," Zhara said softly. "Not when I'm still needed."

Teacher Hu blew out a frustrated sigh. "It's your choice, I suppose," she grumbled, pulling out a low folding table from the corner and setting it up on the floor between them. "But now you must swear to me that you will never reveal the existence of the Guardians of Dawn to *anyone,* or I'll have you placed on the next caravan headed to the outermost west, just see if I don't."

Zhara frowned. "Just what are the Guardians of Dawn exactly? Meng Grandmother said you were an underground magical resistance organization."

"We're more of a secret society than a resistance organization," the herbalist said wearily, as though she had explained this many, many times before. "The latter makes us sound like we're trying to start some sort of uprising."

Zhara thought of the sunburst token, stamped with the symbol of the previous, deposed Mugung Dynasty. "Aren't you?"

Teacher Hu gave a derisive snort. "Certainly not. The Guardians of Dawn are not a political organization; we are a historical-knowledge preservation and mutual aid society. We provide funds, care, assistance, and even escape for those in need. Magicians, anti-magicians, or anyone sympathetic to the cause of magician liberation."

"I don't know, auntie," Zhara said dubiously. "That sounds very much like a political organization to me."

The apothecary groaned. "The function of the times in which we live, I suppose. The very existence of magic has become political." She shook her head. "But the primary aim of the Guardians of Dawn has always been to preserve and protect, not to overthrow or topple tyrants. Despite what some of us might say."

Zhara lifted her brows. "What does that mean?"

Teacher Hu fixed her with a stern look. "Never you mind. I don't want you getting mixed up with any revolutionary rabble, you hear me? We are here to provide aid, not to get you killed. I've seen enough bloodshed to last me through this life and the next." The herbalist found a tea set and set it on the table. She filled the pot with several large handfuls of oolong and poured the now-boiling water onto the leaves. "Now, drink."

Zhara accepted a cup of tea from Teacher Hu with both hands. She took a sip, trying not to hiss with pain as the tea burned her tongue. As per usual, the apothecary had not bothered to check the water temperature before steeping the leaves; the brew was bitter and burnt and far too hot. She coughed and set her cup down.

On the other side of the room, Thanh stirred in his sleep. "Mama," the boy murmured. The herbalist went to tend to the child.

"What happened to the boy's mother?" Teacher Hu asked, wiping away the sweat from Thanh's brow.

"Apparently the Kestrels took her," Zhara said. "I found him alone in an alleyway when he . . . when he . . ." Every time her mind touched on the memories of the night, it recoiled reflexively, as though to protect her from the horror of it all. The coiling, roiling mass of rat bodies and tails, the gurgling squeak and murmur, the voice that called her *Guardian of Fire* . . .

"When he lost control of his magic?" The apothecary studied Zhara through tortoiseshell spectacles, her eyes large and owlish behind the lenses. "Children his age usually start showing signs of magical ability, although rarely do so in such a spectacular manner. Master Cao had quite a mess to clean on his hands."

Zhara stared at the dregs that had settled at the bottom of her cup. Her mind's eye was blurred, and the only thing she seemed to be able to remember with any clarity was that blazing light burning the darkness away. "Is that what happened?" she murmured. "Do you turn into a monster when you don't have any control over your own magic?" She thought of the chaotic nature of her own power, her inability to channel it into what she desired, and felt afraid.

"A monster?" Teacher Hu raised her brows. "I suppose if a magician isn't careful they can unintentionally harm people or cause a lot of damage, but to call them a monster is a bit much, lah?"

Zhara shook her head. "No," she whispered, cringing as the image of myriad oily eyes bubbling in blistered skin grew sharper in her mind. "I mean he turned into a *literal monster*. He turned into an"—she gulped, forcing the word through stiff lips—"abomination."

The word fell with a thud onto the floor between them. She could hear the Second Wife's words echoing in the silence. *There are rumors of monsters in the marsh.*

It was a long while before Teacher Hu replied. "It's happening again," she murmured, her face drawn, lips pale.

Zhara looked up. "What's happening again, auntie?"

The apothecary continued dabbing at the boy's forehead to avoid Zhara's questioning gaze. "The blight," she said softly.

"Blight?" Zhara thought of the darkness on Thanh's magic like spots of disease, and remembered Meng Grandmother and Teacher Hu arguing in the shop about the dearth of crowned fern fiddleheads. "What blight?"

The herbalist smoothed the blanket down over the boy's sleeping form and rose to her feet. "Remind me, child; how old are you again?"

"I'll be seventeen on the Night of the Sevens," Zhara replied.

"Too young to remember then." Teacher Hu began clearing away the cups and tea from the table. "Too young to remember a world where magic was as normal as breathing, let alone how it all changed during the blight." She shook her head. "No one knows how it started," she said, her eyes fixed on the middle distance before her. "Or the cause. But twenty years ago, magicians throughout the Morning Realms began turning into monsters and the very first magician to turn was . . . the last Mugung Emperor."

Zhara nodded. Every schoolchild in Zanhei knew that the transformation of the Mugung Emperor into an abomination was the genesis of the Just War. The Warlord rode down from the north with his horde to put the previous ruler to the sword for the sake of the empire, before installing himself on the Sunburst Throne as the new Gommun Emperor. Before turning that same sword on all the magicians throughout the realm.

"It began with listlessness," Teacher Hu continued. "A curious change in temperament. Then suddenly, without warning, without notice, the afflicted began sprouting scales. Claws. Fangs. Wings." She closed her eyes and removed her spectacles to let them hang about her neck. "Before we knew it, a plague of abominations began destroying the land and its people." She turned her gaze on Zhara, her expression clouded with foreboding. "And I fear it's happening again."

Zhara turned the teacup around and around in her fingers without drinking. "Is there," she said hoarsely, "some way to stop it?"

"They say a pinch of prevention is worth a dollop of cure." The apothecary gazed down at the sleeping Thanh. "I need to go to the marsh and figure out the cause of this strange corruption."

Zhara sat up straighter. "I'll go with you, auntie."

"You?" Teacher Hu looked disapproving. "Why?"

"Because I can sense this corruption," Zhara said, holding out her hands. "And . . . and because I seem to be able to cure it."

The apothecary's gaze was pitying. "There is no cure for abomination, child."

But the existence of Thanh—hale, whole, human—indicated otherwise. Zhara shook her head. "Nevertheless, I can be of use to you, auntie. I am a magician. Let me help in whatever way I can."

Teacher Hu said nothing. "It will be dangerous," she said at last. "I would rather you stay safe."

Safe. For Zhara, the feeling of safety was as fraught as the fragrance of cheap osmanthus perfume. The scent of her stepmother's clothes cabinet as she lay hidden among the robes, the taste of terror souring her mouth. "Will I ever truly be safe," she said, more to herself than to the apothecary, "until the world is safe?"

"Probably not," Teacher Hu said matter-of-factly. "But there's nothing you can do about it except survive."

Survival. Zhara was well acquainted with survival. Survival was the kitchen in which she slept, the room that contained her father's death plaque, her sister's stool in the corner, her romance books, her ash-covered pallet by the hearth. But the world was bigger than that, and the existence of *The Thousand-Character Classic* proved it. It had taken an accidental encounter with a blushing boy in the marketplace to make her understand that surviving and living a full life were not the same thing.

"The world is dangerous," Zhara said softly. "And I don't want to survive; I want to *thrive.*"

14

M AGIC, HAN DISCOVERED, TICKLED.
"Stop squirming," Master Cao snapped, reapplying a glyph for healing to Han's arm for the third time. He had watched in amazement as the diminutive bookseller had done the same for Xu's injuries, soft brushstrokes leaving trails of lavender light as broken skin knit together. His best friend was completely recovered from their fight against the abomination now, with no physical sign of the horrors they had endured earlier that night.

Their eyes, on the other hand, remained haunted.

"Sit still!" Master Cao grabbed Han's wrist and plied his brush a little more firmly against the bruises dotting his arm.

"But it itches," Han complained. He watched as the slash on his arm briefly sealed itself up before unraveling again. "Why doesn't the spell work on me?"

"I don't know," the bookseller said irritably, short-tempered with exhaustion. Master Cao had spent the past several hours setting the devastation and destruction from their battle with the monster to rights, tracing lavender spells in the air with several quick strokes of his brush. Han and Xu marveled as broken bits of building and rubble repaired themselves, cracks healing, smoothing, vanishing. "But we may have to do this the old-fashioned way. You," he said, pointing to Xu, who was staring glassy-eyed into the middle distance. "There's a wooden box carved with Lo's pestle and mortar on the shelf behind the counter. Bring it here so we can bandage up this young man."

Xu did as they were bid, watching as the bookseller clumsily attempted to clean Han's wound before stepping in. "May I?" they asked, gently taking the linen bandages from his hands. "I think I may have more experience with this than Master Cao. I've spent most of my life trying to get my pr—my friend to his majority alive."

"Be my guest." The bookseller relinquished the binding of Han's wounds to Xu.

"I suppose one doesn't need to learn how to do things the old-fashioned way if one knows how to wield magic," Xu remarked, efficiently cleaning and bandaging up the cut on Han's arm.

"Oh, I was useless at anything except books even before I knew I was a magician," Master Cao said wryly. "But I was lucky; those books saved my life when my magic came in."

"*The Thousand-Character Classic?*" Han asked, thinking of the primer on the Language of Flowers the bookseller had given him.

"No." Master Cao smiled. "Novels." He gestured to the shelves around him stacked high with copies upon copies upon copies of titles such as *The Wandering Monk* and *Into the Thick of It*. "Adventure stories. I often dreamed of becoming a hero like the ones I read about in these tales, flying about on a cloud and bringing justice to the world. Like them, I had power." The bookseller raised his hands and laughed. "Unlike theirs, it wasn't much to speak of."

Han sat up straighter in his seat. He recognized the affection in Master Cao's voice; it was the same affection and excitement he had felt reading *The Maiden Who Was Loved by Death*. "What of romance novels?" he asked. "Did you enjoy those too?"

The bookseller chuckled. "I didn't when I was a boy," he said. "But I've come to appreciate them since." Their eyes twinkled. "Do you have any particular favorite?"

"*The Maiden Who Was Loved by Death*," Han said immediately.

"Oh, yes, that writer is quite popular." Master Cao nodded. "And prolific." He gestured to the storeroom at the back of the bookshop, where Teacher Hu, Mistress Brandy, and the boy had disappeared down a trapdoor. Han was astonished to discover the existence of a basement beneath a store so close to the waters of the canal, but Master Cao explained that it was only possible through magic. There were spells carved into the wooden posts and dirt floor that kept the waters of the river at bay. "There are several new titles back there that my scriveners and I haven't yet had time to copy out. I am"—he winced—"a bit short-staffed lately."

"Short-staffed?" Xu asked. "Why?"

Master Cao sighed. "The bookshop is partially a front for the Guardians of Dawn," he said. "And the people who work for me are members of the organization, who help me find magicians throughout the city and help them escape."

So the fishwife was right, Han thought. The bookseller really *was* running an illegal smuggling operation of sorts.

"Escape?" he asked, thinking of Uncle Li and his cousin Ami. "Escape where?"

Master Cao fixed him with a knowing gaze. "I'm not telling you, child," he said. "For their safety, and yours."

"Is the reason the bookshop is short-staffed because all the magicians have escaped to safety?" Xu asked.

"Alas, no." Master Cao shook his head. "If only that were the case. No, several of them have gone missing in the past few weeks and no one knows where. Or why."

Xu worried their lower lip. "The Kestrels?"

"I doubt it." The bookseller absentmindedly played with the braided cord about his waist. "Announcements would have been posted everywhere if that were so."

Han played with the dressing on his arm. "All of the missing are magicians?" He thought of his brother's friend, Yao, the kitchen boy.

"It appears so." Master Cao sighed again. "Anyway, go ahead and take a look at these romance novels, young man. You may borrow what strikes your fancy, providing you return it in good condition, of course."

Han leaped to his feet, wincing a bit as his wound reopened in his excitement.

"Yah!" Xu called. "Don't overdo it!"

But he ignored his best friend, running his fingers over stacks of manuscripts reverently, scanning the titles for anything that struck his fancy.

"Be careful," Master Cao warned. "It's a mess and nothing's organized.

Oh, and watch out for that bookshelf. It's old and rickety from being moved aside so often."

Han gleefully sat down beside the pile of paperbacks behind the counter and started thumbing through the titles.

"*The Pearl Diver*," he read aloud. "*The Conqueror of Beaver Hill*."

From their seat on the other side of the bookshop, Xu gave a snort of amusement.

"*Staff and Rod*," Han continued. "*A Treatise on the Joys of Totem Worship*." He opened to the first page. "This doesn't seem like a romance— Ohhhhhh." He slammed the book shut as Xu cackled with delight. "Shut up," he said, feeling his face light on fire.

It was at that propitious moment that the ground beneath him bucked and rolled. Han gave a shout as he went crashing to his hands and knees.

"Move!" came a muffled voice through the floorboards. "I can't lift you when you're sitting *on* the trapdoor!"

Startled, Han threw himself to the side, wincing as the seams of his borrowed garment popped open along the shoulders. Since he had cast aside the priestess of Do disguise during the fight, Master Cao had kindly lent him a spare set of clothes. Unfortunately, he was several times bigger than the bookseller, and Master Cao's robes barely reached mid-shin.

The trapdoor opened fully, revealing a heart-shaped face with delicate features surrounded by a mass of dark, unruly hair.

"Mistress Brandy!" Han warbled in surprise. He scrambled to his feet and tugged at the hem of Master Cao's robes to make sure everything was covered and in good order. Leaning against the rickety old bookcase, he tried his best to seem suave. Elegant. Sophisticated. "Good to see you're still breathing," he said, several octaves deeper than his normal voice, in what he hoped was a tone of cool disdain. That was the tone the hero seemed to affect most in *The Maiden Who Was Loved by Death*.

She looked up at him with a strange expression on her face. "Have you caught a cold, Master Plum Blossom? What's wrong with your voice?"

Xu sniggered from the other side of the room, and Han felt his face flush even hotter. "I'm fine." He coughed. "Just, uh, a little tickle in the throat."

The shelves he had been leaning on suddenly buckled beneath his weight, sending a pile of books cascading to the floor. Panicked, he leaped forward to straighten them up when his foot slipped on some loose pages. Han went crashing into another set of shelves, which tumbled to the ground, burying him in an avalanche of books. Something jingled, and he sneezed.

He crossed his eyes to find the laughing, golden eyes of Mistress Brandy's ginger cat right before his nose. "This is it," he said mournfully. "This is rock bottom. Buried under the remains of my dignity and a demon cat." Han sneezed again.

"Sajah," she admonished, but Han could hear the smile in her voice. "Be nice."

The cat sniffed then turned to twine itself about Mistress Brandy's ankles, but not without giving him an eyeful of its rear end first. Han groaned, trying to dig himself out from under a pile of books and shelves, and Mistress Brandy bent forward to offer him her hand.

At her touch, something surged deep within his bones and blood, a musical note or sound, a sensation that resonated with recognition. Mistress Brandy's touch felt like a summer's evening in the meditation garden, like the warmth in his limbs after a sparring session in the exercise yard, like his little brother's head resting against his shoulder as they slept. Han fought the urge to both snatch back his hand and give in to that feeling of comfort. Mistress Brandy's eyes widened before she quickly pulled away, her face turned shyly to the side.

"H-hullo," Han said, a giddy grin crossing his face.

She smiled back. "Hullo," she said.

For several long moments, no one spoke as all eyes—human and feline—darted back and forth between them waiting for either Han or Mistress Brandy to say something. Xu and Sajah exchanged glances before Xu rose to their feet with a long-suffering sigh.

"Please excuse my friend's terrible manners, my dear," they said to Mistress Brandy. They gave her a respectful bow, bent at the waist with hands clasped before them. "Allow me to introduce ourselves. I am Chan Xuhei, and this fool"—Xu indicated Han with a tilt of their head—"is Won—"

"Li," Han interjected quickly, giving his mother's surname. Wonhu was the surname of Zanhei's ruling family, and he didn't want his true identity as the Royal Heir known. There was no need to bring the palace—or Anyang—into things just yet. "My name is Li Han."

Mistress Brandy inclined her head. "Jin Zhara," she replied. "It's a pleasure to meet everyone."

"If you are all quite finished," came a disembodied voice from the trapdoor, "we've got a rather large problem on our hands." A plump, bespectacled figure emerged from the basement—*the apothecary, Teacher Yu or Wu or something like that,* Han thought, struggling to remember their name.

"Everything all right, Teacher Hu?" the bookseller asked. "Is something the matter with the boy?"

"In a manner of speaking," the apothecary said. "He apparently transformed into an abomination and back tonight."

All color left Master Cao's cheeks, leaving him pale and ashen. "No," he said, sounding stricken. "That's . . . impossible."

Xu cleared their throat. "I'm afraid we didn't sustain our injuries by accidentally falling off buildings. It's more that the buildings fell on us, in a manner of speaking. Were thrown at us, more like. By a giant, terrifying monster made of a thousand rats and ten thousand eyes." They shuddered with disgust. "My body may be healed, but my mind will never recover. I will have nightmares for weeks."

The bookseller shook his head. "No," he repeated. "No. If abominations are walking among us, then it means . . . it means . . ."

"Don't say it," Teacher Hu said irritably. "Don't say it."

". . . demons," Master Cao finished in a scarcely audible whisper. His nut-brown eyes were round with fear.

"Demons?" Han startled, remembering Anyang's cracked voice crying out about a frog demon knocking at his dreams. "But they're not real . . . are they?"

"Of course not," Teacher Hu scoffed. "Religion is one thing, but demons? Demons are simply what we call the dark side of human nature when we don't want to hold ourselves accountable."

The bookseller crossed his arms. "You wouldn't be so cavalier about the existence of demons if you could be possessed by one yourself." Master Cao's expression darkened. "Possession is a fate worse than death."

The apothecary snorted in derision. "And how would you know? Have you been possessed before?"

"No," the bookseller said quietly. "But my brother was. I had to cut him down myself when he transformed into an abomination."

Silence fell over the bookshop, and Han shifted uncomfortably in his seat. *The frog demon sits beside me and asks me to give him my magic.* "Are there," he ventured, "different kinds of demons?"

Master Cao shot him a sharp glance. "What do you mean, child?"

Han looked to Xu, but his best friend's eyes gave nothing away. "My brother," he began slowly, "sometimes speaks of a frog demon haunting him in his sleep."

Xu stiffened, but kept their mouth shut. At Han's words, the bookseller went very, very still.

"The Frog Demon of Poison and Pestilence," he murmured. "The first Lord of Tiyok?"

"Not this again," Teacher Hu groaned.

"The first Lord of Tiyok?" Mistress Brandy said thoughtfully. "Weren't there four Lords of Tiyok in the old fairy tales?"

Master Cao gave her an approving smile. "Yes. According to *Songs of Order and Chaos,* there were four high-ranking generals of the Chaos realm—the Frog Demon of Poison and Pestilence, the Locust Demon of Starvation, the Viper Demon of Discord, and the unnamed King of Tiyok, called the Ancient One. These generals fought against the Guardians of Dawn while the Sunburst Warrior battled the Mother of Demons, before sealing them all away with the Star of Radiance."

Han thought he could vaguely recall some of this story from the Bangtan Brothers' performance of it last summer, although in truth, he had paid more attention to the action sequences than anything else. But even if this were all true, surely he would know if Anyang were possessed by a greater demon. Wouldn't he?

"What are the signs of possession?" he asked. He thought of his brother's magical temper tantrums, the uncontrolled bursts of power, the panicked resignations of half a dozen nursemaids. *He cracked my ribs open and tried to crawl inside.* "And what causes it?"

"The signs of *corruption*," Teacher Hu interjected with a glare at Master Cao, "are listlessness, a change in temperament, and irritability. As for the cause . . . we still don't know."

"The apothecary thinks abomination is a matter of medicine, not magic," the bookseller said scornfully. "No matter that the afflicted *literally* turn into actual monsters." Master Cao sighed and shook his head. "The truth is, we know very little about demons. What little we do know came from *Songs of Order and Chaos,* an ancient book of cosmology and demonology, but the original was lost centuries ago."

"I thought there was still a copy in existence." Teacher Hu frowned.

"There was," the bookseller said heavily, "one copy our scholars and historians had begun reconstructing from archival and anecdotal sources, but that copy disappeared six months ago with Li Er-Shuan and his daughter."

"Uncle Li!" Han gasped.

The heads of the apothecary and the bookseller swiveled to study his face. "*Uncle* Li?" Master Cao asked with interest. "You never mentioned you were related to him."

"I, uh—" Han felt a warning jab in his side—the butt of Xu's now-ruined fan pressed against his ribs. "He and his daughter are distant cousins of mine. Very distant cousins," he added when Xu jabbed his ribs again.

Master Cao's expression brightened. "Ah, is that why you asked me if I knew where they had gone?" A shadow passed over his face. "Ami was a clever girl," he said. "Her father was a bit odd, and not much of a caretaker. Brilliant, but odd."

"Yes, I know." Jab. "Sir," Han added politely, rubbing his side and glaring at his best friend. "Ami and I knew each other as children."

A furrow appeared between the bookseller's brows. "I thought Li Ami lived in the palace with her father as a child."

"I, er, yes!" Han coughed. "My parents also work at the palace."

Master Cao looked thoughtful. "Do they now?"

"Don't," Teacher Hu said warningly.

"But we could use some eyes and ears in the palace," the bookseller protested. "We were caught entirely off guard by the news of the Royal Heir's engagement to Princess Yulana."

Yes, and so was the Royal Heir himself, Han thought bitterly.

"What would the Guardians of Dawn need?" Xu asked.

"Well . . ." Master Cao pulled at his lower lip. "If someone could find Li Er-Shuan's notes on *Songs of Order and Chaos,* that would be a great asset to our organization. He was working with his daughter and Huang Jiyi, another one of our scholars of magic, on reconstructing the text."

"What makes Master Cao believe there's anything in the palace?" Zhara asked. "Surely this Li Er-Shuan would have destroyed any evidence connecting him to magic." She had kept quiet throughout most of the conversation, her eyes large and round as she tried to process all the new information. That ginger menace of a cat dozed in her lap, but opened one baleful, golden eye at Han before closing it again. He sneezed.

Xu cleared their throat. "If that's what the Guardians of Dawn need, then I might be of some assistance to the organization," they said, glancing sidelong at Han. "Since I live at the palace."

"We *both* live at the palace." Han glared at the subtle shake of his best friend's head. If Xu had their way, Han would stay holed up in the royal palace and well out of harm's way until he reached his majority. But he couldn't bear to remain safe when Anyang's very existence was a danger. Not when he could, at last, *do* something about it.

"You're only children," Teacher Hu said, looking from Han to Xu and finally to Zhara.

"And so were we, when all this began," Master Cao said softly.

Han met Zhara's eyes across the room. He remembered the expression of longing in them as she gazed at the books on display, and the realization that he could live for so much more. "My mother," he said slowly, "was a magician. When the Kestrels took her away, she made me promise to protect my little brother from the Warlord's justice."

He did not look away from Zhara as he spoke. "And until now, I didn't realize survival was not the same thing as living."

Her eyes shone in the candlelight. "We want to thrive, not just survive," she said softly.

A thrill ran through Han, galvanizing him from head to toe with a tingling sensation. *We.*

Teacher Hu and Master Cao exchanged looks. The apothecary shook her head, but the bookseller seemed to disagree with her assessment.

"They're only children," Teacher Hu repeated.

"If they are children now," Master Cao said, "then they won't be children for much longer." His face was grim. "There are no children during war."

Teacher Hu looked sad. "We are not at war yet."

Master Cao closed his eyes. "The war never ended."

The apothecary studied the shining, eager faces of those she had called children and held their gazes for a long time. "All right," she said at last, her voice grave. "Welcome, comrades, to the Guardians of Dawn."

15

THESE DAMN ROYAL ROBES WERE FAR TOO hot for the southern climate, Han thought, feeling beads of sweat trickle down his sideburns and onto one of the three starched linen collars he wore as part of his court regalia. Seven layers of cotton, silk, and silk brocade were simply too much on an ordinary day, let alone the day the Royal Heir was to officially meet his future bride. Han wasn't sure how much of the sweat beneath his headdress was due to being overheated and how much was due to stress.

After all, Princess Yulana was arriving today.

Of course, it didn't help that he was standing in direct sunlight at the top of the steps leading to the Hall of Heavenly Wisdom. Han had never given much thought to just how far the throne room was from the main entrance gate until he had to wait for the northern procession to reach him. Two canopy-bearers on either side of him held a fringed covering between two poles to offer some respite from the unrelenting heat, not that it did much good. The humidity was especially oppressive today, a thick, sticky blanket that draped over the Infinite River basin like a linen cloth over a basket of steamed taro buns. Despite the attendants gently fanning him from all directions, the air felt stale. Suffocating. Han fidgeted on his feet, wishing he could at least sit down.

A sudden blast and blare of horns announced the approach of the northern procession. The shock and surprise further drenched Han in a fine film of cold, anxious sweat, and he found himself unexpectedly grateful for the seven layers of fabric between his armpits and his audience. Drumbeats filled the courtyard, nearly loud enough to drown out the thumping of his heart as he waited to greet his fiancée.

The distance from the gates to the Hall of Heavenly Wisdom was long, and the wait was agonizing. Han's eyes kept sliding shut, the dangling beads of his headdress tinkling as he continually jerked his head back upright. If Xu were with him, they would probably be poking him with their fan to keep him awake, but his best friend wasn't considered high-ranking enough to stand beside the Royal Heir while he greeted a foreign entourage. Besides, they were probably taking a nap at the moment, recovering from their late-night misadventures with the Guardians of Dawn.

Lucky them.

Perspiration slicked his palms with fear as the memory of the monster they had fought returned to him. Han shuddered, and the beads about his head danced in sympathy. That abomination, that . . . thing had been a little boy, a little boy about his brother's age, and the idea of the same fate befalling Anyang terrified him. He wished he could bring Mistress Brandy—Zhara—into the palace to work whatever magic on his little brother she had managed with the Buri child.

Zhara.

As his future bride made her slow, unbearable march toward him from the gates, Han couldn't help thinking of Zhara and wondering how his betrothed would compare. The fierce, late-morning sun beat down on the top of his headdress, while a heat of an entirely different sort crept up the back of his neck as he thought of her smile. He had seen beautiful women before—the palace was filled with beautiful women— but not a single one of them affected him the way Mistress Brandy did. Her presence did funny things to him. His legs went watery, his insides disappeared, his lips and tongue lost all coordination, while at the same time, his blood seemed to fizz with effervescence, making him giddy.

A giggle rose in his throat, and he choked it down with a hiccough.

And another one.

And yet another one.

Oh no.

Behind him, he could sense the Chancellor glaring disapprovingly.

Princess Yulana's entourage was still a ways off; perhaps he could swallow the spasms before she arrived.

Beneath the drumbeats, Han could hear the *clip-clop* of hooves across the courtyard cobblestones. Ahead, several gates away still, he could see a short, stocky rider atop a black horse at the head of the procession, followed by an attendant holding an enormous scarlet banner bearing the sigil of the Gommun Kang—a black bear surrounded by a wreath of thorns. He squinted, looking for the palanquin bearing his bride toward him, but was unable to find it. He resisted the urge to shade his eyes, as the Royal Heir was not supposed to show any emotion in public; he must be still, serene, and like a statue at all times.

Being a prince was ridiculous.

"Remember, Your Grace," the Chancellor murmured at his shoulder, "do not bow when the princess arrives. His Grace ought to make a fist with his right hand and thump it against his chest, over his heart."

"I—*hic*—know that," Han said irritably. "I do—*hic*—pay attention—*hic*—to my lessons—*hic*—sometimes." He rubbed his chest ruefully.

As the procession crossed the final gate to the inner courtyard, the assembled ministers and bureaucrats bowed at the waist, a rippling sea of green, blue, and purple according to rank. The attendants beside Han also bowed as the northern delegation approached, leaving only the Chancellor standing straight by virtue of his title as regent.

By now the lead rider's features were visible, as well as the secondary banner that flew beneath the Great Bear: a golden flag with five tabs—white, red, blue, green, and yellow. The flag of the Golden Horde, the most elite warriors of the steppes. The rider at the head of the procession must be an important warrior, as they were the only one on a mount—a stout, sturdy-looking horse with red tassels on its bridle. A plain, brown-and-white-speckled kestrel sat on the rider's shoulder, curiously tame despite the fact that it was neither hooded nor jessed. The armor worn by the lead rider was also much more impressive than the very practical leather cuirasses and vambraces worn by the other escorts, although much simpler than the ceremonial plate armor Han had seen his father occasionally wear. The leather breast-plate was etched with a gilded pattern of thorns, the hardware and buckles that held the straps together were made of polished gold instead of brass, and instead of a boiled leather cap, the lead rider wore a pointed, golden helmet over a golden mesh aventail. A long, white feather trailed from the comb of the helmet, from a bird Han did not recognize. The rider was much younger than he would have thought an exalted warrior would be.

"Your Grace," the Chancellor hissed.

Han shot the regent another glare out of the corner of his eye. "What?"

"The princess," the minister said with a harsh whisper, "rides at the head of the column. The Royal Heir must salute her *now*."

"She—*hic*—what?"

The drumbeats faded away as Princess Yulana made it to the bottom of the stairs to the Hall of Heavenly Wisdom and dismounted. The kestrel at her shoulder didn't even flap its wings as she dropped to the ground and waited, looking up at Han with an expectant look on her face. He started to bow before remembering that he was supposed to greet her in the northern fashion. With another hiccough, he thumped his right fist against his chest. The princess returned the gesture, standing about awkwardly until a slim attendant in shaman's robes emerged from the entourage to whisper something in her ear. She startled, then held her clasped hands out before her as she bowed in the southern fashion. Her attendant nudged her again and she removed her helmet. Her hair was shaved on the sides and braided in a long horsetail down her back like a steppe warrior, but the most shocking thing about it was not its masculine style, but its reddish color.

"Now, Your Grace," the Chancellor said beneath his breath.

Startled, Han bowed in return, his movements just as stiff as his future bride's. He cleared his throat to give his pre-rehearsed remarks, spreading his arms wide. "Wel—*hic*—welcome, honored guests," he squeaked. "Wonhu—*hic*—Han of the Laugh—*hic*—ing Monkey gladly—*hic*—receives the—*hic*—representatives of the Gom—*hic*—mun Kang."

The sound of his hiccoughs echoed throughout the courtyard, nearly as loud as the drums that had announced Princess Yulana's arrival. Behind him, Han could sense the Chancellor seething with embarrassment and allowed himself a small smile of satisfaction. Formalities observed, he tucked his hands into his sleeves, his part finished.

The regent then stepped forward to take on the role of his father's proxy. "Welcome, Your Highness and esteemed guests," the Chancellor called, but his slimy, unctuous voice did not carry far. "The House of Wonhu is honored by the presence of the Gommun Kang's First Daughter."

From behind the regent's outstretched arms, Han tried to get a better look at Princess Yulana. His future bride was tall and muscular; unsurprising, considering the ease with which she rode her horse into the palace. The heir to the Gommun Kang was no delicate flower to be carried about on a palanquin; no wonder he hadn't seen one in the procession. Her ceremonial armor included a blade at her side, and based on the easy, almost thoughtless way she rested her hand against the hilt, he suspected she was as comfortable with weapons as she was on horseback.

"And the future Grand Kang of the Ten Thousand Families is honored to be invited," said the attendant at the princess's side. Unlike the others in the delegation, the attendant was not dressed in armor but in a simple, sky-blue tunic tied with a red tasseled rope about their waist. The hems of their sleeves were long and made of contrasting bands of red, white, yellow, green, and royal blue, which trailed along the ground. A pointed cap with long, dangling strings of blue and white beads was perched atop their head, and a small gourd and brass gong hung from the rope at their waist. Some sort of shaman, Han supposed.

"The future Grand Kang?" the Chancellor said in a bewildered voice, and for the first time Han heard the man sound flustered and confused. "That was not the arrangement—" He gathered his composure and bestowed a thin smile upon their guests, all teeth and no lips. "Ah, but no matter. We shall discuss this over refreshments, of course."

"Of course," the attendant said smoothly. They turned and nodded at the members of the entourage bearing parcels and chests, indicating they should step forward. When the princess made no movement, the attendant discreetly cleared their throat. The princess started, then bowed stiffly once more.

"In thanks for the Royal Heir's hospitality," she said in a flat voice, "may I offer some treasures of my people as tribute."

Han stifled a yawn and tried not to groan with boredom. The presentation of gifts would drag on for another several moments, and he was desperate to sit down. He was especially desperate to escape the banquet at the Pavilion of Serene Rest that was to follow, where the two reluctant lovers were supposed to get to know each other in a so-called informal setting. As though sitting in the garden surrounded by twenty-five of their closest, most intimate advisors could be considered informal.

His eyes slid to Princess Yulana, who seemed equally bored. He surreptitiously tried to get a good look at her face. From a distance, it was difficult to tell whether or not she was attractive, but Han thought she was the sort of girl people called *handsome* rather than beautiful. She had a rather angular—almost boyish—face, and despite all the armor she proudly wore, her countenance seemed friendly. He realized with some amusement that the bird on her shoulder somehow managed to mirror her expression almost exactly, the way palace ladies and their jowly lapdogs ended up looking like each other. The kestrel's sky-blue eyes were an unusual color. Perhaps it was blind, and that was why it seemed so tame.

"We thank the Gommun Kang for the generous gifts," the Chancellor intoned once all the chests and boxes and parcels had been opened. "Now," he said. "The princess has come from a far distance and must be tired. We have refreshments prepared at the Pavilion of Serene Rest, which we hope Her Highness will find suitable." He clapped his hands as several handmaidens from the Hall of Earthly Delights stepped forward. "These attendants shall guide the princess to her quarters once the Royal Heir sees fit to dismiss us."

Eagerly, Han started to raise his hands when the princess cut in.

"I would rather pass the time in the royal library, if you don't mind," she said bluntly. "I've heard great things about Zanhei's collection." Princess Yulana addressed the Chancellor informally, and the rudeness of it all seemed to slap the Chancellor across the face. Han grinned. Perhaps he and his fiancée would get along after all.

"I see," the Chancellor said, slimy lips pursed in a frog-like frown. "We had not realized Her Highness was a scholar as well as a warrior. She need only mention what she is looking for and we shall bring the texts to her rooms immediately."

Princess Yulana shrugged. "I prefer to browse the stacks myself," she said. "You never know what might strike my fancy."

Han frowned. He found it odd that the first thing the Warlord's granddaughter wanted to do after traveling all the way from Urghud was to visit a *library*. More than odd—suspicious. Cold beads of anxiety gathered in his gut when he realized he, too, was in search of a book. A very particular book.

The Chancellor seemed confused but held his hands before him and bowed. "But of course, Your Highness," he said. "We can discuss the particulars over refreshments."

"Perfect," she said. Her eyes slid up to meet Han's, and even from his distance, he could see her gaze was sharp and intelligent. Twinned with the stare of the kestrel on her shoulder, he felt curiously exposed. He looked to the Chancellor, who signaled him to dismiss the gathering.

He raised his hands once more. "Let us adjourn," he said, relieved his hiccoughs seemed to have subsided at last. "I bid the Gommun warriors to avail themselves of Zanhei's hospitality." He remembered to thump his right fist against his chest this time. "My lady," he said to the princess.

She returned his salute. The kestrel at her shoulder pecked at her ear.

"We accept your—His Grace's—hospitality," she said stiffly. Then, a beat too late, she bent at the waist, holding her hands out before her incorrectly. "I look forward to dining with you—him—at the Pavilion of Serene Rest."

Han felt his lips tighten in some approximation of a smile. "Me— *hic*—too."

Dammit.

16

ZHARA WAITED BY THE LION TEMPLE IN the marsh, trying desperately to scrape the muck off her shoe with a reed. The roads in the lowlands were perhaps less *road* and more *ox path,* and more than once she had found herself up to her ankles in what she hoped was mud.

She and Teacher Hu had agreed to meet with Meng Grandmother on the outskirts of the Buri settlement, which was in the floodplains a league or so upriver from Zanhei. The apothecary had sent Zhara on ahead of her, as she had to finish up with the last few clients in her shop, and didn't want the Buri matriarch to wait. Meng Grandmother was supposed to meet them at the Lion Temple, one of the landmarks on the road used by travelers for worship of their various gods.

Zhara had been the first to arrive. She studied the modest little stupa, which was littered with half-burned sticks of incense, flowers, food, and joss paper around its base. The Lion Temple was older than Zanhei itself, built for an unknown god of the marsh long since forgotten. Whatever relic the stupa had housed was long gone, replaced by the everlasting flame of truth. Zanhei, like the other southern provinces in the empire, made devotions to the six Immortals, celestial beings who each governed a different mansion of Reason—language, astronomy, martial arts, music, math, and medicine. Their symbols were painted onto the base of the Lion Temple: the brush for Yuo, a compass for Tendi, a sword for Wu, a flute for Omhak, a pair of scales for Shua, and a mortar and pestle for Lo.

She frowned, noticing a strange seventh symbol with the others, a hollow circle with a dot in the center, painted in red. It reminded her of the shape of the sunburst token the Guardians of Dawn handed out. Cautiously, she ran her fingers over the mark. Still damp.

"Ho, Jin Zhara." She looked up to see Meng Grandmother coming up the road, hobbling on the arm of a young person, hand raised in greeting. "I thought Teacher Hu was supposed to be with you."

"She'll be along soon, I hope," Zhara said. "She had to close up shop. How is Thanh?" The apothecary had taken the boy back to his people the day before, once he had fully recovered from his ordeal.

"Fine," the Buri matriarch said. "Back to his usual, cheerful self, in fact." She frowned. "He says he doesn't remember what happened, which is a blessing, I suppose." She sighed and turned to the youth at her side. "This is one of my other many, many great-grandsons, Kam." Kam hailed Zhara with an upraised arm as she returned the gesture. "He will show us where the children were playing before they . . . changed."

"Where was it?" she asked.

"By the fountain," Kam said. "The city built a new one a few months ago, but I'm afraid we don't use it much."

"Can't trust anything built by you city dwellers," Meng Grandmother muttered, gesturing to the crumbling roads around her. "Nothing is made to last." She tapped the base of the Lion Temple with her cane. "Only the ancient structures stand the test of time. Bah," she spat, staring disapprovingly at the symbols painted along the base of the stupa. "Look at this nonsense. Keep your gods to your own temples in the city, I say!"

"Does Meng Grandmother know what this means?" Zhara asked, pointing to the last symbol—the circle with the dot in the center. "It looks new."

"Ah," the Buri matriarch said. "That's Mara's symbol."

"Mara?" Kam asked. "Isn't that the name of the first abomination?"

Meng Grandmother smacked her grandson on the back of the hand. "Don't let these city dwellers hear you besmirch the name of the Seventh Immortal with your nonsense," she said sternly.

"The Seventh Immortal?" Zhara asked. "But I thought there were only six mansions of Reason." She counted on her fingers, starting with her thumb. "Language, astronomy, martial arts, music, math, and medicine."

The Buri matriarch looked at her with an expression akin to pity. "You install your gods on our land, turn our children to their worship, and yet you know so little of them," she said, shaking her head in dismay. "Magic. Magic is the seventh mansion of Reason." The old woman tapped the base of the stupa with her cane as she moved along the symbols. "Yuo, Tendi, Wu, Omhak, Shua, Lo, and the last and youngest of the Immortals— Mara."

"I've never heard of Mara before," Zhara marveled. "What happened to their worship?"

"The Warlord happened is what," Meng Grandmother said in a grim voice. "The old bear destroyed all evidence of the Seventh Immortal, and every other reference to magic he could find, when he installed himself on the Sunburst Throne as Emperor of the Morning Realms."

Kam looked as though he were still trying to wrap his mind around the concept. "Then . . . Mara was not the first abomination?"

The old woman shifted on her feet. "Well," she hedged. "They weren't *not* the first abomination. According to the legends, anyhow."

Zhara raised her brows.

The old woman sighed. "All right," she said grudgingly. "Mara was indeed the first abomination. But that's not a story magicians like to tell." She looked up at the dome of the sky, the stars bigger and brighter out in the marsh where no city lights could blot them out. "They say that all children born under the mansion of the Seventh Immortal are blessed—or cursed—to walk with one foot in the realm of Order and the other in the realm of Chaos. That magicians, like Mara, are the children of Tiyok, the Mother of Ten Thousand Demons."

Zhara went still. "Then . . . are magicians also part demon?" Her magic flickered in protest.

"You know the story of how this world came to be?" the old woman asked.

"Of course." Every child in the Morning Realms knew the story of the origins of the cosmos. How Do, the place of beginnings and endings, created Jun and Yan, the divine embodiments of Order and Chaos. How Jun and Yan together created light and dark, matter and void, reason and madness, with humanity caught in between. Order and Chaos within a single being. Forever in balance.

"When the world was first created," the old woman continued, "the heavens and the abyss fought for the soul of humanity. The Immortals and the spirits on one side, Tiyok and her ten thousand demons on the other. Locked in eternal battle, a fairy and a demon sought peace between them by joining together in love. From that union came Mara, who, like humanity, was born of Order and Chaos."

Zhara furrowed her brow. "If Mara was born of a fairy and a demon," she said slowly, "why does that make them an abomination?"

"Because it violates reason," the old woman said. "Because it makes them something uncanny. Something that shouldn't exist." She glanced down the road. "Ah, there's Teacher Hu now."

Once the apothecary joined them at the Lion Temple, the foursome made their way to the heart of the Buri village together. Camp settlements began sprouting up like lotus flowers along the shores of the Infinite River as they drew nearer to the lowlands. The refugee section of the Pits was farther upriver along the floodplains, where the land had not yet been drained to make way for human habitation. Stilt-houses banded together like storks along the banks, spindly legs propping up the wobbly wattle-and-daub bodies of hasty housing. The evensong of delta crickets rose and fell around them like the tides as fishermen and their tame cormorants poled home on their rattan skiffs after a day's work on the water.

As the reed houses hove into view, Zhara's magic began to tingle along the ki pathways of her body. It was as though there was a pucker to the smooth flow of the universe around her, like water parting around a rock, and the rock was the village ahead of them. The marshy wetlands started giving way to packed-dirt paths as they approached, the scent of damp and brine dissipating into the aroma of curried stir-fry.

"There," Kam said, pointing to a long, raised house on stilts at the far end of the street, some ways apart from the other buildings. "That's the sick house where the other, uh, corrupted children are."

"We should examine them before we go out to the fountain," Teacher Hu suggested.

"All right," Meng Grandmother said. "But we shouldn't stay too long."

As they approached, Zhara could feel the currents of the universe swirling faster about her, like a whirlpool spinning around a void. Pressure filled her ears, and an uncanny quiet fell over them. Even the crickets had fallen silent; the only sounds were the quiet murmur of the river in the distance and the gentle shushing of reeds dancing in the spring breeze.

"Here we are." Kam pushed aside the woven reed mat that covered the doorway. Zhara listened for the sounds of breathing as she ascended the rickety bamboo ladder into the sick house. Nothing. No low voices. Just the thud of her rapidly beating heart as she pushed aside the mat and followed after Meng Grandmother and Kam.

"Leave your shoes at the door!" the old woman shouted. "We may be lowland bumpkins, but we're not *barbarians*."

The first thing that struck Zhara was the smell. It was close and stuffy inside the sick house, the air thick with the all-too-familiar reek of humanity. Sweat, tears, undigested food, and dirty hair, yet beneath it all was a curious, sickly sweet scent that she could not quite name.

The second thing that struck her was the bodies.

She hadn't noticed just how many there were at first, having taken them all to be empty sleeping pallets and bundles of blankets laid out on the floor. It wasn't until she saw the blankets moving that she realized there was a small, brown body curled beneath each one. A few adults were clustered here and there, hovering over each bed, each child. Parents, she assumed, or other family members.

"There are many more corrupted now than there were before," Teacher Hu observed in a soft voice.

Meng Grandmother nodded. "Two when the last foraging party returned from Mount Zanhei yesterday, and another one who came back from playing by the fountain a little ways upriver. The rest"—she gestured with her cane—"are all adults. They've been like this for weeks now."

"Why did the government build the fountain?" Zhara asked.

"The groundwater around the marsh isn't good for drinking," Meng Grandmother said. "So we used to draw our water from the wells down near the Pits."

Zhara was taken aback. "So far away?"

She nodded. "The government began building a new fountain much closer to the lowlands a few months ago, and it's only just recently been finished. About three weeks ago, I think." The matriarch's face tightened with silent fury. "They didn't care when our people started going missing. The ministers only cared that there were enough bodies to exploit for labor. To build this useless fountain."

Teacher Hu cleared her throat after a moment. "Where is the water in the fountain coming from?"

"The springs up by Old Changxi," Kam answered.

The apothecary made notes. "And when did the corruption begin to take hold among your people?"

Meng Grandmother drew her brows together. "About three weeks ago?" She startled. "Do you think this is all related?"

"Could be," the apothecary said in a noncommittal voice. "Old Changxi sits right at the base of Mount Zanhei. Zhara," she said, turning to her assistant, "would you mind examining the patients to see if they're all afflicted with the same, ah, blight you sensed in Thanh?"

"Yes, auntie." Zhara nervously wiped the sweat from her hands onto her tunic and approached the nearest sickbed. "May I?" she asked the parent. They gave her permission, and she knelt beside the child and laid a hand on their cheek.

As it had with Thanh, her magic immediately responded to the presence of another magician, only now she was better able to differentiate between what was magic and what was not. Magic was home, familiarity, comfort; the blight was . . . rotten. Diseased. With sight that was not sight, Zhara traced the meridian pathways throughout the child's body, seeing the same darkness, the same *emptiness* dimming the light inside. She removed her hand and moved on to the next patient, and then the next, and the next, and the next, examining them all before turning to Teacher Hu, and nodding her head in confirmation.

"All right," said the herbalist. "Let's go investigate this fountain."

The fountain was at least an hour away by foot, and by the time they arrived, night had fallen completely. Teacher Hu carried flint and steel in her satchel, but all the vegetation around them was too wet to make for good tinder or a torch. So they trudged along after Meng Grandmother and Kam, who seemed untroubled by the utter darkness.

"It's a good thing you came, Zhara," Teacher Hu muttered. "I had hoped to run some tests at the site, but there's no point of running them if you can't see two inches in front of your face."

The barest sliver of a moon was visible in the sky, and the myriad stars cast only the faintest glow. Near the horizon, Zhara could see the thick band of silver that comprised the Gleaming River and by habit sought out the stars on either side that represented the woodcutter's daughter and the fairy prince. In a week's time, they would be celebrating their reunion at the Night of the Sevens.

"Here we are," Kam said, pointing ahead. "The fountain."

It was a big, ugly, hulking thing, hunched over like a monster squatting on the marsh. At first glance, it seemed more like a temple than a fountain, an enormous structure built of what looked to be quarried limestone from farther upriver. Four giant columns rose from a flat paved bed, each carved with what seemed to be a different guardian animal. At first, Zhara thought they represented the traditional cardinal beasts of the Morning Realms—the Lion of the South, the Unicorn of the West, the Eagle of the North, and the Dragon of the East—but upon closer inspection, they seemed to be different creatures entirely. A . . . frog? Some sort of moth? A wolf? The last figure was completely unrecognizable as either animal or human, appearing as a horrible, horrifying chimera that seemed to undulate and shift in the darkness.

At the center of the structure was a pool of water dug into the flat surface, perfectly round and perfectly still. Its smooth, glassy surface mirrored the skies above, and for a moment Zhara felt dizzy, as though the world had flipped over. She was no longer sure whether she was looking down into the water or up into the heavens. Zhara blinked, and the world righted itself again.

"How bizarre," Teacher Hu remarked, sitting down at the water's edge. "The fountain seems more like a ritual bath than a well." The apothecary reached into her satchel and removed several small ceramic vials fitted with cork stoppers, filling each one with samples of water from different sides and depths of the pool.

"Don't drink it," warned Meng Grandmother as Teacher Hu brought her face down to the surface for closer examination.

But the herbalist ignored the Buri matriarch, dipping a wooden cup into the well and taking a sip. The others held their breath, waiting for Teacher Hu to fall into a trance or for some other change. But when several moments passed without an adverse reaction, the apothecary frowned and took another sip.

"It's not poisoned, at least, not by any means I can detect," Teacher Hu said. "In fact, I'd say this was some of the sweetest water I have ever tasted. Zhara, come here, child, and let me know what you think. If what is tainting the water is magical in nature, you should be able to tell."

Zhara had been lingering at the edges of the fountain, unwilling to cross the threshold and pass under the watchful, otherworldly eyes of the stone gargoyles. A shudder passed over her as she entered the fountain. She felt suddenly cold, as though she had been plunged into an icy bath.

Meng Grandmother and Kam also joined the apothecary at the fountain's edge, cupping their hands into the pool and tasting the water. "It's good," the old woman said in surprise. "Less mineral than I expected, considering its source from the slopes of Zanhei."

"It doesn't smell earthy," Kam added. "Or stagnant like other wells farther out in the marsh."

Following their lead, Zhara dipped her own fingers into the water, then jerked her hand back in surprise.

"What's wrong?" Kam asked fearfully.

Frowning, she dipped her hand in the pool once more, swirling her hand around in the cool depths. "It's not water," she said slowly.

"What do you mean it's not water?" Meng Grandmother asked in confusion.

Zhara shook her head, frustrated that she lacked the words to describe what she was feeling. "It's just . . . not water," she said. "It's as unlike water as the color red is to a duck." Hesitantly, she touched a drop of liquid to her tongue. Again, she was overwhelmed with the sensation—the conviction—that what filled the well was not water, but something *else* turned liquid.

She could feel Teacher Hu's gaze on her face. "Perhaps," the apothecary said slowly, "for us non-magicians, we are sensing only the physical essence of the liquid before us. But to a magician . . . perhaps there is another dimension."

Zhara sucked in a sharp breath in understanding. "The water has been transformed," she said. "Like Thanh's ki before he—before he became an abomination. No longer human, but *other*." She turned her face up to those gathered around her. "Something . . . demonic."

Silence fell over the marsh, as though the entire world held its breath.

"Is that even possible?" Teacher Hu asked in hushed tones.

"I don't know," Zhara whispered. She looked to the northwest, where the stark silhouette of the volcano dominated the landscape, crowned by its ever-present veil of clouds. "But I think we will need to travel to the source to find out."

17

ZHARA SUPPOSED IT SHOULD HAVE TROUBLED HER how easy it was to sneak back into Zanhei after nightfall, but she wasn't going to complain. Teacher Hu had shown her the crack in the city walls on the southwestern side, hidden from the watchful eyes of the night guard and the casual observer by a hedge of azaleas. They had both easily slipped through and gone their separate ways with nary a good night, hurrying home to catch as much sleep as they could before dawn.

The streets were dark and quiet, the lanterns lining the second-floor balconies extinguished. The light of the disseminating moon illuminated the empty lanes with a fading silver glow, and Zhara was careful to watch her step on the uneven cobblestones. Her slipper had started to unravel again, and she would have to repair it when she got home. She yawned. Or first thing when she woke up.

As she turned onto her street, the convivial laughs and inebriated murmurs from the local tavern on the corner spilled into the night. Zhara usually tried to avoid passing by the tavern after nightfall, mostly to avoid running into the Second Wife, although occasionally she had had to fend off the amorous and indiscriminate advances of the neighborhood drunks.

"And who might this little stranger be?" came a light, sweet voice. The hairs stood up on the back of Zhara's neck.

The Second Wife.

Zhara ducked behind a tree, heart pounding.

"A friend," came another voice, high-pitched, reedy, and oddly familiar, although Zhara did not know why. She thought she might have heard it very recently. Somewhere dark, or hidden, and smelling of damp . . .

"Are you?" the Second Wife said, her tone insolent, direct. "Then why have I never seen you before?"

"The lady may not know me," the stranger said. "But she knows my master."

"And who is your master?"

"Lord Chan."

There was a long moment before the Second Wife spoke. "Don't jest, you little gnome," she said bitingly. "Why would Lord Chan send you to speak to me? Especially after my stupidly shortsighted Suzhan refused to marry him?"

Zhara sucked in a sharp breath, then clapped her hands over her mouth.

"Because," the stranger said, "things have changed."

The Second Wife scoffed. "Of all the eligible daughters in Zanhei, your master wants to marry mine. Mine! A poor, plain, unattractive oaf of a girl. A *blind,* poor, unattractive oaf of a girl. Utterly useless."

Rage boiled through Zhara's veins, every muscle and nerve alert and alive with fury. Suzhan was so much more than her looks, her poverty, her disability. She was musically gifted, she was kind, she was sweet, she was loyal. Any person would be lucky to marry her.

"My master has never cared about her blindness," the stranger said. "Your daughter has . . . other assets."

The Second Wife snorted. "What assets? Her stepfather left us with barely two coins to rub together."

Just then, a rowdy group of ruffians stepped out from the tavern, their boozy shouts echoing off the roof tiles, and the stranger's reply was lost. Zhara strained to listen to the rest of her stepmother's conversation over the ruckus.

"—bring her to—"

"—the other girl—"

"—why her—"

"—because she is a magi—"

By now the crowd of carousers had stumbled upon Zhara—quite literally. "Well, what do we have here?" the nearest one slurred, blowing a breath full of beer and vomit in her face. Zhara coughed and tried not to gag. "A pretty little girl out for a stroll at this hour of the night?"

"Might not be pretty, and might not be a girl," said one of their companions.

"Don't care!" said the first. "Any port in a storm, lah?"

Her power prickled at her palms, but Zhara didn't need magic to deal with these poor, drunken sods. A well-placed stomp or a kick would do just as well, if not better. She brought her foot swiftly down on the instep of the one trying to proposition her, drove her elbow into their stomach, and ran down the road. Behind her she could hear the laughter and the jeers of the unfortunate fool's friends as she unlocked her courtyard gate and stepped over the threshold. Zhara peered behind her to make sure she wasn't being followed.

Sajah greeted her with a grumpy *prrrrt?* as she entered the kitchen and slipped into bed, her eyelids sliding shut despite her best efforts to make sense of what she had overheard between the Second Wife and this mysterious friend of Lord Chan. But the events of the day were catching up to her, overtaking her, and before long, Zhara fell asleep.

The banging of city drums jolted Zhara out of bed the next morning. Sunlight streamed in through the kitchen window and she threw her hand over her eyes, disoriented by the brightness. It was usually darker than this when she got up.

The realization that she had overslept struck her a moment later, and Zhara reflexively threw herself out of bed, scrabbling for the folded clothes on the stool beside her sleeping pallet. The Second Wife would be expecting breakfast at any moment. Bleary-eyed and exhausted, Zhara thrust one leg into her trousers, then the other, and it wasn't until she had secured her tunic about her waist with a sash that she noticed she had put them on backward.

Congee. Congee would have to do for breakfast. Zhara still had leftover rice that had not yet gone bad. She poured several ladlefuls of water into the wok and set it on the burner ring, stirring the coals in the oven with a poker to stoke the flames. She scraped the slightly burnt and stale rice at the bottom of the pot with a spoon and dumped it all into the wok, covering it with a lid so it would come to a boil faster. In the meantime, she found another pot and added a half dozen eggs for hard-boiled tea eggs.

"Ah, good, you're awake."

Zhara startled, nearly burning herself as a tall, willowy silhouette appeared in kitchen threshold. Sajah hissed at the intruder from his perch on the pantry shelves—the Second Wife.

"M-Madame," Zhara stammered, hastily clasping her hands before her and bowing. "I had not thought she would be awake so early. I—I promise breakfast shall be ready shortly."

"Relax." Her stepmother waved a hand as she stepped into the kitchen. The Second Wife's long dark hair was loosely gathered in a ponytail at the nape of her neck, and Zhara could see through the threadbare silk of her dressing gown to the courtyard beyond. "I just wanted to apologize for my behavior the other night. After we came back from our first meeting with Lord Chan."

Zhara flinched. "N-no need, M-Madame." She wasn't sure which stunned her more—her stepmother's apology or that it seemed . . . almost sincere. Gratitude and suspicion snaked themselves around her stomach, squeezing tight like a girdle. Fragments of a conversation floated through her memory, and Zhara thought she could recall two voices raised in quiet argument, but the thought dissipated before she could grasp it.

The Second Wife squinted. "For heaven's sake, child, why is it so murky in here? Light some candles, my dear."

Zhara ordinarily worked in darker conditions than these. The light from the tiny kitchen window was practically incandescent by comparison. "I—I don't keep candles in the kitchen, Madame."

"Oh?" Her stepmother lifted a shapely brow. "Why not?"

"The—the fire in the hearth is—is usually more than enough for me."

The Second Wife sighed. "Child, honestly, it hurts me that you would think I would begrudge you a few candles to light the kitchen as you work. You may take some from the chest of drawers later today if you wish."

"Y-yes, Madame."

Her stepmother brushed past her to the seat beside the hearth. Up close, Zhara could see more clearly the pillow creases against the Second Wife's cheek, the fraying collar and hems of the silk dressing gown, and the puffiness of sleep and too much rice wine about her dark, dark eyes. She was somewhat shocked to see threads of gray glittering at her stepmother's temples and lines engraved about her mouth—without makeup, without the daily armor of glamor she wrapped about herself, the Second Wife's age was beginning to show.

"Anyway, I wanted to talk to you before you left for work, Jin Zhara."

She stiffened. She knew she couldn't trust the Second Wife's reformed manner; her stepmother's tendency toward malice always lay in wait. Like Zhara's own magic. "Of—of course, Madame," she said, panicking as she saw the faint, rosy glow of her magic crack through the lines of her palms. She clasped her hands even harder as she held her bow.

"Oh, do get up," the Second Wife said. "It makes my back hurt to see you hunched over like that all the time."

"Yes, Madame." Zhara straightened and immediately dropped her hands to her sides. "May I—may I return to making breakfast while Madame speaks?" The eggs were rattling in the pot as the boiling water tossed them about, and Zhara immediately pulled them off the burner ring.

The Second Wife yawned and waved her on. "Go on," she said. "I won't be long, but I have a favor to ask."

Zhara paused rinsing the hardboiled eggs. "Of course, Madame," she said, resuming the task of gently cracking the shells and returning them to the pot.

"It's about Suzhan, you see."

Zhara refilled the pot with more water from the cistern, adding black tea leaves, cinnamon, orange peel, hot pepper, fennel seeds, and star anise along with some soy sauce. "What about Suzhan, Madame?" she asked carefully, setting the pot back on the burner ring.

Her stepmother shook her head. "While I do love my treasure very much," she said, "Suzhan's willfulness does try my patience." She gave Zhara a wistful, watery smile. "And I'm afraid I've never been able to control my temper well. How unbecoming, I know."

Zhara thought of the bruise on Suzhan's cheek. She grabbed a few scallions from cold storage and began chopping furiously. Beneath her hands, the wooden handle of the knife grew warm and malleable before turning into a leek. Startled, she dropped the leek where it clattered against the cutting board, a knife once more.

"Is everything all right, child?" The Second Wife's voice was all syrup and solicitousness. "You didn't cut yourself, did you? Let me see." She rose from her seat beside the hearth and reached for Zhara's hand.

"I'm fine, Madame." With immense effort, Zhara willed her magic to subside so as not to sting her stepmother.

The Second Wife made a show of studying Zhara's hand. "You're a good girl, Jin Zhara." Her stepmother ran light fingers over her work-roughened skin in a soothing gesture. "I wish Suzhan was as good as her big sister about this entire marriage business, but my daughter refuses to even consider things from my point of view. Especially as Lord Chan is willing to overlook her . . . youthful contrariness and extend his offer to us again."

"Again?" Something tickled at Zhara's mind, a persistent niggle at her thoughts, trying to get her to remember . . . what? She couldn't think through the distracting thrill of her stepmother's concerned touch.

"Yes." The Second Wife continued tracing Zhara's calluses. "Lord Chan is not an unreasonable man. He's arranged for another meeting, and I want you to accompany us this time— Aiyo!"

There was a discordant jangle as a dusty ginger streak tore across the kitchen, hissing and spitting and scratching at the Second Wife's legs.

"Sajah!" she cried, swooping down to scoop the cat into her arms, but he slipped out of her grip, limbs flailing at her stepmother.

"What is this nasty thing?" The Second Wife swiftly lashed out with her foot, sending Sajah flying toward the hearth. "You," she ordered Zhara. "Get the broom and shoo this flea-bitten thing out."

Reluctantly, she went to grab the broom from the corner, but the cat had already fled into the shadows. Zhara breathed a sigh of relief and returned the broom to its place beside the fireplace. Behind her, she could hear the pot of tea eggs overflowing, so she quickly excused herself to take it off the burner ring.

"Disgusting," the Second Wife sniffed. "Make sure that creature doesn't return. Imagine what diseases it might be carrying. And where our food is prepared too!"

"Yes, Madame. A thousand pardons, Madame," Zhara said, bowing over and over again. She thought of how cats were sacred to the Lion of the South, of how they were supposed to drive pestilence away, not bring it in. She made a note to visit the Lion Temple later to make an offering in penance.

The Second Wife lifted her chin, dismissing her as she began pacing the kitchen floor. "Well," she said. "Before we were so rudely interrupted, I came to ask you to accompany Suzhan to meet Lord Chan at a teahouse."

Now that she was free of her stepmother's distracting touch, the memory of that odd overheard conversation between the Second Wife and a strangely familiar stranger struck Zhara like a slap to the face. "Madame will forgive me," she said slowly, "but why me?"

"While I love my treasure dearly"—her stepmother's serene facade cracked—"she does not trust me. That's where you come in, my dear. To convince her to say yes. You will do that for me, lah? You are my good girl, Jin Zhara."

But Suzhan had not wanted to marry this man. Her sister had been terrified of him. The desire to please her stepmother warred with the need to protect her sister. Zhara knew she had to try to speak out on Suzhan's behalf, even as her resolve withered to nothing in the face of the Second Wife's silken sweetness.

"Madame," she said tentatively. "What does Madame know of her daughter's future husband?"

Her stepmother seemed surprised. "What I told you before. That he is very rich and very powerful. That is all we need to know."

Zhara bit her lip. "There are . . . unpleasant rumors about Lord Chan's past, Madame."

"Oh?" The Second Wife had gone still.

"They say," Zhara began carefully, "that he is known by another name in the lower parts of Zanhei." When her stepmother did not dismiss her, she continued. "The Black Widower."

"The Black Widower?" The Second Wife laughed. "How quaint."

"He has married and buried many wives, Madame."

"All nasty rumors spread by his rejected brides, I'm sure." Her stepmother sniffed. "Ah, Jin Zhara," she said, and her voice was nearly . . . kind. "I know you are worried for Suzhan. And worried about what will happen to you too, aren't you? Where you will go when she marries? What you will do?"

Zhara looked up the Second Wife, caught off guard by her stepmother's intimate—nearly gentle—tone. "I—I—" she stammered. She had never given her future much thought before. The need to keep safe, to survive, had narrowed Zhara's focus to the next meal, the next bit of cash, the next sunrise. *Be good, and be true,* her father had said. It was the only way she knew how to live—to make sure her stepmother remained pleased.

"I can see the thought hasn't even occurred to you," the Second Wife said pityingly.

"N-no, Madame."

"Well," her stepmother said, her voice smooth, soothing . . . seductive. "Going forward, Suzhan is going to need a handmaiden in her new life as a palace official's wife, and who better to look after her than the one person who knows her better than anyone in the world?"

Zhara was stunned. "M-me?"

Your daughter has . . . other assets.

"Yes, you." The Second Wife stepped closer, her long, elegant silhouette as slim and as balanced as a blade. Sweat broke out along Zhara's hairline even as goose bumps broke out along her arms. She had never been so close to her stepmother before, and her proximity was both terrifying and intoxicating. "You are family after all, Jin Zhara."

The words struck her in the ribs, and she found herself unable to breathe. The twin snakes of gratitude and suspicion slithered frantically in her stomach, at odds with each other, struggling for dominance. Zhara didn't know what to think. She didn't know what to feel. She waited for the barbs in her stepmother's bait, to feel both the hook and the catch.

"Wh-what of Madame?" Zhara asked. "Who will take care of her?"

The Second Wife's smile was both winsome and wily at once. "How thoughtful of you to think of your poor old mother," she said, and there it was—the hook in Zhara's heart, tugging at the strings. "But I'll be fine. Suzhan's future husband has already been incredibly generous to us. Here." She removed a nugget of silver from her sleeve and set it down on the counter. "Buy yourself something nice," she said. "Maybe a new pair of shoes. A whole new ensemble, even. After all"—her stepmother scanned her up and down—"you'll need something decent to wear for the meeting at the teahouse."

With trembling fingers, Zhara picked up the nugget of silver. It was worth more than three months' wages from Teacher Hu.

"See?" the Second Wife said. "I'll be fine, just as I said."

City drums began sounding the late-morning hour. "Madame," Zhara started. "I'm late—"

Her stepmother waved her off. "Go," she said. "We don't want you to be late to work. I'll finish making breakfast." Zhara hesitated, but the Second Wife pushed her toward the door. "Shoo."

She bowed as she unwrapped the apron from her waist, rushing to hang it on the peg beside the door.

"Zhara." The morning light blurred the lines from the Second Wife's face and the gray from her hair, but her expression had calcified—her eyes glittering chips of obsidian, her lips a graven slash. "Diligence, duty, and dedication to the family. Isn't that what you said before?"

It wasn't a question. "Yes, Madame," she replied.

"Good." The Second Wife rolled up the sleeves of her dressing gown and began pulling bowls from the shelves for breakfast. "Make sure you don't forget. After all," she continued sweetly, "a good girl wouldn't disappoint her poor old mother, now would she?"

18

WONHU HAN, THE ROYAL HEIR OF ZANHEI, was a young man of many talents—fencing, archery, equestrianism, poetry—but breaking and entering was not one of them.

"Mother of Demons," he muttered, stabbing himself with a hairpin for the seventh time. "They make it seem so easy in detective stories."

The bronze padlock fastened to Uncle Li's doors was in the shape of a lion, its roaring mouth the keyhole, its body the combination dials. The only key was in the Chancellor's quarters, and in the absence of a password to his cousin's rooms, Han had attempted to pick the lock. The fruits of his labors included a handful of misshapen hairpins, a rather wicked wound in the pad of his thumb, and several strangled screams of frustration.

"I believe I could help with that, my prince." Han turned to see Xu standing behind him, rouged lips twisted into a smug smile. They dangled a key on a chain before his nose. "Looking for this?"

"Xu!" Han leaped to his feet, wincing as he stepped on a hairpin. "How did you get that?"

"I found it in my father's office." Xu stepped forward and slid the key in the lock. With a turn of their wrist and a click, the padlock fell away from the doors. "There are some advantages to being the Chancellor's only child. Not many. But some."

"Right," Han said, pushing his way into Li Er-Shuan's quarters. "Let's see what we can find for this Huang Jiyi, lah?"

The Guardians of Dawn had relayed the message that they were to meet with Huang Jiyi on the morrow. Master Cao had said Huang Jiyi— one of the scholars who had worked with Uncle Li on the reconstruction of *Songs of Order and Chaos*—was a poet living in the pleasure district at a teahouse called Wisteria Court, and that they were all invited to a verse party to share their findings. Han was rather excited at the prospect of meeting a real poet; maybe he could show them some of his own works.

This, of course, necessitated a trip to Uncle Li's quarters to see what—if anything—his cousin had left behind.

Uncle Li's rooms were very much as he remembered them from the last time he set foot inside six years ago, just before the Kestrels dragged his mother away. The writing desk was covered with several sheafs of loose paper and unwashed brushes and inkwells, as well as several half-crumbled ink brinks, long since cracked and dried with age. A thick patina of dust covered everything—the drapes, the bedding, the furniture, the empty shelves.

"For an astrologer," Xu remarked. "Li Er-Shuan didn't keep too many reference books or charts."

"Uncle Li was always a bit odd," Han agreed. "*Eccentric* is what my mother used to call him."

Li Er-Shuan had been a strange fixture in the palace, a thin, twiggy man in oversized robes and owlish spectacles who had served as the Royal Consort's astrologer for years. Uncle Li was technically his mother's cousin, a remnant from her old life as a courtesan down in the pleasure district before her marriage to Prince Wonhu. As an astrologer, Li Er-Shuan didn't seem to have much skill or talent, and he had been widely and roundly ridiculed in the palace for his bizarre behavior and manic moods. But the Royal Consort had protected him against any and all detractors, telling Han that there were some bonds that could not be broken.

Like the bonds of blood and magic.

Han looked around the room. Several low wooden cabinets lined the walls. An eating table. Two wooden chairs without seating cushions, and a strategy game set on the floor. A simple platform bed. But no bookshelves, no books. No notes. No hint as to where his cousin might have disappeared.

Xu moved toward the nearest cabinet and began opening the drawers, then moved on to the cupboards and wardrobes. "I don't know where Li Er-Shuan ran off to," they said, "but I don't think he was given much notice." The wardrobes and cupboards were full of clothes, pressed and neatly folded, while the dresser drawers were filled with clean socks and undergarments.

"Why would someone run off with their books and not their clothes?" Han asked.

"I don't think he did," Xu said. "There's no way he could have taken everything on such short notice. And if he was an agent for the Guardians of Dawn like Master Cao said, then he must have kept anything related to magic hidden."

Han riffled through Uncle Li's trinket boxes. His cousin had little in the way of valuables, but he also seemed to have left behind anything of worth or sentimental value. Enameled brooches, jeweled belt buckles, and even a Wulin silk fan lay untouched and gathering dust in its case, and a silk painting of his wife and three daughters was left hanging on the wall. He knew the youngest, Ami, who had been near his age. Master Cao had called her clever, but in his memory, she was a quiet, mousy sort of girl who had worked as her father's scribe. He moved to Li Er-Shuan's desk for a closer look.

Uncle Li's writing space was a disaster, notes and papers scattered everywhere. Han ran his fingers over page after page after page of half-finished thoughts, the ink long since dried and faded. The words seemed scribbled down in haste, rambling and nonsensical, the thoughts dark and tortured.

> Twenty years ago, a ritual gone wrong. A summoning?
> Demons. Nightmares. Poison. Infection.
> Guardians. Guardians. She is a Guardian. I must protect her.

As Han shuffled the papers together, something slipped from the pages and fell to the desk. With a frown, he picked it up—a small brown-and-white-speckled feather with a bead attached to the shaft. A niggle of dread tickled at the base of his neck.

"Xu," he said quietly. "Look."

His best friend studied the feather with a frown. "This looks like it might have been part of a hair ornament," they said. A look of horror dawned on their face. "Kestrels."

"They were here," Han said grimly. "And recently too. It's one of the few things in here not covered in dust." His heart fell. "Do you think they managed to get their hands on Uncle Li's notes for *Songs of Order and Chaos?*"

Xu took another sweep of the room. "I don't think so," they said. "We would have heard about it. A list of all banned books confiscated and destroyed is published every year, and I've never seen *Songs of Order and Chaos* on it." At the astonished look on Han's face, Xu shook their head in exasperation. "Does His Grace have *any* idea as to what goes on in his city?"

"No," he said simply. "Why should I, when I have you by my side?"

Xu shook their head again. "No, I don't think the Kestrels got their hands on this book. Despite his, ah, eccentricities, I don't think Li Er-Shuan would be so foolhardy as to leave anything incriminating just . . . lying about. More likely he hid his things in plain sight." Xu stopped pacing. "Oh. Oh no."

Han gave his friend a sharp glance. "What is it?"

"If His Grace wanted to hide a book in plain sight, where would he put it?"

He narrowed his eyes. "Among other books of its kind, I suppose. Why?"

"And aside from the university, where might His Grace find a copy of every book in Zanhei, including those that were banned, but not burned?" Xu flicked their gaze from Uncle Li's desk to the corridor outside, toward the archives beyond the door. "A place so easily accessible that Li Er-Shuan, an astrologer and historian with access to the archives, might not have had to keep his personal collection in his own quarters?"

Han was bewildered. "Speak plain, please."

Xu groaned and threw up their hands. "The royal library, you dolt," they cried, unable to maintain their courtesy any longer. They buried their face in their palms. "Sometimes, my prince," they said in despair, "I worry for Zanhei's future."

"I don't," he said cheerily. "Not with you at my side."

To Han's surprise, he found a familiar ruddy-haired person in the library searching through the stacks.

"Your—Your Highness!" he stammered. "What is the princess doing here? Wasn't she just here yesterday?" He recalled her unusual request for access to the library when she first arrived. "Did Her Highness, er, find everything she was searching for?"

Princess Yulana was intimidating, with or without armor. She was plainly dressed in the long tunic and trousers of her people, the top stitched from yellow silk and the trousers from leather. Despite being indoors, she still wore her boots, leaving dirt tracks up and down the polished wood floors. Perched on her shoulder was her ever-present kestrel with its unnerving, blue gaze. Han wondered if the bird slept under the covers with her, tucked in against a pillow like some of the lapdogs he had seen court ladies carry. He dismissed the idea as ridiculous; it was far more likely that *the princess* slept in the mews, dozing atop a perch alongside the creature.

"I, ah, finished everything I borrowed, so I'm looking for some more light reading." The princess's eyes shifted from side to side. "You wouldn't happen to have any recommendations?"

Han looked his intended up and down. She didn't seem like the bookish sort, although he supposed he shouldn't judge based on appearances alone. Still, her presence in the stacks troubled him, suspicion churning his gut like indigestion.

"Recommendations? I, uh—" He racked his brain for something that might sound impressive or educated, something a young man of his status would definitely have read and enjoyed, but the only title that came to mind was *The Maiden Who Was Loved by Death*. "Do you like . . . romance novels?"

"Romance novels?" The princess was amused. "You southerners

really are soft. No," she said hesitantly, "I'm not looking for a love story. I was hoping to find a, uh, rare text."

"Does the princess happen to know the name of the author?" Xu asked helpfully. "I'm sure the library clerks would be far more knowledgeable than we are as to the inventory."

She frowned. "I can't quite remember the name. Li Something. I don't know much else about them, but I do know that they were an astrologer of some renown."

Astrologer. Han shared a panicked glance with Xu. "I was not aware that Her Highness had an interest in astrology," he said.

"Oh, it's not for me," the Warlord's granddaughter said. "It's for my auncle Mongke. My mother's younger sibling," she said, seeing the confused look on Han's face. "The shaman."

"Ah." Han recalled the slender figure in multicolored robes standing beside the princess at her arrival. "So." He cleared his throat. "Why is your auncle interested in astrology?" *And why are you the one searching the library instead of them?* he wanted to ask.

Princess Yulana shrugged. "Shaman stuff, I suppose," she said in what wasn't quite a convincingly nonchalant tone. "I think they were comparing myths between the different regions of the Morning Realms. My grandfather," she said with a slight tightening of her jaw, "was unfortunately rather indiscriminate when it came to the destruction of forbidden texts, so Auncle Mongke is looking to rebuild our own base of knowledge and perhaps reclaim a bit of what was lost."

Han wasn't sure, but he thought he could detect a slight hint of criticism in her voice when it came to the actions of the Warlord during the Just War. The bird on Princess Yulana's shoulder suddenly flapped its wings, batting its feathers against the side of her head in what seemed like a rebuke. She flinched and glared at her avian companion, looking both sheepish and rebellious at once. "You're right, you're right," she murmured.

He winced. Not only was his future bride the granddaughter of the man who wanted people like his little brother dead, she also seemed to be a few arrows short of a full quiver. Han cut his eyes to Xu, who appeared just as mystified.

"Anyway." Princess Yulana coughed. "Apologies for taking up so much of your time." She nodded at Xu, then at Han. "Your Grace."

And before he could offer his farewells in return, she was gone.

Han and Xu spent the rest of the afternoon in the archives room of the library, sorting through piles upon piles of old manuscripts, loose sheafs of paper scribbled with notes, and disintegrating texts. The library clerks had been bemused but all too happy to relinquish their organizational duties for the day, leaving the Royal Heir and his right-hand person alone with their work. It didn't take either Han or Xu too long to figure out why. There was a never-ending deluge of books to inventory, catalog, repair, and discard, with more coming in every hour, and Han realized sorting through it all would be like bailing a sinking ship with a thimble.

Xu had already given up and was lounging on the floor of the cataloguing room with a plate of sliced dragonfruit and peeled lychee nuts. A stack of texts sat at their elbow, half opened and half read.

"*A Meditation on the Color Brown,*" they called out as Han searched for the title in his ledger. "*A Treatise on Benefits of Cat Ownership.*" They flopped onto their back with a groan. "And to think I skipped out on physical training for this."

Han squinted as he scanned the inventory list for a mention of either work. "I thought you preferred sashaying to swordplay."

"Depends on the sort of swordplay," Xu said slyly. "I don't mind engaging in a little practice with a willing partner."

"But you hate exercise."

"Oh, I don't know." Xu grinned. "Sometimes all that grunting, grappling, and sweating can be a bit of fun."

Han sighed. "I think we're starting to repeat ourselves." He set the ledger aside and rubbed his eyes. The words were beginning to blur together. "I've already marked *A Treatise on the Benefits of Cat Ownership.*

That's all the books." Disappointment and fatigue pinched at the bridge of his nose. "Everything's been accounted for."

"What about the rubbish pile?" Xu asked, pointing to a large bin full of books so battered and beaten they were practically falling apart.

"If they're all going to be thrown out anyway, I don't see the point."

They shrugged. "If I was going to hide something potentially treasonous and incendiary, the rubbish bin is as good a place as any to keep it. I don't think these get emptied all that often."

Han groaned. "Fine. Let's just go through them and get it over with."

The two of them dragged themselves to the enormous wooden tub and began sorting through the contents. Some of the books in the bin were so worn they weren't books so much as a loose assortment of pages barely bound together by broken thread.

"Hold a moment, I recognize this." Han picked up a piece of paper stamped with a sunburst in red ink and reached for the token around his neck, comparing the two symbols. Although faded on his pendant, the shapes were the same on the coin and on the page. He scanned the words, which seemed to form part of a poem. "*Nestled between your rosy, peaked hills, my mind wanders to the valleys of our love*," he read aloud. "*I knock at the gates to a forbidden garden, starving for a taste of your fruit.*"

Xu lifted their head, ears perking with interest. "Ooh, is that *Tales from the Downy Delta?*"

"Is it?" Han scanned the lines of the poem again. "I thought that was supposed to be pornographic."

His best friend opened their mouth, then shut it again with a shake of their head. "Never mind."

"Look." He thrust the paper beneath his friend's nose and pointed to the red sunburst stamp. "I recognized *this*."

Xu frowned. "I've seen this symbol before."

"Yes," Han said, removing the pendant from his neck and handing it to his friend. "It's the mark of the Guardians of Dawn."

"No," Xu said in a distant voice, a furrow deepening between their brows. "I've seen it somewhere else. In a book, maybe . . ." They trailed off, face pale beneath their makeup. "Your Grace," they said in a hoarse voice. "This is a symbol of the previous dynasty."

"The Mugungs?" Han scratched his head. "But I thought they flew the standard of the Four-Winged Dragon during the Just War."

Xu shook their head. "Someone wasn't paying attention during his history lessons, I see."

"Yah," Han protested. "I paid attention during the battles."

They sighed. "Your Grace. Why is the seat of the empire called the Sunburst Throne?"

"Because, er," he began weakly, "because we are called the Morning Realms and the sun rises in the east?"

Xu took a deep breath and closed their eyes. "Yuo, give me strength," they murmured, entreating the First Immortal, patron of scholars, for guidance. "Because," they said slowly, as though explaining to a particularly thickheaded student, "the throne traces a lineage all the way back to the first emperor of the realms—the Sunburst Warrior."

Han flopped down on the floor with a petulant huff, covering his face with the page. He felt like a child again, sitting at his tutor's feet and reciting works by dusty old philosophers and historians. He wasn't much of a scholar; he was much more comfortable with the sword than the brush. Of all the subjects Han had been forced to endure, only poetry had ever excited him. Partially because poems were short, but also because his mother had been a poet herself. He still had a few of her poems hanging from scrolls in his quarters—the few he had managed to save from his father's grief.

"The Mugungs were directly descended from the first emperor," Xu continued. "They believed themselves responsible for maintaining balance between order and chaos by any means necessary, including the use of magic."

"Yes, yes, I know." Han puffed his cheeks and blew, watching the smutty words flutter up and down before his eyes. The paper smelled strange—almost like lemons, tangy and sour. In a room that smelled of nothing but dried ink and dust, the scent was noticeably sharp. "But the world fell out of balance, which is why the Warlord usurped the throne to rid the realms of all magicians. But what does the Mugung Dynasty have to do with the Guardians of Dawn?"

"In all the myths, the Guardians of Dawn were the Sunburst Warrior's loyal companions," Xu said softly. "Dedicated not only to holding back the forces of darkness, but to maintaining the Sunburst Warrior's right to rule."

Han sat up straight, understanding seeping into his bones like water seeping into a well. "Are you saying that *our* Guardians of Dawn, this magical mutual aid society—"

"—may also be Mugung loyalists as well," Xu finished, their voice scarcely audible.

A buzzing drone filled Han's ears, a high-pitched whine that sounded like the word *treason* whispered over and over and over again in his mind. "But that's ridiculous," he said, throat dry. "The last Mugung princess perished when the Warlord razed the old imperial palace to the ground. If she still lives, and the Guardians of Dawn want to restore her to the Sunburst Throne then . . ."

"Civil war," Xu whispered. "What have we gotten ourselves into, my prince?"

Han looked down at the page of pornographic poetry stamped with the treasonous sunburst. An underground resistance organization dedicated to magician liberation. But by what means?

"Your Grace," Xu called. "I've found more pages." In their hand they held several loose sheets of paper, each bearing the symbol of the Mugung Dynasty. Frowning, they brought their fingers to their nose and sniffed. "Ugh," they choked. "It smells like someone's orange blossom perfume gone bad. Like vinegar."

Vinegar. A sudden olfactory memory assailed Han's nose of the time he had broken a bottle of perfume on his mother's vanity and spilled it all over his clothes. But it hadn't been perfume; it was apple cider vinegar. The Royal Consort had later shown him how to dip his brush and write with it, and he'd watched as the words faded from the page.

Like magic, he had said. It was the only sort of magic he could ever have.

"Xu," he said. "You're a genius." Han held up his page to the window, where the late-afternoon light streamed through the latticework. "Invisible ink."

And there, shining behind the words of the world's most infamous poem, was another set of lines.

The Star of Radiance binds the darkness
And the heir survives

"What does this mean?" Han asked, squinting at the page. "What is the Star of Radiance?"

Xu sighed. "At some point, my prince, it would behoove His Grace to read through a history book instead of one of his romance novels. The Star of Radiance is the imperial jewel, said to have been wielded by the Sunburst Warrior during their battle against the Mother of Ten Thousand Demons."

Ah. Han now remembered the final climactic dance scene from the Bangtan Brothers' performance of it last summer. "To seal her into the abyss, lah? With the help of the Guardians of Dawn?"

"Yes, my prince."

He frowned as he continued to scan the lines.

The heir survives and blossoms beneath the tree of immortality
In the lands of the furthermost west
The domain of the Unicorn King

"Unicorn King?" Han tried to remember a fairy tale with a character called the Unicorn King but came up short. "Do you know what the Unicorn King is?" he asked his best friend.

Xu stroked their chin thoughtfully. "No, but *the lands of the furthermost west* sounds like it could be a clue. Ugh," they said in disgust. "How is it that I shaved this morning and I'm already growing a beard?"

"Truly?" Han stroked his own chin with envy. He grew so few hairs that he wondered if simply plucking them every few days wouldn't be more effective. "I'm jealous."

Xu shook their head. "Does His Grace think that Li Er-Shuan may be hiding in the lands of the outermost west?" they asked, lowering their voice so that they would not be overheard. "Among the Free Peoples living there?"

Han studied the sunburst symbol at the bottom of the page. "It's as good a place to hide as any," he conceded. "There are hundreds— thousands—of clans among the Free Peoples, and they are loyal to no one but their shaman-king."

"The Qirin Tulku," Xu supplied. "Although I am impressed His Grace remembered that much."

"Yah," Han said. "I may not care for lessons, but I'm not *that* stupid." He sighed. "Let's look through the rest of the bin to see if we can find any more of these notes and pages to bring to Huang Jiyi at Wisteria Court tomorrow."

"Straight away, my prince."

As the two of them rummaged through the rest of the rubbish pile for more of Li Er-Shuan's work, Han couldn't help wondering what had compelled his cousin to take refuge in the wilds of the outermost west instead of trusting to the Guardians of Dawn. He touched the sunburst pendant at his throat.

"Oh, Uncle Li," he murmured. "What have we gotten ourselves into?"

19

THE POETS WHO COMPARED ZANHEI'S PLEASURE DISTRICT to a night-blooming jasmine had either never smelled a jasmine flower or had never set foot in Flower Town by day.

Zhara wrinkled her nose as she made her way beside the canals that smelled more strongly of sewage than of perfume, passing through narrow alleyways crisscrossed with dripping laundry lines and saturated with the dank reek of garlic and accumulated mold. Although it was just over the canal from the covered market where she worked, Zhara had never set foot in the pleasure district before. The reality did not live up to her imagination, and she was a little disappointed.

Flower Town was said to come to life once the sun went down, but the streets were busier than expected for the middle of the afternoon. Vendors, merchants, delivery children, and other ordinary people bustled back and forth down the alleyways and along the canals, going about their day-to-day business. Zhara walked along the main waterway that ran from the city of Zanhei to the center of the pleasure district. The main canal was called the Gleaming River, an homage to the story of the magpie lovers, but also a reference to the shimmering poets, philosophers, and other pleasure seekers who arrived by barge or gondola. The ferrymen who carried these dignitaries to their destinations were called magpies in reference to the tale, but also for the black, white, and red clothing they wore.

As the wild tangle of streets and alleyways straightened into respectable walking lanes and avenues, the beauty of Flower Town unfurled itself. There were elegantly proportioned teahouses made of wood and stone that overlooked the waters, graceful gardens with carefully cultivated flowering trees, and a musical, murmuring water feature at every turn. Red lanterns and brass wind chimes decorated the doorways and the signs above the lintels were carved of wood and lettered in gold. The walls here were made of white stone instead of the clay found in the Pits, and the roofs were made of tile instead of thatch. The latticed windows were sculpted into intricate patterns that suggested a leaf, a flower, a bud.

At last Zhara found the blooming wisteria tree that marked the entrance to Wisteria Court and also gave the teahouse its name. The tastefully painted black-and-gold gates were shut, but there was a bellpull to the right. Zhara rang the bell, which gave off a sweet, silver sound. The gates cracked open, and a beautiful young attendant appeared.

"How may I help the customer?" they asked, bowing with their hands out before them. It was a moment before Zhara realized that the attendant was a servant and not a courtesan, due to the grace of their manner and dress. The attendant's hair was pulled back into a simple bun held with a wooden hairpin decorated with a cluster of dangling wisteria blossoms. They wore a simple lavender gown of silk and chiffon, much plainer than something a noble lady or courtesan would wear, but much finer than anything Zhara would ever touch in her life. She touched the purse tied at her waist, feeling the weight of the Second Wife's silver nugget against her hip.

"I, um." Zhara removed the sunburst pendant Teacher Hu had given her from her neck and showed it to the attendant. "I'm here to see Huang Jiyi."

"The Ice Princess?" they said, face screwed with distaste. "Oh. The guest must be here for the verse party. Some of your party are already here. Follow me."

The world inside the gates was even more beautiful than the building's elegant facade. Polished wooden walkways with railings carved into graceful patterns formed paths around pools of water with lilies and lotus flowers. The walkways were covered, blurring the lines between what was inside and what was out in the world of nature. The empty space between posts and railings framed picturesque scenes like windows, so that every view in Wisteria Court was a work of art.

The attendant led Zhara past a small courtyard and into a garden, where Han and Xu were already seated in a pavilion that overlooked a perfectly round reflecting pool. Master Plum Blossom's face brightened at Zhara's arrival and he jumped to his feet.

"Good afternoon, Mistress Brandy!" He dimpled excitedly. "Are you ready for the verse party? Did you prepare anything?"

Beside him, Xu made a face. "Don't encourage him, please," they begged.

Zhara glanced at Han, who was practically vibrating on his tiptoes in anticipation. "I wasn't aware I was supposed to prepare anything," she said with a smile. "I've never been to a verse party before."

"You can recite someone else's poems, or you can offer up one of your own, and then the judge will make a decision," Han said. "Do you want to hear some of mine?"

Xu made a desperate gesture behind Han's back, slicing a hand across their throat and shaking their head, but Master Plum Blossom looked so eager that Zhara was loathe to refuse him.

"All right," she said. "Recite me some of your poetry." It was probably dreadful, but she was willing to make allowances for someone so good-looking.

"Really?" He looked so happy, smiling so wide his nose scrunched up with delight. He reached behind him and pulled out a tiny scroll from his sash. "I wrote this last night in preparation for today. An acrostic syllable poem for—for you." A dark red flush spread up his neck to his cheeks, and he ducked his head, suddenly shy. Unrolling the scroll, he read aloud, "*Mistress Brandy*—that's the title." He cleared his throat. "*Mistress Brandy. Mis*—*mysterious, mischievous maiden. Tress*—*treasurer of cabinets containing herbs. Brand*—*brandishing romance novels. Y*—*Eeeffortlessly.*" Han beamed at her expectantly as he finished.

Zhara pressed her lips tightly together. "That's, um, that's very . . . unique, Master Plum Blossom."

He beamed. "What do you think, Xu?"

"I think," they muttered, "that you may have something worthy of wiping the bums of every citizen from the palace to the Pits."

"Thanks," Han said, nodding his head. Then he scowled. "Wait."

Zhara hid a giggle beneath her hand. "I'm afraid I don't know much about poetry," she said. "Although I have read some."

"Do you recall any lines?" Han asked, rolling up his scroll.

"The petals of twilight unfurl with beckoning glances," she declaimed in a soft voice. *"And the air grows redolent with sweetness and sandalwood, fragrant with frangipani."* She grinned at Han's astonished expression. "I thought it appropriate."

"*The Pillow Book of Cheng Na!*" Xu exclaimed. "I see Mistress Brandy is a person of exquisite taste."

"What's a pillow book?" Han asked.

Xu caught Zhara's eye and winked. "You should be grateful you've never heard Han recite his *Odes to Physical Pleasures*. It was the most traumatic thing I've ever experienced in my life."

"Oh?" she grinned. "Have we another Kui-Shung the Lewd on our hands?"

"More like Kui-Shung the Lunkheaded," they muttered.

"Who's Kui-Shung?" Han swung his head back and forth between Zhara and his friend, a bewildered look on his face. "Do they also enjoy working out? My odes are all about the pleasures of lifting weights."

"Ah, there you are!" Master Cao approached, crossing the courtyard with a tall, slim figure at his side. One of the courtesans of Wisteria Court, judging by their dress. "May I introduce you children to Huang Jiyi, the Guardians' most esteemed historian and scholar of magic?"

The courtesan bowed, and the force of her glamor struck Zhara like a blow. Huang Jiyi's slender dancer's frame was draped in delicate robes of blue, with several layers of silk, brocade, and chiffon that shimmered like water as she moved. Her oval face was bare of any makeup or ornamentation, and her ink-black hair was smoothed back in a simple bun at the nape of her neck so nothing could distract from the terrifying symmetry of her features. The faintest trace of rosewater and neroli oil lingered about her, bright and seductive.

"Welcome to Wisteria Court," the courtesan said in a less-than-welcoming voice. "Are we all here?" she asked, looking to the bookseller. Master Cao nodded. "Good, then let's head inside and get down to business." She turned and headed into the shadows of the teahouse, beckoning them to follow.

"You mean we aren't here for a verse party after all?" Han asked in a disappointed voice. "But I had four other poems planned!"

The courtesan brought them to her private quarters, a set of surprisingly large rooms at the back of the establishment, very private and enclosed. "I make my mistress a lot of money with my writing," she said by way of explanation, seeing Zhara's surprised expression. "So she lets me have whatever I want."

Master Cao, Han, Xu, and Zhara all sat down on the floor cushions arranged around the low table in the middle of the room while an attendant brought them several pots of tea and plates of beautifully cut fresh fruit. Peaches, apricots, giant gooseberries, and even mangos and dragonfruit from the southern archipelago.

"So," Huang Jiyi said, flopping down on the cushion beside Zhara. Her dark, intelligent eyes took in every feature of Zhara's face, and she found herself blushing under the intense scrutiny. "You're the girl who faced down an abomination and survived. I'm impressed. You don't look like much."

"Yah," Han protested. "Xu and I were there too."

"Be kind, Huang Jiyi," Master Cao admonished.

"I thought I was being kind," the courtesan said. Only the barest hint of a wrinkle between her brows betrayed her confusion. "I didn't expect such a powerful magician to be so young."

Not that Huang Jiyi seemed much older than Zhara herself. She guessed the courtesan to be about twenty-one years of age or so. "I am honored to meet the treasured one," she said politely. "Is she a magician as well?"

Huang Jiyi shook her head. "No. I do come from a family of magicians though, or I did. Once."

Her lashes flickered and her nostrils twitched and Zhara wondered if the courtesan wasn't trying to hold back tears.

"Anyway." The courtesan crossed her arms. "What have you got for me?" Her voice was neither friendly nor rude, but oddly cold, dispassionate, as though Zhara were some specimen to be examined. "Master Cao says you have some magical developments of interest."

"Teacher Hu and I went out to the lowlands last night to investigate some claims of what the Buri are calling *corruption* among their people." Zhara reached into her satchel and pulled out a vial of water, setting it on the table before them. "And found this."

Jiyi picked it up, studying it curiously. "What is it?"

"Water," Zhara said. "It's tainted with some sort of . . . magical essence. Demonic essence, we think. We took samples from the fountain near the settlement. The Chancellor had it built a few months ago, and it channels water from the springs near Mount Zanhei."

"Mount Zanhei?" the courtesan asked. "Now, that's fascinating. According to the texts I've read, whatever caused the volcanic explosion a thousand years ago was some sort of ritual gone wrong. Maybe even a demon summoning."

"Why would anyone want to summon a demon?" Zhara asked.

Jiyi studied her for a long moment. Zhara quailed under the focused intensity of the courtesan's eyes. "For more power," Jiyi said, as though the answer were obvious.

"But magicians can already alter the elements to suit their whims," Xu said. "What more could they possibly want?"

The courtesan shrugged. "There are limits to magic," she said. "Just as there are limits to the rules governing the natural world. For example, a magician does not produce water from nowhere; they can draw moisture from the air to collect into a stream of water. Or they could take a solid piece of wood and manipulate the spaces between matter to shape a flute. But despite their access to the void, a magician cannot violate the laws of the universe. They cannot turn rice into jewels, change night into day, read minds, or produce money out of thin air. That would be a violation of order and reason."

"Wait, I'm confused," Han said.

"Of course you are," Jiyi said, looking him up and down with disdain. "All brawn, no brains, this one. I can tell."

"Jiyi!" Master Cao said disapprovingly.

Zhara shifted uncomfortably in her seat. She thought of the times she had transformed salt into sugar and wine into water, all violations of order and reason according to the laws of magic.

"Is that why magicians used to summon demons then?" Xu asked. "To be able to do things that are a violation of the natural order?"

Jiyi nodded. "Anything a magician can do, a man can do, it's just that magicians . . . take a shortcut through the void, I suppose. But sometimes a person wants . . . more. To bring someone back from the dead. To cloud the minds of others. Any number of reasons, really."

"But if summoning a demon turns a person into an abomination, then why risk it at all?" Zhara asked.

The courtesan's face was hard. "Desperation. Ignorance. Arrogance. Some don't know what the consequences are. Others don't care. Still others think it is a price they can bear. They're all wrong, of course."

Han tugged at the weedy, wispy little hairs on his chin. "I still don't understand," he said. "Why is it that a demon can do all these things when magicians cannot?"

"Because," the courtesan said slowly, as though speaking to a very dull-witted child, "demons are creatures of chaos, but magic is a mansion of Reason, and therefore bound by the same laws that govern the rest of the natural world. Chaos has no laws. Chaos is boundless."

Xu ate the last slice of dragonfruit, chewing thoughtfully. "Then . . . magicians who become possessed turn into creatures of chaos themselves?"

Jiyi gave them a look of begrudging respect. "I suppose not all of you are hopeless. The monster that is the abomination is chaos made matter. We think."

Han raised a brow. "We think?"

"To be honest, there's never been a lot of information on possessions and abominations, even before the Warlord destroyed all the books of magic," the courtesan admitted. "As far as I know, there was only one—*Songs of Order and Chaos*."

"Which disappeared with Uncle Li," Han said, pulling a rolled leather folio from his waistband. "But the treasured one worked on reconstructing the text with him, did she not? Can't the courtesan remember what she worked on?" He unfurled the folio, revealing what looked to be pages torn from several different books. There was a faint vinegar tang to the air.

Jiyi shot him a glare. "If you must know," she said, "I mostly worked with Li Er-Shuan's daughter, Li Ami. She transcribed most of her father's work into something legible—practically translated the manic thoughts in his head into something more intelligible."

"So the courtesan didn't work directly on *Songs of Order and Chaos* at all?" Han asked with dismay.

It was a moment before she replied. "No," she said in a grudging voice, as though she had not wanted to admit this to anyone. "Not directly."

"Huang Jiyi." The courtesan did not meet Master Cao's gaze. "Is this true?"

She closed her eyes. "Yes," she said at last.

Han and Xu gave audible groans of disappointment, but Zhara studied the courtesan's face. Beneath the brusque tone and haughty manner, she sensed there was someone incredibly lonely, someone who was afraid of letting anyone in lest they leave her. Again. "I think," Zhara said softly, "that Huang Jiyi is still the best scholar of magic we have." She turned to Master Cao. "Isn't she?"

The courtesan gave Zhara a sidelong glance.

The bookseller sighed. "Yes, she is," he admitted. "She comes from a family of spell-mongers."

"Spell-mongers?" Xu asked. "What's that?"

"People who create new spells." Jiyi absentmindedly swirled the last of her tea in her cup. "We study the Language of Flowers, maintain the histories and etymologies of how each logograph was created and occasionally"—she met Zhara's eyes—"we create new ones." The courtesan gave a crooked little half smile, which softened the unrelenting symmetry of her features and made her seem more approachable. "So yes, I am the best scholar of magic the Guardians of Dawn have." She set down her teacup and reached for the stack of papers on the table—Li Er-Shuan's notes. "Let's have a look."

"They're are written in apple cider vinegar," Xu supplied. "If you hold the pages up to the light—"

"Master Cao," Zhara said quietly, so as not to disturb the others poring over the pages, "does the bookseller really think the answers to possession and how to cure it lie in *Songs of Order and Chaos?*"

"Yes, and no," he replied. "If we look to our myths and legends, the answers are right there, staring us in the face."

Zhara was taken aback. "They are?"

The bookseller fixed his nut-brown eyes on her, his expression unreadable. "Yes," he said simply. "The Guardians of Dawn. They say that the souls of the Sunburst Warrior's companions are reborn whenever the world is out of balance."

Guardian of Fire . . . there you are . . .

Zhara looked down at her hands folded in her lap. Magic bristled beneath her skin. She thought of the searing light that had burned away the corruption within Thanh, revealing a human boy where a monster had been. "Reborn?" she whispered. Was this power even hers? Or did it belong to some creature of chaos she carried within her, like a parasite waiting to burst out of her body and harm those she loved when she could no longer control it? Was this the power that had blinded Suzhan? Was she also an abomination?

"Hold a moment," Jiyi said, interrupting her thoughts. "Where did you say this water came from, Jin Zhara?" The courtesan picked up the vial sampled from the fountain.

"Out in the marsh," Zhara answered. "But the water is channeled from the slopes of Mount Zanhei."

"There's something here about a ritual for summoning"—Jiyi's brows furrowed as she tried to decipher the astrologer's hand—"something I can't quite make out, but I think it might say *greater demon.*"

Master Cao started in his seat. "Greater demon? A Lord of Tiyok?"

"This ritual was supposed to have taken place at the Guardian of Fire's resting place—Mount Zanhei." The courtesan looked up at them. "Near the ruins of Old Changxi."

"*Have taken?*" Xu asked. "Does the treasured one think that someone *actually* tried to summon a greater demon?"

"I don't know." She set down the notes and fixed her gaze on the bookseller. "But it may explain your missing magicians, Master Cao."

"Oh?" He sat forward, eyes eager. "How so?"

Jiyi grimaced. "The ritual calls for the ki of *many magicians*." She bit her lip. "But I don't know what that means."

The bookseller hung his head. "Nothing good, I fear."

"I'll arrange a riverboat captain to take us up to the ruins of Old Changxi tomorrow," the courtesan said. She looked at Zhara. "Do you want to come?"

"Me?" Zhara blinked. "Y-yes. Yes, I do. I appreciate the offer, treasured one."

"We're coming too!" Han said. "Aren't we, Xu?"

His best friend grinned, but their smile failed to reach their eyes. "Does the treasured one really think that going up to the volcano will provide answers?" they asked. "I'm not one for unnecessary physical exertion—"

"Then you don't have to come," Jiyi said simply. "Although," she said, eyeing Han's broad shoulders, "I could use a couple of mules to carry my equipment."

"Equipment?" Xu asked. "What for?"

"So I can take some readings, measurements, and samples, of course." The courtesan turned to Zhara. "You can detect demonic essence, right?"

Zhara nodded, then looked away. "What if . . . what if I become possessed?" she asked quietly. "Up there by the volcano? What if all this exposure turns me into an abomination?"

Jiyi tilted her head. "You touched the tainted water down at the marsh, lah? That's how you discovered it was tainted with demonic essence in the first place."

"Yes." Power roiled in Zhara's veins, and she curled her fingers into fists.

"I doubt you'll be affected by whatever is up by Mount Zanhei," Jiyi said. "It's likely a matter of exposure time and exposure amount. Those so-called corrupted children have been drinking from those waters for months now and only one of them turned into an abomination."

The magic simmering beneath Zhara's skin receded.

"Unless, of course," the courtesan said, "you're already possessed, in which case I don't think the presence of another demon will do you much harm." She set down the papers and made a face, looking from Zhara to Han to Xu. "You can laugh, you know," she said imperiously. "That was a joke."

Zhara gave her a thin smile.

"Ugh, no sense of humor, any of you." Jiyi rose to her feet and rang the little triangle hanging by the door to the room. A servant materialized with a bow just outside the threshold. "Clean this up," the courtesan said, gesturing to the table. "And find Captain Shang down by the docks. Tell him I would like to hire him for a trip upriver tomorrow."

"What of Master Cao?" Han asked, sneaking a glance at the bookseller.

"I have to man my shop," the bookseller replied. "But if you find any of my missing scriveners . . . well." He tucked his hands into his sleeves. "Let's hope they're none the worse for wear."

The servant immediately cleared up the remains of sliced fruit before disappearing with another bow. Jiyi turned to the others, a knife's-edge grin on her face.

"Be down by the docks by morning light," she said. "This may be the most memorable pleasure cruise of your entire life."

20

IF IT WEREN'T FOR THE THREAT OF abominations, demon possession, and magicians gone missing, Zhara could nearly believe she was
on a pleasure cruise up to Mount Zanhei. The day was fair and mild,
and the breeze along the water pushed away some of the humidity that
had begun to descend on the city farther downriver. She watched the
tame cormorants on fishing skiffs dive and splash, their wings spray-
ing droplets into the air and making rainbows along the surface, and
allowed herself to pretend she was just another rich young noble on a
scenic trip to see the ruins of Old Changxi. Everything was perfect—
the weather, the scenery, the people.

Well, almost everything.

"Just kill me now," Han groaned, hunched over the side railing. His
normally healthy glowing skin was replaced by a sickly green pallor,
and even his hair seemed limp and lifeless, hanging in stringy strands
about his face as he heaved into the water. "This is worse than the time
I got into Uncle Li's liquor cabinet and thought the raspberry brandy
was a funny kind of fruit juice."

"Just throw up," Xu said cheerfully. "You'll feel better."

"I would if I could," moaned the unfortunate sailor. "But everything
I had for breakfast is already feeding the fishes several miles downriver."

"Gross," Xu said mildly.

Zhara couldn't bear to listen to the wretched retching any longer.
"Here," she said, coming to stand beside Han. She took one of his
wrists in her hand and gently but firmly pressed her thumb on a spot
three finger-widths below his palm. "This meridian point can help

with nausea. Teacher Hu often teaches this to pregnant people suffering from morning sickness."

"Just go lie down," Jiyi said grouchily. "And stop subjecting the rest of us to your bodily agony."

"But what if I miss something?" he whined, head still hanging over the side of the barge.

The courtesan tapped Zhara on the shoulder. "Come," she said with a tilt of her head, indicating Zhara should follow her toward the canopied seats. "I have a gift for you."

"Ooh, a gift?" Xu asked in a bright voice. "She shouldn't have."

Jiyi shot them a glare. "Did I say it was for you?"

They pouted. "If the treasured one brought treats, I hope she brought enough to share with everyone on board."

Zhara sat down on one of the cushions in the middle of the deck beneath the canopy, bewildered as the courtesan held a long, slim ebony box out for her to take. It looked like some sort of case, lacquered with a motif of water lilies. Stunned, Zhara accepted the gift with both hands and a bow. "A th-thousand thanks," she stammered. "I don't know what I did to deserve this."

"Oh, stop with the false modesty," the courtesan said grumpily. "It wasn't out of the goodness of my heart or anything. You're a magician, Jin Zhara, and you should have the tools of one."

"The tools of a magician?" Zhara opened the box to find a brush nestled against a plush, dark blue velvet lining. Han managed to rouse himself from his queasy misery to stand beside Xu, curiously peeking over her shoulder. Mystified, Zhara pulled the implement out of its case.

"A brush?" Xu asked.

"It belonged to my father," Jiyi said shortly. "It was his favorite brush for spellwork."

The brush was surprisingly heavy, its handle made of polished mahogany, the bristles both stiff and soft at once. There were scuff marks along the tip, worn from use. Zhara replaced the tool in its lining before closing the box. "A thousand thanks, treasured one," she repeated in a quieter tone. "It must have meant a great deal for her to give it to me."

"Didn't I tell you to stop it with the false modesty?" Jiyi made a disgusted noise as she swept forward and flicked the case open again. "And stop calling me *treasured one*. It makes me feel like I'm a shiny bauble in a shop, a curio on display." Her face softened. "Just call me Jiyi," she said gruffly. "It'll make it easier for the both of us. Now"—her face resumed its customary hauteur—"take the brush out and let's get to work."

"Work?" Xu whined. "And we were all having such a good time."

"Speak for yourself," Han muttered.

"The two of you can go back to whatever it was you were doing," Jiyi said, waving them off. "You're not important."

"Yah!" Han protested. "We're very important! I'm—" He choked back his words and Zhara wondered if he wasn't going to vomit again.

"*You're* not a magician." The courtesan crossed her arms. "This is magician business."

"You're not a magician either," Xu grumbled.

Jiyi gave them a sharp look. "Did I give you permission to address me so informally, Chan Xuhei?"

Xu muttered something obscene beneath their breath. "Fine," they announced sulkily. "I can see we're not wanted." They wrapped an arm about Han's shoulders. "Come, Your Gr—Han. You'll feel better when you lie down."

Once they were alone, Jiyi gracefully sat down in a cross-legged position, then—almost as an afterthought—rearranged her limbs to hunch over like an old man, raising one knee to rest an arm atop it. She was plainly dressed in a tunic and trousers, which sat on her elegant frame almost like a costume. While it was impossible to overlook the other girl's beauty entirely, Zhara couldn't help thinking Jiyi tried her hardest to make everyone forget just how stunning she was.

"So," the courtesan began. "What do you know about magic? The channeling and working of it, I mean?"

Zhara ran her fingers lightly up and down the length of the brush.

"Hardly anything," she admitted. "My father died before I was old enough to understand much of what he taught me."

"Hmmm," Jiyi said noncommittally, although Zhara could hear a wealth of judgment within that sound. "I suppose we'll have to start at the very beginning then." The courtesan yawned and pulled her long, straight hair over her shoulder, toying with the ends. "So," she said. "What makes a magician different from other humans?"

Zhara raised her brows. "The ability to wield magic?"

"But what *is* magic?" When Zhara couldn't answer, Jiyi gave an impatient snort. "Really, I knew you were uneducated, but I didn't expect you to be *this* ignorant."

Zhara flinched. "I'm sorry," she mumbled, fumbling with the brush between her fingers.

Jiyi scowled. "Would you stop that?" she snapped.

The brush clattered to the deck of the ship, and Zhara scrambled to pick it up before it rolled away. "Sorry," she repeated.

"Stop apologizing," the courtesan said in exasperation. "It's very annoying." When Zhara cringed again, Jiyi sighed. "I'm not going to box your ears for a wrong answer, you know," she said in a kinder tone.

Zhara bowed her head. "I'm sor—" She stopped herself at the courtesan's expression. "Please, continue," she said meekly.

Jiyi drew in a deep breath. "What distinguishes magicians from other people is their ability to shape the chaos void," she said. "A house is made of wood, wood comes from trees, trees grow from seeds, and so on and so forth, until we get to the smallest building blocks of matter. What holds the universe together? That invisible force is what we call the chaos void, and magicians have the unique ability to manipulate that potential for change."

Zhara had always thought of her magic as a force unto itself, something active not passive. Her fingertips prickled, as though her very thoughts had summoned her power. "So magic is not something to be wielded?"

"It is not magic but the magician that is a weapon to be wielded," Jiyi intoned, lifting her chin as though passing down a proclamation from on high. She held her pose for a few moments, but when Zhara did not respond in the way she had hoped, she groaned. "From the *Annals of Wei Kai-war*?" At Zhara's blank expression, the courtesan shook her head. "Moving on. Your brush," she said, nodding at the implement in Zhara's hand. "Do you know what it's for?"

Zhara hesitated. "I'm assuming *writing spells* is not the answer you're looking for."

The slightest hint of a smile touched Jiyi's lips. "Uneducated but not hopeless." She gestured toward Zhara's satchel. "Did you bring your copy of *The Thousand-Character Classic*?"

With a nod, Zhara reached into her bag and pulled out the primer. Jiyi flipped it open and pointed to the first set of characters. "What do you think this is?"

"The Language of Flowers," Zhara hedged, looking not at the primer but at the courtesan's face.

"You didn't say *spells*. Good. Because this"—Jiyi flapped the primer at her—"is useless for creating spells. Magicians don't learn the Language of Flowers because magic is done with the right words, the right incantations, or the right glyphs. The Language of Flowers has no power in and of itself."

Zhara was surprised. "If the Language of Flowers has no power," she said, "then why were all the books of magic burned during the purges of the Just War?"

"Why does any conquerer destroy the writings of the conquered?" Jiyi said in a grim voice. "If you erase their past, you deny them a future. Those books of magic?" She ran her fingers over the worn cover of *The Thousand-Character Classic*. "My father used to say that those books were more than just spells. They were history. Poetry. Art." A muscle along the courtesan's jaw tightened as her eyes stared into the middle distance, looking at a memory Zhara could not see. "Magic is more than ability; it was a culture too. And the Warlord took them—that—away from me."

An old but unhealed wound ran beneath Jiyi's words, pain throbbing through every wobble of her voice. Zhara looked down at the brush in her hand. *It was my father's,* Jiyi had said. Like her, the courtesan had had a magician father. And like her, she had also lost him to the Warlord's fanaticism.

"I'm sorry," Zhara said softly, and this time the courtesan did not berate her.

"Anyway." Jiyi cleared her throat and Zhara discreetly averted her eyes while the other girl surreptitiously wiped at her wet cheeks. "The brush." The courtesan reached forward and wrapped her fingers around Zhara's, correcting her grip on the writing implement. "You may wonder then what the point of a magician's brush is if the Language of Flowers is in itself powerless."

Zhara held her tongue, letting the other girl lecture her through her grief. She knew all too well the enormity of loss, the all-consuming wave that threatened to submerge all rational thought. She knew too, that sometimes the only way through sorrow was to keep swimming, to keep living or drown.

"What are words?" Jiyi went on, not expecting an answer. "What is the Language of Flowers? Nothing but symbols. Representations of sounds or syllables or even entire sentences. Of intention. And what is the brush? It is also a symbol, an extension of your arm. The appendage that *does*. That creates. That acts."

By now Zhara was entirely lost. When the courtesan caught sight of her bewildered expression, she sighed and shook her head.

"I suspect by the look on your face that you're the sort who learns by doing rather than theory," Jiyi said wryly. "You'd rather just try to create a spell, wouldn't you?"

Sheepishly, Zhara nodded her head.

"Fine." The courtesan opened *The Thousand-Character Classic* and pointed to the first set of characters. "Let's start here. What does this say?"

"*The sky was black, the earth yellow,*" Zhara read aloud. She had practically memorized the first chapter when she tried working with it before. "*The universe vast and limitless.*"

The courtesan gestured for her to continue.

"*The sun and moon both wax and set,*" Zhara went on. "*The stars and constellations spread throughout the heavens.*" She glanced up at the courtesan.

"I don't mean to offend," she said, "but I'm just reading the translations written down beside the original lines. What good does that do?"

Jiyi snorted. "You're too literal-minded, Jin Zhara." She tapped the first line of *The Thousand-Character Classic*. "See here, there are four characters that make up the first set. What does the first one mean?"

Zhara squinted at the blurred lines beneath the courtesan's fingertip. "*Sky?*" she ventured. Jiyi moved to the second. "*Black?*"

"No." The courtesan pointed to the next character. "This is *black*. The second one is *earth*." At Zhara's confused expression, she rolled her eyes. "When it comes to translation, there is no one-to-one exactness. Each character has a definition in isolation, yes, but it is only in context with other characters that we understand the fullness of its meaning. That is how spells are created."

"I see," said Zhara, although she didn't.

Jiyi slumped. "Jin Zhara," she said, slouching back and spreading her legs. "Why do you think I'm the greatest verse master in Zanhei?"

Based on the courtesan's smug expression, Zhara suspected Jiyi didn't want to hear her actual answer, which was that she was privileged enough to have had the sort of education denied to most everyone else. "Is it because those with whom she spars are mean in thought and narrow in imagination?"

Jiyi grinned. "You're not wrong there, but that's not the reason." She crossed her legs and leaned forward, resting her chin on her hand. "It's because I understand it is not the beads on a necklace which make it beautiful, it is how the beads are arranged."

Zhara glanced down at the lines of indecipherable glyphs on the page. "So you're saying that the Language of Flowers is a language of poetry?"

"Poetry?" Han called. "Did someone say poetry?"

"I thought you were feeling sick!" Jiyi shouted at him.

"I'm feeling much better now, thanks to some advice about pressure points." He smiled and winked at Zhara, and the urge to giggle overcame her. She turned her head away to avoid the full force of his dimples.

"That and he finally managed to heave the last of his breakfast into a sick bucket," Xu added. "Gross."

Han glared at them. "Must you always humiliate me like this?"

"Would the two of you please shut up?" Jiyi closed her eyes and massaged her temples. "We're trying to learn about magic here and don't need any distractions."

"They're no trouble," Zhara said in a mild voice, sneaking a sidelong glance at Han.

"I said *distractions*," the courtesan said pointedly, and Zhara's cheeks flushed with embarrassment.

"Right," she said with a cough. "The Language of Flowers is a language of poetry?"

"Yes," Jiyi said. "In a manner of speaking. There is an art to translating and interpreting it, and it relies as much on understanding nuance as it does on holding the meanings of all the characters in your head."

Zhara nodded, although it was more to humor the courtesan than it was to agree with her. Jiyi closed her eyes and threw up her hands.

"All right," she said irritably. "Let's start with something simple." She turned the page to the second chapter of *The Thousand-Character Classic.* "Why don't we begin with *fire*?"

After an hour, the *only* spell Zhara could manage was fire.

The first attempt was a raging success—rather literally, as she caused a sudden conflagration to break out on the barge. Han and Xu had run to the railing and thrown the bailing bucket into the river, then doused the deck with water. The captain came running at the sight of flames on his ship, shouting about the destruction of his property at the top of his lungs.

"I'll pay for any damages," Jiyi said dismissively, waving him off with an elegant flick of her wrist. "Incredible," she murmured, studying the still-smoking scorch marks on the deck. "I've never seen anyone take to this so quickly."

But despite the initial surge of confidence, every other spell Zhara attempted ended in abject failure.

"Feel your way along the void," Jiyi instructed. "Sense it at the tip of your brush. Do you feel it?"

Zhara did not, although she had tried her best. She did not understand what the courtesan meant by *the void,* and as Jiyi was not a magician herself, she could only relay what other magicians had described in their writings.

"It's the space between matter," Jiyi said, stamping her foot in frustration. "I don't know how to put it any better than that. How did you do it when you started that fire?"

The honest truth was Zhara did not know. The theory, according to the courtesan, was that a magician would find the void within the object or thing they wanted to set aflame, concentrate on it, then channel their intention through their brush, using the character for *fire* to generate heat by shifting matter fast enough to cause friction, then combustion.

But that was not how any of it felt when Zhara started that conflagration on the deck. There was no void she manipulated, no space between matter she sensed at the tip of her brush. It was as though fire and heat and flame were just waiting beyond her senses for her to grab and bring into existence from nothingness. Apparently, creation, like transformation, was another violation of the natural order.

"I'm sorry," Zhara repeated over and over, despite Jiyi's increasingly exasperated scolding. She glanced down at her hands, faintly glowing in the late-morning sun. Curling them into fists, she tucked them behind her back so the others wouldn't see. "I guess I'm just a dunce."

"*Stop. Saying. That,*" Jiyi growled. "I can't tell if you're putting yourself down because you want my pity or if you truly believe yourself to be worthless. Either way, it's very irritating."

"Leave her be," Han said. "This is all very new for her."

Zhara gave him a sidelong glance and a shy smile. No one had ever stood up for her before. The urge to giggle returned.

The courtesan shot him an annoyed look. "If anyone should be apologizing for being a dunce, it's this one," she muttered, jerking her chin toward Han. "Shouldn't you be attending class at the university or something?" Jiyi narrowed her eyes. "You *are* a student, yes?"

He coughed. "Classes were, ah, canceled this morning." Behind him, Xu flicked their fan open, hiding their face behind the brilliantly colored silk.

Jiyi rolled her eyes before turning back to Zhara. "We might as well stop your lessons for now," she said grudgingly. "I suspect you're tired. We'll try again some other time, when you're fresher."

Zhara pressed her left fist into her right palm and bowed. "A thousand thanks, Teacher Huang," she said in a formal voice. "I am grateful for her instruction."

"Enough," the courtesan said. "You make me feel more ancient than Lo's mountain." But she couldn't help the slightly pleased smile that quirked the corners of her lips at being accorded the respect.

Zhara smiled back. "Of course, Teacher Huang," she intoned as she rose to her feet.

Jiyi scoffed and joined Han and Xu at the bow. The scenery around them had changed as they traveled upriver—the marshlands further south giving way to irrigated fields of rice, then tame grasslands, then scrubby little forests as they approached the ruins of Old Changxi. Sandy banks had turned into rocky cliffs, the waters from a muddy gray-brown to a brilliant emerald green as their barge navigated through a narrow channel of towering limestone walls.

"Wah," Zhara breathed. "It's stunning."

Beside her, a tall, broad shape cleared their throat. "It is," said Han, his voice squeaking a little. "Seems a nice destination for a romantic date, lah?"

Zhara looked askance to find him gazing at her and not the scenery. His ears were bright red in the sunshine. "A date?" she asked lightly.

He tugged at his earlobe, which was growing redder by the moment. "Yes, right," he hemmed and hawed. "It's a beautiful setting."

"A beautiful setting for potential death by volcano," Xu called from their side of the boat.

Han glared at his best friend. "You always do like to ruin the mood, Chan Xuhei!"

As the channel narrowed even farther, the current became even swifter, rocking their barge back and forth atop the choppy waters. Zhara stumbled back from the railing and straight into Han's arms. He set her upright and wrenched himself away.

"You, um, all right?" The redness had spread from his ears down his neck as he looked away, careful to keep his gaze focused straight ahead.

"I'm fine, Master Plum Blossom." She grinned, then noticed his white knuckles as he clung to the railing. Despite the blush staining his neck and ears, the rest of his face was wan and sallow. "Are *you* all right?" she asked. "Feeling queasy again?"

"No, I'm good," he said brightly. He shot her a big smile, which immediately turned into a panicked grimace as he gripped the railing even tighter. "Never better," he said through gritted teeth.

The waters were becoming quite turbulent, and Zhara felt the churning of her stomach as their craft was tossed about on the current.

"It's going to be a rough ride!" the captain called. "Best hang on— won't be long!"

Ahead, she could see the passage widen into a secluded lake, with Mount Zanhei's lonely peak in the distance, dominating the landscape. Zhara held her breath as their craft raced along the channel, bobbing and bucking like a horse trying to throw its rider. Water splashed onto the deck, turning the surface slick and slippery. Behind her, Xu cried out as they got caught in the spray.

"This is Wulin silk!" they wailed in agony.

Presently, the river calmed as they emerged from the narrow passageway and onto the lake. Zhara gasped as the vista opened up before them. The lake was much larger than it appeared from the limestone channel, the color an astonishingly bright turquoise blue, as though reflecting the sky of another world entirely. The water was surrounded on three sides by towering white cliffs, topped with the remains of ancient watchtowers, while the fourth opened into the ashen remains of a petrified city surrounded by a lush, dense forest.

"Oh," she murmured as Han stirred beside her.

As the captain brought their vessel closer to shore, Zhara could see signs of life—human life—among the ruins. The docks were clean and well-maintained, and the harbor was lined with what looked like storefronts and cafés selling souvenirs and things to eat and drink. The scene reminded her of Zanhei's covered market, hustling and bustling with customers haggling and bargaining with vendors for the best deals. If it weren't for the enormous volcano towering over them, she could imagine Old Changxi to be just like any other city in the Morning Realms.

"I thought this place was abandoned," Han said in confusion as workers began swarming the quay to bring their barge to dock.

"No one lives here," the captain explained. "But there's a good living to be made on all the tourists coming to see the ruins. As I know well," he said wryly. He looked around in confusion. "Where did the other young lady go? I want to settle the account before everyone disembarks."

"You'll get your money, don't worry." Jiyi emerged from below-decks carrying a large, bulging bag. "Here, take this," she said, unceremoniously handing it over to Han as she passed. He fumbled as it fell to the deck with a heavy thud.

"What am I, a mule?" he complained, slinging the satchel over his shoulder with a grunt. "What did the courtesan put in here—rocks?"

"No, your head is stuffed with rocks," Jiyi said as she handed over a large purse to the captain. "The bag is stuffed with books and a few other supplies to bring some samples back to study."

Han thrust his head into the bag, which clanked and clattered with the weight of its contents. "She needs all this? Why?"

Jiyi ignored him and watched as the captain meticulously counted out the cash. Twice. Once he was satisfied he hadn't been cheated out of what he was owed, he gave the four of them a grave nod.

"Six hours," he said. "Be back here before sundown. I want to be gone before it gets dark."

"But it will take us at least two hours to hike to the foot of the volcano and back," Xu said in dismay.

"Six hours," the captain repeated firmly. "Nothing good happens here after nightfall, trust me."

Jiyi eyed the man with disdain. "You don't believe in the ghost stories, do you?"

"What ghost stories?" Xu asked anxiously.

The captain looked grim. "They say these ruins are haunted, but it's not the dead that worry me."

Xu sidled toward Han, hiding behind their friend's broad shoulders. "Then what does?"

The captain did not answer straightaway, gazing at the forest beyond the borders of Old Changxi. "Abominations," he murmured.

Zhara exchanged looks with Jiyi, who subtly shook her head. "We'll be back before sundown" was all the courtesan said.

The captain nodded. "Six hours," he said again. "Or you're on your own."

21

UNDER DIFFERENT CIRCUMSTANCES, HAN THOUGHT VISITING the ruins of Old Changxi would make for a rather romantic—if somewhat macabre—date. The petrified buildings were quite picturesque, and walking around the empty and preserved streets gave the entire outing an illicit feel, as though he were somehow sneaking around his own city at night after curfew. The thought of stealing secret kisses with a girl in such a setting was a dream of Han's he didn't know he had, and he kept glancing Zhara's way, wondering if—hoping—she was having similar thoughts.

"Would you hurry up?" Jiyi shouted from the front, where she led the group by several paces. "Captain Shang said to be back by sundown."

"Then the courtesan can carry this satchel herself!" he yelled back. "We'll see how fast she moves then."

"I thought you said you worked very hard on maintaining your physique," Zhara said, looking over her shoulder to smile at him.

"Yes, well," he hedged. "It's really more for aesthetic reasons than practical ones."

"What's the point of having an impressive body if you don't put it to good use?" Xu winked at Zhara, who laughed and gave them a playful smack on the shoulder.

"I am putting it to good use!" Han protested. "I'm carrying Madam Fussybritches's bag up a mountain, aren't I?"

"I'm sure Mistress Brandy can think of other uses for an impressive body, lah?" they said, nudging Zhara with their elbow as her cheeks turned bright pink in the late-morning sun.

"What?" Han asked in confusion. "What other uses?"

"Shut up and save your breath," Jiyi called. "The trek's only going to get more difficult from here."

They approached the crumbling northern wall of the petrified city, beyond which the wilds began. The walls here were taller and more massive than the walls surrounding Han's home city, and he marveled at their size—thicker than four horses abreast, with several enterprising trees growing through the cracks along the top. Despite the destruction wrought by the eruption all those years ago, the gate was still intact, having been carved of stone instead of wood. There was only one remaining guardian beast statue at the city gate, remarkably unscathed. Han had never seen a creature like it before—some fantastical feline chimera with the mane of a lion, the tail of a peacock, and two small, rounded horns on its head.

"The Lion of the South," Zhara murmured. "Protecting the citizens from plague and pestilence."

"What in heaven were these people afraid of?" Xu murmured, eyeing the old capital's defenses as they entered the forest. "No walls, no matter how massive, will keep an angry volcano at bay."

"Perhaps they were afraid of monsters," Zhara remarked, patting the guardian beast's paw as she passed. "They say the woods around Mount Zanhei were once teeming with ravenous beasts, restless dead, and hungry ghosts." The light fell away as they pressed deeper into the woods, blotted out by the impenetrable canopy above. Han thought he heard the slight ringing of a bell and looked up to find a large bird with reddish feathers perched atop a nearby tree. He sneezed multiple times.

"It was likely abominations," Jiyi said. "If we're right about our suspicions that the source of the demonic poison is the volcano, then Old Changxi was probably overrun with them back in the day. So if there were any magicians in the city, they were probably thrown into the woods and left to fend for themselves."

"Wasn't Mount Zanhei supposed to be a magician holy site?" Han asked.

"And how would you know?" Jiyi asked scornfully.

Han looked away. "My mother was a magician too," he said in a low voice. "And despite what the treasured one thinks, I'm not *that* ignorant."

The courtesan didn't reply, but he liked to think that her back looked contrite as they made their way through the forest.

"Mount Zanhei was a magician holy site?" Zhara prodded gently.

"Yes." Han dimpled at her. "Old Changxi was once a thriving community of magicians." He noted her admiring gaze and puffed out his chest, strutting a little as they walked. "Mount Zanhei is apparently the loc—locust—location of a lot of magical energy."

"That's certainly true," Zhara mused. She tilted her head to take in the summit of the volcano, hidden by clouds. "There's something . . . tugging at my ki." She turned to the others. "Can you feel it?"

Han, Xu, and the courtesan all exchanged glances and shook their heads.

"What does it feel like?" Jiyi asked, curiosity and longing in her eyes.

Zhara shuddered. "Like something is siphoning off my energy and strength," she said. "It feels . . . off."

"That's likely the demonic essence," the courtesan said.

"Is demonic essence even real?" Han asked. "Isn't a demon a being of pure chaos? How can chaos and the world of order coexist?"

"So he has a brain after all," Jiyi said teasingly. "And here I thought you could barely read."

"Yah!" Han pouted. "I do too read! I read . . . lots of things!"

"Like what, *Tales from the Downy Delta?*"

"Has *everyone* read that except me?" There was a noticeable incline to the path now, and Han was starting to sweat with the effort of hauling Jiyi's bag up the slope. "Why does everyone like to pick on me?" he panted, lagging behind the others.

"Because it's cute when you're flustered." Zhara waited, allowing him to catch up to her on the trail.

"Cute?" He sneezed again and found the reddish bird cackling nearby, its brilliant scarlet plumage catching the light of the sun as it flapped its wings. "I'd rather be cool. Calm. Collected, even."

"Not handsome?" She smiled.

"Well, I'm already handsome, so that's beside the point."

She laughed and shook her head.

"What, do you not think I'm handsome?" Suddenly Han was fearful that all the times the Royal Consort and her handmaidens had told him he was attractive growing up had been nothing but well-intentioned lies. "My mother always told me I was good-looking."

She gave him a sidelong glance, eyes dancing. He felt a curious stab to the gut, almost like a stitch in his ribs, but in the wrong place. "Your mother was right," she said shyly. "You are, in fact, very good-looking."

The *very* in that sentence did strange things to his body. That stab to the gut melted into hot molten lava, dissolving all his bones and leaving his hands floppy and limp. "I—ah—uh—" All feeling seemed to have disappeared from his lips as well. "Thanks?"

Zhara chuckled. "So, books," she prompted. "You were talking about your preferred reading materials."

"Oh. Right!" He sheepishly scratched his head and gave an awkward laugh. "Well, I did like that book I accidentally stole from you the first time we met."

"*The Maiden Who Was Loved by Death?*" she asked, eyes widening in surprise.

"Yes!" he said. "It was *so* good. I'm all caught up now. The way Little Flame gave herself up to the Death Lord in exchange for her sister's life! And the Death Lord himself? So charming yet so scary all at once? I mean, their love is going to kill her, but I kind of want them to kiss at the same time?"

Zhara broke out into delighted laughter, the sound ringing through the forest like the clarion sound of a bell. "Why, Master Plum Blossom," she said. "I didn't know you were one for light romance novels."

"Me neither, to be honest." He shrugged. "I just assumed books were supposed to, you know, make you smarter or improve your character or something. I didn't realize they could also be entertaining."

"The next installment should be coming out next week," Zhara said.

"Ooh, we should read it together!"

She laughed again. "If I can find a copy, perhaps," she said. "I usually borrow them from Master Cao once the demand has died down."

"I'll buy you a copy," Han said. "I owe you one anyway."

Zhara rested her hand lightly on his shoulder, and his entire body broke out in goose bumps despite the heat and humidity of the day. "I appreciate the sentiment," she said softly. "But you don't owe me anything, Master Plum Blossom."

"Consider it a favor to me then. He smiled. "To spare me the agony of waiting for you to catch up."

She smiled back and they fell into silence, saving their breath as they continued their climb. The incline was noticeably steeper now, and the sounds of their panting echoed loudly throughout the forest. The air was thick and oppressive beneath the canopy, unbearably hot despite the shade it offered from the noon sun. Everything felt muffled, deadened, slow, and even trudging along the trail was like moving through glue. The only sign of life aside from Han and his companions was that reddish bird, flitting from branch to branch with a jingle of the bell around its neck. He thought it might be someone's pet. He sneezed again.

Presently, the trek began to flatten and Han could see the slope of Mount Zanhei itself, rocky and barren, its bare face rather stark against the wild, overgrown landscape. Ahead there were several pools scattered about, steam rising from bubbling surfaces.

"What's that smell?" Xu asked, reaching into their sash and pulling out their fan.

"We're coming up on some hot springs," Jiyi replied. "Lots of people go bathing here."

"This place has hot springs? And me without my bathing attire," Xu lamented. They dabbed delicately at their brow with a piece of cloth while they fanned themself. "I could use a refreshing dip."

"No one's going near these hot springs," the courtesan said sternly. "We're only stopping by to take a sample to compare with the water Teacher Hu brought back from the marshland reservoir. It could be tainted with a demonic essence for all you know."

"But look at me," Xu moaned as their rouge came away on their handkerchief. "I must seem like a ghoul."

They did, in fact, look rather ghoulish, with rouge smeared across their lips like bloodstains and kohl smudged beneath their eyes like the illustrations of hungry ghosts in Anyang's storybooks. "It's true," Han said as their best friend wilted in dismay. "You do look—"

"You look fine, Xu," Zhara interrupted, shooting Han a warning glance. "I'll clean up your makeup when we get to where we're headed."

Their group came upon the hot springs at last, three small pools surrounded by volcanic rock with a stunning view of the city and lake below. From this vantage point, the lake was a different color than seen from the barge—a shocking pale green tinged with aqua where the waters touched the shore. Below them the ruins of Old Changxi gleamed silver in the summer sun, shining like a jewelry box nestled amid the dark green jade of its surrounding woods.

"I can see why people would come here to bathe," Zhara murmured, standing at the edge of the outcropping and gazing out over the landscape. "It's so picturesque."

"Yes, nothing adds to the ambiance of a place more than the possibility of dying horribly, at any moment, in a terrible volcano explosion," Xu said drily, tugging at Zhara's sleeve. "Can you fix my makeup now?" they whined.

"*A candle unused is but wax and wick,*" Han quoted, setting down Jiyi's bag and working out the knots in his back. "*I would rather light the flame, knowing it will go out, than sit forever in darkness.*"

"Why Won—Li Han!" Xu said in astonishment. "Was that . . . the work of some noted philosopher you quoted to me?"

"Yes." He beamed at his best friend. "Jae Hyun, the author of *The Maiden Who Was Loved by Death.*"

Zhara chuckled as she wiped Xu's face. "See? Books *do* improve your character."

"Everyone be quiet," Jiyi ordered. "The entrance to the cave system is somewhere around here and I can't hear myself think with all the incessant flirting." She walked around the overlook, carefully examining the hot springs and the surrounding area. "Help me look."

"What are we looking for, exactly?" Han asked. The pools must have been a popular bathing destination at one point, for he could see the neglected paths around the springs and carved stone benches to the side. But it appeared as though tourists now preferred to bathe elsewhere—weeds and weather had worn the wooden walkways to rotten remains, and time had ground the carvings on the stone benches to mere hints of their former glory. Zhara and Xu were examining a stone pavilion a little ways off, one of the few intact structures left.

"I'm not sure," Jiyi murmured, running her fingers over the stones surrounding the hot springs. "I think there are some carvings here— the Language of Flowers, but an older style. I'm not as familiar with it." She thrust her hand at Han without looking at him. "Hand me my bag."

He dutifully jogged to where he had dropped it and brought it back for the courtesan. Jiyi retrieved a book and some charcoal, tearing out a page to make some rubbings against the rocks. Han circled each of the pools, looking for more carvings. "There's more here," he called, pointing them out as the courtesan made her way around the hot springs.

"I think these mean *cleansing*," Jiyi muttered to herself as she worked. "Maybe some sort of spell of purification? Were these ritual baths, perhaps? Ritual baths for what?" She thrust out her hand again. "Hand me a jar so I can collect a sample of this water," she demanded.

"Over here!" Zhara called from the pavilion. "I think I've found something!"

Jiyi stuffed her rubbings into the bag before handing it over to Han. "Yah," he complained. "Carry your own satchel this time."

She ignored him, joining the others at the pavilion. "This is an altar or some sort of holy site," the courtesan said with some surprise as she entered, scanning the carvings on the ceiling and columns. "These all indicate this is a Lion Temple. Look," she said, pointing to a faded painting of a feline chimera, identical to the carved guardian beast standing watch just outside the gates of the old city below. "I think this is supposed to be the Lion of the South." She ran her fingers along the inscription below the image. "*The Lord of the Fanged and Furred*," she read aloud. "*The Lion of the South can take on any shape or form, for his power—like that of his master—is the power of transformation.*"

"His master?" Zhara asked, peering over Jiyi's shoulder. "Who's that— Aiyo!" She startled as a bell rang and that large, reddish bird flapped onto the railing beside her.

"I swear this bird is following us," Xu muttered, glaring at the creature. "Wasn't it down by the old capital ruins before?"

"Birds like these are probably native to the area," Zhara said. "I'm sure this is one of many that live around here."

The creature in question ruffled its feathers in an avian huff. Han tried to stroke the bird but it cawed and hopped away, fixing him with its golden glare. The bird's stare seemed rather familiar to him, but he couldn't pinpoint why. He sneezed again. Odd, he wasn't allergic to birds.

"Anyway, these aren't the carvings I wanted to show you," Zhara said, drawing Jiyi away from studying the columns. "It's this." She pointed to the floor, where one of the stone tiles bore a symbol—a circle bisected by a vertical line.

Jiyi tilted her head to one side, crouching down to get a closer look. "This is a symbol against the evil eye." She began digging her fingertips into the crevices around the tile. "I think," she said distractedly, "that this is some sort of hatch. This is probably the entrance into the caves." She held her hand out to Han. "Bag. I've got some tools in there."

"Hold a moment." Zhara knelt beside the courtesan, hand hovering over the symbol. "Maybe it's something that can only be opened by a magician."

"Doubtful," Jiyi said with a frown.

Zhara hesitated, biting her lip and tucking her hands into her sleeves. Han could see her reluctance to speak, her inclination to fold herself back into something small, inoffensive, and insignificant. The sparkle was gone from Zhara's eyes, and she suddenly seemed dull, as though she had drawn a cloak over herself in order to disappear.

"The treasured one might be learned in magic," he said pointedly. "But Zhara is the only one of us who is actually *gifted* with it. Maybe we should let her speak." She caught his eye and he gave her a small nod of encouragement.

"True," Jiyi said grudgingly. "I apologize, Zhara. Go on."

Zhara gave Han the smallest smile of gratitude. He was already hot from their hike up the mountain, but he felt warm in an entirely different way now.

"It feels like—it feels like when I come into contact with another magician," Zhara said. "There's a . . . resonance, perhaps. Recognition. It's as though the carving itself has magic."

The courtesan crinkled her nose. "Inanimate objects can't be magical," she said, not unkindly. "There are stories of enchanted weapons and the like throughout history, but they're just that—stories."

"Still," Han insisted. "It doesn't hurt to let her try, lah?"

Zhara looked to Jiyi, who pursed her lips before giving her a nod. Slowly, uncertainly, Zhara pressed her palm against the symbol and closed her eyes.

Han held his breath.

Nothing happened.

"Zhara," Jiyi said gently, "you can barely manage the simplest spell, I don't think—wah!"

There was a grinding, rumbling noise as the earth beneath their feet began to tremble. Dust and debris fell from the ceiling of the pavilion, clattering about them in a shower of pebbles. Jiyi flailed about for something to brace herself against, but Han kept his eyes on Zhara, who had not moved from her spot beside the hatch.

"The volcano is erupting!" Xu cried, clutching at their face. "Oh, I knew this trip was a bad idea!"

Zhara snatched her hand from the carving and jumped to her feet, swaying a little as the ground shuddered beneath them. Han leaped forward to keep her steady as she stepped back. The symbol seemed to glow a faint rose-gold where she had touched it and the tile sank, revealing a flight of steps leading down into darkness. The tremors immediately ceased.

"How—how did you do that?" Jiyi ran forward to examine the newly revealed entrance, her eyes alight with awe and disbelief. "Did you use a spell? If so, what? And how did you manage it without a brush?"

Beside him, Zhara seemed unusually pale, her normally rich brown skin a dull ashen color. She held her hands beside her, elbows locked and rigid, and Han tried wrapping a tentative arm about her shoulders. She flinched and he immediately retreated, embarrassed and not a little chastened.

"Are you all right?" he asked instead.

After a long moment, she nodded. "I'm all right," Zhara said in a hoarse voice. "Just a little, um, shaken."

Xu nervously approached the hole in the ground. "What does everyone think is down there?" they asked, peering down the steps.

"That's what we're here to find out," Jiyi said, rubbing her hands together with glee.

"Not me," said Xu emphatically. "I only tagged along to make sure my pr—my *friend,* Han, makes it to his majority."

Jiyi waved distractedly at them, circling the entrance excitedly. "Well, if you're not going to come along and make yourself useful down there, make yourself useful up here and get me some samples of hot-spring water," she said, confidently striding down into the unknown. "I'm going exploring." A few steps in, the courtesan looked over her shoulder at Han and Zhara. "Are you two coming or not?"

22

THE AIR BENEATH THE PAVILION REEKED OF brimstone. Zhara discreetly kept her nose buried in the crook of her elbow, trying not to gag. The sulfurous stink was one thing, but the faint, sickly sweet scent of decay lurking beneath it was another. A smell like the butcher shops and abattoirs of the Pits hung heavy over her like a miasma, the reek of fear. It was the smell of animals being led to slaughter, of prey caught in a predator's talons, of magicians dragged before the Falconer to be executed. It was the smell of death and it made Zhara want to throw up.

"Isn't this exciting?" Jiyi asked, either oblivious or completely indifferent to the atmosphere. Zhara had never seen her so energetic before, so enthusiastic, so . . . young. Stripped completely of her apathy and contempt, the courtesan was almost like a little girl, cheerfully chattering away about anything and everything that interested her. "Think of all the things we're about to learn about ancient magicians. Rituals and spells that might have been lost to time! Characters in the Language of Flowers we've never seen before! Maybe even *books*!"

"The treasured one and I have two very different definitions of *exciting*," Han muttered in a slightly muffled voice, free hand covering his nose. The other was braced against the wall as he descended, as the steps were uneven and the incline rather steep. "Personally, descending into the bowels of Tiyok itself isn't exactly my idea of fun."

"Tiyok isn't a place," Jiyi said scornfully. "The realm of Chaos is a state of existence."

He glared at the courtesan. "Regardless," he said. "The heart of a volcano seems to be both literally *and* figuratively *Tiyok*."

"Ooh, look at you," she cooed. "I'm impressed you even know what *figuratively* means."

"Yah," Han protested. "I've been very well educated!"

Zhara kept her hands to herself as she followed a few paces behind, careful of her step and balance. Her palms still itched after unlocking the hatch, and she worried what else she might accidentally stir with her magic. Touching the mark on the tile had been like coming into contact with Thanh, with that bone-deep—soul-deep—sense of recognition, that sense of her magic leaping to life as though called awake. But like with Thanh, there had been something unsettling in that touch, the feeling of something rotten, something . . . corrupted. She curled and uncurled her fingers, trying to rid herself of that lingering sensation.

"It's getting dark," Han complained as they walked. "I can hardly see anything. Yah!" he yelped. "Something just brushed past my leg!"

"Likely a rat," the courtesan said dismissively. "I'm sure the caverns around here are teeming with vermin— Aiyo!" she said in surprise. "Something just nipped at my ankle." She looked at Zhara and frowned. "Do you have a light?"

Zhara glanced at her fingertips, which glowed faintly in the dimness. "I don't," she said, tugging at her sleeves to pull them down over her hands. "Did anyone bring a torch?"

"Han, hand me my bag," Jiyi said. "There should be a couple of torches in there."

"I don't have it," he said, sounding bewildered. "Why would I have it?"

"Ugh." The courtesan sighed and rolled her eyes. "Well, go fetch it then," she said impatiently.

Han huffed with irritation. "For the last time, I am not your mule," he said petulantly. "Fetch it yourself!"

"Fine." Jiyi immediately turned and started making her way back up the stairs. "You're lucky I'm in such a good mood." Zhara thought she must be in a good mood indeed not to berate Han for addressing her so informally. "You two go on ahead," the courtesan called over her shoulder. "I'll catch up in a bit."

Han craned his neck as he tried to peer down the steps. "Go on?" he asked in bewilderment. "How? Does she think we're bats or something?"

"First a mule, and now a bat." Zhara smiled. "She must think of you as an entire menagerie of animals."

"Makes sense," he groused. "Since she doesn't seem to think of me as human." He froze, eyes fixed on a point somewhere below them in the gloom. "Zhara," he said in a strained voice. "Do you see that?"

She tried to follow his gaze. "See what?"

"Down there," he whispered. "Is it just me or are those . . . eyes staring back at us?"

Zhara squinted into the darkness, a blackness so black as to be impenetrable. It was the sort of darkness that had a shape, weight, and texture of its own, where light and life were swallowed up and lost forever. Dread drenched her in a cold wave as her magic stirred uneasily, nervy and anxious like a forest creature poised to flee . . . or fight. Power raced along her ki pathways to pool in her palms, making them tingle and itch.

"I can't see anything," she said slowly. Then something flickered ahead, like the shine of light against gold coins. "Wait."

Then she saw them—a pair of glowing eyes, burning like the last two embers in a long-dead furnace. Zhara sucked in a sharp breath and unthinkingly reached for Han's hand, remembering a heartbeat too late the magic lurking beneath her skin. Yet he immediately turned his palm over and laced his fingers with hers, completely unaffected by her touch, the touch that had burned nearly every other non-magician with whom she had come into contact. She held herself still, marveling at the feel of his bare skin against hers, despite the power that hummed and thrummed in her hand.

"It's just a—just a trick of the light, lah?" Han asked in a cracked voice. "Just the light above reflecting off . . . something."

The glowing golden eyes slowly blinked—once, twice—before winking out of existence entirely. All the hairs rose along the back of Zhara's neck. There was another presence waiting in the darkness with them, and she realized with a jolt that she had known it was there all along.

They were not alone.

"Perhaps—perhaps we should head back," she said uncertainly.

"Right," Han said readily. "No point in heading down without—"

There was a grinding, scraping sound, and the walls of the stairwell began to shudder. Zhara glanced behind her to see the stone tile above them slowly moving back into place. "Han!" she cried. "The hatch!"

He was already bounding up the steps two to three at a time, long legs pumping hard. "Jiyi!" he called. "Jiyi! Xu! The door!" He was nearly to the entrance when the stone tile slid back into place with an echoing thud, sealing them both in total darkness.

"Jiyi!" Han shouted, fists pounding against the stone entrance. "Jiyi, open the hatch! Xu!"

"Han?" Zhara dropped to all fours and carefully felt her way back up the stairs on hands and knees. She had never known a darkness so complete, so stark as to have a weight and menace all its own. It pressed against her face like a film, a mask, and Zhara felt as though she were suffocating, even though she knew she could breathe just fine. "Han?"

Ahead, she could hear him pounding away at the stone tile that covered the entrance. "Yah!" he yelled. "Let us out!"

There was a muffled response from the other side—either Jiyi or Xu.

"What?" Han bellowed. "I can't hear you!"

Behind her, Zhara knew the glowing, golden eyes were still staring. The stare clawed at her for attention, an insistent tickle at her back that she wanted neither to engage nor acknowledge. Magic roiled her blood, pushing and straining at her skin as though desperate to break free, and she had to sit down to focus on keeping her power contained. She hugged her knees to her chest and closed her eyes, even though it was too dark to see. "I won't look, I won't look, I won't look," she murmured.

Through closed lids, she could sense the presence creeping closer. Her magic quivered and vibrated, and the effort of holding it back was nigh intolerable. Zhara hoped Han could get through to Jiyi and Xu and get the door open; she wasn't sure if she could hold out much longer. She wasn't sure what was worse—the power she could scarcely hold back or the golden eyes hovering just beyond the edges of her senses.

Something warm and fuzzy brushed her leg with the tinkling of a bell.

There was a burst of flame.

"Zhara!"

She opened her eyes, wincing against the flood of brightness that assaulted them. For a moment she was disoriented, lost as to the source of light before she realized it was her. *She* was the source of light.

Or rather, her hands.

They were wreathed in flames from fingertip to wrist, as though her flesh were a candle and her skin the wick. She could feel the incredible heat of it all as the fire slowly spread up her arms to the rest of her, yet there was no pain, no burning, only light and life and warmth. Zhara thought of what Jiyi had said on their boat ride up to the ruins of Old Changxi, that magic must follow the rules of nature lest it be a violation of order. To create fire, she had to *intend* for it to happen, to feel along the void to manipulate matter. She had done none of those things. She had not intended for her hands to burn.

And yet here she was, her hands and forearms doing a passable impression of a torch. The hairs on the back of her neck prickled as though the breeze had whispered in her ear.

Violation.

"Zhara!" Han came running to her side. "Are you all right?"

"Stay back!" She brandished her flaming hands before her, and he fell back against the steps, eyes round with both awe and alarm. "I don't want to hurt you."

"Easy there." He held up his own hands in a gesture of surrender. "It's all right."

"It's not all right!" Zhara tried thrusting her hands behind her, singeing her clothes in the process. Although the fire on her body did not hurt her, the flames were real, and the heat of it made her sweat. She wanted to cry, she wanted to scream, she wanted to lie down and make it all go away. "I'm a monster!"

"You are not a monster," Han said quietly. He got to his feet and took a step forward.

"I am!" Her hands shook, making the shadows around them flicker and dance. "Look at me!"

"You're trembling." He took another careful step closer, hand outstretched—not in a gesture of surrender, but of kindness.

"Please," she repeated. "I don't want to hurt you."

"Shhh," he soothed. "It's all right. No one's going to get hurt."

Zhara barked a harsh laugh, wiggling her fingers at him. "Oh, I'm sorry, did you miss the part where my *hands are on fire?*"

He came to a standstill. "Does it hurt?" he asked gently. "You, I mean. Are you in pain?"

Her throat tightened and she closed her eyes at the sting of sudden tears. She could so easily hurt him, burn him, scar him the way she had Suzhan all those years ago, yet he was the one standing there asking if she were in pain. Zhara had thought that nothing could hurt her more than the Second Wife's cruelty, but she was wrong; the compassion in Han's large, round eyes hurt even worse.

"I'm fine," she said, turning her face away. But she was not fine. "Please. Go away. I don't want you—anyone—to see me like this."

"What do you mean?" His voice was closer now, but she did not back away. "Like what?"

Zhara closed her eyes. "An abomination."

"Last I recall, an abomination was this beastly thing made of thousands of oozing, oily eyes trying to kill us," Han said lightly. "And unless you've got several dozen eyes hiding beneath your tunic and trousers, I'd say we're in the clear."

A soggy chuckle escaped her despite herself. "I'm afraid I can't prove otherwise." She waved her hands, then attempted to bat her lashes. "Unless you want to check for yourself."

Han cleared his throat, and even though the flames cast harsh shadows on his face, Zhara could see his face darkening in a blush. She laughed again, and the fire wreathing her body began to retreat, fading slowly down her arms to her wrists. He stepped closer and she did not pull away. His hand hovered near her arm, but his gaze was steady on her face, a questioning look in his eyes, as though seeking permission to touch her. She did not move as he inched ever closer, unflinching before the fire. Zhara bit her lip, holding her breath as slowly, hesitantly, Han wrapped his fingers gently about her wrist.

The flames winked out.

The darkness that doused their eyes was so complete that Zhara stumbled back, but Han tightened his grip and pulled her into his embrace. She stiffened, then relaxed by degrees as she realized he was unhurt, that neither the fire nor the touch of her magic had burned him. The rush of magic that had filled her body receded, and a deep chill settled in the void left in its wake.

"You're . . . an anti-magician," she said in some awe.

"A what?"

"An anti-magician," Zhara said shakily. "You have magic in your bones, but it doesn't affect you."

"So you're saying I'm a useless magician," Han said in dismay. "Fantastic."

Zhara laughed. Relief and disbelief kept battering her body in wave after wave of exhaustion, and she couldn't stop trembling, though she wasn't cold.

Han wrapped his arms tightly about her. "It's all right," he said over and over. "You're all right."

Zhara buried her face in the crook of Han's shoulder, allowing herself to be *held,* if just for a moment. The subtle pattern of his silk brocade overgarment was smooth against her cheek, the faint scent of sandalwood, ylang-ylang, and a boyish musk clinging to his clothes. He coughed and subtly shifted to one side, and Zhara realized with embarrassment she had been rubbing her nose against his chest.

"So." Han cleared his throat. "It wasn't my intention to put out our only source of light."

Zhara gave a nervous giggle. Although her power had faded, her entire body still tingled with a sensation both more and less dangerous than the thrill of magic thrumming through her veins. "I'm sorry," she said.

"What for?"

Zhara could just imagine the look of confusion on his face, the full brows drawn, the corners of his lips turned down. "For . . . for turning off the lights, I suppose," she said. "And . . . for being a histrionic, melodramatic mess."

"Well, we all have our bad days." She could hear the smile in his voice. "So I guess we'll just have to sit here and wait in the darkness until Jiyi and Xu come back with tools to break the hatch open."

"Is that what they said?"

She felt his shoulders move up and down in a shrug. "It was either

Stay here and we'll go get help or *Day fear underground more sell.* I'm betting it was the former— Aiyo!" Han jumped back with a jangle. "Something just swiped at me." He sneezed.

"What is it?" Her pulse began to race, but curiously, her magic remained calm. Zhara looked down to find the golden, glowing eyes had winked back into existence.

Niang, said a grumpy voice. A voice she recognized.

"Sajah?" she asked in amazement. She startled when something warm and fuzzy wrapped itself about her ankles, but then it started purring, sending comforting vibrations up her leg. She reached down, fingers searching for the cat. "Is that really you?"

A cold little nose bumped against her knuckles. *Mrrrow,* came the reply.

"Is that . . . your cat?" Han sneezed again.

Sajah hissed.

"Yes, that most definitely sounds like your ginger menace," he grumbled stuffily. "He hates me. *Achoo!*"

The cat unwound himself from her legs, and Zhara could hear the light padded sounds of his dainty paws tripping down the stairs. The golden eyes appeared, staring at her from several steps farther down. They blinked out of existence again before reappearing several more steps away.

"I think he wants us to follow him," she murmured.

"Where? Down there?"

There was a pause, as though Han were peering farther down the stairwell, nose scrunched, lips pursed in a pout, and shuddering as he imagined what potential horrors they might find. With a start, Zhara realized that she could recall every detail of his expressions, that he had become so engraved in her thoughts that she could summon his face at will. A furious flush swept her from head to toe, so hard she could feel her blood pulsing against her face.

"I think so," she said, grateful that her blush—like the rest of her— was invisible in the dark.

"I suppose it's not like we have other options while we wait," he muttered. "Might as well finish what we started, lah?"

23

AFTER SEVERAL MINUTES OF STUMBLING AROUND IN the pitch-black, Han sheepishly asked Zhara if she could try the flaming hands thing again.

"Not if it makes you uncomfortable," he added quickly. "Or if it pains you in any way."

They had been making their way down inch by agonizing inch, carefully feeling out the edge of each stair with their toes before advancing another step. Their progress was careful, slow, and Han wanted to punch the wall with frustration. If he could be sure just where the wall *was*.

"I'm afraid I can't," Zhara said softly.

"Why not?"

There was a long pause before she answered. "I—I don't know how."

Han recalled her terror on the stairwell, her unwavering belief that her magic somehow made her a monster, and thought of Anyang. His little brother also believed himself a monster, because he believed he had somehow driven his one friend away with his inexplicable powers. "Does your magic just . . . lash out like that?" he asked, treading carefully around her feelings.

"Sometimes." He could hear her footfalls lightly scraping against the stone steps beneath them. "Jiyi talks about *the void* between matter all the time, but to be honest, magic has always felt like a force beyond my control." She fell quiet. "Sometimes it lashes out and hurts others."

"You can't blame yourself for things beyond your control." Han could feel her flinch beside him, even though he could not see her.

"Nevertheless," she continued. "I've hurt people before."

The rest of that story hung in the air between them, as suffocating as the unrelenting darkness. Han desperately wanted to ask her about it, but he didn't want to press the matter and push her further away. "I'm sure it was an accident," he said uncertainly.

"It wasn't." Her voice was flat.

He was taken aback. He couldn't envision sweet little Mistress Brandy ever harming someone intentionally. "You mean you wanted to hurt someone?"

"No, of course not." He imagined her closing her eyes, her brows furrowed in pain. He had seen that look of regret on her face before, so at odds with her bright and cheerful countenance. Han had often wondered at the circumstances of her life that caused her features to fall so easily into the lines of cowed submission and sorrow. "But it doesn't matter what I intended. She got hurt, and it was my fault."

He knew so little about her, he realized, and she him. They were both so guarded, so careful about their truths. Yet Han sensed Zhara's guardedness had to do with a lifetime of expecting pain, while his came from the simple, selfish notion that he didn't want to scare people— her—away. If he told her who he truly was, would she hate him for lying to her? The gulf between a prince and an apothecary's assistant seemed so insurmountable. But when he was just Han, when he was just a boy, and she a girl, the distance wasn't so frightening. Guilt trickled down the back of his neck, cold and damp.

Then he realized something was dripping from the ceiling. "Augh!"

"What?" Zhara asked in a panicked voice. "What is it?"

His hand came away from his neck and shoulders wet. He gave his fingers a cautious sniff. They smelled faintly mineral, like the hot springs above. "I think there's water dripping from the ceiling."

A jingle, and two glowing, golden eyes briefly reappeared a few steps below them. Mistress Brandy's nightmare of a cat opened its mouth in a yawn, the feline equivalent of a laugh. He glared at Sajah before he realized he could make out the barest outline of the creature in the dark.

"Zhara," he said hesitantly. "Is it just me, or is the darkness getting less . . . dense?"

"Maybe?" She sounded dubious.

The black around them was definitely thinner now, more gray than black. Han could make out the vague shapes of things around him—Zhara's hair, her shoulders, her arms, her legs. Ahead, where the cat's eyes had been, he thought he could see a faint, eerie, blue-green glow. He could still hear the far-off ringing of a tiny bell on a collar, but the glowing eyes had disappeared.

"Is that . . . light up ahead?" Zhara asked disbelievingly.

"I—I think so." He was starting to be able to see the edge of each step as they went down and the curve of the wall as it spiraled down and down. The blue-green light grew stronger with each step and gave everything a surreal quality, as though he were descending not into the heart of a fiery volcano, but to the bottom of an ocean's jade depths. Han looked down at his clothes, the subtle pattern of white clouds glowing faintly in the dimness. The cat was nowhere to be found, vanished as quickly as it had appeared.

Presently, they came to the end of the stairs, and Zhara gasped.

"Are those—are those *stars*?" she asked, tilting her head back to gaze at the ceiling in wonder.

They had entered an enormous cavern both taller and wider than the Hall of Heavenly Wisdom at the palace. The source of the eerie, blue-green illumination was dozens—hundreds—of little lights dangling above their heads, like strings of beaded curtains made of the heavens. Like stars, they chased away the shadows around them, limning everything in a watery, otherworldly glow. Han glanced askance at the girl beside him, the blue light tracing the features of her face and the line of her neck with a magical brush. She looked like a fairy, or a celestial maiden from one of his mother's bedtime stories; an otherworldly being of light and darkness.

"Beautiful," Zhara murmured.

"Yes," he whispered, but he wasn't looking at the underground galaxy above them.

She caught his gaze, eyes shining with the reflection of myriad terrestrial stars, and smiled. It lit her face brighter than the false galaxy above and he had to look away, feeling as though he had been caught unclothed. He took the opportunity to survey the cavern, which was much larger than he had realized, nearly the size of the palace courtyard in Zanhei. The ceiling was several stories tall, seemingly supported by several pillars made of glittering stone that sparkled and shone like gems. The air was fresher here, smelling less of brimstone and more of damp. There was a dripping noise coming from somewhere, like the musical plinks of a lute string being plucked, echoing throughout the cavern.

"Look," Zhara said, pointing to a pillar beside him. "There's something carved here. I think it's the Language of Flowers." She drew in closer to examine it, fingers hovering over the mark. "Oh, Jiyi would love to see this."

As they moved through the cavern, the uneven stone floor gave way to smooth packed earth before widening into an enormous open expanse. In the center was a circle of large rectangular blocks, each about waist-high, too even and angular to be anything but man-made. Behind the structures, on the far side of the cavern, was a pool fed by enormous stone teeth dripping from the ceiling. The water was ringed by more of those blue-green lights, giving it an ethereal glow.

"There is a strange sort of energy about this place," Zhara murmured as they approached the blocks.

"Really?" Han rubbed at his forearms to chase away the invisible ghosts that clung to his skin. "I don't feel anything. Except a little creeped out."

"It's hard to explain," she said, "but it feels like putting my hands on that symbol on the hatch upstairs. Like something is *pulling* my magic from me."

He frowned. "Do you think it's whatever might be causing possession downriver?" He glanced at the pool on the far side of the cavern. "What about that?" he said, pointing at the water. "You said the well and dam in the marsh were contaminated by demonic essence."

Zhara moved past the circle of blocks toward the pool and tentatively dipped the tip of her ring finger in the water. She immediately snatched it back as though she had been burned. "It's not the pool," she said, shaking her head. "But the water is definitely tainted like the well in the marsh."

"Tainted? Do you mean poisoned?"

She paused, as though gathering her words before laying them out. "Not exactly," she said slowly. "It's more as though the *essence* of the water is no longer water."

Han blinked. "I'm confused."

Zhara laughed. "Me too, but it's the only way I can describe it." She waved her hand toward the pool. "I mean, this looks like water. For all intents and purposes, it *is* water. But at heart, at its very core, it's something else, something . . . demonic."

He mulled over her words. "Nope, still confused."

She smiled and shook her head. "The pull on my magic feels stronger over there," she said, pointing toward the circle of granite blocks. "It's almost as though I can feel my energy being drawn out of me toward the middle."

They made their way to the structures at the center of the cavern— twelve rectangular blocks arranged in a radial circle like the points on a compass. As they drew close, Han could see a large, circular piece of stone embedded in the packed-dirt floor, white and gleaming as though made of limestone or marble.

"What do you think these are?" He ran his hands over the top of the nearest block, which was carved with several symbols in what he assumed was the Language of Flowers. There was a funny sort of smell lingering about the blocks, almost sweet, yet cloying at the same time.

Zhara drew up beside him and examined the structures. "Some sort of monument, perhaps?" She coughed and covered her nose with her sleeve. "What stinks?"

He knelt beside the block for a better look. There was a groove running along the side near the top, about a hand's breadth down. The sickly sweet smell was stronger here, and strongest along the groove. "Yah, I think you can open this," he said. "I think this slab on top moves." He dug his fingernails into the groove, which was just big enough for him to wedge his hand in. "Help me."

She backed away slowly. "I don't want to touch it."

"No? Why not?"

Zhara pointed toward the carvings in the Language of Flowers etched onto the sides of the granite blocks. "Those carvings. I don't know what my touch will do."

"Your touch opened the hatch upstairs."

"I know." She brought her hands up to nervously toy with the ends of her braids. "But there's something . . . not right about these carvings. When I touched the mark on the hatch, it didn't just feel as though something were pulling my magic; it felt as though it were"—she bit her lower lip—"stealing my ki."

"And that's . . . not a good thing, I presume?" He never did have a particularly good grasp on this notion of ki. His fencing master, Teacher Kang, would talk about it all the time, especially in the moments when they were meditating instead of fighting. Han hated meditating.

She raised her brows. "No," she agreed. "It's like . . . like someone sapping your strength, leaving you weak. But instead of your strength, it's your life force." She shuddered. "Standing here, among these blocks," she murmured, "it feels like someone's thrown a net over me, and there are hidden barbs among the knots." Zhara looked thoughtful as she studied the carvings on each of the stone structures. "What are these?" she asked. "The same glyph is traced on each of them." She slowly turned around as she counted. "Twelve in all."

"I don't know." Han moved to the center of the blocks, where an enormous circular piece of white marble was embedded in the dirt floor. He sat back on his haunches, studying it closely. The same symbol as the one on the hatch upstairs was carved into the smooth surface, along with a myriad of other glyphs in the Language of Flowers. If Jiyi were here, she probably would have been taking a thousand charcoal rubbings. "Look," he said. "I keep seeing that symbol everywhere. I wonder what it means."

Zhara went to look over his shoulder, then cringed, nearly tripping in her haste to get away. "That pulling—that grasping feeling is strongest here." She eyed the marble slab fearfully. "There's . . . something beneath that stone," she said slowly. Then she shook her head. "No, there's nothing beneath it."

Han was bewildered. "Which is it? Something or nothing?"

She retreated toward the granite blocks. "It's a nothingness that has its own presence," she whispered. Her eyes widened in wonder. "It's . . . the void."

He looked at her with concern; the nonsense made her sound like a soothsayer or some of the broken-minded wanderers down in the Pits. "I don't follow," he said carefully.

Zhara took his hand. Every part of his body sang at her touch, a jubilant shout of joy, and Han struggled to keep his expression under control. "Do you feel that?" she asked.

"Y-es," he cracked.

"That resonance between us," she said. "The chaos in our blood?"

Chaos was perhaps too accurate of a description of what was happening to Han's blood, but he swallowed hard and strove to keep his cool. "Yes," he whispered, stepping in close. He felt the inexorable pull of gravity between them, trying his best to resist falling into it and making a fool of himself.

"That's the void."

Well, that put a bit of a damper on his enthusiasm. "Why, Mistress Brandy," he said lightly, in order to disguise his disappointment. "How romantic."

She chuckled. "The void is where magic begins," she said, repeating the lessons the courtesan had taught her. "The place of potential." Zhara turned back to the structures, her expression growing serious. "This . . . white stone *radiates* nothingness," she said with some surprise, then went still.

"What is it?"

She swallowed. "Didn't Jiyi say this was a place of demon summoning as well?"

Han looked down at the slab of white stone, then at the granite blocks around him. "You think," he said hoarsely, "that this is where the ancient magicians of Changxi used to summon demons?"

"Perhaps," she said. "But whatever this place is, it is drawing magical energy toward . . . *that*." She pointed toward the slab beneath his feet and he leaped aside. "Swirling around that—that lodestone." She circled the carving. "Is it just me, or do these carvings seem newer to you?"

He hadn't even noticed there were other carvings inside the ring of the bisected circle. Zhara was right; the bisected circle looked weathered and worn by time, as though thousands of other hands and feet had crossed paths here before, but just inside the circle was another set of characters, the lines and strokes sharper and cleaner, as though they had been made more recently.

"I think it's a spell," she said. She groaned. "I wish we had something to make rubbings with so we can bring it back to Jiyi."

Han took it upon himself to examine the marks more closely. "What do you think these are for?" he asked Zhara.

Her eyes swept around her at the rectangular structures. "Markings for an altar?" she suggested weakly. "Did ancient magicians perform some sort of sacrifice in their rituals?"

"You're asking the wrong person." He studied the groove running near the tops of the blocks and was even more convinced that there were lids fitted on top of them. Curious, Han pressed his palms against the top and pushed. It moved, but barely. The lid was heavier than he'd thought, and he reminded himself not to skip squats the next time Teacher Kang assigned them. With a grunt, he managed to topple the lid to the floor with a thud that echoed throughout the cavern.

The first thing he noticed was the smell. That sickly sweet stench was unbearable and he buried his nose in his sleeve, eyes watering.

The second thing he noticed was the body.

"Oh," Zhara said weakly. "These aren't sacrificial tables or altars." A look of horror dawned on her face. "They're *tombs*."

"Well," Han said weakly, "I think we've found our missing magicians."

24

THE SMELL THAT WAFTED UP FROM THE casket was dreadful—sour, sharp, and sweet all at once. Zhara coughed and threw her sleeve over her face. Beside her, Han choked, trying not to retch as he leaned over the tomb, scanning the remains for signs of life.

"Are they—are they dead?" she asked.

"I think so," he said grimly.

Zhara swallowed down her bile. "Do you know how they died?"

He shook his head. "There are so many bodies in here," he said, voice shaking with horror.

Screwing up her courage, Zhara stepped forward to take a look for herself. The open casket held the remains of several different corpses in varying states of decay. She recognized the blue-and-white-patterned wrap and the red-beaded bracelet on the topmost corpse. Dieu.

"Oh, Thanh," she whispered. "I'm so sorry."

By the looks of things, the boy's mother had not been dead for very long. Her body, though gaunt and emaciated, was still whole, and her clothes were still fresh. The forager lay supine in the casket, surrounded by bones, with her eyes closed and hands crossed over her chest.

"They almost look like they're sleeping," Han said in a tone of discomfort.

Zhara had to agree. If it weren't for the dry, gray tinge to Dieu's skin and the withered, wasted look to her mouth, she could almost believe Thanh's mother would wake up at any moment.

"We should . . . we should say something," Han said awkwardly. "Some prayer to send their soul back to Do."

"The Buri don't believe in the place of beginnings and endings," Zhara said softly. "They believe in the Great Wheel, and that their earthly vessels must be burned before they can be returned to the cycle of rebirth." She studied Dieu's face, which looked at peace in its final repose. "We should probably bring her remains back with us."

Han glanced to the other eleven coffins in the chamber. "I don't know about you," he said with a wince, "but I somehow doubt Captain Shang would appreciate us using his barge to bring corpses back to Zanhei with us."

She couldn't gainsay him. "All right," she said reluctantly. "Let's open the rest of these caskets and see if we can't at least identify them to inform their loved ones of their final fate."

Han braced himself against the next tomb. "Hold your breath," he warned as he slid the lid off. This casket didn't smell quite so terrible as Dieu's; its topmost inhabitant was a desiccated skeleton.

"I—I think this person was a palace official," Han said in a strangled voice. Zhara peered around his shoulder for a closer look. The skeleton was dressed in disintegrating rags that might have been silk. The warped and wasted remains of their golden, embroidered patch of office rested on their chest beneath their hands, and the stiff, rectangular, tortoiseshell belt that was part of an official's regalia was still intact. Han fell to his knees and began rummaging through the bones.

"Han!" she said in alarm. "What are you doing?"

"Looking for their personal seal," he said. "I need to know who this person was."

"Do you . . . do you have an idea who they were?" she asked quietly. She suspected he did.

Han closed his eyes. "I don't know for sure," he whispered. "But I'm afraid it's . . . I'm afraid it might be Uncle Li."

His magician cousin. The one who had gone missing. The one who had been in possession of *Songs of Order and Chaos*. Zhara placed a comforting hand on Han's shoulder.

"Help me look," Han said, looking at her with desperate eyes. "Please."

Zhara eyed the spells carved onto the lids and sides of the tombs; these caskets were clearly some sort of enchanted vessels created to funnel energy from magicians, and the thought of climbing in one didn't strike her as particularly safe.

But after a moment Han got to his feet, clutching a jade medallion in his hand. "It's not Uncle Li," he said, half relieved, half regretful. "This is a seal from the Ministry of Interior Affairs. Uncle Li worked as my m——the Royal Consort's astrologer."

Zhara gingerly took the medallion from his hands. The stone was cool, but it wasn't tainted with demonic essence like the waters of the cavern. "Do you know the person this belonged to?" she asked, turning it over. Inscribed on the back was the name *Chow Danzhi.*

"No," Han said. "But when we get back, Xu and I can check the archives in the Ministry of Records to see when they disappeared." He took the medallion back and tucked it into his sash before turning to the skeleton. "My apologies for disturbing the minister's rest," he said with a bow.

She gave him a sidelong glance and gently nudged him with her elbow. "Say a prayer to send their soul on to Do."

"Me?" He looked around. "Here?"

"You suggested it before," she said. "With Dieu."

Han shifted on his feet. "All right." Straightening his shoulders, he held his hands outstretched over the skeleton of Chow Danzhi as Zhara had seen the death nuns do at funerals. He cleared his throat. "*In Do, all things begin and all things must end,*" he declaimed stiffly. "*Man, born of both Order and Chaos, returns to the cauldron of consciousness to become one with Do. Farewell,* Chow Danzhi, *may your ghost know peace.*"

He clapped his hands four times, and the two of them got on their hands and knees and pressed their foreheads to the floor, sending off the official's soul to the place of beginnings and endings. "Was that a real prayer?" Zhara asked as they got back to their feet.

"Ahaha," Han said, rubbing the back of his head. "I might have, er, just made that up."

Zhara smiled. "It was beautiful," she said sincerely. "Like a poem."

"Truly?" He looked surprised.

She shook her head. "Come on," she said. "Let's see if we can't help any of the others find peace."

The next casket revealed another Buri forager in a much more advanced state of decomposition than Dieu. Both Han and Zhara threw their sleeves over their noses, choking as the stench of rot hit them in the face. She didn't want to look too closely at the body, then berated herself for being such a coward. But there wasn't much to identify them with—the blue-and-white-patterned wrap they wore was similar to Dieu's, but they had no other distinguishing marks or jewelry.

The next casket revealed another skeleton wearing what looked to be the remains of a gown at the top of the bone pile. The silk had long since rotted away, but several pieces of jewelry remained—strands upon strands of turquoise and jade, a golden ornamental hair comb, and several rings about their fingers. Han and Zhara got on their hands and knees and pressed their foreheads to the floor to send this soul on to Do as well.

"I wish we knew their name," Han fretted. "Who knows what hungry ghosts we might have unleashed by opening up these tombs?"

Boom!

They froze, looking at each other in alarm. A resounding thud shook the cavern, the echoes bouncing and building off each other until they could no longer tell from which direction it had come.

"What was that?" Zhara whispered. Her magic immediately sprang to life, its power running down her ki pathways, hovering at her fingertips.

They say these ruins are haunted, Captain Shang had said. *But it is not the dead that worry me.*

"I don't know," Han whispered back, large eyes even wider with fear. He raised his gaze to the cavern ceiling and pressed his palms together. "O Lion of the South," he said. "Please protect us from the devouring dead." Then he sneezed.

Prrrt?

Two glowing eyes appeared in the shadows among the glittering stone pillars. "Sajah!" Zhara cried. "There you are!"

The ginger cat materialized out of the darkness, his bell ringing as he made his way toward them on padded feet. "This wasn't the fearsome protector I had in mind, O Lion of the South," Han muttered stuffily.

Sajah scowled and swiped at his ankles.

Zhara held her breath, listening for another thud in the darkness, but all she could hear was the faint *plink plink plink* of water dripping somewhere. After a moment, she let out a sigh of relief. "It likely wasn't anything," she said, although doubt niggled at the back of her mind. "Let's move on."

They opened the rest of the coffins, each containing the remains of many magicians. Han and Zhara said prayers for those they could and made note of any identifying marks on the bodies to bring back.

"I'm sorry," she murmured to each magician as she and Han bowed to pay their respects. "I'm sorry the deceased one did not get the farewell they deserved." The tears that leaked from Zhara's eyes were as much from sorrow as they were from the overpowering smell of putrefying flesh. "I wish we could grant them peace."

"We'll go to the temple when we return to Zanhei, and find a priestess of Do to perform the last rites." Han laid a gentle hand on the small of her back and she tried not to flinch. He quickly withdrew his hand and she felt emptiness where his touch had been. "They can say their prayers, even without a body."

They had come at last to the final coffin. With some trepidation, Zhara helped Han open it, fearful of what might be inside.

It was a child.

She gasped and covered her mouth, feeling tears prick and sting her eyes. Like Dieu, they seemed to be asleep, pink still in their cheeks. The child was so young, perhaps the age she had been when the Kestrels took her father away. Who were they? Did they have anywhere to go? Did anyone miss the child the way she had always wanted someone to miss her?

"I think—I think this is my brother's friend," Han said softly. "Yao. A kitchen maid's son." Gently, he reached down into the casket and pushed the boy's head to the side, revealing a large, purplish birthmark on his collarbone. "It is." His voice was heavy.

The child pursed his lips.

"Han," she said, grabbing his arm. "I think—I think he's still alive."

"I don't know," Han said dubiously, watching the hands clasped over the chest. "I'm not sure he's breathing." He leaned over the lip of the casket and held two fingers beneath the child's nose. "Hold a moment," he said excitedly. "I think I felt a breath!" He gently shook the boy's shoulders. "Yao!" he said. "Yao, wake up!"

The boy did not move, did not react to the sound of Han's voice. Zhara reached down to take his hand. "Yao," she called. "It's all right. You're safe."

It was only then that she realized something was deeply, dreadfully wrong. The boy's meridian pathways were drained of his magic, as though something had siphoned off his power. But beneath that sense of emptiness was a deeper sort of void.

Chaos.

Corruption.

Yao opened his eyes and hissed. Zhara jumped and dropped his hand, as a sudden drop in pressure made her ears pop. The boy crawled out of the tomb and began convulsing on the dirt floor of the cavern, fur erupting from the skin along his spine. Grotesque cracking, popping, and stretching noises bubbled up from the boy's body as he suddenly tripled in size.

Zhara stumbled and fell back.

Abomination.

25

WHERE A CHILD HAD BEEN WAS A monster, twice the height of a grown man, bow-legged and ape-armed, with bulging, rippling muscles. Gray fur covered the creature from head to toe, and the boy's legs transformed into a wolf's, with paws sporting foot-long claws. The head was long and snoutlike, with enormous tusks protruding from its mouth, and six red, glowing eyes bubbled up along the bridge of its nose, opening and closing as they appeared.

"Zhara!" Han shouted.

Scrambling to her feet, Zhara ran for the pillars as Yao roared behind her, shaking the very foundations of the cavern. Rocks and pebbles crashed down about her head, shattering into dust. The abomination ran clumsily but swiftly, using its apelike arms to propel its legs forward. The claws that sprouted from its knuckles scraped along the ground as it chased her, scoring deep ridges into the earth.

"To the left!" Han called. "Left!"

She threw herself to the left and tripped, falling to her hands and knees. Yao leaped toward her and she rolled away, just barely missing being raked by the monster's enormous claws.

"Toward me!" Han stood in the middle of the cavern, frantically waving his arms. In his right hand he appeared to be holding an ancient, rusted blade. Zhara hauled herself to her feet and ran toward him, lungs bursting.

"Where—on earth—did you—get—that?" she panted, pointing at the sword.

"Does it matter?" he cried, standing between her and the abomination.

"It was buried with one of the bodies." He brandished it at the monster. "Stand back!"

For the briefest moment, the creature paused. Six red, glowing eyes stared back at them, blinking all at once as though it understood Han's words. Then the monster threw its head back and roared, showing a mouth full of rows upon rows upon rows of razor-sharp teeth.

Han roared back, holding his blade with both hands.

The abomination paused as though taken aback.

"I can't believe that worked," Han murmured.

A piercing ray of light struck the creature in the face and it threw its arm up with a cry of pain. Zhara and Han shaded their own eyes, trying to figure out the source.

Mrrrow!

Out of the shadows a reddish shape came flying, hissing and scratching at the abomination's face. As her eyes adjusted to the brightness, Zhara could see a cat furiously tearing at the creature's head with its claws.

"Sajah!"

"Zhara! Han!" Two silhouettes cut through the shaft of light, and she turned to see Jiyi and Xu running down the stairs. They must have been able to open the hatch.

"Oh, Immortals preserve me," Xu stammered upon seeing the monster in the cavern. "I knew coming down here was a bad idea."

"Shut up and come help us!" Han yelled.

"With what? My fan?"

Jiyi reached into her satchel and withdrew two flasks. "Watch your heads!" she called, hurling them toward the abomination.

Her aim was good, striking the creature in the chest. The ceramic flasks shattered, coating the monster with a dark liquid that smoked and bubbled. The abomination stumbled backward, howling with pain as its skin blistered and burned. Han leaped forward and slashed at its legs with his blade, causing it to trip and fall. He lunged forward to drive the tip into the monster's heart, but a gargantuan hand came up and swatted Han away, sending him flying across the cavern. He landed with a rather sickening thud before sliding to the ground, limp and lifeless.

"Han!" Zhara cried, running to his side. She dodged another swipe of the monster's claws and kneeled beside him, her fingers seeking out his pulse. He stirred and groaned beneath her touch.

"I'm fine," he ground out between clenched teeth. "Just a little bruised. My ego, that is."

"Leave him!" Jiyi screamed at her. "Focus on the abomination!"

Zhara snatched up the fallen blade beside Han and held it before her with shaking hands. The weapon was old, the steel pitted with rust and overuse.

"Not the sword, you idiot!" The courtesan dodged the creature's attacks, nimbly leaping from one side to another. The abomination roared and brought a hand down to smash one of the granite caskets, showering them all with bits of rock and stone. "Your magic! You are the only one of us who might be able to stop this thing!"

Xu ran to Zhara's side, taking the sword from her hand. "I'll protect him," they said, holding the blade inexpertly in their grip. "Go."

She reached for the magician's brush tucked into the back of her sash as she ran toward the abomination, quickly sketching the character for *fire* in the air.

Nothing.

"The void, the void!" Jiyi called in exasperation. She grabbed her satchel as the monster swung at her head, tripping as she ducked. Several small ceramic flasks rolled out from the bag as she frantically tried to recover them. "Reach through the void and *shape* it to your desire!"

Zhara dared not close her eyes to concentrate, and tried her best to recall the lessons she had had with the courtesan on Captain Shang's barge. But her mind was blank, filled only with the horror of facing down an unholy creature whose very existence defied reason. Her magic rioted and roiled within her, and she didn't know which was more terrifying—the abomination or the unpredictability of her power. The brush felt flimsy between her fingers, the wood fragile against the power of Tiyok.

"Jiyi!" Xu cried as the monster lurched toward the courtesan still scrabbling and scrambling for her flasks on the ground. Thinking quickly, Jiyi threw a handful of dirt in its face, but six translucent, membranous eyelids slid down to protect its eyes. The creature opened its enormous maw wide and roared, leaning forward to swallow the courtesan whole. A tall figure suddenly appeared before Jiyi, barreling headlong into the abomination and knocking it onto its side.

"Your Gra—you imbecile!" Xu hollered. "How am I supposed to get you to your majority alive when you're *trying* to get yourself killed?"

"Payback!" Han crowed, taking a large rock and smashing it repeatedly against the creature's head until it went limp. "Although," he said, ruefully rubbing his shoulder, "I didn't think payback would hurt so much."

Jiyi pulled out a length of rope from her satchel and tossed one end to Han. "Now's our chance," she said. "Tie it down."

Han wound his end around the abomination's snout and yanked it tight while the courtesan made short work of its hands and feet. A twinge of pity stabbed Zhara through the gut; that monster had been a human child once, a little boy whose only flaw was that he was a magician. Despite the snout, the claws, the fur, and the six eyes that were half open with pain, all she could see was a little boy in a palace attendant's uniform.

"Zhara!" Jiyi cried. "Now!"

She stumbled forward with the brush held before her. "What—what should I do?"

"I don't know," the courtesan said irritably. "Something. Anything! Fire's as good a spell as any." The abomination began to stir and strain against its bonds. "Hurry before it breaks loose!"

Zhara placed the tip of her brush against the monster's fur, hand trembling so hard she could scarcely tell if she even wrote the glyph correctly. "There is no magic but intention," she murmured, and thought *flames.*

Nothing happened.

"I don't mean to rush things," Xu said from a healthy distance away, "but it appears as though the creature just managed to break the restraints about its snout."

Han and Jiyi pulled harder on the ropes. "The void!" the courtesan shouted. "Think of the void!"

But the void had no meaning for Zhara. What she knew of magic was a positive force, not a negative one. A presence, not the *absence* of anything. She felt magic bursting along the seams of her very being, pushing at her eyes, her skin, her hair, searching for a way out. Hesitantly, she held her hand out over the creature. There was a snapping sound as the rope holding the creature down began to fray.

"Zhara," Han said warningly. "We can't hold on much longer—"

With a roar, the abomination broke free, sending Han and Jiyi head over heels in opposite directions. Zhara fell backward as the creature advanced, looming menacingly over her. Her eyes met theirs, and although she knew it was hopeless, she couldn't help searching for some bit of humanity—of the child—left in its gaze.

There was none, only the void and Tiyok.

The abomination opened its maw in a monstrous grin.

Mrrow!

Sajah came soaring to her rescue, claws sinking into the creature's myriad red eyes. Its shriek echoed throughout the cavern, dislodging a rain of pebbles and sand. The monster blindly lashed out with its claws, catching Zhara across the cheek and sending the brush spinning into darkness. She got to her hands and knees to look for the writing implement when Sajah gave a warning cry. She had the barest moment to think before a giant hand came crashing down beside her. Another yowl, another roll, another crash.

"Zhara!"

She could hear Han's voice, but she couldn't see anything except the rise and fall of furred hands swinging at her head. Her legs burned, her lungs burned, her entire being felt as though she were on fire even though the flames merely lurked beneath her skin. She could feel each of her movements growing slower, heavier—

"Zhara!"

An enormous paw came down and she thrust her hands out before her, too tired to scramble out of the way. Her palms caught the creature's wrist as the claws came within a hairsbreadth of her throat.

Her magic exploded.

There was a howl of pain as Zhara went up in flames, as fire leaped to her skin, as her power finally burst free. The abomination staggered back, clawing at its fur with screams of agony. Zhara looked down at her hands as the flames flickered over her skin, causing all the shadows around her to dance. Out of the corner of her eye, she could see Han's wide, round eyes, Xu's open-mouthed gape, and Jiyi's astonished brows.

"H-how—" the courtesan croaked.

The monster recovered from its burns and lunged forward. The fur of its hands was singed and smoking, and Zhara just barely missed being impaled upon one of its claws as she dove to the right, out of its reach. She waved her arms at it frantically, as though trying to chase off a wolf in the fields. It snarled and cowered, crouching down as it creeped toward her. In the light of her fire, she saw that two of its eyes were shut and bleeding where Sajah's claws had injured it.

"Just burn it!" Xu yelled. "Grab ahold of its arm and don't let go!"

Zhara leaped back, avoiding swipes of the abomination's claws. "You try it then!" she cried.

"Come on!" Han jumped to his feet, picking up the remains of the rope. "We have to figure out a way to restrain it."

"We tried that already," Jiyi said. "And see how well it worked?"

"Zhara didn't have her magic fire-hands going then," he said, casting about for an idea. "Here!" He pointed to two crystalline pillars. "Set up a tripwire and *boom!* While it's down she can crisp the creature to a char."

Jiyi and Xu took the rope from Han's hands and ran to lay the trap. "This way!" Xu waved. "Bring the abomination over this way!"

"Again," Zhara said through gritted teeth, dodging left and right, "you're welcome to try it yourself." She was being backed into a corner, and if she didn't make a play soon, she was going to find herself between a rock and an enormous monster. Desperate, she caught Han's eye and he leaped for the ancient blade that had been tossed aside earlier.

"Yah!" he hollered, rattling his weapon at the creature.

But the abomination ignored him, pressing on toward Zhara.

"Yah!" Han yelled again, and this time, he hurled his sword like a hatchet, blade over hilt.

It glanced harmlessly off the creature's hide.

Zhara had run out of room. Behind her was the cavern wall, and to either side were large rocky outcroppings too cumbersome to clamber over quickly. She covered her face with her hands, feeling the heat of the fire against her cheek.

Jingle, jingle.

Sajah slithered in to stand between Zhara and the abomination with a hiss, the fur along his spine raised and his tail puffed out. To her surprise, the monster paused, as though fearful of the scrappy little house cat, and shuffled awkwardly away. For a moment, Sajah's body seemed to ripple. Zhara couldn't tell if it was a trick of the light or a heat mirage from the flames engulfing her hands, but Sajah seemed to grow in size—a thick, luxurious mane bursting from the ruff around his neck, his tail tripling in width to fan out like a peacock's tail.

"Zhara! Go!" Han yelled.

She dove for the opening between the creature and the rocky outcropping to her right, tumbling head over heels before getting to her feet and running for Xu and Jiyi. Behind her, the abomination roared in confusion before turning around to lumber after her in the semi-darkness.

"Over here!" Xu beckoned.

Zhara pumped her legs harder, crossing the pillars where the trap had been laid before bending over to catch her breath.

"Get ready," Jiyi muttered to Xu as the abomination lowered its head, feet scratching the floor as it prepared to charge.

With a cry, the creature lurched forward on all fours, galloping toward them.

"Will the rope hold?" Xu asked fearfully.

"Pray to the Lucky Star it does," Jiyi said. "Now!"

The two of them snapped the rope taut between them, catching the abomination about its knees. It tripped and fell to the ground with an earthshaking thud. Jiyi threw herself atop the creature's back, bellowing at Xu and Han to help her.

"The arms, the arms!" she cried. "Keep the arms pinned down!"

Han grabbed the abomination's wrist, straining with all his

considerable strength to prevent the claws from doing any more damage. On the other side, Xu stood on a ledge, feet braced as they pushed at a boulder with their back, the scraping noise grating on Zhara's ears. It teetered before tumbling down and crashing onto the monster's other wrist with a stomach-churning crunch. The creature screamed in agony, thrashing about even harder.

"Now, Zhara, now!" Han yelled, hanging on to the abomination's arm for dear life.

She rushed toward them, hands outstretched. The abomination cringed as she approached, its uninjured four eyes blinking against the light. For the briefest moment, Zhara held its gaze, and for the first time, she saw the hint of fear in its face. She hesitated, thinking of that little boy with the purplish birthmark on his collarbone. He had looked at her with such an expression of fear when he transformed, and she couldn't help wondering if he was still looking at her now.

"What are you waiting for?" Jiyi screamed. "Kill it!"

By now the abomination had gone quiet, as though resigned to its fate. Zhara's heart caught in her throat, pity squeezing it tight. That little boy might be a monster now, but he had been just a magician once. An unlucky one, to be caught in a demon's clutches.

"I'm sorry," she whispered. "I'm so, so sorry."

Then, taking a deep breath, she placed her burning hands on the creature's chest.

It roared in pain, making her ears ring. The skin around its chest cracked and blistered, but something else was happening. As the fur burned away, beneath the raw and weeping hide was not flesh, but another body. The abomination began to shrink in size, its claws retracting, the red eyes disappearing.

"Wh-what's happening?" Xu asked.

Where her palms met the abomination's flesh, Zhara could feel their magic connecting—hers and the abomination's. Along their meridian pathways she could feel the flow of power cycling between them, and the memory of the night she fought Thanh returned to her. She'd had little control over what she was doing then. The need to survive had ripped the magic straight out of her, transforming the darkness within Thanh back to light, turning a monster back into a human. But now that she could *see* the flow of energy between her and the abomination who had once been Yao, she knew what to do. Closing her eyes, she let herself burn away the corruption.

When she pulled her hands away, a naked little boy lay where a monster had been.

But when she raised her eyes, her friends were looking at her as though *she* were the monster. Zhara drew back, feeling the eyes of the others on her—Xu's incredulous, Jiyi's disbelieving, and Han's . . . she dared not look at Han. She could sense the smile on his face, and she was afraid to look at him, afraid to read more into that smile than was truly there. She turned her focus to her hands, the fingertips still smoking, the lines of her palms glowing with a faint, pinkish glow.

"How did you do that?" Jiyi demanded. "Tell me!"

The courtesan's voice was harsh, but not frightened. Not yet, at any rate. Zhara wasn't sure how Jiyi was going to react when she told her.

"I—I don't know," she said.

Jiyi narrowed her eyes. "Liar."

Zhara flinched.

"Leave her alone," Han said quietly. He stepped forward and took off his outer garment, covering the child on the ground with it. The boy shifted and murmured as though dreaming, unresponsive to Han's gentle attempts to wake him. "She's been through a lot."

"We've all been through a lot," Jiyi growled. "I just want to know *what* it is we've gone through."

"We've fought an abomination, isn't that enough?" Han carefully wrapped Yao in his outer garment and picked him up. "We can answer questions once we get back to Zanhei and the rest of the Guardians of Dawn."

"No." The courtesan slammed her bag down, heedless of the ceramic flasks and equipment she had brought with her. "I need to know who—or what—we're bringing back to the city. So tell me what happened, Jin Zhara. Now."

Zhara's spirits sank, dread and disappointment clenched tight about her heart, making it difficult to breathe. All her worst fears were about to come true; she could see judgment written all over Jiyi's beautiful features. *Monster,* it said. *Aberration.* "I—I changed the boy back from monster to human."

"I saw that," Jiyi said icily. "But what I want to know is *how.*"

She bit her lip. "I—I burned away the emptiness," she stammered. "In the boy, I mean."

"With magic," the courtesan said skeptically.

"Yes." Zhara brought her hands to her solar plexus. "I . . . feel my power as a living thing," she whispered. "As a force unto itself, not as a—as an ability." She raised her gaze to Han, who gave her an encouraging nod. "That force is like the ki of any living thing, only mine can—can *change* things." She thought of the custard buns and of the wine she had changed into water. "Transform them. Including"— she swallowed, looking to the unconscious child in Han's arms— "monsters."

Jiyi said nothing, and Zhara lowered her eyes to floor, not wanting to look at the courtesan's face to see judgment turn into disgust. Han sneezed and Sajah materialized out of the darkness, rubbing his face against her shins with a purr.

"What you're telling me is impossible, Jin Zhara," the courtesan said in a low voice. "A violation of the natural order."

Abomination. Jiyi didn't have to say it, but the word lingered in the air like the reek of rot and decay. Zhara turned her face away, closing her eyes to keep the tears at bay. The courtesan's words hurt more than she had expected. She wrapped her arms about herself, wanting nothing more than to melt into the shadows, to vanish from her friends' memories.

A slim shadow moved to her side and laid a comforting arm about her shoulders. Zhara looked up to see Xu beside her. "Is it a violation of the natural order?" they asked. "We've witnessed an actual, literal abomination turn back into a human child before our very eyes. If that isn't the restoration of order over chaos, then I don't know what is."

The fear clamped tight about her chest loosened slightly. She lifted hopeful eyes toward Xu, who squeezed her shoulder lightly in response.

Another presence came to stand at her other side, hop-stepping in surprise as Sajah hissed. Han.

"You don't know everything about magic, Huang Jiyi," he said. "You may have grown up around it and you may have studied it, but you still don't know what it's like—not truly—to *have* it. You've admitted yourself that there's so much that's been lost, especially when it comes to"—he gestured vaguely to the cavern—"all this. So who is to say what Zhara can do is impossible?"

There was a silence and Zhara steeled herself to look at the courtesan. Jiyi's expression wavered between uncertainty and fear, the corners of her mouth downturned and firm but her eyes questioning and soft. The disgust Zhara was afraid she would find on her friend's face was absent; instead, there was a yearning sort of . . . curiosity. She realized the courtesan wanted to be swayed, persuaded, convinced. Jiyi wanted to *know,* not condemn. The courtesan pressed her lips together, and Zhara held her breath.

After a moment, Jiyi closed her eyes and shook her head. "Well," she said brusquely. "I look forward to writing a treatise about new discoveries in magic in the future then. Let's go." She turned and headed toward the stairwell leading back to the outside world. She paused on the bottom step and looked over her shoulder. "Are you coming?"

The grip about Zhara's heart vanished entirely, and her body was flooded with a different sort of warmth than that of the flames that had engulfed her before. She tripped after the courtesan, feeling more hopeful than she had in days.

"Wait." Jiyi turned, holding her hands out to Han. "Give me the child. You and Xu stay here."

"What? Why?" He relinquished the boy to Jiyi. Zhara helped Han drape the child over the courtesan's back, taking his outer garment and tying it around the courtesan's waist to help support the boy's weight.

"We need to take him back to Captain Shang's boat before sundown." Jiyi tied the sleeves of Han's tunic tighter about her slender waist.

Xu placed their hands on their hips. "And what about us?"

"You and your friend stay here and take some charcoal rubbings of the carvings." The courtesan pointed to the bag on the floor by their feet with her chin. "There's paper in the satchel over there."

"Why can't Zhara stay with us?" Han complained.

"Because," Jiyi said impatiently, "we don't know how her magic will affect the spells written there. I suspect they're for some sort of demon summoning."

"Then why can't the treasured one stay?" Xu asked. "She's the only one who can even read these stupid carvings."

"Because," the courtesan said, hitching the boy's weight higher on her back, "it's a beautiful day and I want to enjoy my outing while there's still light left. The ruins of Old Changxi are most picturesque, aren't they, Jin Zhara?"

Zhara smiled. "Indeed they are, Huang Jiyi."

"Come on then." The courtesan began ascending the stairs. "And do us a favor and bring a torch, will you?"

She grabbed a torch with an apologetic look at Han and Xu before running after her friend. She lit the torch with her magic, feeling both proud and surprised that she could so at will now.

"Wonderful," Han muttered behind her. "I think I preferred it when they treated me like their mule."

26

NIGHT HAD FALLEN BY THE TIME THEY returned to the docks of Zanhei Port. The journey downriver had been easier on Han's stomach than the one upriver, but perhaps that was due to what he had experienced in the bowels of the volcano's cave system. Like an entire child turning into a monster. Nothing cured motion sickness like a little abomination, apparently.

That was the second time in as many weeks that he had witnessed something so mind-bendingly horrifying. He truly must have been born under the Wanderer's star. Han didn't know what he had done in a previous life to deserve such twisted luck, but it must have been terrible.

Captain Shang had been none too pleased when they returned from the caves with an extra passenger in tow, but shut up when Jiyi shoved another envelope stuffed with cash at him. Yao slept the entire ride back, seemingly none the worse for wear, although they would need to take him to the Guardians to be sure. Han was glad he could bring one piece of good news to his brother, at least.

"I'll take Yao back with me to Wisteria House," Jiyi said once they had docked. "The rest of you are welcome to stay as well. It's late and it's a long walk back into the city after curfew."

Zhara shook her head. "I have to be back before dawn to make breakfast for my family."

Jiyi narrowed her eyes. "Can't they make it themselves?"

Zhara gripped the railing as she disembarked, limping a little as she made her way down the gangplank. "My sister? No. She's blind." Han hurried to her side and offered his arm. She gave him a grateful smile and his insides went missing again.

"Hmm." The courtesan's lips tightened. "All right then. What of you two?" she asked, looking at Han and Xu.

Xu yawned and glanced sidelong in Han's direction. "It all depends on what my pr—what Han wants to do," they said.

Han looked down at Zhara, still clinging to his arm. "I, uh, I'll walk Mistress Brandy home," he said. "I think she hurt herself during the fight."

Zhara's lashes fluttered in surprise. "You noticed?"

He felt the tips of his his ears go red.

"Well then," Xu said, giving Han an encouraging wink. "I'll help Jiyi bring Yao to Wisteria Court and spend the night there."

"We'll reconvene soon to discuss . . . everything." Jiyi yawned. "I'll send a message." And with that, she set off without even a bow of farewell, leaving Xu holding the sleeping Yao in their arms.

"What am I supposed to do with the boy?" they complained. "Carry him all by myself?"

Han clapped his friend on the back. "Time to start working out!" he said cheerfully.

Xu grunted, and Han and Zhara helped them shift the sleeping Yao to their back. "I should hire a magpie," they grumbled, making their way down to the pleasure district.

"Now you, Mistress Brandy," Han said, turning around. He crouched down and presented his back to her.

She stared down at him in confusion. "What are you doing?"

"Climb on."

"A piggyback ride?" Zhara said incredulously. "I'm not a child, you know. I can walk."

"No, no, no," Han insisted. "Take it from someone who's gotten a lot of injuries while working out. You'll want to rest that leg so you don't damage it further, maybe even permanently."

She eyed him skeptically, but after a moment, she hesitantly clambered onto his back.

"Oof," he grunted as he stood up. "You're denser than you look."

Zhara gave him a light smack across the back of his head.

"Aiyo! I mean that as a compliment!" he cried. "It means you have a lot of muscle mass!"

"Is that a good thing?"

"I think so?" Han resettled her weight and wrapped his arms about her legs. It would have been easier to hold her if he could get his hands beneath her thighs, but he was already quivering from such close contact as it was. Any closer and he would dissolve into jelly. "All right, Mistress Brandy. Where to?"

Han didn't want to admit it, but he was getting tired.

When he first made his offer of carrying Zhara home on piggyback, he hadn't realized just how far she lived from the docks, and he was starting to regret his offer. He paused before a particularly steep hill and readjusted his hold on her legs, hitching her forward so she had less of a stranglehold about his neck.

"Are you sure you don't need a break?" she asked for the seventh time. "I can walk on my own for a bit, you know."

"I'm fine," he panted. "This is good for me. I've been neglecting weight training lately."

"If you're doing this to impress me or prove a point, you can just let me down now."

Han knew she was giving him a gracious way out, but his pride dictated that he suffer through the consequences of his decisions. "No need," he said through gritted teeth. "How much farther now?"

"Just a bit."

He could hear the smile in her voice, but ignored it. "You've been saying that for the past several streets."

"I thought you said you've been neglecting weight training?"

He grunted. "Just keep talking to me, Mistress Brandy. Take my mind off the pain." He began climbing the street, thighs burning as he tried to keep a steady, even pace so as not to further embarrass himself.

"About what?"

"Anything," he said between breaths. "Favorite food. The life cycle of crickets. What you think will happen in the next installment of *The Maiden Who Was Loved by Death*. Anything."

"I don't know." She laughed, causing her weight to shift in his arms. "What do *you* think happens?"

"The point is—for you—to talk—not—me." Biceps screaming, he continued trudging determinedly up the hill.

"All right," said Zhara. "I'll ask questions, and you can nod your head for yes or no. Will that work?"

Han nodded and they continued traveling in silence for a while.

"I—thought—you—were—going—to—ask—questions," Han panted.

"Give me a moment! I'm trying to think."

Han gritted his teeth. "Hurry—up."

"All right, all right." She paused. "What's it like living at the palace—no. Sorry, that's not a yes or no question. Are you afraid, living at the palace?"

He nodded. *Yes.*

"Because of your brother?"

He was afraid *for* his brother. *Yes.*

"How did you know about the Guardians of Dawn? No, wait. Sorry, sorry. Let me think." Then, "Are you afraid someone will discover your brother is a magician, or . . . something worse?"

Han walked several agonizingly slow steps before he could think of how to reply. He tilted his head to the side.

"You're afraid that someone will discover your brother is a magician," Zhara supplied.

It was several steps before Han gave a little half nod.

Zhara was quiet for a long moment. "But you're starting to become afraid that he's corrupted," she said in a low voice.

He paused for a breath. *Yes.* He shifted his grip and walked on. He hadn't had a word for it then. He had only known of his brother's night terrors and the frog demon. But now he knew it could be so much worse. Corruption. Possession.

"Is that why you sought out the Guardians of Dawn?"

All he wanted, all he had ever wanted, was to keep Anyang safe. Back then it had been simple. Find help, have someone else take care of it. Just as Xu had done for him all their lives. But Han was coming to realize that intentions were not enough. Not when there was so much at stake.

Yes.

They had crested the top of the hill. The climb was even steeper on the way down, with stairs and railing leading down into the heart of a residential quarter. Han knew from experience that going downhill was worse than climbing up.

"Not long now, I promise," Zhara said. "Unless you want to set me down and catch your breath."

"I'm fine, I just need to adjust my hold," Han managed in a strangled voice.

"Put me down, Master Plum Blossom," she ordered. "Let's take a break." She pointed to a low stone wall a few steps ahead of them, the boundary of a wooded park. "We can sit there for a while, at least until the night watchmen come."

She slid off his back, and he gratefully shook out his arms. He wasn't quite sure when he would get feeling back in his fingers. Han fanned himself with the neck of his tunic—now damp with sweat—and gingerly sat down next to Zhara, careful to maintain a proper distance. Which seemed silly, considering the closeness of the contact between them up until that moment, but still.

"Here." Zhara took his hands and began massaging the circulation back into his extremities, although he wasn't sure how much good it would do if all the blood in his body was going to his face. "Better?"

"Yes," he squeaked, then coughed. "Yes," he repeated, lowering his voice.

Near the entrance to the park, the air was cool and damp, ripe with the smell of green and growing things, and Han felt the tightness of his muscles begin to relax. He took several deep breaths in an effort to slow his pulse. Zhara wasn't using magic or a spell, but he felt ticklish all over just the same.

The hill on which they sat overlooked the river, beyond which they could see the lights of Flower Town. A small, steady stream of wish lanterns floated into the sky from the pleasure district, where vendors had gotten a head start on the Night of the Sevens festivities by selling wishes to tourists. Zhara watched the scene below, both stars and wishes reflected in her eyes. The soft glow from the lanterns warmed her skin, and Han remembered how she had looked when facing down the abomination—Yao—in the caverns of Mount Zanhei. She had been beautiful and awe-inspiring then, but he found her even more terrifying now. An awkwardly ordinary girl. Sitting next to an ordinary boy. On a gorgeous early summer night in Zanhei.

"Pretty," Zhara murmured.

"Yes," he said thickly.

She turned to look at him and he flushed. He fought the instinctive urge to look away, to flee and hide, and forced himself to hold her gaze. Her lips parted, and he found himself drawing close, their faces falling toward each other like gravity, like inevitability.

The image of Princess Yulana swam before his eyes, and he tried to push thoughts of her away. The northern princess was the Royal Heir's betrothed and the Royal Heir's problem, and right now he wanted to be Han. Just Han.

But he couldn't.

He pulled back. He didn't miss the look of disappointment on Zhara's face, and his stomach burned with both guilt and pleasure at once.

"So," he said, clearing his throat. "While we're here, I can answer some more of your questions, if you'd like. Ones that require more than a yes or no answer, that is."

Zhara was quiet for a moment, swinging her feet back and forth. "Master Plum Blossom and I are hardly acquainted," she said softly, her tone suddenly distant and formal. "It wouldn't be appropriate to pry into his private life."

The careful civility in her voice hurt, and he realized then that she had been hurt by his retreat from their near-kiss.

"After all we've shared, you're going to revert to using honorifics?" he said, striving to keep his tone light. "I mean, I've had your legs wrapped around my waist."

She blinked. "I—wh-what?" Even in the darkness he could see her cheeks glowing, and not from magic either. To his surprise and delight, she began giggling, the sound bursting like bubbles of brightness around him.

He grinned. "Who's the innocent one now?"

She shook her head as her giggles blossomed into full-blown laughter. "I'm impressed, Master Plum Blossom," she said, and the familiarity, the intimacy, the warmth was back in her voice. "And here I thought you were afraid of girls."

"Why does everyone say that?" he complained.

Zhara raised her brows. "If everyone says it, then, well . . ."

"Hurry up and ask me something," Han said crossly. "Before I leave you here on his wall by yourself."

She smiled at him. "All right." Zhara turned her face back to the lanterns hovering over Flower Town like fireflies, and once more he caught that look of longing on her face, the one that had snared his heart the first time he saw her outside Master Cao's. "Have you ever been to the Night of the Sevens masquerade ball at the palace?"

"Yes," he said, unsure of where she was headed. "Every year."

"What's it like?" she asked softly. "I've always wanted to go."

He paused. The honest truth was that the masquerade ball was his least favorite part of the Night of the Sevens celebrations. The traditions surrounding the so-called most romantic night of the year seemed ridiculous and performative, done more for appearances than for pleasure. Marriage proposals were common on the Night of the Sevens, as were partner dances where lovers spent the entire evening in each other's arms. On second thought, Han thought he could understand the appeal, painfully aware of the scant inches between their littlest fingers as they rested their hands on the low rock wall.

"It's . . . nice?" He surreptitiously slid his hand closer so that their skin just barely brushed. Beside him, Zhara tensed, but did not pull away.

"Describe *nice*." Zhara laughed, a little breathlessly. "Come, come, Master Plum Blossom, I thought you were a poet."

"Yah, give me a moment," Han said, panicking a little. "I can't declaim off the cuff, you know."

She chuckled. "It's all right," she said. "Just . . . tell me about your favorite part."

He didn't have any. "Well," he said slowly. "It's not directly related to the ball, but . . . back when my mother was still alive, she would take my brother and me to—to the Royal Consort's meditation garden to watch the fireworks." He fell silent as the memory returned to him in waves. "In the northeast corner of the garden was a three-story moon-viewing pagoda," he went on, "and we used to sit there in the darkness while bursts of colored light rained down around us like a shower of stars." Han looked up at the night sky, spangled with the same constellations that he and Anyang used to draw with their fingers as they waited for their father to arrive. "And then, at the end of the night, when his duties were done, my father would sneak away to join us and we would all fall asleep there. Together."

Zhara's hand shifted ever so slightly so that her littlest finger rested over his. "Oh, Han," she said. "That's beautiful."

It was the feeling of her skin against his that brought him out of his reverie. He felt his pulse knocking against hers, his ears burning from both the audacity and the hesitancy of that simple touch. "Yes, well," he said, clearing his throat. "What about you? Why are you so interested in the Night of the Sevens?"

She was silent a long while before she answered. "Because," she said softly, "I was born on the Night of the Sevens." Zhara looked toward the Gleaming River, that milky swath of stars that cut through the heavens like a ribbon of dust and light. On either side were two bright stars, the Fairy Prince and the Woodcutter's Daughter. "I've never had a birthday present," she murmured. "Or if I did, I don't remember. Ever since I was very young, my father and I had been on the run, so there was no time to celebrate my birthday. So every Night of the Sevens I would pretend the celebrations at the palace were for me." She ducked her head, looking embarrassed. "I know it's silly," she said. "I'm sorry, I—"

"I'll take you."

Zhara lifted her head in surprise. "What?"

Han took her hand in his. "I'll take you to the celebrations at the Night of the Sevens. Declare the holiday in your name."

Again, that sensation of closeness, of gravity between them, inexorable and irresistible, pulling their faces together. Mistress Brandy's eyes, her lips, her skin were luminous in the moonlight, and Han wanted nothing more than to close the distance, to touch her, to kiss her.

Their lips brushed, barely more than a breath.

Warmth exploded in his bones, lighting his insides like fireworks on the Night of the Sevens, brilliant, dizzying, terrifying. Han thought of himself as a brave person, but found himself quivering, quaking, shaking, trembling harder than a leaf in a gale.

Zhara laughed as she withdrew. "Who are you that you can so boldly claim to declare a holiday in my name, the Royal Heir?"

The mention of his title brought his mood crashing to his feet. No matter how much he might want to be Han, just Han, there was no escaping who—or what—he was. He pulled back his hand. "I'm rested enough now," he said. "Come on, let's get you home."

They continued on without talking, save for the occasional directions given out by Mistress Brandy.

"Here," said Zhara as they rounded the corner onto a small side street, completely dark save for a small candle shining in the upstairs window of a narrow house at the far end. "That's where I live."

Han looked up at the second floor of her apartments and thought he saw the flicker of a shadow pass behind the rice-paper screen that covered the window. "Someone waiting up for you?"

"No. I sleep in the kitchen on the ground floor." Zhara hesitated at the door. "Thank you," she said. "For the piggyback ride."

He dimpled, and this time, he saw them work their full effect on her. She quickly dropped her gaze, unable to meet his eyes, suddenly shy. Han couldn't help puffing out his chest a little.

"Will you be all right getting home yourself?" Zhara asked.

He nodded, working out the crick in his neck. "It's a short walk to the palace from here."

"All right," she said. "Good night, Master Plum Blossom."

But it was several more moments before Han finally forced himself to turn back and set out for home. When he reached the end of Zhara's street, he paused to glance over his shoulder. She still stood in the doorway of her house, watching his figure grow smaller and smaller in the distance. She raised her hand in farewell, then disappeared into the shadows of her house. Heart buoyant with hope and happiness, Han found his footsteps lighter than they had been in days. He could still feel the touch of her eyes watching him leave and he was glad that, at last, someone could appreciate the view.

27

SUZHAN WAS ALREADY AWAKE WHEN ZHARA CAME bearing the breakfast tray.

"Mimi," she said in surprise. "What are you doing up so early? It's not even dawn." She kept her voice low; the welts on her calves had only just healed from the last time she accidentally woke the Second Wife from a drink-induced stupor.

"I couldn't sleep," Suzhan said, the dark circles beneath her swollen eyes lending truth to her words. She looked almost haggard, but there was a curious serenity to her features, as though she had passed the night in meditation and had come to an epiphany. She sat on her pile of blankets on her side of the partition—a single cotton sheet that served as a makeshift privacy screen—hair loose about her shoulders, arms wrapped about her knees.

Zhara set the breakfast tray before her sister and removed the linen cover that kept it warm—a bowl of congee drizzled with soy sauce and sesame oil, topped with sliced scallions and a tea-soaked egg. "Have something to eat then," she whispered. "Something in the belly should help you fall back asleep."

Suzhan shook her head. "I'm fine, nene," she said, but there was a strange tightening of her voice, as though she were consciously swallowing down words that wanted to be said. "I—I just want to be left alone."

Unexpectedly hurt, Zhara covered the tray once more. "All right, mimi," she said. "I'll be late coming back from Teacher Hu's tonight, but I made duck and fire-lotus-root soup that can be reheated for supper. There's also rice in the steamer."

Her sister said nothing, gazing through the windows. "Will you be meeting them tonight? Is that why you'll be late?"

Zhara was taken aback. "Meeting who, mimi?" she asked in confusion.

"Whoever it was you were speaking with last night."

A chill fell over her bones. "I—I don't know what you're talking about." She realized with sudden panic that she could not hear the Second Wife's soft, even snores on her side of the partition.

"Don't play coy with me, nene." Even though Suzhan could not see in the dark, Zhara felt her sister's eyes fixed on her face. "It sounded like a boy."

"Shhh." Zhara knelt before her sister, wrapping her hands around her wrists to convey her anxiousness. "What about Madame?" she murmured, listening hard to the silence empty of heavy breathing.

"Mama's not here," Suzhan said. "She was out all night too. Doubtless she'll be back from the taverns soon." She tilted her head. "It's all right, nene; you can tell me. Who were you with?"

All the fear and dread Zhara had been holding seeped out of her like water out of a leaking pot. "Oh." That giddy feeling from the previous night returned with a rush. Her blood fizzed and her lips tingled with the memory of Han's near-kiss. She wanted so desperately to share what had happened with her sister, to tell Suzhan *everything*. Happiness threatened to spill over into her daily life, and she needed someone to help her contain it so she wouldn't make a fool of herself to the entire world.

"I—he—" she began, then bit her tongue. What could she tell Suzhan without revealing . . . everything? That she had met Han because they were both involved in a clandestine group of resistance fighters dedicated to magician liberation? The Guardians of Dawn, abominations, possessions, her own magic . . . what could she possibly tell Suzhan without endangering herself, her new friends, and their cause? Without endangering their . . . sisterhood? She had kept her powers secret for so long, she wasn't sure which would be the bigger betrayal—the blindness or the silence. "He—he's a . . . friend," she finished.

"Didn't sound like a friend," Suzhan said softly. "He sounded like a beau."

Again, that flush and flare of pleasure. Zhara pressed her hands to her cheeks, feeling them warm beneath her palms, and willed herself to remain calm. She thought of Han in the marketplace as they fought off the abomination that had been Thanh—the lines of his neck straining, the muscles in his arms flexing as he threw rocks and other projectiles at the monster. The power in his thighs as he leaped away from attacks, the breadth of his shoulders and the slimness of his waist. The feel of that lean muscle beneath her body as he carried her home on his back. "Just a friend," she repeated weakly.

Her sister closed her eyes. "Are you going to run away with him?"

"What?" Zhara clapped her hands over her mouth before she remembered the Second Wife wasn't on the other side of the partition, listening to their conversation. "Don't be ridiculous, mimi," she said. "Of course not."

"Why not?" Suzhan's tone was strange, high-pitched and strangled. "I would, if I were you."

Zhara was taken aback. "Mimi," she said. "I would never leave you."

"Maybe you should," Suzhan whispered. "And live out your happy ending, just like in your romance novels, nene."

Zhara frowned, trying to decipher her sister's curious expression. With a start, she realized that Suzhan's face was no longer an open book to her. "What brought this about?" she asked, her throat tight. When had they suddenly grown so far apart?

Her sister looked away. "Lord Chan," Suzhan said stiffly, "has renewed his offer of marriage."

Immediately, Zhara's hand flew to the silver nugget still in her pocket. In the whirlwind of what was happening with Han and the Guardians of Dawn, she had completely forgotten about her conversation with the Second Wife.

"You knew." Suzhan sounded neither sad nor accusatory, merely resigned. The defeat in her sister's words churned Zhara's gut with guilt.

"Yes, mimi," she said, unable to lie.

Her sister bit her lip. "He wants to meet you."

Zhara said nothing.

"You knew that too." Suzhan faced Zhara again, eyes narrowed. "When were you going to tell me, nene?"

"I—I f-forgot." It was the truth, but it sounded like a lie on her lips.

"Your tongue betrays you," Suzhan said. She closed her eyes, pain darkening her brow.

"I'm sorry," Zhara whispered. She didn't know what else to say.

"I suppose Lord Chan just wants his money's worth," her sister said bitterly. "Two for the price of one."

Your daughter has . . . other assets.

The acid in Suzhan's tone burned, but it burned Zhara more that there was nothing she could say to gainsay her sister. Money—and the want of it—ruled their lives, the tyrant that dictated every step, every move they made. If Suzhan did not marry someone rich, then they would be turned out into the streets to beg for their suppers. Zhara would spare her sister that if she could.

"Run away, nene," Suzhan said softly. "Run away with your not-a-beau while you can. Take your chance."

Zhara tried to imagine what life would be like if she ran away with Han, and to her surprise, she found she could not envision it. Not yet. The future was too much, too big for her mind to encompass. She could only hope for the little things—a look, a touch, a kiss. It had never occurred to Zhara to dream of anything bigger than small pleasures in life; she had never been able to afford anything more.

"No," she said with a shake of her head. "I would never abandon you, mimi. I would never choose my own happiness over you. *Never.* If I run away, I'm taking you with me."

Suzhan gave her a soft smile. "Oh, nene," she said. "Don't sacrifice yourself for me." She fixed her sightless eyes in Zhara's direction, her gaze unfocused yet piercing. "Because I won't sacrifice my happiness for you."

Zhara blinked. "Mimi, what—"

"If I run away," her sister continued in a louder voice, "I'm running away to Jingxi. To the music academy." Her hands plucked at invisible zither strings, the memory of music still lingering in her fingers.

Once upon a time, like any other well-bred girl, Suzhan had received music lessons from the finest tutors in Zanhei. And unlike most other well-bred girls in the city, Suzhan had had a gift. Her last tutor had told them she was good enough to attend the academy at Jingxi, the premier music institution in all of the Morning Realms. Mistress Yifei had forwarded on a letter of recommendation to the academy, and a place had been held for Suzhan. But they could not afford the tuition fees, and of all the dreams they had had to give up as their funds and futures dwindled, this had been the hardest for Suzhan to bear.

"I see," Zhara murmured, an unexpected lump rising in her throat. She reached out to smooth the hair back from her sister's face. "Then I will follow you, mimi. I will follow you to Jingxi and take care of you."

Suzhan brushed Zhara's hand away. "No, don't," she said. "Don't follow me, nene." She shook her head, staring angrily into nothing. "Don't you ever get tired of it all?"

"Of what?" Zhara was almost afraid to ask.

"Of being a good girl." Her sister's lip curled. "Of taking care of an invalid."

"Mimi—"

"No." Suzhan's tone was forceful. "That's my truth. I'm an invalid. And unlike you, I've made peace with it." Her voice softened. "But what about you, nene? What is *your* truth? What is your happiness?"

Tears prickled along Zhara's lower lashes. "I don't know what my happiness is," she said quietly. "I only know that I am happy with you." Unbidden, the image of Han's eyes, large and shining in the moonlight, returned to her. *I'll take you. I'll take you to the celebrations at the Night of the Sevens.*

Suzhan snorted. "That's not your truth."

"Oh?" Zhara was amused. "What is my truth then?"

Her sister's expression was serene. "You want to be loved, nene."

Zhara was taken aback. "But I am loved," she said hesitantly. "By you." She wondered if it was still true.

"Yes," Suzhan said, and it was her matter-of-fact nonchalance more than her words that soothed Zhara's troubled heart. "But you don't want to be loved like that." The slightest teasing smile tilted the corners of her lips. "You want to be loved like Tiny Light or whatever her name is. From *The Girl Whose Lover Died*."

It was a moment before Zhara understood what her sister meant. Then she laughed, the sound wavering and watery in that quiet upstairs room. "*The Maiden Who Was Loved by Death*," Zhara corrected. "And her name is Little Flame."

"Same difference." Suzhan waved her hands indifferently. "All those stories are the same."

"They are not!"

Her sister merely gave her a dubious look.

"They're not," Zhara insisted.

Suzhan shrugged. "The details may differ," she said. "But the endings are all the same."

Zhara supposed she couldn't argue with that. "That's true," she conceded. "A story needs to have a happy ending in order to be a romance."

Suzhan tilted her head as she considered her sister. "Why do you love romance novels so much, nene?"

Zhara wrapped her arm around Suzhan's shoulders, resting her head against her sister's. "I don't know," she admitted. "I suppose . . . I suppose I find comfort in the idea of love conquering all hardships, all obstacles. They give me hope that someday, someone might find me . . ." She trailed off.

"Find you what?" Suzhan asked quietly.

"Worthy," Zhara finished. Sudden shame crawled over her skin and she resisted the urge to pull away and hide her face, even though she knew her sister couldn't make out the expression of embarrassment there.

"Worthy of what, nene?"

"Just . . . worthy." Again, the image of Han's eyes floated through her memory, soft and gentle and concerned as he wrapped his hands around her flaming arms in the caves beneath Mount Zanhei. There had been no fear in his eyes then, only compassion. Only kindness. "Someone of worth."

"Oh, nene." Suzhan said nothing for a long while. "You want to be cherished." She laughed, but it sounded more wistful than mirthful. "You really are an incurable romantic."

Discomfort churned Zhara's insides. "You make it sound as though I'm suffering from some sort of chronic ailment," she said with mock indignation.

Suzhan snorted. "If delusional escapism can be considered a chronic ailment, then yes, you're terminal, nene."

"Ah." Zhara nodded. "Perhaps there is no hope for me. It's true I used to dream a handsome prince would fall madly in love with me and make me his princess."

"Well, Zanhei's Royal Heir is still unwed, so no need to abandon hope just yet."

"He's engaged to Princess Yulana, mimi."

Suzhan raised her brows. "Is he? Well, engaged is not yet married." She smiled. "Plenty of time to make him yours."

"I said I wanted a *handsome* prince," Zhara said severely. "Based on his betrothal portrait, his chin is receding faster than his hairline."

Her sister broke into peals of laughter, as Zhara had intended. The tension dissipated with the darkness as the sun broke the undivided horizon into dawn. "Promise me you'll live your truth," Suzhan said. "For I promise I will."

Zhara held her sister's hand. "I promise."

28

To Han's dismay, when he arrived at the training yard the next morning, there was a crowd gathered there. The second-floor landing was stuffed with curious onlookers watching as Princess Yulana sparred with the captain of the guard. His fencing instructor would have had a field day with her stance and grip, which was—to put it delicately—inelegant. Southern women were not inclined to take up the art of steel, although he knew that northern women rode into battle alongside men in the Golden Horde. Han couldn't tell if the captain of the guard was going easy on the princess for courtesy's sake or if he was merely incompetent—a concerning thought—but she was roundly besting him left and right, dodging the guard's attacks before returning several of her own with ruthless efficiency.

Despite the roughness of her technique, he had to admit that Princess Yulana was good.

Very good.

"Stab me with Wu's blade," Xu said, joining him by the railing. They blew out an appreciative breath. "She's something, isn't she?"

"You've never picked up a sword in your entire life," Han remarked. "How would you know?"

"Oh, I know my way around all kinds of blades, my prince," they said coyly, flicking open their fan.

"But I've never seen you in the training yard."

As though sensing their gaze, the northern princess glanced up at the second-floor landing. Xu gave a little wave of their fingers and winked, flirtatiously fluttering their fan before their face. She rolled her eyes and tossed her ruddy hair, but not before returning Xu's wink with a feral grin. His best friend pressed their hand to their chest in exaggerated mock pain.

"There are plenty of other battlefields on which to engage," Xu said with a sly smile. "After all, Wu was a prodigious lover as well as a prestigious warrior."

"She was?" Han blinked before remembering the Third Immortal was also known for her numerous amorous affairs. "Right." He could feel the tips of ears burn bright red in the morning sun as he turned to his intended bride in the training yard. "Well, Princess Yulana is impressive, I'll grant you, but not really my type."

Xu watched as she skillfully deflected a round of blows from the captain of the guard to a chorus of cheers from the stands, several of them coming from palace handmaidens. "I don't think His Grace is her type either," they murmured.

"Yah," he protested. "I've been told I'm very handsome." He had never cared much about his looks; his face was just another fact of life, as sure as the sun rising in the east every morning. But these days, he had cause to consider whether or not he was attractive to other people, and the thought that his looks might not be appealing to . . . to people to whom he wanted to seem appealing made him panic a little. He brought his fingertips to his lips, thinking of his near-kiss with Zhara last night.

"His Grace is very handsome," Xu said soothingly, patting him on the shoulder. "But the Royal Heir could be the most handsome man in all of the Morning Realms, and I still think the princess wouldn't care."

Han was confused. "What do you—" He watched his intended bride blow a kiss to the gaggle of handmaidens gathered in the stands beside him, who giggled and hid their faces behind their fans. "Oh," he said. "*Oh.*"

"Ha!" The northern princess exchanged several more blows with the captain of the guard before barreling him to the ground, the point of her blade lightly pressed against his throat. The handmaidens cheered, their appreciative applause ringing off the stands.

Captain Yen held his hands up in surrender. "I yield, Your Highness."

Princess Yulana tossed her practice sword to the ground in disgust.

"Is that the best you can do?" she said scornfully. "Soft. All you southerners are soft." She toed her blade with the tip of her leather boot.
"Wood," she scoffed. "Back home we practice with steel."

Her undisguised disdain rankled Han's pride. "Southerners care
about *safety*," he called from the landing. "We care whether our soldiers
live or die before they even reach the battlefield."

The princess tilted her head up to look at him, curly wisps of ruddy
hair peeking out from beneath the brim of her fur-trimmed hat. She
wasn't pretty, exactly, but Han had to admit her unusual hair and
freckles were striking. "If your soldiers die in the training yard before
they reach the battlefield," she replied. "Then they will have proven
themselves unworthy to ride beneath your banner."

"Is there no value to human life?" he challenged.

Princess Yulana held his gaze, eyes beady and hard. "If you truly
valued human life," she said, "then you wouldn't send your men to war
at all."

Although he knew that northerners did not observe formality
in their speech, her intimate tone felt like a slap to the face. As the
granddaughter of the Warlord and the niece of the Gommun Kang,
Yulana would have known this, and yet she chose to deliberately
flout southern courtesies. Han didn't mind a little rudeness, but
this was more than rude; it was insolent. His blood heated with
indignation.

"Fine," he said. "Why don't we go a round ourselves, Princess? Steel
against steel." After his encounters with abominations, Han had intended to practice javelin-throwing, but it appeared as though a change
of plans was in order.

The princess lifted her brows and her expression softened into a
look of grudging interest. "Oh?" she said. "You think your dancing,
southern ways can best me?"

Xu elbowed Han in the ribs. "What is His Grace doing?" they hissed.

"Showing a little southern pride," he hissed back. He straightened and
addressed the northerner in the training yard below. "The priestesses
of Do perform sword dances," he said mildly. "The princes of the south
don't dance with steel." He lifted his chin. "They kill."

S. JAE-JONES

Out of the corner of his eye, he could see Xu smack their forehead with their palm.

Below, Princess Yulana studied him with a furrowed brow, keen eyes taking his measure. Then she threw her head back and laughed. "You're funny," she said in surprise. "This marriage might not be a disaster after all."

Han walked down the steps to the sawdust-covered training floor. "A disaster?" he asked, beckoning to a waiting page to bring him a sword.

She snorted. "If you thought this alliance of political convenience would turn out to be a love match, then you're even softer than I expected."

The page returned with Han's ceremonial sword, a beautifully intricate, ornate . . . and utterly useless weapon. "Not this one," he said, feeling embarrassment creep up the back of his neck. "Get me something a bit more practical."

"Here." His fencing instructor, Teacher Kang, stepped forward and held out his own blade, a slightly battered double-edged sword with a rounded pommel. "For all her forward aggression, she favors the edges of her weapon, not the tip," he said in a low voice. "The princess appears to be more comfortable with something like a saber rather than a straight blade, likely a holdover from fighting on horseback." His tutor nodded toward Han's torso. "Keep an eye on your periphery, but don't be careless with your guard either."

Han accepted the sword from his master with both hands, discovering to his dismay that it was heavier than the wooden practice one and his ceremonial blade put together. He gave it a few experimental swings, testing its weight and balance. Behind him, another page offered the princess a steel weapon of her own, which she confidently twirled about with one hand, showing off her impressive wrist strength. Now that Han was on the training floor, he wondered what on earth had possessed him to offer her a challenge. He was a decent swordsman, and very athletic, but unlike the Warlord's granddaughter, he had never been tested on an actual field of battle. Teacher Kang patted him encouragingly on the shoulder, which suddenly felt very naked without padding or armor.

Stepping out onto the ring, he reversed his grip on his blade, holding the hilt in his left and covering the pommel with his right in readiness. Princess Yulana mirrored his gesture, and the two of them bowed in salute before moving into guarded stances—she holding her weapon in her right hand, he in a defensive posture with both hands on the hilt.

"The match will go until first blood, or until one surrenders," Teacher Kang said. "Are both parties agreed?"

Han and the princess nodded. He hadn't realized just how tall and well-muscled she was until he saw her up close, standing nearly eye level with him. He swallowed nervously.

"Then begin."

She immediately launched into an attack, catching him off guard. He parried clumsily, taken aback by the brute force she was able to wield. Her aggressive fighting style left no room for forethought, only reaction, and all his moves felt clunky and stiff as he fended off her attacks. Above them, onlookers cheered from the stands on the second floor, although he wasn't sure for whom they were cheering.

"Is this the infamous southern style I've heard so much of?" Yulana taunted. "Where is the grace? The elegance?"

Irritation burned his ears, and he sidestepped one of her swipes, hearing the keen edge whistle past his ear. He pressed from her unguarded side, but she was faster than he expected, switching hands to bring her blade to meet his.

"There it is," she said. "The fancy footwork I was told about."

He could sense Teacher Kang watching critically behind him, and above him, he could sense Xu's disapproval radiating from the stands. Regret warred with indignation in his veins; Han was ordinarily quite easygoing, but there was something about the princess's insolent smile that made his hackles rise, even though a rational part of his brain knew there was no just cause for his annoyance.

By now he had gotten into the rhythm of the bout—the princess liked to overwhelm her opponents with a flurry of attacks, leaving them no room to think. Dodging was a better defense than parrying, as she wasn't comfortable with long techniques like lunging, and getting on her flanks afforded better openings, since she tended toward straightforward aggression.

"Are all northerners this slow?" he taunted when he had managed to spin toward her unguarded side once more. "I could run circles around the princess."

"And tire yourself out faster," she returned. She too was getting into the rhythm of the bout and was now standing just beyond engagement distance, anticipating his next move. He feinted to the left before driving forward with the point of his blade in a lunge. The princess easily deflected his attack and clucked. "You're far too easy to read," she said condescendingly. "You wear all your thoughts on your face."

"And his shoulders," he could hear Teacher Kang mutter off to the side. Han shot his master a glare as he engaged the princess in another round of blows.

After a while, he was beginning to feel that the princess was either toying with him or going easy on him. More than once she could have drawn first blood with a flick of her wrist, but pulled back, allowing him to sidestep or parry. He wasn't sure which was worse, her contempt or her pity.

"You're holding back," he said angrily.

"I'm sorry, did you want to get hurt?" she asked, lips tugged to one side in a reckless smile. "My uncle would be most displeased if I accidentally killed my future husband in a friendly duel."

"Uncle?" Their blades crossed with a clang before they sprang apart. "I thought His Imperial Majesty arranged this marriage."

She gave a harsh laugh. "No, my uncle needed a convenient place to dump me so I wouldn't yank the bear claws of the Gommun Kang off his neck."

Han knew little of northern politics, although he did know that the head of each major clan was called the kang. He had always fallen asleep beyond that point in his history lessons though.

"I thought northern women had license to do whatever they pleased," he said, dodging a series of cutting attacks.

Princess Yulana sneered. "We do," she said. "Insofar as it contributes to the good of the kang."

"I thought women could also claim the title of kang."

"They can." She ducked as he took a swing over her head. "And I intend to."

"Then why agree to this marriage at all?"

A strange expression crossed Princess Yulana's face. "It was the safest place Auncle Mongke could think of," she murmured. "Who knows what my grandfather's plans for me would be if he found out what I really was?"

Xu's words returned to him. *I don't think His Grace is her type.* His irritation suddenly melted away in a wave of compassion, and his desire to best her in the training yard vanished. "I see," he said.

"Do you?" For the first time since they met, her eyes turned cold, and Han realized he had mistaken her previous tone for insolence when she was merely being insouciant. "And what would you know, O Prince of Zanhei?"

He flinched as the edge of her weapon passed within a hairsbreadth of his neck. Zhara's face flashed before his eyes, the memory of her soft, full lips parted in surprise after he had nearly kissed her. That almost-kiss had been established on a lie; Zhara did not know who he was. Not truly. To her, he was Li Han, the son of a palace bureaucrat, who had a magician younger brother he was desperate to protect. It had started out as a little falsehood, a tiny seed, innocuous and insignificant. But now that seed had sprouted, blossoming into a sprawling lie he was not sure he could control.

"I know a lot of things," he said quietly. "I know what it's like to have to hide who you truly are from those you love."

She paused, and Han immediately seized upon the opportunity, thrusting at her open side. Yulana sidestepped with a curse and attacked from his left. He fell for her feint, and she dodged to the other side as he stumbled forward, flailing as he tried to block her next blow. He overbalanced and fell to his hands and knees, rolling onto his back to find the point of her blade in his face.

"Ha," she said, breathing hard.

With a groan, he dropped his blade and brought his hands up in surrender. "I yield," he grumbled as the onlookers from the stands burst into applause.

A puzzled expression crossed the princess's features and she glanced down at her side. She fingered a small cut at her side, where the barest tip of Han's sword had managed to score a hit.

"I believe that was first blood," he said, unable to keep the smug grin off his face.

"Ugh," she said grudgingly. "That was a dirty trick, catching me off guard with your soft emotions." She snorted with disgust. "My fault for falling for it, I suppose."

He shrugged as he sat up. "It wasn't a trick," he said, nodding at Xu coming down the stairs to join him. "I meant every word I said."

The princess stared at Han, sharp eyes scanning him for any sign of disingenuousness. "Hmm." She reached a hand down to help him to his feet. "Well played. Shall we call it a draw then?"

"A draw," he agreed as she hauled him rather roughly upright, nearly sending him flying. Xu caught him before he tripped headlong into a pile of sandbags.

"Ugh, the Royal Heir is all sweaty," his best friend complained. They grabbed a cotton cloth and threw it over Han's face. "I would be most grateful if His Grace cleaned himself up." Handmaidens brought forth more cotton cloths and hand towels steamed with rosewater and patchouli while a page returned Han's blade to Teacher Kang.

"You're not what I expected, southerner," the princess said, winking as she accepted a hand towel from a handmaiden. The handmaiden blushed fiercely, hiding her face behind her tray with a giggle.

Han quickly wiped his face. "What was Her Highness expecting, exactly?"

Princess Yulana smirked. "A soft-skinned idiot who's never lifted a finger in his life, not even to feed himself."

"Her Highness is not entirely wrong," Xu said beneath their breath, grabbing another clean cloth to rub the spots Han had missed.

"Yah!" he protested, grabbing the hand towel from his best friend. "I can do it myself. I'm not entirely helpless, you know."

"I was half right," Yulana mused, grabbing his hand and turning it over. "I thought the skin of all southern nobles was as pale and as soft as steamed rice cakes, but you've got some hard-earned calluses, I see."

"See?" Han crowed. "We're not all soft; we're just idiots—wait."

The princess threw her head back and laughed, a full-throated, deep-bellied sound that rang throughout the training yard. A few of the guardsmen shot her a disdainful look, as though her unbridled expression of delight were somehow an affront to their sensibilities. Han looked around to the court ladies—the older ones tight-lipped and sour-faced, the younger ones hiding their feigned expressions of shock and distaste behind brightly colored fans. With some discomfort, he realized that perhaps there was some merit to Yulana's distaste for southerners.

"You're all right, Prince Rice Cake," the princess said. "Perhaps this won't be a disastrous marriage after all."

For the briefest of moments, Han was pleased, as though he had won a victory far more significant than a mere fencing match, then the memory of the near-kiss he had shared with Zhara stabbed him through the gut.

Presently, a page appeared, whispering in Xu's ear as they handed them a message. They unrolled the scroll before quickly crumpling up the message. "Your Grace," they said quickly. "There is a matter that needs his attention."

"Anyang?" Han asked fearfully. He hadn't seen his little brother or Yao since they returned from Mount Zanhei. Xu gave a slight shake of their head and the dread eased a little.

"The Second Heir is fine for the moment," they said. "This pertains to the ah, issue, we've been dealing with the past few days. Yesterday, in particular."

"I see," he said. "I'll be right there." He dismissed the page and turned to the princess. "I'm afraid I must take Her Highness's leave."

She frowned. "Is something wrong?" she asked. Her intense eyes were far too canny for his comfort.

"No, nothing's wrong," Han said brightly. "It's just my brother is prone to, ah, occasional tantrums. It's been hard for him ever since our mother died."

Yulana stiffened. "Ah," she said. "I heard the Royal Consort was a magician. My condolences."

He eyed her with suspicion, unsure whether her condolences were for his mother's death or for the fact that she had died a traitor. "Yes, well," he said. "His brother becoming engaged to the young woman whose grandfather put his mother to death hasn't been too easy for him either."

She narrowed her eyes. "No, I imagine it hasn't."

Han could feel his angry dimples making their appearance and smiled hard to disguise his discomfort. Their previous rapport from the match had dissipated, and the guilt and dread he had felt ever since their engagement was announced returned full force. She was too observant by half, this northern warrior princess. No matter how much he wanted to like her—to be her friend—she was still the Warlord's granddaughter, and her very presence was a blade held to Anyang's throat.

"My apologies, Your Highness." He bowed from the waist. "But I must go." He turned and gestured to the disapproving court ladies on the landing above them. "I'm sure there are plenty of people at court willing to show off the many delights Zanhei has to offer in my absence." He beckoned to one of the older ones, the sternest and most disapproving of them all, and tilted his head toward the sweat-stained princess beside him. "Wei Tianjin," he said, mustering the sweetest, most poisonously polite southern tone he could manage, "I do believe Princess Yulana is in need of a palace chaperone. As the most senior of the court ladies, I believe you are the most qualified to accompany her, as well as show her some of the sights of our illustrious city."

"Of course, Your Grace." The court matriarch bowed her head, the golden flowers of her headdress trembling. "Come, my lady," she said, turning to Princess Yulana with such a look of scarcely concealed disdain that Han felt like applauding. "Let's get Her Highness cleaned up."

His fiancée shot him a sour look as she was escorted out of the training yard, but what made Han uneasy was not the intensity of her glare, but the glint of revenge in her eye.

"So much for avoiding a disastrous marriage," Xu murmured at his side.

29

THE SUMMONS TO MEET LORD CHAN AND the Guardians of Dawn arrived on the same day, and the meetings were to be held at the same time and the same location.

Zhara had been on her way back from getting lunch at the street vendors when a runner from one of the local taverns came to deliver a message from the Second Wife, their breath already stinking of beer and rice wine. "Lord Chan requests the honor of Jin Zhara's presence at Wisteria Court later this afternoon," they slurred as they held out their hand for coin. "Just past the long-shadow hour."

Her hands were laden with plates of black-bean noodles and a few of her favorite steamed cassava cakes wrapped in banana leaves. She had no coin with which to tip the messenger, and neither was she inclined to pay them the silver nugget lying heavy in her purse. "I'm sorry but I have no money," she said apologetically.

"That's all right, pretty little thing," the messenger said, leaning in close with a leer. "I'll take a kiss as payment instead." They shut their eyes and pursed their lips, and Zhara stung them with her magic as they drew near. "Aiyo!" they hissed. "What was that?"

"Perhaps it was a fire wasp," she said in a mild voice. "They're attracted to the smell of fermentation and"—she added wickedly—"their venom is said to cause a painful swelling of the genitals, infertility, and possibly even death."

The messenger's hands dropped to their crotch with a yelp as they scuttled away, and Zhara walked back to the apothecary feeling smug and full of good cheer.

"Message for you," Teacher Hu said without looking up as Zhara entered the shop, brows furrowed as she made lists of stocks that needed resupplying. "From Huang Jiyi. She wants to meet up with you and the others this afternoon at Wisteria Court during the long-shadow hour to discuss her findings from your excursion up to Mount Zanhei."

Zhara froze. "*This* afternoon?"

"Yes." Teacher Hu glanced at her over the tops of her spectacles. "Is something the matter? Ooh, hand that over, child, I'm starving." She reached for the black-bean noodles, rummaging about the myriad drawers for a pair of chopsticks.

Zhara retrieved the utensils from their box beside the rest of their meager cooking implements. "I can't go, auntie," she said. "I have . . . another engagement at Wisteria Court."

The apothecary raised her brows. "Another engagement? What sort of engagement?"

Zhara picked at her noodles, suddenly without appetite. "To meet with my sister's intended."

"You?" Teacher Hu paused mid-slurp. "Why?"

Why indeed? She thought of the strangely familiar stranger making a bargain with the Second Wife in the wee hours of the morning, and of her stepmother's insistence that Zhara accompany her and Suzhan to this meeting. Her stomach churned with dread. *Don't follow me,* Suzhan had said. *Promise me you'll live your truth.* But that was a promise more easily made than kept. "What of you, auntie?" she asked. "Can you meet with Jiyi in my stead?"

The herbalist shook her head. "I promised Meng Grandmother I would tend to the afflicted children today," she said regretfully. "I've been studying the samples of water we drew from the well and attempting to find some sort of treatment, if not a cure, for this blight. There are some remedies I would like to try."

Zhara bit her lip. "What do I do?" she whispered. "I must meet with this Lord Chan."

"Or what?" Teacher Hu removed her spectacles with a frown. "Your wicked stepmother will turn you over to the Kestrels?"

Zhara winced. "No," she said, but her voice was uncertain. "She wouldn't."

"Wouldn't she?" When Zhara did not answer, Teacher Hu grunted with disgust. "What sort of mother holds the knowledge of her daughter's magic over her head as some sort of collateral?"

"It's not like that," Zhara insisted weakly. "The Second Wife saved my life." But that excuse was wearing thin from overuse. "She's given me the clothes on my back, the food in my belly, and the roof over my head. She's given me a home, at great personal risk to herself and her daughter by blood. My sister, Suzhan. An orphan like me can't ask for more, especially a magical orphan girl. I can't ever repay the debt I owe her, so I do whatever I can. Cooking, cleaning, bringing home my wages from my work here with you, auntie."

"So you work like a servant in her household," Teacher Hu said. "That's what your stepmother gets out of this arrangement, as far as I can tell."

"Sh-she c-cares for me." It wasn't until Zhara said the words aloud that she knew them to be a lie. Her tongue had betrayed her yet again, tripping over the truth that lay lodged in her throat.

The apothecary studied her with a pitying expression, and somehow it was the gentleness in her gaze that hurt more than the admittance that the Second Wife did not love her. "Jin Zhara," Teacher Hu said in a gruff voice, "didn't you once tell me you didn't want to survive; you wanted to *thrive*?"

She had. She just hadn't expected Teacher Hu to throw her words back in her face with such kindness. "But where would I go?" Zhara whispered. "What would I do?"

"You could stay with me until you found a more suitable living arrangement," the herbalist said. "Or you could take refuge in the lands of the Qirin Tulku with the other magicians the Guardians of Dawn have smuggled out of Zanhei."

"The Qirin Tulku?"

"The Unicorn King."

Zhara knew of the Unicorn King, which was what the rest of the empire called the spiritual leader of the varied clans of the Free Peoples of the West, who swore fealty to no royal or chieftain, no sovereign but the Sunburst Throne. The Free Peoples alone rejected the

Gommun Emperor's claim after the Just War, and the Unicorn King declared that any magician could claim his protection from the War-lord's justice. "I thought the Unicorn King was some sort of shaman or hierophant," Zhara mused, "not a political leader."

Teacher Hu's lips thinned. "He's not, but as I've said, we live in political times."

Silence fell over the apothecary as Zhara considered the possibility of a life separate from the Second Wife. From Suzhan. *Don't you ever get tired of being a good girl?* For so long Zhara had believed that to be safe was to be subservient, that if she were good enough, well-behaved enough, the world would treat her the way she wanted to be treated. *Be good, little magpie,* Jin Zhanlong had said. *Be good, and be true.* It was the only way she had known to survive. But perhaps she had focused too much on the first part of her father's advice and not enough on the lat-ter. Perhaps the only way to thrive was to be true to her own happiness.

Whatever that was.

Teacher Hu watched as Zhara listlessly poked at her noodles with her chopsticks. "You need not make any decisions straightaway," she said. "Whether or not you attend this meeting with the Guardians of Dawn or with your sister's intended is up to you. Your life is your own."

Zhara said nothing and merely pushed her food around on her plate. She could feel the herbalist's eyes on her, considering her, studying her, pitying her. She almost dreaded hearing what Teacher Hu was going to say next.

"Are you going to eat that?" the apothecary asked hopefully. "Be-cause if you're not, I definitely have room for more."

The apothecary gave her the rest of the afternoon off, which allowed Zhara some time to sort through her thoughts. Teacher Hu insisted she go for a walk to clear her head, so Zhara took the opportunity to wander through the luxury-goods sector of the covered market on her way to Wisteria Court.

The bronze sunburst pendant weighed heavy about Zhara's neck, while the silver nugget weighed heavy on her heart and pocket as she walked past stalls selling mangos and spices from the kingdom of the Sindh, rugs and tapestries from the Dzungri basin, and even glasswork from places beyond the furthermost west. Preparations for the Night of the Sevens were underway throughout the southern provinces, with merchants in the luxury-goods sectors doing extra business selling costumes and accessories to all those looking to celebrate the reunion of the magpie lovers in style. Rumors of who had received invitation tokens that year flew fast and far among the gossip-mongers in the Pits, and the bookies laid odds on who would play the coveted roles of the Fairy Prince and the Woodcutter's Daughter at the palace masquerade ball. Although tradition dictated that all unmarried people in the city were eligible to be chosen by chance in a lottery, the truth was that quite a bit of money changed hands in the lead-up to the festival, the choice for the most eligible bachelor and maiden as fiercely political as any match made by the nobility.

"Although this year the Fairy Prince and the Woodcutter's Daughter are likely to be you and your bride-to-be, aren't they?" Zhara said to one of the Royal Heir's betrothal announcements nailed to the boards in the common. She paused and studied the image of Zanhei's future prince with a critical eye, now that there was no crowd to block her view. Whether or not it was a good likeness, she couldn't say; depictions of the Royal Heir were as varied as the artists who painted them, although there seemed to be a some consistencies—round eyes, large nose, square jaw. A good-looking face, she supposed, if a bit generic. Not nearly as handsome as Master Plum Blossom, although she allowed that he and the Royal Heir had features in common.

"His Grace would be more attractive if he just smiled a bit more," she said to the poster, thinking of the way Han's nose scrunched and his dimples appeared when he laughed. She wondered if the Royal Heir had a sense of humor. None of the portraits did him any favors in this regard, for they all depicted him dead-eyed with no hint of laughter at the corners of his lips. If Han ever did make good on his promise to take her to the masquerade ball on the Night of the Sevens, Zhara hoped to catch a glimpse of the Royal Heir. She had never seen a prince before. She moved on, making her way through the fashion sector toward Flower Town.

The Morning Realms had now entered the season of Greater Heat, and the streets of the covered market were unusually sparse as shoppers spent the hottest part of the afternoon cooling off with drinks in cafés by the canals. Even the Kestrel presence was light, with most northerners taking refuge from the unrelenting afternoon sun by resting inside with their eyes closed.

The glitter of glass beading on white satin shoes caught Zhara's eye. The white slippers with pink-and-yellow water lilies embroidered on the toes she had wanted so badly remained unsold all this time. She touched the silver nugget at her waist. She could do it. She could buy the shoes. She could spend the blood wages from her stepmother and buy an entire outfit to wear to the meeting with Lord Chan.

Your daughter has . . . other assets.

Zhara turned away, grasping the sunburst pendant about her neck—

—and ran straight into someone walking out of a wall.

"Gommun's claws!" the stranger swore. "How—" Their eyes widened at the sight of Zhara. "You!"

Zhara recognized the stranger's hair before registering the fact she was able to see *through* this person to the canals on the other side. A reddish, ruddy color, beautiful and unusual. "You," she breathed. "The not-ghost!"

In the golden afternoon light, the redhead's outline was blurry and indistinct, as though seen through a haze or in a dream. Panicking, the youth turned to flee, but Zhara reached out and grabbed them by the arm faster than thought.

A note sounded in her head, deep vibrations of recognition that resonated through her body, her *magic*. This redhead was a magician, but not like any other magician she had sensed before. And by the expression on their face, the redhead felt it too.

"How—" they both began at the same time.

"You first," Zhara said firmly. "Since I'm still not going to be able to explain why I can touch you, because I honestly don't know."

The youth's eyes darted back and forth. "Fine," the stranger said in a low voice. "But not here. Let's go find someplace private to talk."

Nodding, Zhara linked her arm through the stranger's, fingers gripping tight around the wrist that was both there and not there. The redhead looked amused.

"Now, where I come from, only lovers walk arm in arm like this," the not-ghost said. "I promise I won't run away, you know."

"Shush," Zhara said. She led the redhead to one of lanterned footbridges that joined the covered market with Flower Town. "I'm not taking any chances. I've got you and I'm not letting you get away."

"Smart girl. I am quite a catch, it's true." The youth winked at her and Zhara choked on the Good-Looking Giggles rising unexpectedly in her throat.

"Are you all right?" they asked innocently, in a tone at odds with the knowing expression on their face.

Zhara glared at them and continued marching them toward Wisteria Court in silence.

"Where are you taking me?" the redhead asked. "Isn't this the pleasure district?"

"Yes, there is someone I would like you to meet," Zhara said. She had made her decision at last. "Her name is Huang Jiyi."

"The Ice Princess?"

"You know her?"

"I know *of* her," the redhead corrected. "She's said to be the most beautiful woman in all of Zanhei." They grinned, tongue touching the tips of their teeth. "As a connoisseur of beautiful women, I wouldn't mind seeing for myself."

"Good." The purple-covered gate of Wisteria Court came into view. "Because we're here."

The usual servant led Zhara and her guest into a retiring room where they were served plates of freshly sliced mangos, dragonfruit, and a crisp, white melon-squash from the Azure Isles that Zhara had never tried before, and which was lightly sweet and tasted of honey.

"Mistress Huang is still asleep," the attendant whispered. "She doesn't like to wake before dark."

"We have a word for those sorts of creatures where I come from," the redhead remarked. "Ganshi. They're usually beautiful women who like to the suck the—"

"Yes," Zhara said quickly. "But tell her this is important."

The attendant looked terrified. "With all due respect," they whispered, "I would rather be chopped for chum than wake Mistress Huang before she is ready."

"Please." Zhara dangled the sunburst pendant before the servant. "It's very important business."

Resigned, but no less terrified, the attendant touched their forehead to the floor and retreated to wake the sleeping bear from her den.

"These look delicious," the redhead remarked, pointing to the melon-squash. "They *sound* delicious. That crispness, that crunch! I must remember to try some the next time I am here in the flesh."

"In the flesh?" Zhara repeated. "So you're not really, you know"— she gestured to the other person's transparent form—"here?"

"Well, I *am* here," the youth said. "I'm just not here in my *body*. What you're seeing—and touching, apparently—is really more the *idea* of me than the physical me."

Zhara speared herself another slice of melon-squash with a silver toothpick. "Explain."

"You know, where I come from, we usually ask each other's names and share something to drink before revealing our deepest, most intimate secrets. I happen to be fond of grain spirits."

"You're not corporeal," Zhara pointed out. She took a bite of the melon-squash and was pleased to find the redhead looking rather glum. "My name is Jin Zhara, by the way," she said through a mouthful.

The redhead sighed. "You can call me Yuli."

"Yu Li?" Zhara swallowed. "Is your family name Yu?"

"No, just Yuli. It's a nickname. My surname is, well, let's just say I have a rather famous grandfather who I would prefer people not know about as it tends to color their view of me."

Zhara decided not to press. "All right, Yuli," she said. "What are you?"

"Human."

She gestured for the redhead to continue.

"Magician."

"I figured that," Zhara said. "I knew that as soon as I touched you. But . . . what sort of magic is this? Is this the result of a spell you've created?"

Yuli shook their head. "No, I've always been . . . gifted, ever since I was a little girl. My powers were different, but I didn't know that until I met other magicians. Magic was rather frowned upon at home, you see."

"Yes," Zhara said drily. "Magic is rather frowned upon everywhere throughout the Morning Realms, I'm afraid."

The redhead flinched. "As though I could forget," she murmured. A cloud darkened Yuli's expression, and for a moment, she seemed to fade in and out of existence.

"So," Zhara said quickly. "This . . . idea of you. What is it, exactly?"

Yuli shrugged. "It's literally just that," she said. "Right now, my body, the physical part of me, is sitting in my quarters in the palace, pretending to take a nap. But the rest of me—the part that thinks, reasons, has opinions, and does magic—that's the part you see wandering around."

"The palace?" Zhara was surprised. "Are you part of Princess Yulana's entourage?" She resisted the temptation to ask if Yuli knew Han.

"Y . . . es." The redhead's lips tightened. "Part of her entourage, that's right."

Zhara was amazed. "But I thought . . . I thought all northerners were—"

"Anti-magic?" Yuli grimaced. "Unfortunately, for the most part they are. But I hope to change that when I—when I reach my majority."

"When is that?"

"Next year. I'm seventeen."

Zhara raised her brows. "And how do you plan to do that? The Warlord is sure to kill you if you defy him so openly."

Yuli looked down at her hands, or where the idea of her hands rested on the table. "I have some protections against the Warlord," she said softly. Then, shaking her head, she focused her gaze on Zhara. Her brown eyes were warm, almost a dark bronze or copper color to match her hair. "But enough about me," she said, leaning close. "What about you? Who is Jin Zhara?"

Despite the fact that Zhara knew the physical Yuli was somewhere far away in the palace, the Good-Looking Giggles made their reappearance. She took another enormous bite of the melon-squash and swallowed both the fruit and the Giggles down.

"I—" Zhara paused, finding herself unable to answer. "I'm just an ordinary girl," she said. "No one special."

"Lady Tengri's bollocks," Yuli said mildly. "No ordinary girl can transform air into matter." She waved her hand over the plate of cut fruit, trying her best to pick up a slice of melon-squash. "Have you always been able to do that?"

The word *transform* tickled something at the back of Zhara's mind, stirring the magic in her veins. "I don't know," she admitted. "I never learned to use my magic properly. I'm trying to work my way through *The Thousand-Character Classic* with Jiyi, but I'm afraid I'm not a very good student."

"No one ever taught you how to channel the void?" Yuli asked sympathetically. "Not your parents? Or a close relative?"

Zhara shook her head. "My mother died of a fever when I was very young, and my father was taken by Kestrels and killed in the last purge."

Yuli paused in her attempts to get a piece of fruit in her mouth. "I'm sorry," she said quietly. "So many lives lost," she murmured. "All because of Obaji."

"Obaji?"

But the redhead said nothing.

"Anyway, so what about you?" Zhara asked after a moment. "Did you have anyone to teach you magic?"

She nodded. "My auncle, Mongke. They were exiled from my grandfa—my family home," she said. "Ostensibly because of their identity as dual-gender, but it was really because of their magic."

"They're still alive?" Zhara asked with some surprise. "I thought all magicians in the north had been put to the sword."

Yuli's mouth twisted wryly. "Like I said, my family has some protection from the Warlord's edicts."

Zhara studied her companion. Based on the fineness of her clothes (or the idea of clothing Yuli projected onto herself), she must be some sort of noblewoman. Perhaps a lady-in-waiting to the Warlord's granddaughter herself, if she was in Zanhei with the northern delegation. "What are you doing here?" Zhara asked the redhead. "With the princess's entourage, I mean. Aren't you afraid you'll be discovered?"

Yuli shrugged. "Not really. As to why I'm in Zanhei . . ." She trailed off as though unsure of how to answer. "I'm here to find a book."

"A book? What sort of book?"

The redhead squirmed in her seat. "I'm not sure, to be completely honest. Auncle Mongke is certain it exists, and that it's here in the south. It's supposedly a demonology text."

Zhara frowned. "Is it *Songs of Order and Chaos*?"

"That's it!" Yuli was astonished. "How did you know?"

"Because," she said, "we're looking for it too."

Yuli furrowed her brows. "*We?*"

Zhara fiddled with the sunburst pendant around her neck. Although she was certain she could trust Yuli, she wasn't sure the other Guardians of Dawn would feel the same. "Some friends of mine at the palace," she hedged.

"At the palace?" Yuli cocked her head to the side. "What are their names? Maybe I've met them."

"Han and Xu."

A startled expression crossed the redhead's face, but before Yuli could explain, the doors to the receiving room slid open with a bang.

"Master Cao?" Zhara asked in astonishment. On the other side of the threshold stood the diminutive bookseller, an expression of mingled shock and horror on his face. "What is the bookseller doing here? Have the Guardians—" She choked mid-sentence when she saw that the little bookseller had not come alone.

Standing behind him was a slim, slightly stoop-shouldered figure in green, accompanied on either side by Suzhan and the Second Wife.

"Zhara," her stepmother said sweetly. "How good of you to come early. Get up and greet our guest. Lord Chan, this is my stepdaughter, Jin Zhara. Zhara, this is Lord Chan Gobu, the Chancellor and regent of Zanhei, and my future son-in-law."

30

To Han's eternal disappointment, Zhara was not at Wisteria Court when he and Xu arrived. Instead, the courtesan was alone in her quarters, her rooms in a state of complete disarray. Papers, books, brushes, ink, and empty cartons of what looked to be street food were strewn everywhere as though a typhoon had torn through the place.

"You're not the delivery boy," Jiyi snapped as they entered. She sat at a low desk in the center of the room, slurping from a plate of black-bean noodles with such gusto that Han wasn't sure she was even chewing. Or exhaling. As far as he could tell, it was just one long inhale of noodles. She was surrounded by several stacks of loose-leaf pages, which all seemed in very real danger of being rewritten by Master Xin's famous eight-spice sauce.

Xu wrinkled their nose. "From the looks of it, the delivery boy has come and gone several times already." All around the courtesan were half-finished pots of tea and the remains of candles burned to stubs, and by the rumpled state of her hair and clothing, it was evident Jiyi had been up all night working on her treatise on new discoveries in magic. "Do they even feed the treasured one here at Wisteria Court?" They delicately toed several dirty cups and plates out of the way, searching for a clean place to sit.

The courtesan snorted, choked, then coughed. "All the cooks here ever give me," she said hoarsely, "is steamed tofu and vegetables followed by beautifully prepared plates of sliced fruit." She finished swallowing and scowled. "I don't dance for patrons anymore, so what do they care if my figure goes by the wayside? I can pen my poems just as well sitting on my ever-widening hips and never moving again." Jiyi glared up at Han and Xu, then let out an enormous belch. "Where's Zhara? I was hoping she would bring me some of those steamed cassava cakes from the docks. I love those."

"I'm sure she's on her way." Xu grabbed several seat cushions from a cupboard in the corner and cleared a space to sit on the floor. "You told us to be here during the long-shadow hour, and lo"—they gestured to the late-afternoon sun streaming in through the rice-paper panes—"it is still the long-shadow hour."

Jiyi grunted. "I don't remember giving you permission to address me so informally," she said to Xu. "And you," she said, turning to Han. "Why are you so tall? Sit down, you're giving me a headache just looking at you."

Han obeyed with alacrity, sitting down amid the rubbish piles and folding his hands in his lap. The courtesan reminded him of Anyang when his little brother was in desperate need of a nap—cranky, irritable, snappish, and stubborn. The skin beneath Jiyi's eyes was dull with the shadows of fatigue, but her eyes were overbright with excitement and too many cups of oolong tea. Her fingertips drummed a jittery beat against the tabletop as she riffled through her notes over and over again. She was practically vibrating with nervous energy, and Han couldn't tell if the courtesan was anxious or overeager to share her findings. The three of them sat in silence as they waited for Zhara to arrive, the tension keying higher and higher until Jiyi couldn't stand it anymore.

"All-right-I-can't-wait," she blurted out, her words slamming into each other like runners tripping in a footrace. "I'll tell Zhara when she comes later." Rocking back and forth with anticipation, the courtesan clapped her hands for attention. "We have found," she announced in a dramatic voice, "the cure for abomination."

Silence.

There was a wild, nearly feral look in Jiyi's eyes that made it somewhat difficult to take her proclamation at face value. When her declaration did not get the astonished or awed reception that she anticipated, Jiyi grunted and tried again.

"Didn't you hear what I said?" she asked, half annoyed, half sheepish. "I said we have the cure for abomination."

"Yes, we heard the treasured one," Xu said calmly. "We're just waiting to hear what it is."

"Oh." Jiyi cleared her throat. "The cure," she said, raising her hands and looking up at the ceiling, "is the Guardian of Fire."

More silence.

"Ugh, this is why I hated performing," Jiyi groused. "No one ever responds the way I want them to. Writing's so much better."

"Erm, how were we supposed to respond?" Han asked politely. "I mean, it's fairly common knowledge that one of the Guardian of Fire's gifts was the ability to turn abominations back into humans. What?" he said at Xu's look of surprise. "I'm not entirely illiterate."

"Can we please get back to the matter at hand?" Jiyi demanded. "The Guardian of Fire! We have the means to treat the blight of corruption afflicting magicians in the city!" She looked from Han to Xu and back again. "Why aren't you more excited about this?"

Xu shook their head. "Perhaps we would be more excited about it," they remarked, "if the Guardian of Fire were more than just a fairy tale."

"Oh, but the Guardian of Fire *is* real," Jiyi said. "And she walks among us."

"She?" Xu picked up one of the teapots and peered inside. "What has the treasured one been drinking? Are we certain this is just tea?"

Han nibbled at his lower lip. As a child, the ministers had always claimed that the only cure for abomination was death, that the only reason the Morning Realms were free of the blight was because all the magicians had been destroyed during the purges after the Just War. But his encounters with abominations had not ended in death; they had ended in life as they returned to their human forms, seemingly cleansed of possession. He thought of the monster in the cave below Mount Zanhei, of the fire that seemed to consume its body at Zhara's touch, burning away all that was unnatural to reveal a frightened little boy inside. A jolt of realization shot through Han, his blood fizzing with the revelation.

"It's Zhara," he said softly. "Zhara is the Guardian of Fire, isn't she?"

Jiyi almost looked impressed. "It appears you don't just have noodles for brains after all," she said. "But . . . yes. You're right."

"Hold a moment," Xu said, raising their hand. "But I thought Zhara was human."

"She is," Jiyi said.

"Then how can she also be an elemental warrior from legend? I thought the Guardians of Dawn were powerful, immortal beings, not an apothecary's assistant from a little shop in the covered market." Xu shook their head. "If Zhara really were the Guardian of Fire, she would be at least two thousand years old."

"Nothing in the old stories says anything about the way the Guardians looked," Jiyi argued back. "Only that they rose when called upon by the Sunburst Warrior."

Han said nothing, scarcely listening to the courtesan and his best friend debate the nature of Zhara's existence. When he thought of Zhara, he didn't think of the shining girl in the marketplace that night he saw her for the second time, the night he saw an abomination for the first time. Instead, he thought of Mistress Brandy with her longing eyes and heart-shaped face, the girl who had sat with him on a hill overlooking the pleasure district as wish lanterns floated into the night sky. The girl with whom he had shared his memories, his vulnerabilities, and a near-kiss. Whether or not Zhara was the Guardian of Fire was immaterial to him—whatever her extraordinary abilities might be, she was also just an ordinary girl.

"I think," he said quietly, "that if Zhara were here, she would remind us that she is a living, breathing, and whole person with thoughts and feelings about this entire situation."

Both Xu and Jiyi fell silent at that, shamefaced and not a little chastised. "Yes, well," the courtesan said in a gruff voice to cover up her discomfort, "speaking of Zhara, it's not like her to be this late."

The shadows had grown longer since they arrived, and there was still no sign of the girl in question. "Perhaps she's been held up at Teacher Hu's," Xu offered. "Shops do close later during the summer hours."

It was as reasonable an explanation as any, but a niggle of worry remained. Kestrel presence on the streets had increased ever since

Princess Yulana's arrival, and the image of all those missing magicians laid out in their coffins beneath Mount Zanhei lingered in Han's mind. "You don't think she's in some sort of trouble?" he asked, looking from Xu to Jiyi.

They all exchanged nervous glances. "Nah," Xu said. "She's clever, our Mistress Brandy. She's probably been delayed at work."

"Not to mention she's the Guardian of Fire," Jiyi added. "She can handle whatever trouble heads her way."

"The courtesan seems so certain of all this," Xu said, falling right back into their previous argument. "How can she be so sure Zhara is the Guardian of Fire?"

"Because we've seen her change a monster back into a magician," Han said softly. "Isn't that the very definition of the power of transformation?" He held up his hand and lowered a finger as he counted each gift. "Transformation, transfiguration, and transmutation. The Guardian of Fire was said to be able to transform anything into anything else—air into matter, stone into gold, and even human into magician or magician into human—by changing the very nature of their ki. Their souls."

Xu shook their head. "We've seen our Mistress Brandy do impossible things, I'll admit, but being an extraordinarily powerful magician doesn't necessarily mean she is an elemental warrior of old." They frowned. "Unless . . . unless she is, ah, *possessed* by the spirit of the Guardian of Fire?"

"Like a demon possessing a magician?" Jiyi mused, picking at her teeth. "That would make sense."

"But I thought possessed magicians turned into abominations," Han pointed out.

"Not necessarily. There are stories throughout history of possessed magicians who retain their human shape and appearance." The courtesan fished out whatever had been caught in her molars and flicked it at Xu, who yelped in disgust. She reached for her pile of notes on the floor beside her and began riffling through the pages. "No one really knows what causes corruption, but Li Er-Shuan's notes indicate that the act of possession is the act of transforming the *essence* of a human into that of a demon. The more powerful the demon, the less monstrous the result."

"How?" Han asked.

Jiyi shrugged. "I assume it's because the greater the demon, the greater its control over the void and how it manifests."

"I didn't realize there was a hierarchy of power among demons," Xu remarked.

"I didn't either, but here"—Jiyi pointed to a relevant passage—"there's something about the four Kings of Tiyok, the only demons aside from the Mother of Demons herself with a title." She made a frustrated noise at the back of her throat. "The rest of the notes clearly reference some other passage in *Songs of Order and Chaos,* but without the source text, I'm lost." Groaning, she tossed her work aside and tipped open various pots of tea. "Trying to decipher Li Er-Shuan's work is like trying to remember the steps to a dance with no music. Half of what you need is missing."

Han rose to his feet and headed to the windows overlooking a beautiful shaded garden in a private courtyard behind Wisteria Court. A parent and child were feeding the moon carp in a reflecting pond. "What do you think happened to Uncle Li and my cousin Ami?" he asked in a low voice. "Do you think they're still alive?" He thought of the circle of stone coffins, each filled with the bodies of missing magicians. Would it have been better or worse, he wondered, to have discovered his mother's cousin among them?

"Han," Xu began, but Jiyi interrupted them.

"Yes," she said simply. "If Li Er-Shuan and his daughter were dead, we would have found *Songs of Order and Chaos* by now."

"How so?" Xu frowned.

"Do you think the Guardians of Dawn are the only ones searching for the book?" the courtesan asked. "There are people all over the Morning Realms who would love to get their hands on *Songs of Order and Chaos,* including the Warlord and his peacekeepers. It would be worth a fortune on the black market, where we certainly have contacts, or else the Falconer would have made a public showing of its destruction."

With a start, Han recalled his encounter with Princess Yulana in the palace library. She had seemed so cagey standing there with that blue-eyed bird on her shoulder, claiming to be in search of a book on astrology. Was she also looking for *Songs of Order and Chaos*? If so, why?

Xu whistled. "And here I thought *Tales from the Downy Delta* was the most coveted and the most forbidden text in all the Morning Realms."

Jiyi made a face. "I don't understand why people like *Tales* so much," she muttered. "I wrote those poems in half a day after several pots of jasmine green tea. I've put out much better work since."

Xu choked. "You?" they screeched, disregarding all formality. "You wrote *Tales from the Downy Delta?*"

The courtesan shrugged. "What did you think I wrote?"

"I dunno," they said. "Love poems? Or romance novels?"

"Did someone say *romance novels?*" Han asked eagerly.

"Don't you start," Xu said as Jiyi rolled her eyes.

"So just what *is* in *Songs of Order and Chaos?*" Han asked. "And why does everyone want it so?"

The courtesan fiddled nervously with the ends of her sash. "It is rumored," she said in a voice so low it was scarcely audible, "that *Songs of Order and Chaos* was the only text that detailed the rituals of summoning, binding, and banishment of spirits."

"Spirits?" Han asked. "Like demons?"

Jiyi pursed her lips. "Demons could be considered a sort of spirit, I suppose, but anything that deals with the realm of the intangible could be considered a spirit, including the Guardians of Dawn—the legends, not us," she added.

Xu scratched their head. "Why would anyone want to summon a spirit? What if you accidentally summon a demon and unleash it upon the world?"

"Summoning rituals don't work like that," the courtesan said. "There must be intention, and the spirit being summoned must be called by name before being bound to a purpose. After their purpose is finished, they must be dismissed or banished."

"But if you already have magic," Han asked, "why would you call upon a spirit?"

The courtesan shrugged again. "For any number of reasons, I suppose. Knowledge, material gain. Spirits work in the realm of Chaos, and their magic is not bound by the rules of order like a human's magic is. Spirits need a vessel in order to work magic on this plane of existence. There are tales of enchanted weapons and objects, where a spirit possesses a thing, but when a spirit possesses a magician . . ." She trailed off.

"Abomination," Han said grimly.

"Power," Xu whispered. "It's always about more power, isn't it? No matter that you sacrifice your humanity in the process."

Jiyi nodded. "That's why *Songs of Order and Chaos* is both the most coveted and the most forbidden text in all the Morning Realms. Even the Mugungs had ordered all copies to be destroyed. Too much potential for abuse, so they banned the practice."

Han thought of Yao in the cave and remembered how the boy's skin had rippled and burst with spiny, spiky fur, how he had thrown his head back and screamed with pain while he had become a monster. He was only a child of ten, Anyang's age, and Anyang's friend. "But what of Thanh and Yao?" he asked. "They were only children when they became abominations. I don't think they were out there on the slopes of Mount Zanhei creating summoning circles. They didn't become possessed of their own free will."

"No," Jiyi agreed. "But I think it has something to do with the structures we found in the cave. But what their purpose is, I haven't yet figured out." She ran her fingers through her knotted hair as an enormous yawn nearly split her head in two. "I'm working on translating the glyphs we took rubbings of by cross-referencing my dictionaries and Li Er-Shuan's notes, but I'm pretty sure what we saw up by the volcano was some sort of summoning spell."

"Summoning what?" Han asked.

"Shouldn't we be asking *who* is doing the summoning?" Xu remarked.

Jiyi shook her head. "No," she said through another yawn. "Remember that all spirits are summoned by name and bound to a purpose. The who matters less," she said darkly, "than the *why.*"

31

B Y ALL ACCOUNTS, THE MEETING WITH LORD Chan was going well.

The Second Wife was all smiles as she made small conversation with her future son-in-law, while Master Cao finalized the details of Suzhan's marriage contract. Zhara tried to catch the diminutive bookseller's eye, wondering if she would have a chance to speak with him once the meeting was over. She knew that Master Cao had studied law at the university prior to opening his bookshop, but she had not known he still provided legal services. Had he known that Zhara would be here? Had he come to deliver a warning? Or was this all simply a coincidence?

Her mind was awhirl with disjointed thoughts, her magic aswirl in her veins with anxiety. At least Yuli the not-ghost had disappeared as soon as the others arrived. Zhara kept her hands tightly clasped in her lap, her gaze lowered as Master Cao read out the final terms of the contract.

"The bride-price shall be settled upon the mother in the form of an annuity," the bookseller read aloud, "in the sum of ten thousand coins or the equivalent of ten hundred-weight measures of silver every twelve months for the next sixty years, in exchange for the gift of Xiao Suzhan's hand, or until such time as the money should no longer be required due to the end of the mother's natural life."

Zhara startled at the amount of money Lord Chan had agreed to bestow upon her stepmother. The wages she brought home from Teacher Hu's totaled less than a hundred coppers per month, and if half of that had not disappeared down the Second Wife's gullet every night, Zhara could have comfortably supported the three of them. Or at least had enough to pay their rent and fill their bellies, with a little left over for small luxuries. She thought of the white silk slippers in the luxury goods sector of the covered market. Small luxuries.

"His Eminence is generous," the Second Wife said in a fawning voice. Zhara cringed to see her stepmother act so subservient, so eager, so . . . desperate. She didn't know which was worse; the Second Wife's bouts of malicious cruelty or seeing her transform into the cringing, clinging matron at Lord Chan's side.

"And for the bride's stepsister," Master Cao continued, eyes darting from the page to Zhara's face and back again, "every provision for a good life shall be provided, including arrangements for a future marriage on the condition"—the bookseller cleared his throat nervously—"on the condition that she agree to join the Chan household as the bride's companion and handmaiden."

"Not as a concubine," Lord Chan hastened to add. "Nor as a servant. A companion to my lovely wife, with the acknowledgment that I will do everything in my power to provide for her as any father would, including a dowry for a future husband."

Lord Chan gave Zhara what she assumed was meant to be a reassuring smile, but it put her in mind of nothing more than a preening little frog. The man had the slightly slack, slimy features of an amphibian—too wide lips, slightly bulging eyes, with a faint, ever-present sheen of sweat all over his skin. Now that she had met him, she could understand why Suzhan had said the man was empty inside. She had never met anyone so bland, so colorless, so devoid of personality before. There was something off-putting about the slackness of Lord Chan's face, which, when combined with his pallor, gave the impression of some foreign spirit or ghost animating a corpse. Everything from his tone to his manner was modulated to be as inoffensive as possible, and while some of that could plausibly be attributed to a lifetime of learned obsequiousness as a palace minister, Zhara couldn't help thinking that the majority of it was a cunning calculation to disguise something . . . darker. Some unspoken motive or ambition, perhaps, although she couldn't quite discern the nature of it.

"Lord Chan's beneficence is unmatched," the Second Wife cooed. "Is it not, Jin Zhara?"

Zhara flinched to have Lord Chan's focus on her once more. She kept her own eyes fixed on her hands in her lap, trying her best to be inconspicuous, insignificant, invisible. Ever since they had gathered to sit down and drink, Lord Chan's gaze had scarcely left her face— not with prurient interest, but a sort of waiting, watching . . . want. Beneath the table, she could see the lightning flickers of power glow and pulse beneath her skin. She tugged at the too-short sleeves of her too-tight tunic.

"So, child," Lord Chan said to Zhara. "Tell me. How old are you? When were you born?" She knew he meant to sound kind, but something about the flat affect in his voice made her magic squirm and writhe in her veins.

She looked toward Suzhan, who was also taking care to keep her unsighted gaze averted from her future husband.

"Go on," the Second Wife urged. "You can answer him directly, child."

Zhara swallowed. "I am almost seventeen," she whispered hoarsely. "I was born on the seventh night of the seventh month in the Year of the Tiger."

Lord Chan shifted in his seat, his finger tapping the tabletop in an excited gesture. "Good, good," he murmured. "That's the right time frame."

Zhara looked up in confusion, but Lord Chan's gaze was distant. He appeared to be making some private calculations.

"Are we settled then?" the Second Wife asked, not quite able to disguise the quiver of eagerness in her voice. "Are we agreed to this new contract?"

Suzhan shifted on her seat cushion, her sharp shoulder blades poking awkwardly through her new finery, the creases of her silk and ramie shirt still crisp and clean. Zhara could see her sister was no more happy with this renewed marriage offer than before, but dared not speak out against it a second time. Lord Chan's generosity was hard to refuse, especially as he had made special arrangements for a private zither tutor when he'd learned of his new bride's passion for music.

"Suzhan?" the Second Wife asked impatiently.

"Yes, Mama," she said in a scarcely audible voice. "Yes, Mama, I am agreed."

At her verbal assent, Master Cao brought forth a small blue-and-white porcelain dish, onto which he meticulously ground a bar of cinnabar into powder for ink. Once the ink was prepared, the Second Wife wasted no time in dipping her forefinger and pressing it to the paper while Lord Chan pulled a small jade seal from a pouch on his belt to stamp the insignia of his office onto the page.

"Now you, my treasure," the Second Wife prompted.

Suzhan's eyes flickered about the room. Her gaze touched each of their faces as lightly as the brush of a butterfly's wing before landing on the pool of red ink in the dish on the table, bright and vivid as blood against the dark mahogany wood. Zhara could sense her sister's nervousness and hesitation and, with tremendous effort, willed her unruly magic to subside before taking Suzhan's hand. "Do you want to sign?" she whispered.

Suzhan swallowed. Zhara could see the conflict in her sister's expression, the desire to please, the fear of her mother's wrath, and the confusion about her future husband's intentions. "What of you, nene?" she whispered back. "Do you want to sign?"

"Of course she does," the Second Wife said. "She'll never have another offer as good as this." Her smile was smug, triumphant. "Will you, Jin Zhara?"

Zhara thought of Han, of Xu, and of Jiyi sitting just scant feet away in the courtesan's quarters. *I'll take you. I'll take you to the Night of the Sevens.* The girl she was before she met Han in the marketplace that fateful day would have never believed she would be sitting before the regent of Zanhei as he offered to bring her into his household. To care for her. As he offered to provide her with the clothes on her back, the food in her belly, a roof over her head, and even, someday in the far distant future, a husband of her own. The girl she was would have never dared to ask for more; she wouldn't have known to ask for more.

You want to be loved, nene, Suzhan had said.

Before, love had not been possible for someone like her. An orphan of mixed heritage—and a magician—would consider herself lucky to find someone to trust with her secrets, never mind carry them for her. Love wasn't safe for someone like her; it made her too vulnerable. Love and leisure were pleasures that belonged to the privileged, and it was hard for Zhara to think of herself as deserving of anything other than a brief respite from suffering. Girls of her class could not hope for more. A magician could hope for even less.

And yet with Han, she couldn't help hoping for more.

To thrive, not just survive.

Zhara met the Second Wife's gaze. "It's not my decision to make, mimi," she said softly.

"But of course it is, my dear," Lord Chan said smoothly. "I would never force anyone to enter a contract against their will. Consent is of the utmost importance."

Again, the words, the tone, the manner all seemed calculated to put her at ease, only they made Zhara more anxious than ever. She could feel her stepmother's eyes on her face. "M-many th-thanks, Lord Ch-Chan," Zhara stammered.

He inclined his head in the perfect imitation of a gracious nod, although his bulging eyes never left her face. There was something cold about his expression—not emotionless, but physically cold. Zhara shivered as though the heat of summer had turned into the chill of winter, as though her warmth were being pulled from her somehow. Her magic seemed to flicker and struggle against an invisible breeze, and Zhara didn't know whether to fan the flames or blow them out entirely.

"Well?" the Second Wife pressed. "Get on with it."

"Help me, nene," Suzhan said quietly, tapping her finger in the direction of the red ink on the table. "I'll sign."

With trembling hands, Zhara brought the blue-and-white dish close to her sister's right hand. "Are you sure?" she murmured. "What about our promise?"

Zhara didn't dare speak of their pact to live their truths openly, but Suzhan understood. "The zither," her sister murmured back, fingers strumming invisible strings atop the table.

"All right, mimi." With some misgiving, Zhara helped dip Suzhan's forefinger in ink before guiding it to the proper place on the page.

"Aiyo." Suzhan hissed and jerked her hand away, leaving a smear on the contract. "Something stung me."

Zhara immediately dropped her glowing hands to her lap, but she could feel Lord Chan's questioning gaze. No, not questioning. *Hungry.*

"Now you," the Second Wife said, sliding the ink toward Zhara. "Let's finalize the arrangements and celebrate while there is still light outside! This calls for a drink, wouldn't you say, Lord Chan?" She beckoned to the servant standing in attendance just beyond the door and ordered a bottle of rice wine for the table.

Zhara stared at the space on the contract for her own fingerprint as the servant brought the liquor and cups. Although the rice wine they served at Wisteria Court was likely some of the finest in Zanhei, she wasn't sure she could stomach any alcohol. The memory of the last time she shared a drink with her stepmother returned to her, along with the image of the enormous purpling bruise on Suzhan's cheek. The neatly symmetrical irony of it all would be funny, if that were her sense of humor.

"Mama," Suzhan said in a low voice as the servant poured her a small cup. "I'm not sure I can drink this."

"Nonsense," the Second Wife said. "You're old enough to enjoy your first sip of adulthood, my darling." She reached forward and wrapped her daughter's fingers around the cup. "Now drink up!"

Suzhan went pale as she lifted the cup, shaking and sloshing, to her lips. She wrinkled her nose as the smell of alcohol hit it, trying not to gag. Before she could think about what she was doing, Zhara grabbed her sister's cup, changing the wine into water.

"Slowly, mimi," she said. "The first sip is the roughest, as they say."

Suzhan took a small mouthful. Her lashes fluttered with surprise as she swallowed. "It tastes like water!" She frowned as she set down her cup and turned her face toward Zhara. "Did you do something to it, nene?"

"Of c-course not!" Zhara tittered nervously. Suzhan narrowed her eyes at the stutter in her sister's words, but held her tongue.

"Hurry, child," the Second Wife urged Zhara. "Yours is the last fingerprint, and then our business is concluded."

Zhara dipped her finger in the red ink, then hesitated, her hand hovering above the page. The ink pooled and gathered in the whorls of her fingertip, dripping onto the table in big, fat, red drops.

The ink splashed clear.

To thrive, not just survive.

"I—I cannot." With her clean hand, Zhara pushed the contract back in Lord Chan's direction. "Please accept my humblest apologies, but I—I don't think I can sign."

He studied her with his bulging gaze, his expression unreadable. Was it fury? Curiosity? Or simply indifference?

"No!" The Second Wife grabbed Zhara's wrist and forced her hand to the page. "Don't be stupid, girl!" Zhara's fingers left a smear of red that immediately vanished the instant it was committed to paper, the pigment evaporating like water. The Second Wife yelped as Zhara's magic stung her, and she stared in amazement at the rose-gold burn in her palm before it faded away.

"It's all right, my dear," Lord Chan said evenly. "I will not force anyone into an arrangement against their will. I will, of course, still be honoring the contract with my darling wife-to-be," he said with a polite nod of his head in Suzhan's direction, but Suzhan was still study-ing the cup in her hands, tasting the liquid over and over again with a frown. "I only wished to provide for a motherless orphan, but I will not compel anyone to accept my generosity as charity."

The Second Wife seemed taken aback by Lord Chan's equanim-ity and strove to match his composure with her own. "Of course, of course," she said. "It's just that I thought . . . our arrangement—" She broke off, her eyes narrowed to sharp pinpoints of dislike as she re-garded her stepdaughter.

"Our arrangement still stands," Lord Chan said to the Second

Wife. He turned to Zhara and took her still-glowing hand across the table before she could snatch it back. Alarm raced up her spine as she prepared for the inevitable shout of pain or surprise, but none came. Instead, she felt strangely drained by his touch, as though something were drawing her magic out of her. She had felt like this once before— standing in the middle of the circle of coffins up at Mount Zanhei. Her head snapped up in confusion to meet Lord Chan's gaze. He was not a magician, yet there was something decidedly . . . uncanny about his touch.

Guardian of Fire . . . there you are . . .

For the first time since they arrived, Zhara thought she could sense something other than bland pleasantry beneath Lord Chan's expression. Something moved in the depths of his eyes, a darkness so complete it had its own presence, an abyss, a void. All the hairs stood on the back of Zhara's neck as she was reminded of the foreign intelligence she had sensed peering out of Thanh's eyes. With a start, she realized she recognized the gaze of the man staring back at her.

It was the gaze that had stared out at her from every corrupted magician.

It was the gaze of a demon.

32

THE LAST OF THE SUN DISAPPEARED BELOW the horizon, and still Zhara had not arrived.

"His Grace doesn't think something's happened to her?" Xu asked in a worried voice. "All those missing magicians, and with the Kestrels roaming the streets, what if—"

"I'm sure she's fine," Han said curtly, keeping his eyes focused on the game of Sparrow he was playing with his best friend to pass the time. In the corner, Jiyi lay fast asleep on her bed, arm thrown over her face as loud, unladylike snores filled the room.

"We shouldn't stay much longer, my prince," Xu said softly, drawing one tile and discarding another. "We can't keep paying off the night watch to hold their tongues. Sooner or later, word will get back to the palace—and my father—about our excursions to the Pits and the pleasure district."

Han drew a tile from the pile and considered his hand without really seeing what he held. "Just until the sundown hour," he said, discarding a random tile. "Then we'll head back."

"But that won't be for a while yet," Xu said, glancing at the sky outside. As the days drew nearer to the solstice, the sundown hour came later and later each evening, a fact of which Han intended to take advantage. "And we can't leave Anyang alone for that long."

Han cringed as guilt curdled his insides with shame. "I'm doing this for Anyang," he said. "This work with the Guardians of Dawn."

His best friend studied him as they drew another tile and discarded yet another. "Are you?" they asked. "Or are you doing this to spend more time with Mistress Brandy?"

Han said nothing as he played his turn, the silence broken only by the clacking of tiles against the table, accompanied by the snores of the courtesan on her bed.

"Han," Xu said gently. "You're—"

"—engaged, I know." The thought of Princess Yulana made Han's stomach hurt. Despite everything, he liked his betrothed, or rather, he respected her. In another life, another world, he thought that they could even be friends. She was fun to spar with in the training yard, and he imagined she would probably be even more fun on an excursion to Flower Town together, but her infamous grandfather was an enormous obstacle to any intimacy or trust that might build between them.

Xu shook their head. "I was going to say you're playing the wrong hand, but I see you have other matters on your mind."

Han glanced down at the tiles before him, then pushed them away. "My head hurts," he said. "Let's take a break."

"And I was about to win too," Xu said mournfully, then drew all the tiles together and stacked them into neat piles for the next round. "Do you want to play Flowers instead?" they asked, pulling out the deck of cards from one of the table drawers.

"Nah, I'm getting a cramp from sitting still too long." Han got to his feet and began doing some stretches, bending forward at the waist to touch his fingers to his toes.

"It's not that I don't appreciate the view, my prince," said Xu from behind him, "but one does get the sense His Grace is moving mindlessly to prevent his mind from moving."

"Don't," he said. "Don't call me His Grace. Not while others might hear."

Xu cast a sidelong glance at the sleeping courtesan, her mouth slack-jawed and wide open, drooling a little as she snored. "You mean where Zhara might overhear," they said softly.

Han flinched as he grabbed his ankles, feeling the stretch go all the way from the backs of his calves to his hamstrings. "Mistress Brandy isn't here," he said instead of answering his best friend's real question.

Xu sighed. "You'll have to tell her the truth someday. And I think it's better she hear it from your lips than discover you're the Royal Heir of Zanhei from someplace else. Like from your betrothal posters."

"I think we're fine on that front." Han snorted. "None of those portraits look like me."

"That's not the point," Xu said sternly. "The point is that you cannot continue this double life, not without someone paying the price. Either Anyang, or the princess, or Mistress Brandy will suffer, and the longer you continue this deception, the greater the consequences will be."

Han slowly unrolled himself, spreading his legs shoulder-width apart and reaching his head toward his right knee. "I know," he said. "It's just . . ."

He was afraid. He was afraid of losing the light in her eyes when she looked at him. He was afraid she would no longer *see* him, a boy and not a crown. To Zhara, he was just Han, and he was terrified of losing that more than anything else.

Suddenly, the doors to Jiyi's quarters slid open with a bang. A disheveled and distressed-looking Zhara stood on the threshold, startling Han in the middle of his stretch.

"Yah," croaked the courtesan from the bed. "Some of us are trying to get some sleep here."

But Zhara didn't hear her. "I need," she said in a panicked voice, "some way for my sister and me to leave the city. Immediately."

Han looked up so sharply he thought he might have pulled something in his neck. "What?" He straightened in a panic. "Leave? Why?"

"Because," Zhara said, eyes wild, "my sister's husband is possessed by a demon."

Marriage, as Han was coming to discover, was a thoroughly demonic business, no matter who was involved.

It took some time for Zhara to calm down enough to relay the entire story. She had been detained, she said, because she had received a summons to meet with her sister's husband-to-be at the same time she was supposed to be meeting with the Guardians of Dawn. At first Han thought for one heart-stopping moment that Zhara said she received a summons to meet *her* husband-to-be—that she was also hiding a secret engagement—and the relief that he was not alone in his deception was both sudden and sweet. Then he realized his mistake, and the self-loathing that overcame him was both shameful and deserved.

A guilty conscience, as Han was coming to understand, was turning him into a terrible person.

"How do you know your sister's future husband is possessed?" Jiyi asked. The moment the word *possession* had fallen from Zhara's lips, the courtesan had snapped out of her drowsy mood, instantly alert and attentive. It was an impressive feat; Han could barely string two words together before his morning cup of tea. "I'm assuming the man didn't turn into an abomination before your very eyes, and in this very teahouse, or we would certainly have heard about it."

Zhara looked down at her hands, which glowed faintly in the fading light. Han recalled the way her hands had blazed with fire on that dark stairwell in Mount Zanhei, and reached out to take her fingers before pulling back. Xu eyed him curiously, and Han returned his hands to his lap, feeling his cheeks flush with embarrassment.

"I—I'm not sure," Zhara admitted. "Lord Chan didn't feel like the other magicians I've met before, not like Thanh or that little boy we rescued from the caverns beneath the volcano. In fact, there wasn't much I could tell about him at all." She frowned. "It was so strange—my sister had told me this man was empty inside, and I hadn't understood what she meant until I met him face-to-face." She shuddered, and a flicker of flame traced her silhouette with fire before vanishing again. "But when he—when he took my hand, it was as though he was made of nothing but a void. A deep, deep abyss that pulled my magic from me."

Jiyi narrowed her eyes. "That doesn't sound like a corrupted magician, that sounds like . . ." She didn't finish her sentence. Struck by a sudden thought, she began rummaging through the scattered stacks of paper on the floor.

"There is something wrong with him," Zhara whispered. "And I am afraid."

"Is there any way your sister can refuse him?" Xu asked sympathetically. "Some way to call off this marriage?"

She shook her head. "Suzhan has already inked her thumbprint onto the contract."

Xu scratched their chin. "Lord Chan . . ." they said slowly. "I wonder if we're related. Chan is a common enough surname, but there aren't too many Chans of noble blood in the south."

"Lord Chan is," Zhara said, "a high-ranking palace minister." A tiny wrinkle of concentration appeared between her brows. "But I can't remember his exact title."

Across the table from Han, Xu had gone a grayish color beneath their rouge. "It wouldn't be Chancellor of Zanhei, would it?"

She lifted her brows in surprise. "I believe that's correct," she said. "How did you know?"

"Because," they said in a strangled voice. "Because the Chancellor is my father."

A stunned silence fell over Jiyi's quarters.

"*Your* father is the regent of Zanhei?" the courtesan asked in an incredulous tone, pausing halfway through a thick volume titled *The First Tiyok War.* Xu gave a numb, miserable nod of their head. "How did we never know of this?" She turned to Han. "And what of you? Do you have anything you would like to share? Is your father the prince of Zanhei? Are you secretly the Royal Heir?"

Han flinched. He could feel the blood drain from his face at the accusation, but Jiyi was too annoyed to notice.

"Wonderful," she grumbled. "Now I've forgotten entirely what I was looking for." She slammed the book shut and tossed it over her shoulder. "Is Lord Chan a magician?" she asked Zhara. "Because a high-ranking magician in the palace could do wonders for our little secret organization."

Zhara absentmindedly rubbed her fingers over the back of her hand, as though trying to scrub away the memory of someone's touch. "I—I don't know," she said. "I don't think so. He certainly didn't *feel* like a magician." She glanced at Han. "Or an anti-magician either."

"What did he feel like?" Xu asked quietly. Their face was still pale beneath their makeup, although some color had returned to their cheeks.

"Like . . . nothing."

"Nothing?" Han frowned. "What do you mean?"

Zhara's eyes were glassy as she stared into the middle distance before her. "I mean . . . nothing. He didn't feel like a human, or a magician, or anything alive even." She fidgeted with the fraying hems on her trousers, picking at the unraveling threads without thought. "Just . . . emptiness made flesh."

"That does sound like my father," Xu said ruefully. "A black hole devoid of feeling."

Han tried to catch his best friend's eye, but Xu was studiously avoiding his gaze. He knew just how much of a pretense their flippant manner could be, a lighthearted mask to hide their true feelings.

"Oh!" Jiyi leaped to her feet and ran back to the book she had so casually tossed aside before. "Now I remember what I was looking for. In the meantime," she said, furiously flipping through pages, "we should figure out how to get you and your sister out of Zanhei."

"You can do that?" Han asked in surprise.

"Teacher Hu said the Guardians of Dawn help refugees escape all the time," Zhara said quietly. "Usually to the lands of the outermost west."

Something about the phrase *the lands of the outermost west* shook a memory loose in Han's mind, like autumn leaves falling to the ground. The scent of apples, sweet yet sharp, and acrid at the back of his throat returned to him. Vinegar. Secret ink. Uncle Li.

"Is that where all escaping magicians go?" Han asked. He thought of Master Cao's missing scriveners and how the bookseller refused to tell him where the escaping magicians might have fled.

"For the most part," Jiyi said. "Why do you ask?"

"Do you think that's where Uncle Li and his daughter might be hiding?"

The courtesan considered this for a moment. "It's possible," she said. "There are so many tribes and clans out there, it would take several years to search among them all for a single missing astrologer and his clever daughter. And the lands are so vast, they've never been properly mapped out. Although," she mused, "if Li Er-Shuan had escaped to the outermost west, it troubles me that he did not tell the Guardians of Dawn. We could have helped him."

"How?" Zhara asked. "How do you manage to smuggle people out of Zanhei?"

"We have lots of different ways," Jiyi said. "And it all depends on the situation. The Guardians of Dawn have learned to be resourceful and flexible over the years. In fact, the next caravan of refugees out of the city will be on the Night of the Sevens."

Han felt a pang of disappointment. He was supposed to be taking Zhara to the celebrations at the palace.

"Oh." He could feel Zhara cast a wistful look in his direction, and he knew she felt the same twinge of regret. "So soon?"

"Well, the Bangtan Brothers will be in town on the Night of the Sevens," Jiyi said. "They've been instrumental in helping the Guardians of Dawn smuggle magicians to safety."

"The Bangtan Brothers?" Zhara and Xu cried at once, before looking at each other with startled expressions.

Xu grinned. "*I am you,*" they sang, reaching out with their forefinger.

She met their finger with her own. "*You are me,*" she sang back, her voice charmingly husky and out of tune.

"Ugh," the courtesan said with disgust. "What is this?"

"A line from one of their ballads," Xu supplied. Then, "Hold a moment. Since when did the Bangtan Brothers start working for the Guardians of Dawn?"

"A few years ago now," Jiyi said. "Apparently the boys are all magicians."

"They are?" Zhara exclaimed. "No wonder their stage performances look like magic!"

"Are their performances cover for their work with us?" Han asked with some interest. He loved spy stories.

"Yes and no," the courtesan replied. "As far as I've heard, the Bangtan Brothers genuinely enjoy performing. But more than that, no one questions why a traveling troupe needs to be anywhere in the empire,

nor do they need imperial passes to traverse the realm. They're inconspicuous."

"I would hardly say that the Bangtan Brothers are *inconspicuous*,"
Xu muttered. "They're the most popular performance troupe in the
Morning Realms."

Jiyi frowned. "Exactly how popular would you say they are?"

"Very," Xu muttered. "Their last performance was so crowded that
people had to be turned away."

Zhara pursed her lips. "I'd say they're fairly popular," she agreed.
"There are still people eagerly checking the boards in the commons for
an announcement of their next stop in Zanhei. If anyone gets wind of
their appearance in town, there will be mobs of people clamoring for
entrance to the masquerade ball."

The courtesan chewed the tip of her brush distractedly. "Hmmm,
this rising popularity could be a double-edged sword," she murmured.
"We told them to keep a low profile as much as possible so as to not
draw any undue attention to their activities with us."

"Hard to keep talent like that from impressing the people," Zhara
said. "Even now they still talk of their rendition of *A Poem for the Little
Things* down in the Pits."

"To think," Xu moaned, "we've been working with the Bangtan
Brothers all this time and no one thought to tell us. I've been wanting
an autograph from the handsome one ever since I saw him play the
romantic lead in *The Most Beautiful Moments in Life*."

"Aren't they all *the handsome one?*" Han asked in confusion. He recalled the performance of the Sunburst Cycle he had seen the troupe
perform the previous year, but remembered very little of their individ-
ual faces aside from a general notion of overwhelming and intimidating
attractiveness. "I thought they were all good-looking."

"Mother of Demons," Jiyi said irritably. "Well," she said to Zhara, "the
good news is that we have a way to get you and your sister out of Zanhei.
Unfortunately, the bad news is that it appears as though your means of
escape will have the eyes of the entire city upon them on the Night of the
Sevens. Ah." She brought her finger down to a page in the book she had
been perusing and ripped it out from its binding. "Here it is."

"What is it?" Zhara asked. "What were you looking for?"

"A description of possession by a greater demon."

"A greater demon?"

"Yes," Jiyi said, scanning the page before her. "It says here that possession by one of the Kings of Tiyok is the most insidious form of corruption, because the greater demon can disguise its true form in the body of a human instead of transforming its host into something unholy and uncanny."

"So the treasured one is saying," Xu said, blood draining from their lips, "that someone can be possessed by a so-called King of Tiyok without us ever finding out?"

The courtesan nodded. "Only the touch of a Guardian of Dawn will reveal it for what it is"—she gave Zhara a significant glance—"emptiness made flesh."

Xu opened their mouth, then shut it again. "Please excuse me for a moment," they said in a stiff voice. "I think I need some air." They rose to their feet, opened the sliding doors to Jiyi's room in one smooth motion, slipped on their shoes, and disappeared down the hall.

"Are they all right?" Zhara asked.

Han got to his feet. "I'll go after them," he said. "It's a lot to take in, discovering your father might be a literal demon and not just a metaphorical one."

33

THE LAST DREGS OF SUNSHINE STREAKED THE twilight sky when Han finally emerged from the depths of Wisteria Court alone.

"Will Xu be all right?" Zhara asked anxiously. She had been waiting in the main receiving room of the teahouse after Jiyi had shooed her out to catch up on sleep.

"I think so," Han said. "Or at least, I hope so."

"Do they need company?"

He shook his head. "They said they wanted to be left alone."

"Will they be safe?"

Han paused before he answered. "I think so," he said. "Xu is quite capable. After all, they've managed to keep me alive for this long." He dimpled, although his smile didn't quite reach his eyes. "Anyway, let me walk you home, Mistress Brandy. It's a beautiful evening, and it would be a shame to spend it alone."

Although the hour was late, the streets were still thick with shoppers and tourists from other parts of the Morning Realms, browsing wares and wringing out every last drop of daylight they could while the skies were still aglow.

The air was syrupy with the sticky humidity of midsummer, but the unbearable heat had dissipated, leaving behind a pleasant, almost sultry environment as Han and Zhara walked through the luxury-goods district on their way back to the city. The lit lanterns gave everything a hazy, dreamy quality when mingled with the lavender and gold of sundown.

Zhara studied the well-dressed customers around them, feeling acutely aware of the grubbiness of her shabby tunic and trousers that made her stick out like a weed among wildflowers. Everything in this part of the market looked, smelled, and felt like money. No, not money—*wealth*. Even the air was richer here, somehow lighter and more complex than it was just a few streets away—subtly perfumed with incense, sandalwood, ylang-ylang, and jasmine. The heavy scents of fried onions, grease, rice, and fatty meats did not linger far beyond the shops and restaurants serving food, as though ashamed of reminding others of such mundane acts as eating. It all made Zhara's mouth water with want, a pleasant ache in her belly that had nothing to do with hunger and everything to do with longing.

"So." Han cleared his throat as he walked beside her. "Have you decided what you will wear to the masquerade ball on the Night of the Sevens?"

"Am I going?" Zhara asked in surprise. "I thought my sister and I were meant to be leaving with the Bangtan Brothers on the Night of the Sevens."

"Oh, right," he said sheepishly. "I forgot. It's just . . . I said I would take you to the masquerade ball, and I wanted to keep my word."

A warmth that had nothing to do with the heat of midsummer or her magic and everything to do with the heat of her feelings for Han burned in Zhara's chest. "Oh, well," she said, trying not to let the Good-Looking Giggles get the best of her. "Perhaps there will be time for just one dance."

He gave her a lopsided grin, his left dimple deeper than his right. "You know," he said, "I've never really looked forward to the masquerade ball before."

Zhara looked down, feeling overwhelmed by the Giggles. "And I've never been," she said. "But I look forward to going with you, Master Plum Blossom."

True to his nickname, Han turned a brilliant crimson, nearly purple in the growing darkness. "So," he said once again, feet shuffling together awkwardly as they meandered down the stalls together. "Have you decided on your costume yet?"

"Costume?"

"It's a masquerade ball," he said. "Everyone shows up in costume, even if it's as simple as draping a sheet over your head and calling yourself a ghost."

"I—I haven't given it any thought," Zhara admitted. "I suppose I didn't believe I would actually ever be going."

Han pressed a hand over his heart. "You wound me, Mistress Brandy."

She shook her head. "It's not that I doubted your word," she said quietly. "It's just that . . . it's just that I had never dared hope that any of my dreams would come true."

His face softened as he looked at her, those large, round eyes of his gentle and open. "Why not?"

Zhara tried to meet his gaze, tried to have the courage not to look away from the naked kindness she saw reflected there. "Because for the longest time I did not know I *could* dream," she said. "That I could wish—want—for things beyond what I needed. A roof over my head, clothes on my back, and food in my belly."

He was quiet for a long moment. "Do you know," he said in a low voice, "why I noticed you in front of Master Cao's bookshop that very first day we met?"

She was surprised he even remembered the first time he saw her. Zhara could scarcely recall her own first impression of him. "No," she said. "What was it?"

"You were looking at the books on display with . . . longing," he said, and Zhara noticed that his ears were even redder than the rest of him. "And it pierced me to my soul. I've never wanted for much, you see," he said quickly. "Except maybe to be an ordinary boy. It was your wanting that made you beautiful to me. Your desire made the world bigger with possibility."

Something light and airy was fluttering about Zhara's rib cage, nearly ticklish and sweet. She wanted to laugh, she wanted to cry, she wanted to do both at once. "Oh," she said, voice trembling. "Alas, Master Plum Blossom, I'm afraid I can't say the same, since I can scarcely recall anything about our first meeting. Well, except for the Kestrels. And the book of magic."

"Yes, that." He ran a hand nervously over the back of his neck. "I suppose that could put a damper on things." He coughed. "So, about your costume. We could find it here. Looks as though there are lots of shops around here selling outfits and ensembles. I could—I could go shopping with you, if you'd like. Give you my, er, opinion on things."

Zhara smiled. "I'd be honored, Master Plum Blossom."

So the two of them took their time as they perused the clothing stalls. A pretty pink-and-white shirt-and-skirt ensemble caught Zhara's eye, and Han, noticing her interest, encouraged her to ask the merchant if she could try it on. At first, the merchant was disinclined to serve her, but when she pulled the silver nugget from her pocket, they immediately relented. At once, their demeanor changed, becoming obsequious and fawning by turns.

When Zhara tried on the pink-and-white ensemble, she closed her eyes to luxuriate in the smooth, almost slippery sensation of silk against her skin. Luxuriate. Luxury. She wondered what it would be like to wear such things every day. Her customary outfit was made of a rough-spun linen, softened by wear and tear. She had long ago ceased to notice the scratchiness of a new shirt or trousers, ceased to feel any embarrassment over the shabbiness of her clothes. Would the luxury of silk become unremarkable with habitual wear?

"Gorgeous," the merchant cooed, pinning a white silk orchid into her hair as they brought her before the full-length bronze mirror in their shop. "How well this shade of pink sets off the customer's dusky complexion!"

Suddenly Zhara found herself showered in compliments—on the rich darkness of her skin, the roundness of her eyes, the wild fullness of her hair, for each and every one of her features that she had been belittled for in the past.

But it was not the clothes that held Zhara's attention; it was her face. Although she had occasionally caught glimpses of her reflection in the still surface of a pond or a well, she had never truly seen herself as others did before. The girl staring back at her in the mirror moved as she did, blinked as she did, tilted her head as she did, yet Zhara could not connect the person before her with the image of herself in her mind. She had always defined herself in relation to those around her—small, drab, dark, mousy—but the girl in the mirror was none of those things.

The girl before her was *pretty*.

She was pretty.

Zhara's gaze touched Han's in the mirror, and with a start, she realized she had not needed her reflection to tell her she was beautiful. She had only needed to see herself reflected in Han's eyes, in the slightly awed, slightly terrified expression on his face. Beneath his gaze, she understood that she had *felt* pretty long before she had ever known she was pretty in truth, because in Han's eyes, she had been *seen*.

"Does the customer like it?" the merchant asked anxiously. "If not, I have plenty more that might better suit their fancy!"

"No, I love it," Zhara croaked, but she spoke to Han in the mirror, not the merchant at her side.

Thrilled, the shopkeep went about calculating the cost and Zhara paid for it without a second thought. To her surprise, the merchant handed her a large purse full of coins—change, they said—a concept that had been previously unknown to her. She had not known one could have more money than what something was worth. The merchant said the tailored adjustments would be ready in two days' time, at which time Zhara could pick up the outfit.

"Now a mask," Han said. "That's the important part of a masquerade after all."

They were passing a shop selling hand-carved masks when a short, plump merchant in their late middle years with smooth, smiling cheeks emerged from the back of the booth. "Welcome, customer, welcome!" they said cheerfully. "Welcome to Mistress Wen's Magical Emporium!"

The word *magical* sent a shiver down both their spines, but Han and Zhara smiled politely at the shopkeeper, who seemed to be a purveyor of a haphazard collection of various odds, ends, and trinkets. Browsing her wares was something of an adventure; they were never sure what they would find no matter where they turned.

"This place is unbelievable," Han murmured. "So many things I never knew I needed until now." He picked up a small parasol hat and placed it on his head. "Ingenious! For when it rains *and* I need my hands free!"

Zhara laughed. "Do you plan on attending the masquerade ball as an umbrella?"

Han surveyed the hat with a critical eye. "It wouldn't be the worst costume I've been made to wear," he said. "One year my mother thought it was a cute idea to dress me and my baby brother up as steamed rice cakes with banana-leaf hats."

"That sounds adorable!"

"It was," he said drily. "On my little brother. I, on the other hand, was ten."

They each fell silent for a while as they riffled through Mistress Wen's collection, the merchant hovering solicitously over their shoulders in case they found something to their liking.

"Ooh, what's this?" Han plucked a slim book from the shelves and flipped it open. "*Thirty-Six Positions of the Petal and Stamen*," he read aloud. "Poetry?"

Zhara's lips twisted. "Pornography."

"Oh? I've read *Tales from the Downy Delta*," Han bragged. "I'm sure this is nowhere near as— Oh, heavens." He snapped the pages shut and threw the book across the stall in a panic. "They just . . . leave it lying about where anyone can pick it up?"

"I hear erotic prints are all the rage in the fashionable parts of the city," she teased. "Surely the palace must have an impressive collection in the Royal Heir's quarters."

"Hah!" Han barked. "Not even remotely."

After several more moments of digging, Zhara found a mask to match her new ensemble. Carved from wood, it was painted white with pink and yellow water lilies, and she flagged down the shopkeep to purchase the mask, lingering over a tray of earrings glittering in the lamplight as she waited for the tally.

"Oh, yes," said Mistress Wen, pouncing on the opportunity for more patter. "I see the customer is interested in these earrings. What exquisite taste! They say necklaces decorate the clothes, but earrings decorate the face. And what a lovely face it is!"

Zhara's hands flew to her ears. "Oh, n-no," she stammered. "My ears aren't pierced." The memory of the Second Wife forcing Zhara to hold down a screaming, squirming, baby Suzhan while her stepmother mercilessly plunged a hot needle into the girl's lobes returned to her, and she suppressed a shudder with a smile.

"Wait." Mistress Wen snatched up a pair of jade earrings and grabbed her hand. "Buy a pair, and I will pierce the customer's ears for free!"

It was a while before Zhara could extricate herself from the overzealous merchant's clutches. Arms laden with packages and pockets much lighter, she and Han made their way to Lotus Bridge and the city of Zanhei itself. By now night had fallen completely, and tourists were buying and sending wish lanterns into the sky.

"Hold on a moment," Zhara said when they passed the booth selling those white silk slippers she had wanted so badly. They remained unsold and on display, the white of the silk taking on a warm hue from the light of the lanterns outside.

"Yah, you're back," the merchant grumbled. "You touch it, you buy it."

"How much?" she asked again, reaching into her coin purse for what was left of that silver nugget.

"Three hundred coins."

Zhara dropped her hand and jaw at the exorbitant sum. "Three hundred?" That was far more than she had left; far more than the silver nugget itself had even been worth.

"Here," Han said, reaching into his sash and pulling out a hefty coin purse. He dropped a gold ingot onto the table before the merchant.

"Oh, Han," she said, "you don't have to—"

"My lady needs shoes to match her ensemble!" But when she opened her mouth to protest again, he lifted his hand to forestall her. "Please," he said softly. "I couldn't give you a copy of *The Maiden Who Was Loved by Death*. Let me give you this, at least."

Tears pricked at Zhara's eyes, and she blinked rapidly to hold them back. No one had ever given her a gift before, and the joy of it was nearly as painful as loss. Han knelt and guided her foot into her new slipper, looking at up her, *seeing* her.

"There." He smiled, eyes crinkled, cheeks dimpled, and nose scrunched. "Beautiful."

She didn't think he wasn't talking of the shoes.

They continued on through the covered market, and Zhara felt as though she were walking on clouds, both literally, in her new shoes, and metaphorically, in her heart. The sweet scent of steamed egg buns, dragon's beard candy, and other treats wafted from food vendors docked along the waterways, while other skiffs sold painted half-masks and burning sparklers, lending a festive air to the proceedings. Early Night of the Sevens celebrations. Zhara watched as several young people gathered about a peddler selling wish lanterns and floating tea lights. They scrawled their wishes onto the outsides of the paper lanterns before walking down to the pier to release them into the air. *Riches,* said one. *A happy life,* said another. *Marriage to a handsome man. Health for my grandmother. Good grades on my next exam.*

"Shall I buy you a wish, Mistress Brandy?" Han murmured into her ear.

Zhara startled to find him standing so near. "What?" she said breathlessly, caught halfway between the desire to pull away and the desire to press even closer.

"I saw you watching the wish lanterns rising into the sky the other night," he said. "And I thought I might help you make a wish come true."

She bit her lip as she considered his offer. It was a simple yet friendly gesture, an act of generosity from someone who was both too aware and not aware enough at once, yet she found herself hesitating. The memory of their near-kiss still haunted her, and she realized after a moment that she was afraid. Not of being hurt, but of his kindness. She could get lost in that kindness. She could get lost in the hope it could mean something more.

"No, it's all right. It wouldn't matter anyway," Zhara said with a self-deprecating laugh. "I'm not even sure what I would ask for." She thought of the promise she had made to Suzhan, that she would follow her truth. Her dream of being cherished. It seemed such a trivial, frivolous wish, and yet she couldn't help wanting to make it.

"Really?" Han watched the steady stream of wishes drift away, a river of stars to the heavens. "I can think of so many things."

She studied him out of the corner of her eye. The lines of his profile limned by the soft glow of the floating lantern lights were sharp and clean, but there was a softness to his gaze as he looked up at the sky. "And what would you wish for, Master Plum Blossom?" she asked.

"Do I pick just one?"

She nodded. "Just one."

He turned to face her, his dark eyes serious. For once the Good-Looking Giggles didn't bubble up her throat; they withered away under the intensity of his focus. On her. "I wish," he whispered. "I wish I had had the courage to properly kiss you that night I walked you home for the first time."

Zhara sucked in a sharp breath. His eyes never left hers, searching for an answer to a question she did not know. He was standing so close, his face angled toward hers. She trembled, wanting so hard she hurt. Everything hurt. She realized now it was hope that hurt most. Han inched closer, and closer, and closer still, and it seemed as though he would forever come nearer but never touch.

Their lips brushed, tentative, hesitant, shy.

Then she pressed herself against him, deepening the kiss. His hands came up to skim her waist, either to pull her in or to her push her away, she wasn't sure. He was so shy, so gentle, it made her heart go soft with tenderness. But she was greedy. She wanted more. She whimpered and gripped the front of Han's robes tight in her fists. He wrapped his arms around her and pressed back.

When at last Zhara managed to open her eyes, she found him staring at her, slightly unfocused, a goofy, lopsided grin on his face. His dimples were barely there, but when she kissed him again and drew back, she found his nose-scrunched smile, dimples out in full force.

"Wah," he breathed.

"Yeah," she whispered, and then to her horror, the Good-Looking Giggles sprang from nowhere, bubbling up from some invisible well-spring of happiness.

"Er," Han said, blinking in confusion. "What's so funny?"

"N-nothing," Zhara said, trying to keep her laughter in check. "It's j-just th-that——" Another shower of giggles burst from her throat. "I get g-giggly around g-good-looking people."

Han looked smug as he leaned forward to brush the hair from her cheek. "Is that so?" he asked, his lips barely a breath's distance away. "I'm flattered." His gaze softened. "You're crying," he said reverently, wiping away her tears with his thumbs.

To her surprise, she was. "Yes," she whispered. "I am."

"Why?"

She gave a watery laugh. "Because, for once, I'm thriving instead of merely surviving."

Han gave a soft gasp as he took his hands away.

"What is it?" she asked. He held his palms up to her face.

In Han's hands, glimmering in the moonlight and shimmering with the myriad rainbow colors of the fireworks-strewn sky, were several freshwater pearls, each one perfectly teardrop-shaped with happiness.

PART THREE

NIGHT OF THE SEVENS

34

IT WAS WELL PAST THE MIDNIGHT HOUR when Zhara finally got home. All the lights were doused in their ramshackle little house, meaning the Second Wife had either gone out for the evening or she was already asleep. A giddy mood shot through Zhara as she tripped through the courtyard gate and into the kitchen, arms laden with goods from the marketplace. Not even the knowledge that she would have to be up in a few short hours to prepare breakfast could dampen her glee. No, the dawn would bring with it another day closer to the Night of the Sevens, another day closer to the rest of her life. Tomorrow she would tell Suzhan that she need not marry Lord Chan, that her nene had found a way for both of them to live their truths.

"Nene."

Startled, Zhara dropped her packages. Sitting in complete darkness on her usual stool before the hearth was Suzhan, her tall, awkward silhouette scarcely visible against the thin silver light of the crescent moon filtering in through the kitchen window.

"Mimi? What are you doing sitting here in the dark?" Zhara hurried forward to tend to her sister, but Suzhan brushed her off with an uncharacteristically stiff posture.

"The dark makes no difference to me," she said in a strange, high voice. Her words were strangled, thin, and reedy, as though she was struggling for air. "But you knew that already."

Zhara frowned, her previously euphoric mood already starting to dwindle. "Is something the matter, mimi? Are you feeling well?" She laid a hand against Suzhan's brow, but it was cool and dry beneath her skin.

"Don't touch me." Her sister's tone was curt, brusque, and entirely without its usual teasing warmth. "Magician."

Zhara felt that last word like a slap to her face. "I'm not—How did you—When—" She had known she would have to confess her power to Suzhan before she revealed the existence of the Guardians of Dawn, but she thought she had time. Time to formulate her approach, to ease her sister into her identity as a magician, to reassure her sister that she was still the nene who stroked her hair and told her stories before bed. Zhara had thought she could come out to Suzhan on her own terms.

But that moment was gone now—stolen.

"I see you don't deny it."

She couldn't. She wouldn't. "Did Madame tell you?" Zhara asked in a small voice.

She wondered if this was the Second Wife's idea of retaliation for having refused Lord Chan's offer of patronage—taking away the one thing she had always taken for granted: her trust that her stepmother would keep Zhara's secret, even at her own expense. Because the Second Wife . . . cared. *What sort of mother holds the knowledge of her daughter's magic over her head as some sort of collateral?* A lump rose in Zhara's throat as she realized what a fool she had been.

"She knew?" It was the note of utter, utter devastation and betrayal in Suzhan's voice that broke Zhara's heart. "You told Mama . . . and not me?"

Zhara closed her eyes. The Second Wife had kept her secret after all. But that knowledge no longer brought her any hope—it only shattered any possibility this conversation with her sister was going to end well. "I did not tell Madame," she said softly. "Madame has always known."

Suzhan let out a soft hiccough of rage and sorrow. "I see." She was silent a long moment. "And why," she asked in a low voice, "did you never think to tell *me*?"

There were so many reasons, but none of them seemed sufficient in the face of her sister's hurt. Because Zhara wanted to protect her, because she wanted to keep her safe from the Kestrels, because she was afraid. She realized she had been afraid of Suzhan's judgment, because

she had not known what Suzhan's thoughts on magic were. They had
never once discussed the subject of the Just War in all their conversa-
tions in Zhara's kitchen, had never once talked about Jin Zhanlong and
how he died, had never once spoken of the reason Suzhan had woken
up blind all those years ago.

"Because," Zhara said quietly, "I was ashamed."

Suzhan did not reply straightaway, and the silence pressed down on
Zhara's ribs, making it hard to breathe. It was as honest an answer as
she could give her sister, for it said everything and nothing.

"Ashamed of who you are?" Suzhan asked. "Or what you've done?"

Guilt and fear jolted through Zhara's stomach, and she wondered if
Suzhan had guessed at or known of the accident that had robbed her of
her vision. "Both," she said hesitantly. "The empire went to war over
magic, mimi. I was ashamed of who I was for a long time."

Suzhan shook her head. It was too dark to make out her features,
but Zhara dare not light a candle or start a fire in the hearth. The dark
was where Suzhan had power, where her sister had the advantage, and
Zhara knew that her sister had chosen this moment and this setting for
a reason. "Being ashamed of an accident or a quirk of birth is as silly as
it is futile," Suzhan said. "This is who you are, nene. There is no shame
in that."

The words were something Suzhan would have said in any other
situation where she was trying to comfort Zhara, but the tone was still
distant, still remote. Before, Zhara would have been able to bridge
that gap between them with humor, but she sensed that laughter now
would only drive them further apart.

"But shame in your actions," Suzhan went on, and her tone was icier
than ever, "that's something else."

It was in this moment Zhara realized that Suzhan might be her
mother's daughter after all, for that brittle bitterness in her voice was
just as painful to hear in Suzhan as it was in the Second Wife.

"So," her sister said. "What have you done that you are ashamed of,
Jin Zhara?"

Jin Zhara. Not nene. Zhara felt as though she were standing on
the edge of a howling divide, arms outstretched and reaching for

something she feared would be lost forever if she spoke the truth. "N-nothing," she said, and cursed herself for her honest tongue.

Suzhan crossed her arms. "You lie."

Zhara could not deny it. "Yes," she whispered. "How"—she licked her lips—"how did you find out?"

"Give me some credit," her sister scoffed. "I'm blind, not stupid."

Zhara cringed.

"I suppose I've always known," Suzhan said. Her voice was softer, but no less cold than before. "There was always something . . . different about you. An unusual glow that even I could see sometimes." There was a soft rustling sound from the corner as she rose to her feet, followed by the light *tap-tap-tap* of her cane. "But I knew for certain after our meeting with Lord Chan."

When Zhara transformed the wine into water.

"*It is by their touch,*" Suzhan quoted, "*that we know a magician as evil.*" She fell silent for a while. "I didn't understand what that meant until I understood it was *your* touch that hurt me as much as it has healed me."

"Mimi," Zhara began. "I never meant—"

"Did you know," Suzhan continued, "that when Mama took me to the healer when I was little, they said that there would be no treatment or cure that could salvage my vision?"

The darkness forced Zhara to speak lest her sister mistake her silent actions for actual silence. "Yes."

"Do you know what reason they gave me?"

Zhara shook her head, then forced the word through her lips. "No."

"That my eyes weren't eyes. Instead of lens and tissue and fluid and blood, the things that sit in my sockets are neither flesh nor glass, but some unnatural, unholy combination thereof."

The description, delivered so bluntly and without feeling, made Zhara's stomach turn over. Bile rose in her throat and she wondered if she was going to be sick.

"I was obviously not born this way," Suzhan continued inexorably. "So the healer asked Mama what magician had cursed me to live like this, for nothing born of nature could have given me such eyes." She had drawn so close that Zhara could feel her sister's breath against her lips. "And now I know that person is you."

"Yes," Zhara whispered again. There was nothing more she could say.

"Why?" Suzhan's voice broke. "Why did you curse me? Did you hate me? Were you jealous of the attention Mama gave me?"

"No, mimi," she said. "It was an accident. An accident, I swear."

She hadn't meant to hurt her sister; she had only wanted to help. She had been practicing in secret for so long, turning buttons into coins, flowers into ribbons, wood into stone. Zhara had been confident, so confident that she could somehow use her magic to fix her sister's eyesight. Even as a child, Suzhan's vision had been deteriorating by the day, and the heavy glass spectacles that had once been enough to help her see no longer worked.

"I just wanted to help," Zhara said, more to herself than to her sister.

It would be easy, she had thought, so easy to change her sister's eyes, to imagine them whole and hale and healed, Suzhan's vision as sharp and clear as it had been when she first got her spectacles. So when Suzhan crawled down to the kitchen one night, Zhara placed her hands on her sister's head as she slept and dreamed of Suzhan waking up with perfect eyes.

She had woken up blind instead.

"I didn't know," Zhara said. "I didn't know what I was doing, but I thought . . . I thought I could fix you."

"*Fix* me?" Suzhan's lip curled with disdain. "As though I were a broken toy in need of mending?"

"No!" Zhara said. "There was nothing wrong with you. It was only that Madame . . ." She couldn't finish her sentence, but she didn't need to.

"It was that Mama thought I was flawed." Suzhan turned her head away. "And took her anger out on me."

"Yes." As Zhara spoke, her magic rose to the surface and illuminated the kitchen. "I would have done anything to spare you the pain."

Suzhan stepped back. "Is that—is that your magic?" Her eyes quivered as they tried to focus on the source of the light.

"Yes," Zhara said in a hoarse voice. Her sister reached her hand out to touch hers in wonder, but Zhara quickly snatched it back. "No, don't," she said desperately. "I don't want to hurt you."

"Hurt me?" Suzhan laughed without mirth. "But you've already hurt me, nene. In so many ways. What difference would a little magic make?" In the faint glow of Zhara's power, Suzhan's face was harsh, her features twisted and contorted with agony. "You were the reason Mama beat me," she said in an anguished voice. "The reason I could not please her. The reason I am being sold off to the highest bidder like some prize cow at market."

"I know, mimi, I know." She wished there were other words she could say, other platitudes of comfort she could offer.

Suzhan snorted. "Is that all you have to say to me?"

"What is it you want to hear, mimi?" Zhara murmured. "Tell me, so that I might say it and be forgiven."

"As though trust were as easy to repair with words as wounds are with magic," Suzhan said scornfully. "I don't have anything I want to hear, nene. Except one thing. That you're sorry."

"I'm sorry," Zhara whispered. "I know it's not enough, but I'm so, so sorry."

Suzhan's shoulders sagged. "You're right, it's not enough." She paused. "But I suppose it will have to do."

Relief washed over Zhara in immense waves, dousing the flames beneath her skin and plunging the kitchen back into total darkness. She knew her relationship with Suzhan was not the same and might never recover, but at least it wasn't unsalvageable. She had betrayed her sister's trust and her sister's love, but that did not mean either could not be rebuilt again. She just had to prove herself. She had to make things right in whatever way she could. Zhara fell to her knees and pressed her forehead to the floor, and although Suzhan could not see her, she knew her sister could sense her prostrate on the ground.

"Let me make it up to you, mimi," she said softly, her words nearly swallowed up by the packed-earth floor of the kitchen. "Let me find some way to make amends."

"And how would you do that, nene?" Suzhan asked wearily. And while the affection was gone from her tone, Zhara could still hear the echoes of love in her voice. "What's done is done."

Zhara swallowed. "Yes, but what if I told you I can get you out of your marriage to Lord Chan?"

Suzhan went still. "You jest."

She shook her head before she remembered to speak. "No, mimi," she said softly. "What if I were to tell you that I'm in deadly earnest?"

"But . . . how?" In that moment, Suzhan sounded like the girl she was—young, hopeful, not yet hardened or cynical to the world around her. "Why?"

Zhara paused, wondering what she could say that wouldn't make her sound either like an old woman telling tales or like a villain for keeping all this a secret from her sister. *Your husband is possessed by a demon* made her sound delusional, while *I'm part of a secret mutual aid society I did not bother to tell you about* made her seem as though she were being infantilizing. "There are," she said slowly, "other magicians in the world. Magicians in the Morning Realms."

Suzhan paused. "I suppose that makes sense," she said. "Although I can't believe I hadn't considered that before."

"Many of these magicians and their allies have been working together in secret," Zhara continued, "to offer aid and support to each other, as well as to the other magical families and their loved ones, since the end of the Just War." At the words *loved ones,* Suzhan flinched. "The Guardians of Dawn have agreed to help us escape to the outer reaches of the empire, where we might both be free from the long arm of the Warlord's rules and edicts." *And from the Second Wife,* Zhara wanted to add, but she couldn't say the words. To utter them aloud would be too much hope for either of them to bear.

"Why would you do this, nene?" Suzhan frowned. "Why would you do this . . . for me?"

Because you are marrying a demon in disguise. "Because I love you, mimi," Zhara said. "And I would never abandon you."

But instead of excitement, Suzhan was strangely silent. "It is true that I would prefer it," she said at last, "if I did not have to marry Lord Chan."

Her sister was going to come. Zhara's shoulders relaxed. "Oh, good," she said. "Because I have a plan, mimi. A plan to get us beyond Zanhei—beyond Lord Chan, and beyond . . . Madame. We just need to be ready to leave on the Night of the Sevens."

Suzhan furrowed her brow. "Mama said I am supposed to attend the masquerade ball with my future husband and greet the Royal Heir of Zanhei and his bride-to-be. It's part of my new duties as the wife of the Chancellor."

Zhara bit her lip. "But you don't have to be by Lord Chan's side all night, do you?"

"No, I suppose not."

"Good. Then I will meet you at the palace, and we shall escape together then."

Again, that strange silence from Suzhan. "Together," the girl said slowly, rolling the word on her tongue as though trying to categorize all its varied flavors. Her fingers twitched, plucking invisible strings again.

"Yes, mimi," Zhara said. "Together." Slowly, hesitantly, Zhara held her glowing hand out to her sister, illuminating Suzhan's face. Her sister's expression was unreadable.

"A good girl to the end," Suzhan murmured. "Aren't you, nene?" She reached her own trembling hand out to Zhara's but did not touch, eyes fixed on the light before her. "I see you, nene," she said hoarsely. "For the first time, I think I can truly *see* you." She shook her head and gave a cracked laugh. "But you know, I think I preferred it when we were both in the dark."

Zhara pulled the magic back beneath her skin and let night fall around them like a blanket. She reached out and felt for her sister's bony shoulders, pulling her into an embrace. "The Night of the Sevens," she said. "The Night of the Sevens is when the rest of our lives will begin."

"I hope so," Suzhan said softly. "I hope so."

35

A FLURRY OF KNOCKS AND SHOUTS ROUSED HAN from sleep.
"Wake up!" a voice hissed. "It's Anyang! Hurry!"

He sat bolt upright, his mind trying to claw out of the cocoon of slumber that clung to him.

"Xu, is that you?" he asked hoarsely, squinting at the silhouette outside his windows. Han fumbled for a robe or a shawl to throw over his nightclothes and opened the rice paper shutters. His best friend stood in the courtyard, hair mussed and makeup smeared, robe hanging askew off their shoulders.

"Who else would it be?" they asked irritably. They tilted their head. "Why, was His Grace expecting someone else? A certain round-eyed maiden who can produce fire with her bare hands, perhaps?"

"Shut up." Han rubbed his eyes. "What's this about Anyang?"

"The Second Heir is not in his residence."

"What?" Terror slashed through Han's sleepy haze, and he was now wide awake. "Where is he? Should we alert the Guardians of Dawn?" He thought of the corpses they had found up in Mount Zanhei. "What should we do?"

"Shh, shh," Xu soothed. "I found him. He's in the meditation gardens but . . ." They trailed off. "Han," they said, dropping their formal tone. "Something's not right."

Han jumped through the open window and onto the ground, wincing as his bare feet landed hard on the gravel. "Let's go."

"What about the guards—"

"Hang the guards," he growled. "Besides, don't you know the night rotation by heart, traipsing back and forth between people's beds as often as you do?"

Xu sniffed. "I'm choosing to read that as a comment on my superior observational skills and not an indictment of my illicit nighttime activities."

Han rolled his eyes and grabbed his best friend's hand. "Hurry!"

The two of them limped and tiptoed their way through the courtyard and out of the men's quarters. Han crouched behind Xu as they squeezed their way between two buildings, careful to keep to the shadows. They soon emerged from the tangle of residences and into the large, open expanse behind the royal assembly, its gilded gables dull in the moonlight.

"Get down!" Xu hissed, throwing themself on top of Han. A phalanx of ordinary palace guards marched past, oblivious to the two human-shaped lumps pressed against a wall.

"I don't know whether to be relieved or concerned they didn't notice us," Han muttered once the coast was clear.

"Relief now, concern later." Xu scowled as they looked him up and down. "You couldn't have chosen something less conspicuous to wear?"

He glanced at his dressing gown, which was a bright white in the darkness. "It was the first thing I could grab," he grumbled.

With a long-suffering sigh, his best friend stripped off their own robes—a navy blue that was nearly invisible against the inky, black night—and handed it over. Beneath the gossamer and gauze Xu wore a surprisingly utilitarian dark shirt and trousers, more suitable for sneaking about the shadows than lounging around in the pleasure district. Han accepted his friend's robe with a sheepish bow and quickly shed his pale dressing gown in favor of Xu's, wincing as the seams tore along the shoulders.

"Xu," he began.

"Save it," they said curtly. "You can buy me another one later."

Anxiety curdled in the pit of his stomach. If Xu wasn't upset about their clothes, the situation must be dire indeed.

They peered around the corner of the assembly hall. "There," they said, pointing to a pavilion ahead. "That's where I saw the Second Heir. Better make a run for it."

The two of them bolted across the zigzag bridge that led to the moon-gazing pavilion, but the viewing platform was empty.

"Where's Anyang?" Han panted, panic squeezing the breath from his lungs. He frantically searched the dark water of the decorative pond surrounding the pavilion. As a child he had once slipped through the railing and fallen in, and neither he nor his brother could swim.

"More guards!" Xu grabbed Han by the sleeve and bodily threw him down to the floor. If he weren't so afraid for Anyang, Han would have been impressed by their strength. "There."

He followed the line of their finger toward the grove of willow trees on the other side of the pond. Two figures strolled side by side beneath the trees. The moon turned the water into a mirror, clearly reflecting the tufted-feather hairstyle of the Kestrels on them both. A third silhouette could be seen sitting on a stone meditation bench a little ways apart—someone small and familiar.

Anyang.

Han immediately jumped to his feet despite Xu's protests and darted into the bushes. He dropped to his hands and knees and crawled toward his brother and the Falconer's birds. Han could hear Xu hiss "Your Grace!" as he wriggled through the ferns and then a soft *thud!* as they followed suit.

"I'm just trying to get him to his majority alive," Xu muttered. "Six more months, just six more months . . ."

The Kestrels drew close to Anyang on the bench, and Han despaired of reaching his little brother in time. The feeling slowly drained from his fingers as he scraped and scrabbled through the sand and dirt, the memory of the day his mother was taken away returning to him in waves. The taste of ash filled his mouth, and he wanted to choke. He had already lost someone he loved once; he didn't know if he could bear to lose another to the Warlord's justice. If he could get to his feet, perhaps he could run, grab Anyang and—

Too late. The Kestrels had already reached the Second Heir. One of the magician hunters—a tall, spindly one—reached out to touch Anyang on the shoulder, but their companion—short and stout—held them back.

"Wait," the short one cautioned. "The Chancellor will give us the all clear, and then we can carry the kid back to bed."

Beside him, Xu stiffened. Han recalled how their face had blanched when Zhara told them that their father was not their father but a demon wearing their father's face. *Are you*— he mouthed before Xu frantically waved at him to keep quiet.

Anyang sat completely still on the meditation bench, his eyes closed and his breathing even, as though he were fast asleep. Several moments passed while Han struggled to hold his breath, to keep the sound of his racing pulse from betraying their position.

Presently, Anyang lifted his head and opened his eyes.

And the world fell silent.

It was as though Han had been plunged underwater. The air was thick and it was difficult to breathe, but the most unsettling thing of all was the complete and utter lack of noise. No crickets chirping. No frogs croaking. Not even the occasional burble of water from the pond as a fish surfaced for flies.

Dead silence.

Anyang leaned over and picked something up from the ground, cradling it to his chest and petting it. It was a while before Han recognized the thing for what it was—a bird.

A sudden *crack!* broke the quiet as his little brother snapped the creature's neck. Han stuffed a hand in his mouth to stifle his cries. The two Kestrels jerked back in horror.

"Hoy," said the taller one. "That's creepy."

Their stout companion hissed at them to shut up.

Slowly, stiffly, Anyang opened his palms to reveal the dead animal, its head dangling at an unnatural angle. His soft breaths ruffled the broken bird's feathers, and after a moment, its wings and talons began to twitch. Flopping. Fluttering. Flapping. Anyang's hands twitched with the creature, almost as though there were invisible strings tied to the ends of his fingers.

The bird began to fly.

"Yah!" the taller Kestrel gasped.

This was wrong, all wrong. The bird was still clearly dead, its neck bent, eyes glassy, yet it flapped its wings disjointedly, somehow managing to stay aloft. The sensation of little skittering claws ran over Han's skin, and he remembered the dead rats pouring through the streets of the covered market, and the wave of horror and revulsion that preceded the abomination, the same creeping, uncanny feeling that had swept over him in the cave beneath Mount Zanhei.

His stomach churned and he tried not to retch into the bushes. "No," he murmured. "No."

Magic that defied all reason and order and logic. He had been with the Guardians of Dawn long enough to know what that betokened now.

Possession.

Xu tightened their grip on his leg, but Han wasn't going anywhere. He was too paralyzed with dread, not wanting to watch but unable to look away. Wanting to hold on to the last moments his little brother was his little brother, and not a monster.

An abomination.

Anyang dropped his arms.

And the bird fell to the ground.

"A powerful magician," Anyang said. "He's a bit young, but at least when I'm manifest in this world, I will have the the advantage of time as the body grows up."

The Warlord's magician hunters startled. "Is that the Chancellor?"

"Of course it is," said Anyang in an irritated voice. "I told you it would be."

The little boy's face took on a different aspect and expression as he barked orders to the Kestrels. His smile was bland, and his eyes seemed to bulge beneath the moonlight. It was as though someone had slipped on Anyang's skin like a mask, the cheeks curiously slack despite the alien intelligence that animated his features. "We have all the elements of the ritual, save for the sacrificial vessel. This boy is a powerful magician; we must hope he is strong enough."

"Strong enough for what, my lord?" asked the taller Kestrel.

Anyang's smile was not his own. "It is of no concern to you. Just make sure everything is ready on the Night of the Sevens. The ritual must be completed then."

Han and Xu exchanged horrified looks.

Ritual? Xu mouthed.

Han shook his head.

"What of this sacrificial vessel, Your Eminence?" the other Kestrel asked. "What is it for?"

Anyang grunted. "Just do as I ask and don't ask questions. I must go; until the ritual is complete, my control over this body is . . . inconsistent at best. I shall speak with you on the morrow." Then, all of a sudden, all of Anyang's muscles went slack and he crumpled to the ground like a puppet whose strings had been cut.

The taller Kestrel nudged the boy with the tip of their boot. "Is he dead?"

Their stouter companion knelt and pressed a finger to the side of Anyang's neck. "No. Pulse is faint, but steady. I think he's just deeply asleep. Come on." They hoisted the Second Heir over their shoulder and began trudging toward the men's quarters of the palace. "Let's take him back to bed before anyone discovers he's gone." An enormous yawn split their face. "I'm not sure how many more nights of this I—or the kid— can take."

"Tell me about it," the taller Kestrel muttered as they followed their companion out of the meditation gardens. "When all this is over, I'm going to sleep for days."

Han held his breath as he watched the Kestrels carry his unconscious brother back to his rooms. Once the gardens were empty, he got to his feet, but he spotted a flash of something dark and red, the color of spilled blood in moonlight, moving through the underbrush.

They were not alone in the garden.

"My prince," Xu whispered, pointing to the movement.

"I see it," Han murmured back. There was something wispy and insubstantial about the way it moved, as though it were a spirit or a ghost floating through the leaves, a reflection from the world beyond the veil. It made no sound as it traversed the garden, but Han thought he could make out the vague shape of a human as the dappled shadows both revealed and concealed the figure. *Is this the frog demon?* he wondered. Slowly, agonizingly slowly, he made his way through the underbrush toward the silhouette for a closer look.

It was Princess Yulana.

Fear and panic sliced through him when he realized the Warlord's granddaughter must have been hiding there long enough to witness the entire scene between a seemingly possessed Anyang and the Kestrels. He couldn't let her escape and go running back to her grandfather or the Falconer, he couldn't—

"Hoy!" Han leaped out of the brush to tackle her to the ground—

—only to fall straight through her onto his stomach.

"Your Grace!" Xu cried, foregoing all pretense of stealth and trampling through the tall grass after him.

Han groaned as he turned over to see the bemused face of his betrothed staring down at him. "Well, if it isn't Prince Rice Cake," she said amiably. "Fancy meeting you here. I would help you to your feet, except, well . . ." She bent over and tried to grasp his hand, but he felt nothing as her hand passed through his.

"Wh-what . . . h-how—" he stuttered. "How is this possible?"

Yulana rolled her eyes. "I'm not here," she said. "Clearly."

"What do you mean you're not here?" he demanded. He reached out to grab the northern princess again, but his fingers passed through her arm as though she were no more than mist or vapor.

She smiled.

"You're . . . you're a magician," Han said in amazement.

"Well spotted." The princess—or the image of her—crossed her arms. "Are all southerners soft in the brain as well as the body?"

"No, just me, I'm afraid." He looked her up and down, studying her closely. Now that he was aware the princess wasn't *truly* standing before him, he could see there was a slight haziness to her, as though the edges of her silhouette had been smudged by a careless hand. "What sort of magician power is this?" he asked.

"Mine," she said irritably. "I've had it since birth."

"Yes—but—" Han faltered, trying to remember all the things Jiyi had told them about the laws governing magic. "Are you . . . are you an abomination?"

"Do I look like an abomination?"

"I don't know," he said. "I don't know what abominations are supposed to look like, except monstrous."

"I will choose not to take that as a comment on my looks," Yulana remarked wryly. "But no, I am not an abomination. I am"—she hesitated—"special."

"I can see that," Han said. "But forgive me if that isn't quite enough to explain what is happening here."

Yulana sighed. "I am," she said after a moment, "the Guardian of Wind."

At first, he wasn't sure if he had heard the northern princess correctly. "I'm sorry," he said. "Did you say *Guardian of Wind*?"

"Are you slow of hearing as well as slow of wits?" Yulana shook her head. "But . . . yes. Yes, I did say that. You know"—she tilted her head as she studied him—"you're not as, ah, shocked or disbelieving as I thought you would be at this revelation."

"Well, you're not the first Guardian of Dawn I've met this week," he said. "You're not the first Guardian I've met on this day, even. Literally *and* figuratively."

Yulana raised her brows. "Do tell, Prince Rice Cake."

Han pinched the bridge of his nose. "Let's just say I've had an, ah, interesting past couple of weeks." He frowned. "Wait, hold on, hold on, first things first. How are *you* the Warlord's granddaughter?"

"Simple," she said in a dry voice. "My mother's father is the Warlord, thereby making me his granddaughter."

The fact that she was insubstantial made it easier for him to resist grabbing her by the shoulders and shaking some sense into her. "You know what I mean."

Yulana made a face. "Fine. My obaji doesn't know I'm a magician."

"How on earth is that possible?"

She shrugged. "It's easy enough when the idea of your own flesh and blood being a magician is anathema to your entire being." The princess gave a humorless laugh. "It's easy to deceive yourself when you don't want to believe your favorite grandchild is afflicted with the Curse. You make all sorts of excuses." She sobered. "And see only what you want to see."

Han narrowed his eyes. "So why *did* the Warlord arrange our betrothal? I thought that maybe it was because you liked women, and your grandfather wasn't pleased about that."

"Oh, that." Yulana waved her hand dismissively. "Obaji has never cared who his children loved or did not love. No, this marriage was my idea."

"Yours?" Han was startled. "Why? And why me?"

"Well, two reasons," she admitted. "The first was that you had a reputation for being a bit thick in the head, and I thought a dullard of a husband would be a boon, especially as I needed to keep my magic a secret. The second was"—she bit her lip—"I was looking for a book on demons. *Songs of Order and Chaos.* The last copy was rumored to be in the possession of Zanhei's royal astrologer. Unfortunately, when I arrived, it appeared that the copy of the book had disappeared with him and his daughter several months ago."

"So that's why Xu and I ran into you in the library," Han said. "You were looking for Uncle Li's book."

"Yes," she said. "Or anything else that might prove useful on the subject of demons and demonology. We don't have that many sources on that subject in the north, as you might imagine."

He thought of the pages he and Xu had managed to salvage from the rubbish bin in the archive room and of Jiyi's meticulous cataloguing of their contents. "What do you want a book of demonology for?" he asked.

"No." Yulana held up her hand. "You've asked enough questions. It's my turn now."

"All right," Han said amiably. "I'll try my best to answer, but I'll warn you that the rumors were indeed correct that your future husband is a bit thick. In more ways than one."

She snorted, but Han thought he got the briefest glimpse of a smile. "Who is Jin Zhara?"

Han startled. "Zhara?" He straightened. "You've met her?"

"Yes, a few days ago, as a matter of fact," the northern princess said. "She's rather cute, I must say. Not my type, but cute nonetheless." Yulana grinned. "Did you know she giggles when she finds you attractive? It's adorable."

Han did know, but what he didn't know was how to feel about the fact that his betrothed had also been on the receiving end of Zhara's Good-Looking Giggles. He imagined the ease with which the northern princess could flirt with Zhara and felt an obscure pang of jealousy at Yulana's confident charm. "So what do you want to know about her?" he asked.

"Who is she?" Yulana repeated. "Or rather . . . *what* is she?"

"What do you mean?" Han asked, although he suspected he could guess the princess's line of questioning.

Yulana held her arm out to Han. "She is the only person who can touch me in my astral state. Of all the other magicians I have come across, you might say she's the only other one who is . . . special. Like me." She studied his face. "She's another elemental Guardian, isn't she?"

Han fell silent. Although his betrothed had given him her identity as the Guardian of Wind easily and without reservation, he wasn't sure if it was his place to reveal Zhara's true identity to Yulana. "She certainly is special," he said instead, thinking of the teardrop-shaped pearls she had shed the night he kissed her beneath the wish lanterns in the city. He had taken the pearls to the palace jeweler and asked to have them set in a pale rose quartz bangle so he might present them back to her as gift on the Night of the Sevens.

He cleared his throat. "She is also a member of the mutual aid society called the Guardians of Dawn."

"Mutual aid society?" Yulana asked in some surprise. "I thought they were a terrorist organization."

"What? No! Who says that?"

Yulana frowned. "In the north, I heard rumors of a secret resistance group fomenting unrest out west under the banner of the Four-Winged Dragon, looking to restore the last Mugung heir to the Sunburst Throne. They call themselves the Guardians of Dawn."

He thought of what Jiyi had said about the western reaches becoming dangerous with rebel groups forming under the banner of the Four-Winged Dragon. The courtesan had dismissed them as *hotheads,* merely warning Zhara that the journey to the land of the Qirin Tulku with her sister would not be an easy one. "I suppose there is a contingent of the organization with more political aims," he admitted. "But labeling them a terrorist organization is just propaganda designed to enforce the status quo. Especially since it's the magicians who are the ones being oppressed."

"True," Yulana conceded. Her outline was beginning to waver under the moonlight as she gave an enormous yawn. "If you would excuse me, Your Grace. It's getting late and I'm exhausted. The effort it takes just to keep myself visible for you is becoming increasingly burdensome, especially when it would be easier to talk to each other in the flesh on the morrow."

"All right," he said, before an enormous yawn cut off his words as well. "Listen, why don't you just come to a meeting of the Guardians of Dawn with me? There are a lot of scholars and historians who can answer your questions far better than I can."

Yulana pursed her lips thoughtfully. "That sounds reasonable, although," she said with a teasing twinkle in her eye, "what will your adorable giggle girl think when you bring your ersatz fiancée to the meeting?"

It was then, Han realized, that he had deeply, completely, and utterly messed up.

36

ZHARA DIDN'T KNOW WHAT TO BE MORE excited about: going to the palace masquerade ball with Han or meeting the Bangtan Brothers on the Night of the Sevens. In person. In the flesh. In such a manner that they might even learn her name. Or who she was.

"Are you paying attention?" Jiyi said, snapping her fingers before Zhara's face.

"Yes," she said, bringing her focus back to the matter at hand—namely, the details of her and Suzhan's escape from Zanhei. "The Bangtan Brothers will find me at the masquerade ball. They will be wearing the sunburst pendant of the Mugung Dynasty, and then Suzhan and I are to join in the procession of animals, dressed as magpies."

The plan was simple enough; Han would get Zhara an invitation token to the Night of the Sevens, where they would spend a few hours mingling among the masked attendees before the Brothers arrived to take the sisters away. She tried not to think overmuch about what would happen next; the world beyond Zanhei was too much to take in. Where would she and Suzhan live? How would they support themselves? Would she ever learn to control this strange magic of hers that existed outside the void? Would she be expected to join in the more political aspects of the Guardians of Dawn? And who would take care of Sajah? So many unanswered questions, and if Zhara spent any time dwelling on them, her anxiety would rush up to drown her with dread. She had to keep treading, to keep her head above water and focus only on the immediate future.

Which was the Night of the Sevens.

Her seventeenth birthday.

Suddenly, the doors to Jiyi's quarters slid open with a bang.

"Can none of you use my doors properly?" the courtesan shouted at the newcomers. "Why must you always be throwing them open so dramatically?"

"Jiyi, I need your— Oh." It was Han at the threshold, but the figure standing behind him wasn't Xu; it was someone else, dressed in northern-style finery and a pointed hat. "You're not alone, I see," he said uncertainly, eyes darting from Zhara to the courtesan and back again.

"When did I *ever* give you leave to address me so informally?" Jiyi grouched. "Ugh, come in, come in." She tilted her head at the stranger who entered behind Han. "Who's this?"

Han and the stranger exchanged glances. "Yuli?" Zhara asked incredulously.

The not-ghost girl winked at her. "We meet again, Jin Zhara." She turned to Jiyi. "Ah, the Ice Princess of Flower Town, I presume," she said, tapping her right fist over her chest in a northern-style greeting. "She is even more beautiful than the poets have claimed."

"Treasured one, this young lady beside me is, er—" Han cleared his throat, looking to the girl beside him uncertainly. "How would you like to be introduced?"

There was something strange and stilted about the way Han addressed the redhead, his tone formal even as his mode of speech was intimate.

"Just *Yuli* is fine." Her teeth were very white against her wind-tanned skin as she gave the courtesan a flirtatious grin. "Although this beautiful lady may call me hers, if she wishes." To Zhara's surprise and delight, Jiyi turned an uncharacteristic shade of apple-blossom pink beneath the northern girl's relentless onslaught of charm.

The courtesan coughed. "Yes, well, it's nice to make Yuli's acquaintance," she said brusquely, although the flush did not leave her cheeks. "How may I be of assistance?"

"Prince Rice Cake here says that the treasured one knows where *Songs of Order and Chaos* might be found," the northern girl said bluntly.

"I didn't say we knew *where*—" Han began.

"*Songs of Order and Chaos*?" Jiyi said in surprise. "How does she—"

Zhara frowned. "Prince Rice Cake?"

Yulana's copper-brown eyes flitted in her direction, and for the briefest moment, Zhara thought she saw a flicker of guilt cross the other girl's expression. "Ah," she said, "just a nickname that popped into my head when I saw him for the first time," she said. "I do that a lot, Bubbles," she said with another wink. "Nickname people, that is."

"*Bubbles?*" Zhara asked.

"For your laugh," the redhead said.

And to prove the northerner's point, Zhara was overcome with another attack of the Good-Looking Giggles. Han looked as though he had just swallowed a frog, his mouth set in a slightly jealous frown. She found herself attacked by another round of the Giggles, this time from a different source.

"Would everyone just stop flirting and get back to the matter at hand?" Jiyi interrupted. She pointed a finger at Yuli. "Now, miss," she said. "What's this about *Songs of Order and Chaos?*"

Yuli leaned against the doorframe, arms and legs casually crossed. "I don't believe I've been offered a seat yet. I don't know how things are done in the south, but where I come from, hospitality is of the utmost importance."

The courtesan made a sound halfway between disgust and a squeak, cheeks pinking even harder as she cleared space around the low center table for the redhead to sit down. Jiyi gestured to the empty seat cushions with a dismissive gesture, unable to fully meet Yuli's eyes.

The northern girl sat cross-legged with a grin. "My thanks," she said to the courtesan with a nod of her head.

"*Songs of Order and Chaos?*" Jiyi asked irritably. "The young lady said she was searching for it?"

"You can drop the formalities with me, treasured one," Yuli said. "It's not the northern way to be so distant with those to whom we wish to get closer." She sobered. "And yes, I am searching for *Songs of Order and Chaos*. I've been searching for a long, long time."

"Why?" Jiyi asked.

Yuli's gaze slid toward Zhara again. "Because," she said quietly. "I am looking for protection from possession."

Beside the redhead, Han sucked in a sharp breath. "You never told me that," he said accusingly.

The northern girl glared at him. "Why would I? You don't go around telling complete strangers your brother is possessed by a demon either, do you?"

At her words, Han went deathly pale, the healthy, golden glow of his skin sallow with fear. Zhara remembered the night he had given her a piggyback ride home, how he had confessed to her that one of his biggest fears was that his little brother's magic had been corrupted. She reached out to touch him, but Han held himself rigid.

"Hold, hold, hold," Jiyi said. "Are the two of you saying that there are abominations running amuck? That we haven't heard about yet?"

Han shook his head. "No," he said. "My brother hasn't turned into a monster, but . . ." His words faded away into uncertain silence.

"But what?" Jiyi prompted.

"I think . . . whatever demon is possessing the Chancellor is trying to possess my little brother."

"A greater demon," Zhara whispered.

Han gave a miserable nod.

"There are four Kings of Tiyok," Yuli said, staring into the middle distance before her. "The Frog Demon of Poison and Pestilence, the Locust Demon of Starvation, the Moth Demon of Discord, and the Ancient One. Your Chancellor is one of these four, but I don't know which one."

"How do you know that?" Jiyi asked, looking impressed, annoyed, and charmed all at once.

Yuli lifted her gaze to meet the courtesan's. "Because," she said, "someone dear to someone I love has been possessed by a greater demon too. And I would do anything—*anything*—to prevent her from becoming the next vessel for this monstrosity. That's why I came in search of the book."

Someone dear to someone she loved, Zhara thought. But not someone the northern girl loved directly.

"Protection from possession," Jiyi said thoughtfully. She looked to Zhara. "If we have a cure, then surely we have a preventative as well."

Zhara wasn't sure why the courtesan and Han were both looking at her with such interest. She drew the collar of her tunic tighter about her throat, feeling curiously exposed and vulnerable. Yuli followed their gazes to stare at Zhara as well, her eyes as keen and as penetrating as a hawk's.

"Why—why is everyone looking at me like that?" she asked.

Jiyi grunted. "You didn't tell her?" she said to Han.

"Tell me what?" Zhara was bewildered.

"That you're the Guardian of Fire."

Zhara blinked. The revelation was dropped in front of her like a stone in the middle of a pond, sending ripples of distortion everywhere, yet the others did not seem at all surprised by the announcement. "The . . . elemental warrior of legend?" she asked weakly.

"Yes," the courtesan said, glaring at Han. "The one who can transform magicians into monsters and back again." She crossed her arms. "You really didn't tell her?"

"I was, uh, preoccupied with other things at the time," Han said sheepishly, turning a deep, plum red. Zhara's lips tingled as she remembered the touch of his lips against hers, soft at first, then more and more insistent, matching her own eagerness with his. She felt her own cheeks heat in response.

"But how—how is that possible?" Zhara glanced down at her hands, at the ever-present fire lurking just beneath the surface of her skin. She thought of the sibilant voice hissing *Guardian of Fire* in the back of her mind every time she encountered a demonic presence—before Thanh had turned into an abomination, and again when she sat before the Chancellor at the meeting with Suzhan, the Second Wife, and Master Cao.

"Ugh, I've been through this with Xu already." Jiyi threw up her hands in frustration.

Across the table, Yuli gave her a crooked smile. It was soft and gentle, meant to comfort instead of charm. "If there are greater demons possessing the bodies of magicians and walking around looking normal, then it stands to reason the Guardians of Dawn—the real ones, not this mutual aid society or whatever—would be able to do the same." The northern girl did not seem in the least bit surprised, overwhelmed, or even fussed about the notion that elemental warriors from legend were walking among them.

After all, said Yuli's voice in Zhara's mind, *if I am the Guardian of Wind, then the Guardians of Fire, Wood, and Water must also be out in the world.*

Zhara started, staring at the redhead before her, who sat calmly with a serene smile on her face. "H-how—"

Jiyi narrowed her eyes at them. "What's going on?"

I've known since we first met that you were special too, Yuli continued. Her grin stretched wider across her face. *It's nice to know I'm no longer alone.*

No longer alone. A sense of familiarity resonated through Zhara's bones, deeper than the sense of recognition that came with the touch of another magician. Yuli had known loneliness too, and Zhara could see the isolation they had both endured without knowing why reflected in the northern girl's coppery eyes.

"You," Zhara breathed.

The redhead smiled, but it was downturned. Sad. "Me," she agreed.

"Would someone please explain to me what on earth is happening?" Jiyi demanded.

But Yuli ignored the courtesan. "Is that your power, Bubbles?" she asked softly. "Can the Guardian of Fire cure a magician of possession?"

Zhara thought back to the times she had met an abomination face-to-face—first with Thanh, then with Yao. She remembered so little of the actual fights themselves, but she recalled clearly the sensation of her magic burning away the rot corrupting their magic, her light chasing away the shadows of chaos. "Yes," she said with amazement. "Yes, I can."

The northern girl let out a sigh of relief. "If that's possible, then you must be able to somehow protect a magician from possession as well." She looked to Han. "We should try that on his little brother."

"Try what?" Han looked back and forth between them, his round eyes even rounder with bewilderment.

"But I wouldn't even know where to begin," Zhara began, before Jiyi interrupted.

"Would someone *please* let me in on this conversation," she said angrily. "Since I am the only person here with any knowledge of the Language of Flowers, the history of magic, or anything at all, really."

"You really don't like not being the smartest person in the room, do you, Ice Princess?" Yuli shot the courtesan another smile, and this one was clearly intended to disarm. Zhara boggled at the range of the northern girl's grins, and envied it not a little.

"Last night," Han said dully, "Xu and I found my little brother wandering the grounds of the palace in a trance. He was clearly under the influence of a demonic force."

"That's when I found them," Yuli said. "I had been following the Chancellor with the suspicion that he was possibly a King of Tiyok in disguise." A wrinkle of concern creased her brow. "From the looks of it, this greater demon has been grooming the boy for possession ever since he discovered he was a magician. It's halfway to possessing a new host but needs some sort of ritual to complete the process."

"That must be what the structures in the cave beneath Mount Zanhei are for," Jiyi breathed.

"What structures?" Yuli asked. "What caves?"

As Han quietly explained their not-so-pleasurable cruise upriver, the courtesan began tearing her quarters apart, turning out drawers, searching beneath cushions, peeking behind bookshelves. Everywhere she looked, there seemed to be yet another stack of papers. "Aha!" Jiyi snatched a page from inside a book and slapped it onto the table before them. "See this?" She had made a crude drawing of the scene in the cave beneath Mount Zanhei, marking out a rough map of the positions of the stone coffins laid out according to the points of a compass, the stone slab in the center, and the position of the glowing pool. "According to Li Er-Shuan's notes, this is an ancient technique for summoning the forces beyond mankind."

"I thought we had all agreed that Mount Zanhei was the site of a summoning ritual," Zhara said.

"Yes," said the courtesan excitedly, "but what we found under Mount Zanhei was not a typical summoning-ritual circle." She shuffled through her notes again and pulled out another piece of paper. This drawing looked nearly identical to the one she had laid down before, but Zhara noticed she had written the glyph they had seen carved on the stone caskets on top of their markers. "This," she said, tapping the character with her fingertip, "is new, this spell. It took me a while to figure it out, but it's the character for *soul,* modified by a fire radical."

Blank stares met the courtesan's explanation.

"Ugh." Jiyi rolled her eyes. "In ancient times, before the Language of Flowers became codified, the glyph for *fire* took on other meanings,

especially when added as a modifier to other spells." When this explanation was met with even more blank stares, the courtesan threw up
her hands in frustration. "What happens when you throw earth into
fire? You get *metal*. Or when you boil water? You get vapor. *Air*. Fire is
the essence of transformation."

Yuli let out a slow breath. "A spell to transform souls," she whispered. "From human . . . to demon?"

Han frowned. "I still don't understand."

The look the courtesan gave him was almost pitying. "Of course
you don't. Apparently your brain lives in your thigh muscles, because
they're bigger than your head."

"Yah, I worked hard for these thighs," Han said, slapping them
proudly before shaking his head and returning to the conversation at
hand. "No, I mean I don't understand the *why*, not the what or how."
He waved his hand over the drawings. "Who abducted these magicians? And for what purpose?"

For that, Jiyi had no answer.

"When we were standing in the middle of the summoning circle,"
Zhara said slowly. "I felt as though something were draining my energy." She thought of that mysterious seal in the middle of the cave
floor, the void into which her energy had disappeared. "As though
someone were *stealing* my power to use it themselves."

The courtesan knit her brows together. "Magic as fuel, perhaps," she
murmured. "Multiple sources of energy." Struck by a sudden thought,
she started sorting through her papers again. "Here it is." Squinting
at her own scribbles, Jiyi read aloud haltingly, "*Rituals, bindings, sum-
monings, and banishments are one and the same, and the number of magicians
required for each spell commensurate to the power of the forces beyond the realms
of order and reason. A single magician may handle a lesser demon, but it may
take several magicians to deal with a demon of greater provenance. The cur-
rency, as always, are the souls of the Gifted.*" She paused and looked up at
them. "Another word for *magicians*," she clarified.

Silence fell over them again, and Zhara knew they were all working
through the implications of the abduction of that many magicians for a
summoning spell.

"*When Tiyok stirs to life again,*" Han sang softly, more to himself than anyone else, "*darkness falls and chaos reigns.*"

Without thought, Zhara completed the next line of the lullaby. "*Summer, fall, winter, spring, Guardians rise and justice sings.*" She looked up at the others, eyes wide. "*Guardians rise . . .*"

Horrified understanding dawned upon them all.

"If," Han whispered, "Zhara is the Guardian of Fire reborn, and Yulana is the Guardian of Wind, then does that mean . . ." He trailed off.

Jiyi swallowed. "That the Mother of Ten Thousand of Demons has awoken?" she finished.

None of them dared voice the answer. And although Zhara's mind was whirling with anxiety and the possible implications of what it all meant, the one thing her thoughts kept tripping over was the fact that Han had called Yuli by a different name. A name she had seen on betrothal announcements throughout the city.

"Yuli," Zhara said slowly. "Is that short for . . . *Yulana?*"

The northern girl flinched, eyes flitting to Han, who looked stricken. "Yes," the redhead said reluctantly. "It's a nickname my obaji gave me when I was a little girl."

Zhara closed her eyes. "Obaji," she said. "Is that the northern term for *grandfather?*"

A pause. "Yes."

"And would that grandfather happen to be the Warlord, the Great Bear of the North and the current emperor seated upon the Sunburst Throne?"

An even longer pause. "Yes."

Zhara looked to Han, who kept his gaze averted, unable to meet her eyes. "Prince Rice Cake," she murmured. *Prince.* She understood then just why the relationship between Han and Yuli seemed so stifled and strained.

Because they were engaged.

Because Han was the Royal Heir of Zanhei.

37

HAN KNEW THE MOMENT ZHARA DISCOVERED THE truth.
The rest of their meeting was concerned with the logistics of getting Zhara into the palace in an effort to preemptively cure Anyang of possession so that whichever greater demon was currently inhabiting the Chancellor's body would not be able to use his little brother as a vessel. But Han's mind couldn't focus on the details; he could only focus on Zhara's face, which looked wan and drawn and without its usual vivacious expression.

Jiyi and the northern princess were getting into heated arguments about the nature of summoning circles (or flirting, he couldn't tell), but Zhara sat completely still and completely quiet. Beneath her skin, he could see the lightning flashes of emotion scattering across her veins, faint but noticeable to someone looking for it. She had never been able to hide her feelings well, and her curious trick of being able to turn into a living column of flames did not make things easier.

But it was the look in her eyes that cut him deepest. Those eyes that had once looked at him as a boy, an ordinary boy, now gazed upon him as though he were a stranger. He didn't know who he wanted to curse more—himself for slipping up and using Yulana's full name, or Zhara for being clever enough to pick up the clues he had inadvertently dropped.

Halfway through the planning session, Zhara quietly got to her feet and walked out the door.

Leaving Jiyi and his betrothed to their cantankerous courtship, Han stepped out into the corridor just in time to see Zhara slip around the corner. Without bothering to put on his shoes, he tiptoed on silent sock feet after her.

Han found her crouched by the meditation pond, running her fingers lightly over the dark surface, breaking the reflection of the moon into silvery ripples. Golden carp periodically came up to nibble at her fingertips, accustomed to being fed by many of Wisteria Court's patrons.

"I'm sorry, little fishies," she murmured. "I don't have anything for you."

Han hung back, reluctant to disturb her. Zhara rose to her feet, shaking the droplets from her fingers and tilting her head to look up at the night sky. She let the light of the Gleaming River bathe her face, that thick band of stars clustered in an arc across the heavens. On either side of the Gleaming River he could see the bright points of light that were the Fairy Prince and the Woodcutter's Daughter—the magpie lovers whose reunion they were to celebrate in three days' time.

"I know His Grace is there," Zhara called softly. "And it's rather creepy having him stare at me without a word."

Sheepishly, Han stepped off the covered passageway and into the open courtyard. She was being formal with him, and it was the distance in her voice that hurt the most. He hadn't known just how much he had come to rely on that intimacy between them, that sense they were more than just peers, but equals, and even . . . friends. "Zhara," he began, but didn't know what to say.

The two of them stood in silence for a long while, contemplating the golden carp swimming beneath a star-spangled sky. "Was His Grace ever going to tell the truth?" she asked at last.

Han pressed his lips tightly together. "Yes." Then, "No." Then, "I don't know."

"Why not?" She kept her gaze averted from his, showing him only the curve of her cheek and the line of her neck in the moonlight. He wanted nothing more than to touch her, to place his fingers against the pulse on her neck, to feel her heart beat in time with his.

But he held back. "Because . . . because I didn't want to," he said at last.

Her eyes were sad as she finally turned to look at him, and he thought of the night he had taken her home for the first time, when they had watched wish lanterns rise from their vantage point atop the hill. The wishes had reflected in her eyes like stars.

"Why not?"

Because he liked the way she looked at *him*. Just him, not the Royal Heir or His Grace or the future prince of Zanhei. Because to her, he was just Master Plum Blossom, just another boy. And he had liked it. He had liked it too much.

"Because then I wouldn't have to be *him*," he whispered.

"Him?"

Han turned his head away. "The Royal Heir."

He could sense Zhara's curious gaze but dared not turn around to see the disappointment in her face. "But His Grace is the Royal Heir."

He shook his head. "I'm just . . . me. Han. An ordinary boy who likes to work out, write poems, and read romance novels."

It was a while before she spoke. "But he is also the heir to the throne of Zanhei."

"Yes." He could not gainsay that. "I don't want it," he said fiercely. "I have never wanted it."

But was that true? For the longest time he had been so concerned about keeping his brother safe, keeping Anyang's magic hidden, that he had had no time or space in his life to think beyond that. Any time the idea of being Zanhei's future sovereign came up, Han had pushed it aside to look at another day, wanting nothing more than one small moment of rest, of time to himself and just himself.

He only ever felt that he had that while working up a sweat in the training yard.

And in Mistress Brandy's presence.

"It doesn't matter what His Grace wants or doesn't want," Zhara said softly. "He is who he is, just as I am who I am. An orphan girl, a magician . . . and the Guardian of Fire."

"Please," he said. "Just Han. Please just call me Han."

But Zhara shook her head. "It would not be appropriate for a girl of my status to address someone so far above me as such."

And this was the reason he hadn't told her of his true identity, he wanted to scream. He hated sitting in his tower, high above the world, isolated by birth and by speech from anyone who could offer him true intimacy. Not even Xu, his best friend, could scale that height with ease; getting them to call him by his name and not his title was like trying to wake them up after a long, raucous night out in Flower Town.

"Never mind that," Han said fiercely. "I don't care about that."

Zhara closed her eyes. "His Grace may not, but the rest of the world does." She wrapped her arms about herself as though hugging herself against the cold, although the night was pleasant and warm. "To the rest of the world, Princess Yulana is someone who is considered his equal."

"Yes, but I don't—"

"—love her?" For the first time that night, the barest hint of a smile tilted the corners of Zhara's lips. "Yes, it appears as though her affections don't lie with people of the masculine persuasion."

Han thought of the courtesan and the northern princess still inside Wisteria Court, and wondered if they had progressed from bickering into something more pleasurable instead. "Yes." He coughed.

"But it still doesn't matter," she whispered. "Whether or not you love her. What matters is that she is the one worthy of being your wife."

It didn't escape his notice that Zhara had dropped back into a more intimate mode of speech with him without thought. Hope rekindled in his breast, a small flame, but steady all the same. "Not more worthy than you," he breathed.

Zhara opened her eyes and looked up at the stars again. "But I was not worthy enough to know the truth, was I?"

He didn't know how to respond to that. If he could respond. If he should respond. "You'll . . . you'll still come to the palace with me?" Han ventured. "On the Night of the Sevens?"

She was silent a long while. "I will go to the palace to see if I can't somehow prevent your brother from becoming possessed. The Second Heir," Zhara murmured, as though realizing anew just who Han really was.

"I didn't mean—that is, of course, I would love your help with

Anyang—but . . ." The words dribbled into nothing at Zhara's re-proachful expression.

"I don't think it's appropriate," she said softly. "Not anymore."

They stood in awkward silence for a long time.

"Let me walk you home," Han said at last. *Let me walk you home for the last time,* he thought.

It was several more moments before she replied. "All right," she said softly.

And this time, they cut through the covered market toward Zan-hei in silence. No piggyback ride, no hands linked in companionship. They walked an appropriate and seemly distance apart, as befitting an unmarried boy and an unmarried girl without a chaperone.

As they passed through the commons, Han could see the announcement of his engagement to Princess Yulana, complete with his picture. This time, it wasn't one of the lesser facsimiles produced by one of Master Kong's assistants. This time, it was an image created by the hand of the royal portraitist himself, complete with angry dimples.

Zhara paused before the poster. "That's you," she said in a quiet voice.

He could not deny it. "Yes."

There was nothing more that could be said.

38

To Zhara's surprise, Suzhan was waiting for her beside the unlit hearth when she returned home.

"Mimi?" she asked. The embers in the fireplace were burned out, and it was pitch-black in the kitchen, save for the light of the crescent moon streaming in through the window. "What are you doing here?"

There was no answer. Zhara could just make out the silhouette of her sister in the darkness of the kitchen, slumped over on her customary low stool and leaning against her ever-present bamboo cane.

"Mimi?" she repeated. "Is everything all right?" She reached out her hand to touch her sister on the shoulder.

Wham! Zhara whirled around to see the heavy wooden doors to the kitchen slam shut, then heard the squeal, grind, and click of the bolt sliding into place. Beneath her hand, the figure on the stool crumpled to the floor, revealing sacks of rice stacked together and covered with a piece of cloth.

"Mimi?"

"I'm sorry," came a muffled sob from the other side of the door. "I'm sorry, I'm sorry, I'm sorry."

"Suzhan!" Zhara hurried to the kitchen doors, trying the enormous iron handles. In the eight years they had lived in this little apartment, she had never shut or locked these doors, the mechanism too heavy to close on her own. There was a gap about a hands-breadth wide between the bottom of the door and the tall threshold on the other side, and through it, Zhara thought she could make out the shapes of two distinct shadows. "Madame?"

One of the shapes walked away, but the other lingered.

"I'm so sorry, nene," it said. "Please, please forgive me."

All the hairs at the back of Zhara's neck stood on end. "Let me out, mimi," she said, gently pounding on the door with the heel of her palm. "What's going on?"

"I can't let you go," Suzhan whispered. "I can't let you out."

Zhara pounded harder. "Mimi? What are you doing?"

The only sounds on the other side of the door were muffled, anguished sobs. "I'm sorry, nene," Suzhan choked out. "I'm so sorry."

Zhara dropped to her hands and knees and tried to peer through the gap between the threshold and the door. She couldn't see her sister's face from her vantage point, but she thought she could make out a small, slight figure waiting for Suzhan at the courtyard gate. The figure was too short to be the Second Wife.

"Mimi?" She slipped her hand through the gap, reaching for her sister. "Let me out."

"I can't," Suzhan said brokenly. She crouched beside the door, fingers fumbling for the gap. "I'm so sorry" was all she said. "I'm so, so sorry."

Zhara gripped her sister's hand in hers. "Why?" she asked hoarsely. "Why, mimi?"

It was a long moment before Suzhan replied. "Do you remember," she said in a raw voice, "when I told you not to follow me? That I would not sacrifice my own happiness for you?"

Zhara closed her eyes. "Yes," she whispered, feeling hot tears slide down her cheeks.

"Do you remember the promise we made each other then?"

It was hard to speak through the lump in her throat. "That we would—that we would each live our truth."

"Yes." Suzhan tightened her grip on Zhara's fingers through the crack beneath the door. "And that's what I'm doing now."

"Being the Chancellor's wife cannot possibly be your truth!"

"It isn't." A hiccough, then a sniffle. "But the academy at Jingxi is."

The premier music institution in all of the Morning Realms. Just as Suzhan had said she would. "But how?" Zhara asked.

The silence spoke volumes. "Lord Chan promised to pay my tuition fees and provide me with an escort to Jingxi. If . . ." She didn't finish.

If she betrayed Zhara. "How bad," she asked in a quiet voice, "are the bruises?"

Suzhan gave a despairing laugh. "Let's just say that if I weren't already blind, I would be now."

Zhara closed her eyes. "Oh, mimi," she said, crying freely now. "Oh, mimi."

"I'm so sorry" was all her sister could say. "I'm so, so sorry."

And it was as Suzhan had said: sorry was not enough.

It was amazing how quickly and how slowly the days passed when there was no work to do and nowhere to go.

Zhara marked the passing of hours with lines drawn in chalk on the stones of the hearth—dawn, daybreak, midmorning, noon, early afternoon, midafternoon, long shadow, sundown, sunset, twilight, nightfall, midnight—over and over and over until she gave up.

What would happen on the Night of the Sevens? Would she turn seventeen with no one to celebrate her birthday but the mice and her father's death plaque on the wall?

No, Zhara decided. There would be palace fireworks at least. She had watched them many times as a child from the very kitchen in which she was imprisoned.

At least she hadn't lacked for food, or even entertainment. The stacks of yellowed romance paperbacks had kept her company well enough in between the Second Wife's visits, and her copy of *The Thousand-Character Classic* provided ample opportunity for frustration as every single spell she tried came to naught.

"What is the use in being a magician," Zhara moaned to her father's death tablet, "if you can't *do* magic?" She tossed the brush Jiyi had given her aside and buried her face in her pillow. "It's all your fault, baba!" She made a muffled scream into her bedclothes.

She lifted her head and glared at the wooden plaque on the wall.

"It's all your fault, baba," she repeated, softer this time. "Your fault you are dead and gone and I'm left here with nowhere to go and no one to turn to." The thought of Suzhan was a stab to her heart, and Zhara closed her eyes against the pain. She hoped her sister was at least happy now that she was on her way to Jingxi. "Of the two, it's the loneliness that's the hardest to bear."

Zhara rose to her feet and removed the death tablet from the wall. She ran her fingers lightly over the carved letters of her father's name. Her mother did not have a death tablet, having been cremated and her ashes scattered in the manner of her—their—people.

"I've always known I was different," she said, replacing the plaque. "So I kept everyone at arm's length, afraid that once they got to know the true me, they would abandon me." She turned her head away. "Just like you abandoned me, baba."

Be good, little magpie girl, her father's voice admonished in her head. *Be good, and be true.*

"Be good," Zhara said bitterly. "I have been good, baba, and look where that's gotten me. Locked up in my own kitchen by my stepmother and betrayed by my sister. So perhaps I should have been true instead of good."

She sat down on Suzhan's low stool and started to cry.

"If I had been true to myself instead of trying to be good, I would have left town the instant I discovered Lord Chan was a demon," Zhara murmured. "After all, my sister stayed true to herself, and now she's on her way to the academy at Jingxi to study zither and become a famous musician." Despite everything, she smiled her herself. "Good for her."

A jingle, and two golden eyes blinked at her from the shadows.

"Sajah?" Zhara wiped her tears. "Is that really you?"

The ginger cat padded toward her on silent feet and butted his head against her hand affectionately. Zhara swept Sajah up in her arms and buried her face in his fur despite his vociferous protests. "You didn't leave me," she said over and over into his soft, white belly. "You didn't leave me."

Mrrrow, the cat said irritably, twisting this way and that to get out of Zhara's grip.

"How did you get in here?" she asked, holding Sajah before her face. "I didn't think there was an opening big enough to let a cat in and out."

Sajah gave her a long-suffering look and then, before Zhara could even blink, transformed in her hand into a tiny mouse with a ruby tail.

Shrieking, she dropped the rodent, and it transformed back into Sajah before her very eyes. "Wh-what—"

Tok-tok-tok!

A series of gentle taps at the kitchen door made Sajah scurry for the shadows. Zhara couldn't be sure if he hadn't transformed into something small again, but his telltale golden eyes gleamed in the darkness.

Tok-tok-tok-tok!

"It's me, child," came a familiar voice, high-pitched and reedy. "Master Cao."

A profound stillness overcame Zhara as the pieces finally clicked into place. The conversation she had overheard between the Second Wife and the stranger. Why she thought she had recognized their voice. It was because she had.

"*Your daughter has . . . other assets,*" she murmured.

"What was that?"

Zhara did not answer, merely watching the play of shadows beneath the kitchen door.

"I brought you some food," the bookseller said, sounding nervous. "Here, I'll slide it beneath the door."

"Where is my stepmother?" Zhara asked. Her voice did not sound like hers—oddly calm, collected, cool.

A pause. "Gone," said Master Cao.

"Gone?" Zhara was taken aback. "Gone where?"

"I'm not sure," the bookseller replied. "But she took the money my master gave her and left Zanhei."

His master. Zhara scoffed. "How could you?" she asked, foregoing politeness and addressing Master Cao directly. "How could you work for Lord Chan knowing what he was?"

"The regent of Zanhei?"

"A demon," Zhara retorted. "A greater demon, no less."

"Ah." The shadows of Master Cao's feet shifted back and forth. "Well, yes, I didn't know Lord Chan was the Frog Demon of Poison and Pestilence until much later."

Zhara rolled her eyes. "But you knew he was a demon?"

It was a long moment before the bookseller replied. "He promised that as long as I worked for him, I would be safe from possession."

The answer was so unexpected that Zhara wasn't sure what she could possibly say in response. "Are you really so terrified of becoming an abomination?" she asked.

"There is no cure for possession," Master Cao said in a hard voice. "I saw that firsthand with my own flesh and blood. My older brother."

Zhara said nothing.

"Do you know what the worst part of becoming an abomination is?" he continued. "It's the knowing. A human consciousness lurks behind that monstrous form and you are trapped forever by your own power. I could see my brother in the eyes of the monster he became, and I was horrified. Aware, and powerless. I tried everything to bring him back. Every spell I could think of. But in the end, the only cure was death."

Until the Guardian of Fire came along. A rosy glow glimmered in the veins of Zhara's hands. "I would have cured you," she said softly. "Little though you deserve it."

Master Cao laughed, but it was a humorless sound. "I didn't know that then. None of us did. So I've made my bargain and now I must live with it. The moment I break my contract with Lord Chan is the moment I will turn into a monster."

"I could still bring you back," Zhara said. She got to her feet and walked to the door, pressing her hand against the wood. "If you open this door, if you break your oath to Lord Chan, I promise you I will cure you of possession. Please."

"I can't," the bookseller said, and he sounded truly regretful. "My master needs you out of the way for the ritual tomorrow night."

"Ritual?"

"Something to do with the Second Heir," Master Cao said. "I imagine he wishes to possess the body of a younger host."

"What is tomorrow night?"

"The Night of the Sevens."

Zhara's mind whirled. She had been imprisoned in her kitchen for two days.

"Please," she said, and she dropped all pretense of pride. "Please let me out." She thought of Han and the promise she had made to try to prevent his little brother from becoming possessed. She had to get out of there. She had to try.

"I'm sorry," Master Cao said. "I truly am."

And then he was gone.

Zhara didn't know how long she sat in dumbfounded silence, but presently, Sajah emerged from the shadows with a jingle of his collar.

Niang, he said, rubbing his face against her shins.

She looked down at her hands. The glow still traced her veins and Zhara wondered if she could somehow use the Guardian of Fire's abilities to transform matter from one thing to another to escape.

She pressed her palms against the kitchen door and thought of ice, of melted water, of—

—stone.

Zhara stepped back and observed her handiwork with dismay. Where a wooden door had been was now a wall of solid granite, save for a bit of space between the bottom and the threshold.

"Blast," she muttered. "What good is it being the Guardian of Fire when you can't *use* your stupid, special ability?" She sighed. "I wonder how Yuli mastered her power." She gasped. "Yuli!"

Zhara turned to Sajah, who looked up at her quizzically. "Can you get a message to Princess Yulana at the palace? She can read your mind, lah?"

The cat tilted his head, the tip of his tail swishing back and forth.

"Is that a yes?" Zhara asked weakly.

Sajah gave her a slow blink.

"Tell Yuli that I'm imprisoned in my house, and that the Second Heir must be protected at all costs. The Guardians of Dawn have been betrayed by one of their own: Master Cao, the bookseller. He has been working at the palace with the greater demon, who is planning to perform some sort of ritual on the boy tomorrow night. The Night of the Sevens. Got that?"

Sajah gave her another slow blink.

"Good."

And he was back in mouse form immediately.

"How—how are you doing that?" Zhara marveled.

Sajah the mouse gave her an exasperated expression before transforming into a monster.

A beautiful monster, certainly, nothing like the abominations she had encountered before. No, Sajah had become a large, leonine creature the size of a pony, with a lion's mane made of fire, a peacock-like tail, and two small, rounded horns on the top of his head. His fur was an incredible mix of gold, scarlet, vermillion, and orange, and flickering within the depths of his coat were electric crackles of lightning.

"Sajah?" she asked incredulously.

The feline rolled its golden eyes and swished its peacock tail at her, causing the bell at its neck to jangle. The bell she had tied around Sajah's neck when she first met him as a kitten, when she claimed him as her own.

"Sajah," she said in wonder, running her hand lightly over one of the horn-like nubbins at his brow. "You're . . . the Lion of the South."

He blew out a sigh.

"*The Lion of the South can take on any shape or form, for his power—like that of his master—is the power of transformation,*" Zhara murmured. "My power. The Guardian of Fire's power." She understood now why the cat had come to her and realized that Sajah had always been looking out for her in his many different forms.

Sajah turned his impatient, glowing, golden eyes on her.

"All right, all right," she said. "I'll let you go."

He immediately transformed back into a mouse and scurried through the gap beneath the door. Then a scarlet bird with a bell around its neck flew past her window, winging its way toward the palace and Princess Yulana.

A booming knock and a searing light jolted Zhara out of bed.

"Zhara?" came a light, familiar voice. "Zhara, are you in there?"

The source of both the knocking and the light came from beyond the kitchen door. A glowing glyph was beginning to eat through the solid stone door, shimmering red-hot like flame. A spell. She couldn't read it, but she recognized it for what it was—the Language of Flowers.

"Xu?" Zhara croaked.

"Yes, it's me! We're here to get you out of there!"

"Stand back," came a different voice. "We're going to get the young lady out of there, but things might, uh, get a little messy."

"It's because you're the clumsiest person I know, Junseo," came a third voice, low-pitched and quiet.

Zhara frowned, trying to count the number of shadows beneath the threshold. "Who are you?"

"Stand back!" said the one called Junseo. "This spell can have the tendency to—"

Kaboom! Crash! Zhara ducked and covered her head as pieces of the door went flying, showering her in grit and gravel.

"—explode," they finished, coughing a bit.

She lifted her head and squinted at the figures silhouetted by the light behind them. She counted eight in all. "Xu?"

The slender youth knelt beside Zhara and helped her to her feet. "At your service, my dear."

"How—how did you know to find me?"

"Well," Xu said, stroking their chin. "I got a very interesting message delivered by a very interesting bird from a very interesting person in the palace."

She frowned. "What on earth are you talking about?"

They grinned. "Yuli got your message."

Tears stung Zhara's eyes. "I'm glad."

"Me too," Xu said. "Now come, your carriage awaits."

"Where are we going?"

"To Wisteria Court. You have a masquerade ball to get ready for, if I'm not mistaken."

An emotion halfway between happiness and regret stirred in Zhara's chest, both tickling and painful at once. "Do I?"

"You do indeed," Xu declared. "Because these fine fellows"—they gestured to the seven young men in the courtyard—"are going to be your escorts."

The tallest of them smiled at her and beckoned his brothers with a brush in his hand. "Two, three!"

All seven of them bowed at once. "Hello, we are the Bangtan Brothers!"

Zhara was stunned. "What?"

Xu smiled. "Looks like it's your lucky day."

39

ZHARA WONDERED IF THE BANGTAN BROTHERS WERE always this chaotic or if it was simply pre-performance nerves.

Jiyi's quarters were in absolute shambles, as seven boys—young men, rather—were in various stages of preparation for the Night of the Sevens. In between getting dressed and doing each other's makeup, they stole snacks off each other's plates, played games and pranks with and on one another, and generally acted like seven unruly brothers instead of seven professional performers.

Of course, none of the chaos was helped by the fact that Xu was fluttering from one boy to the next, trying to get them all to sign their names on their fan.

"Would you all just shut up!" the courtesan bellowed when the shouting, singing, and laughing had grown so loud it was impossible to hear oneself think, let alone coordinate with the various attendants having fits of excitement over having *the* Bangtan Brothers grace the halls of Wisteria Court. "Xu, leave those boys alone and come help Zhara get ready!"

"One moment," they said, making eyes at the second tallest. "I just need an autograph from the handsome one." *Bohyun,* Zhara thought his name was. The eldest. His ears turned red from Xu's incessant flirting, although he kindly obliged by drawing an illegible scribble in ink on Xu's incredibly expensive Wulin silk fan.

"Chan Xuhei!" Jiyi cried. "Stop flirting and get your ass over here. Ugh!" She threw up her hands and rolled her eyes. "I don't know what the big deal is," she said sourly. "There are plenty of attractive people in the world. I don't understand why people lose their heads over *these* particular boys."

Zhara privately suspected that Jiyi was immune to their charm partially because she was far more enamored of the likes of Princess Yulana, but said nothing. "I think they're sweet," she said, smiling and blushing a little when one of them—*Mihoon,* she thought—brought her a plate of Azurean melon-squash he had peeled and sliced himself. Of the seven, he seemed the quietest, less interested in participating in the others' rambunctious readying rituals and more concerned with reading a book or taking a nap. "Many thanks."

Once Xu had finished pestering the Bangtan Brothers to sign their fan, they made their way to where Zhara sat on the floor of the courtesan's quarters, already dressed in the pink-and-white ensemble she had purchased with Han. The weight of the silk and ramie jacket was both soothing and stifling at once, and she had never been more conscious of being in costume, of pretending to be someone she was not.

"Cheer up," Xu said as they combed Zhara's hair. "It's the most romantic night of the year, and you're going to a masquerade ball with seven of the most attractive young men in the Morning Realms. What more could a girl ask for?"

Zhara tried to give them a smile, but the edges of her lips were unexpectedly heavy. Despite all she had ever dreamed about coming true, a leaden ball of ice sat in the pit of her stomach, slowly leaking numbness into her veins. She glanced down at her feet, at the white slippers Han—the Royal Heir—had given her, and the numbness intensified.

"Zhara?" Xu's hands were gentle against her scalp as they gently detangled her unruly waves. "Is everything all right?"

"Xu," she said quietly. "Why didn't you tell me?"

Their fingers paused against her head. "Tell you what?" they asked lightly, but she could sense the hesitation, the flinch, in anticipation of what she was about to say.

Zhara hugged her legs to her chest. "About you and Han. Who you—he—really is."

"Ah." Xu continued playing with her hair for a long time without speaking. "So he told you."

She shook her head, feeling Xu tug at her locks to keep still. "Yes," she said, then paused. "No. He let it slip."

"I see." They started brushing sweet almond oil through her strands to prepare her hair for the hot styling wax. "How?"

She closed her eyes, allowing the smooth, even, repetitive strokes of the brush lull her into a sense of calm, if only for a little while. "He called her *Yulana* instead of *Yuli*."

Xu sighed. "That would do it. I really do despair of getting my prince to his majority alive." An attendant brought a tray with a bowl and two sticks of warm styling wax. "Zhara," they began hesitantly. "Han doesn't love—"

"The princess?" she asked. "I know." Something hot dripped down her face and Zhara was astonished to discover she was crying. She felt nothing—no sorrow, no disappointment, no hurt—yet tears continued to trace their way down her cheeks, hot and stinging.

"You do?"

She nodded again, earning herself another hissed reprimand. "I'm not upset about the engagement," she said, although somewhere past the numbness, she knew this was a lie. The memory of his eyes, large and yearning in the moonlight as he leaned down to kiss her, returned to haunt her like a ghost. "It's just . . ." She bit her lip.

"He lied to you," Xu finished softly.

Her throat tightened as the tears slipped faster down her cheeks. "Yes."

"Oh, Zhara," they said, and it was the kindness in their voice that undid her. She buried her face in her hands as the numbness dissipated in a flood of tears.

"I know it's silly," she said, breaths hitching in her chest. "I know why he did it. He lied to protect the Second Heir. His brother." An-yang. She realized she hadn't even known the names of Zanhei's royal family members, that hardly any of the regular citizens of the city and the Pits did. Zhara tried to reconcile the idea of Prince Wonhu's younger son, a sheltered, pampered little boy living in a gilded palace, with the reality of Han's little brother as he had described Anyang to her. Tenderhearted, sensitive, a little defensive, and emotionally attached to anyone who would show even in the barest bit of love.

"Yes," Xu said. "He did. His mother, the Royal Consort, had already suffered a terrible death at the hands of the Falconer; he wasn't going to risk giving his little brother up to the same fate."

"I *know* that," Zhara said. "It's just"—she glanced around Jiyi's private retiring room, where she and Xu and Han had spent so many afternoons simply laughing and enjoying each other's company—"I trusted you all," she finished. "I trusted every one of you with all my secrets, even the ones that could destroy me. I did so because I thought— because I *believed*—you were safe. All of you."

Xu said nothing and continued to brush sweet almond oil into her hair. "Trust is not a river that flows in only one direction," they said gently, after a long moment. "Nothing can be received without something being given in return."

Trust. The ghost of the kiss she shared with Han returned to her, whispering doubts into her mind. What was intimacy without trust? Without trust, there was only desire, a shallow, fleeting thing that could be easily erased by someone prettier, someone funnier, someone more attractive all around. She thought of the way Han's large, innocent eyes went round with embarrassment whenever she teased him, the way his nose scrunched when he smiled, the way his dimples appeared when he was both happy and upset. He was probably the most handsome boy she had ever met, made all the more attractive because he was sweet and kind and just a little bit thick. Her heart ached with tenderness when she thought of him, because she cared about him. Because she had trusted him. And now it was all ashes in her mouth.

Xu sighed as they tied half her hair into a bun at the crown of her head, winding the rest into elegant shapes and swirls around it. "I wanted to tell you," they said. "I thought it silly that you should be the last to know, especially considering how close we—the two of you especially—had become. But"—they started pinning ornamental flowers made of mother-of-pearl and silk into the mass of hair at the top of her head—"you can't always force someone to admit to something before they're ready."

Unbidden, the image of her sister's glassy, tear-filled eyes rose up in Zhara's mind. For years, she had kept her magic hidden from Suzhan, and for the longest time, she had told herself it wasn't because she didn't trust Suzhan, it was because she wanted to protect her.

But was that true? In the light of Suzhan's sudden betrayal, Zhara wondered if perhaps she hadn't been right about her sister after all. That no matter how much love might exist between two people, without trust, nothing was ever safe.

"I know," she said in a small voice. "But I thought that . . . I thought that I had been—had been . . . worthy."

Xu's hands paused in doing her hair before resuming their work. "You are worthy, Zhara," they said softly.

"Am I?" She thought of her broken relationships, of Suzhan's anguished voice when Zhara admitted to being the one who had damaged her eyesight permanently. "Then why do I feel so worthless?"

To that Xu had no response. Instead they helped get her ready for the ball in silence, painting her face with a delicate touch—rouging her lips and cheeks, darkening her brows and lashes with kohl, and drawing a small lotus flower on her forehead between her brows with red lip paint.

"There." Xu placed the mask on her face. "You look beautiful. You'll be the prettiest girl at the ball, and Han will regret ever hurting you."

The mirrors were currently occupied by the Bangtan Brothers, who were crowding around and fighting for space, but it didn't matter. It didn't matter whether she was seen by anyone tonight, because the one person by whom she wanted to be seen couldn't look at her. She had always known there wouldn't be a fairy-tale ending for the two of them, but it didn't make the reality hurt any less.

"Thank you, Xu," she said.

They waved her off. "It was nothing."

"No, not just for this," she said, gesturing to her hair and makeup. "But for being my friend."

They patted her on the back before handing her the white silk slippers Han had bought for her that night they had kissed for the first— and likely last—time. As they had been when she first put them on, the slippers were light and comfortable, as though she wore nothing on her feet at all.

"Dancing shoes are ready." Xu smiled. "Now go enjoy yourself at the ball."

Despite the terrible circumstances in which she found herself, Zhara was having the night of her life.

The Night of the Sevens masquerade ball was everything she had dreamed it would be as a child. The rafters and columns of the palace were strung with paper lanterns and fairy lights—little candles hung from miniature cradles—painting gold onto the glass mosaics on the walls of colonnades, giving them a flickering, lively quality. The shapes cut into the lantern shades cast dancing shadows on the scenes depicting the founding of Zanhei by the Monkey King, the founder of House Wonhu, while the fairy lights illuminated the darkness like earth-bound stars.

But it was the people—oh, the people!—who captured Zhara's attention and imagination. Although she was well accustomed to the diversity of culture and skin color within the Pits, seeing a vast array of faces and features from all parts of the Morning Realms in one place was overwhelming, especially when they were all dressed so beautifully. Gowns of silk and chiffon mingled with robes of brocade and tulle, leather tunics and trousers, gilt armor and jewelry. Although the ball was a masquerade, not everyone had bothered to come masked; some held theirs loose in their hands, more like a fashion accessory or a fan, and still other had painted elaborate patterns in gold and silver and other colors across their faces.

"Put your eyes back inside your head," teased Taeri, one of the two tumblers of the troupe. He sat with Zhara, Jiyi, and their music director Mihoon in their painted wagon, along with their props, backdrops, and instruments. Getting into the palace itself had been simple enough; their leader, Junseo, had simply presented the performance token to the guards at the eastern gate, who let them in without further examination, either too giddy or too tipsy to be thorough or meticulous. It was the most romantic night of the year, and everyone was more preoccupied with pleasure than with enforcing order.

"It's a shame we're not performing for real tonight," said Sungho wistfully, the troupe's other tumbler, clown, and stage director. He surveyed the enormous courtyard with starry eyes that shone bright with the reflected twinkling of the fairy lights. "I've always wanted to play for an audience in a venue as beautiful as this."

"We'll get our chance someday," Junseo said. "When the world is finally safe for people like us."

The brothers murmured in agreement as they went about preparing themselves for the night ahead.

"Remember the plan, boys," Jiyi said, hopping down from the wagon. Her years of dancing in Wisteria Court served her well in her costume as a celestial maiden. Her diaphanous white gown, with its long, trailing sleeves that covered her hands, fluttered and flowed around her like water bubbling in a brook. "The Ha family, the Chu twins, and the Lok sisters are all dressed as magpies *and* wearing a sunburst token about their necks. Mingle with the attendees as you look for them, and try not to draw too much attention to yourselves. We'll meet back here when the tocsin strikes the midnight hour and head out."

One by the one, the members of the Bangtan Brothers gave the courtesan a bow and then melted into the crowds of the Night of the Sevens in search of refugees to smuggle out of Zanhei. Zhara watched them go with an unexpected twinge of her heartstrings. In a different world, she and Suzhan would be two of the refugees leaving Zanhei for the outermost reaches of the empire, looking to start their lives over among the Free Peoples of the West. In a different life, Zhara might have been here with Han, searching through the crowd for magicians and their families, all while stealing a kiss or two beneath the stars as they waited for the fireworks to begin. Just like that night they had watched the wish lanterns float into the sky from their perch on a hill overlooking the city.

But that life was a lie. It had always been a lie.

"Zhara!" Jiyi hissed. "Stop dawdling and follow me. Getting close to the royal dais won't be easy, especially when we don't have special dispensation to approach the prince and his family."

The two girls sidled along the edges of the grand courtyard, taking the longest route possible to the Hall of Heavenly Wisdom at the center of the palace. Even from this distance Zhara could see the platform set up at the top of the stairs leading up to the hall where the prince and his heirs held sessions of government, complete with a tasseled canopy. Beneath the tasseled canopy sat four chairs—one for Prince Wonhu, two for his sons, and a smaller stool for the Chancellor at the sovereign's feet. At present the seats were empty, as the members of the royal family would not emerge until the sun had set completely to kick off the festivities with the procession of animals.

Zhara adjusted the mask on her face and made her way to the dais.

A sudden clash of gongs and the rhythmic throb of drumbeats rang across the courtyard. A hush fell over the crowd as torchlights were extinguished, lamps were lit, and candles twinkled into existence. *The work of magic or ingenious stagecraft?* Zhara wondered. Either was certainly possible with the Bangtan Brothers, especially now that she knew all seven of them were magicians.

Through the open southern gate came a procession of creatures from the otherworld. Zhara counted—there were at least twelve among them, which meant that the Brothers had managed to find all the refugees they were to escort out of the city. At the front of the procession, Taeri and Sungho, the two best tumblers in the troupe, whirled down the promenade, long, trailing sleeves flying in their wake. Zhara couldn't tell who was who under the identical spirit masks they wore, painted white with exaggerated expressions, representing creatures from the otherworld. A tall performer in a spotted deer hide costume and a wooden antler headdress led the procession from the gate, while a lone figure in blue and brown descended the steps in front of the Hall of Heavenly Wisdom, trailing an enormous banner of silver silk behind them. Zhara couldn't recognize either of them.

"The Fairy Prince," the crowd murmured appreciatively. "And the Woodcutter's Daughter!"

Zhara watched as the heroes of the tale danced on opposite sides of the silk banner, reaching for each other across the Gleaming River that divided the world of men from the world of the spirits. Two more performers, in black and white with bird masks perched on their heads, leaped over and across the silver banner—magpies flitting across the divide between mortal and fey. She thought they might have been the refugees, for they moved stiffly and awkwardly, nervous and unused to performing before a large crowd.

The doors to the Hall of Heavenly Wisdom opened with a loud gong, and from the depths of the building emerged a figure in royal red accompanied by two in princely blue and a third in imperial gold. Even from her distant vantage point, Zhara could immediately pick out Han on the platform, his height and muscular breadth giving him away beneath the blue silk robes patterned with golden monkeys and the tall headdress draped with a curtain of beads. He was not in costume, unless the regalia of the Royal Heir of Zanhei was considered a costume. As she drew near, she realized that the Chancellor was not on the dais with the rest of the royal family; the fourth chair that she had assumed was for Lord Chan was in fact for the redheaded northern princess, for it was she who was clad in an imperial gold robe trimmed with black fur that looked far too hot and heavy for the summer night.

She didn't know why it hurt to see Yuli standing on the dais beside Han. Zhara knew there was no regard between them, that their arranged marriage was just that, yet the fact that the northern princess had been complicit in hiding the truth from her stung. She understood that none of what had transpired was Yuli's fault, yet her feelings were just as unpredictable and chaotic as her magic sometimes, blazing up and down at will.

As though she had heard Zhara's thoughts (which was certainly possible), the redhead immediately turned her head and caught Zhara's eyes in the crowd.

Bubbles, said the coolly amused voice in her mind.

Zhara waved back, but Yuli gave the slightest shake of her head.

Kestrels. Even the redhead's mental tone was grim. *In plainclothes tonight. And don't try to communicate with me; I can't hear you. I can only project my own consciousness into yours. Nod if you understand me.*

Zhara gave a barely perceptible nod.

Good, the northern princess said. *I don't know where the Chancellor is, but Han and I think he is still getting ready. It will take some time to get up to Mount Zanhei from here, so he will need to make his play for the Second Heir soon if he is to make it up to the volcano by midnight to complete the ritual. Make your way here, and we will find some way to "accidentally" come down to meet you and you can place your hands on the boy to do your Guardian of Fire thing. Nod if you understand me.*

She nodded again.

"Oh, beg pardon." A thrill of magical recognition went up Zhara's spine when a large person dressed in a bear costume collided with her. One of the other magician refugees? But they wore no sunburst pendant about their neck. Instead, to her horror, she saw the subtle detail of black wings stitched onto the shoulder of the bear's sleeve.

A Kestrel.

A Kestrel whose touch rang the same bell of familiarity within her bones as Thanh, as Yao, and . . . as Han. A magician . . . and not, all at once.

She suddenly understood how the Falconer had tracked down and discovered so many magicians all those years.

Kestrels were anti-magicians.

"Seize her," came a voice to Zhara's right. Whirling around, she saw Master Cao standing behind her, wearing the costume of a magpie. Two more figures dressed as bears flanked her on either side, and when their skin touched hers, she knew them for what they were.

The Warlord's peacekeepers.

"It was never about the Second Heir, or your sister," Master Cao said, and his voice sounded almost sad. "It was always about you, Jin Zhara. It was always about you."

With a whip-fast motion too quick for her eye to follow, the little bookseller drew out his brush and sketched a glyph into the air before her face, leaving a trail of lavender light. All at once, the scene around Zhara began to darken as consciousness began to fade from her body.

"No," she said, but her lips seemed too thick, her tongue too swollen to properly form words.

"I'm sorry," Master Cao said, and the sorrow in his tone seemed genuine. "I'm truly, truly sorry. But you are expected on the slopes of Mount Zanhei, and we cannot be late."

Yuli! She tried calling for the northern princess with her mind, but remembered too late that the redhead could not hear her. *Yuli!* Zhara struggled with all her might against the Kestrels and their grip, but Master Cao's spell was working, and she was losing consciousness.

And as everyone else's attention was focused on the dazzling performance of the Bangtan Brothers, Master Cao and his Kestrels smuggled Zhara out of the palace, leaving only one perfect, pristine, white silk slipper behind.

40

THE BANGTAN BROTHERS' PERFORMANCE WAS DRAWING TO an end, and Zhara was nowhere to be seen.

"Are you sure you were able to relay the message properly?" Han muttered beneath his breath to the redhead standing by his side. "You're sure she heard you?"

I'm sure. The slightly irritated touch of Yulana's voice in his head nearly caused him to trip over his chair. The sensation of having someone else sitting in his mind was both unsettling and invasive, as though his betrothed had walked in on him while he was getting dressed. He wondered if she could read his thoughts and scrambled to cover them up, the way he would cover himself with a robe on the way back to his quarters from the bath.

No, I can't read your thoughts.

Han jumped.

But your face certainly gives everything away.

The sensation of someone laughing inside his head tickled. It made him want to sneeze.

Several bursts of colored firecrackers snapped and popped on the courtyard floor below the dais on which Han stood with his brother and Princess Yulana. The show was now officially over.

"Gogo," Anyang said, tugging on his big brother's hand. "I thought you said someone was going to kick the frog demon out of my head."

"Shh," Han urged. Yulana had warned him there were plainclothes Kestrels scattered among the ball attendees that night. "Yes, she should be in the crowd somewhere."

"Where?" His little brother craned his neck. "What does she look like?"

"Pretty," Princess Yulana offered. "She's quite pretty."

Han tried not to pout. "Indeed."

Boom!

The entire courtyard shuddered and shook, the bells and wind chimes hanging from the columns and rafters sending up a cacophony of jangling.

"Was that . . . was that an earthquake?" Yulana asked with a frown.

Boom!

Screams and shouts arose from the crowd, but Han couldn't see what was causing the commotion. The ground buckled and rolled beneath their feet again, and Han threw himself on top of Anyang to protect him from any sort of debris.

"Abominations!" Prince Wonhu gasped. Han's father had gone chalk-white, the whiskers of his wispy beard dark, crinkled, and stark against his bloodless complexion.

"Where—" Han began before he was interrupted by another shout from the crowd.

Several grotesque figures began bursting forth from magpie costumes, their bodies tripling in size, tearing the seams of their clothing and their human skin.

"My prince," Xu cried, huffing and puffing as they ran up the stairs, heedless of the guards shouting at them to back away. "Look!" They held in their hand something small and white, and with a sinking heart, Han realized it was one of the slippers he had bought for Zhara the night they kissed. Zhara *had* been here. And now she was gone.

"It's a summoning circle!" Jiyi shouted, running up behind Xu. "The whole palace courtyard. It's a summoning circle!"

From their vantage point, Han could see the stone structures he had taken to be decorations laid out in a perfect circle below him. Anyone with magic caught in the center was jerking, tearing at their clothes and skin in agony as spines, teeth, fur, and feathers burst from their bodies, the echoing sounds of broken and popping bones bouncing off the courtyard walls.

There was another shriek of alarm and then another creature bounded in through the main gate—its fur made of lightning, a lion's mane of flame about its ruff, and a tiny little bell around its neck.

Han sneezed.

"Sajah?" he asked in amazement.

The enormous leonine chimera turned its head in Han's direction and scowled. He shook his head. That was Sajah, all right.

"The Lion of the South," Yulana said in awe.

"How do you know?" Xu asked.

"All Guardians of Dawn have a companion beast," the northern princess said.

"Yes, yes, this is all well and good, but we can't just stand here gawping." Han ducked as an enormous piece of rubble shattered above his head. "Mount Zanhei is several hours upriver." He took in the chaos around them—the abominations tearing through the palace grounds as though its stones and beams were made of soft tofu, the Bangtan Brothers wielding their brushes and drawing spells of protection while the creature known as Sajah tore through the abominations with several swipes of its mighty paw. "What are we going to do?"

"Fortunately," said Yulana, "I may have a solution for that." She tilted her face up to the heavens and closed her eyes as they rolled back into her head, lifting her arms above her head.

The others waited.

And waited.

And waited some more.

"Er, is she all right?" Xu whispered to Jiyi.

The northern princess pressed her palms together and slowly brought her hands down to touch her thumbs to her forehead, her lips, her throat, and her heart before her opening her eyes. Her dark brown pupils were gone, replaced by a glowing blue so pale they were nearly white. Xu gave a shout of surprise, grabbing Jiyi's shoulders and darting behind the courtesan in fear. Jiyi shoved them aside as she grabbed Anyang, wrapping her arms protectively around the Second Heir.

"What is this?" she shouted. "Han!"

Han stood in front of his brother, hand hovering over the ceremonial dagger he wore at his belt, but he did not think Yulana meant them harm. He watched as the northern princess held her position, her blue-blind and far-seeing eyes looking toward something none of them could see.

Then a sharp, piercing cry rent the night air.

Their heads all jerked upward, and Han spotted a dim, bird-shaped shadow circling overhead. He blinked and rubbed his eyes, wondering if he was seeing things or if the bird had two sets of wings. He glanced toward Yulana, whose pupils had returned to their ordinary, earthy brown. She smiled and winked at him when she caught his gaze, pointing her chin toward the sky.

At first glance, he thought the bird was some sort of raptor—an eagle or a hawk perhaps—but now he wasn't sure. Two long, kite-like ribbons trailed like streamers from its tail, and its long neck was nearly serpentine as it dove down to meet them. But it was the size that astonished Han most; it was absolutely enormous . . . and growing bigger and bigger as it came closer and closer.

He threw up his hand to shield his eyes from the dust swarms stirred by the bird's gargantuan wings as it landed. It was like no creature on earth. Then he glanced behind him at the giant glowing feline protecting them from abominations.

"Say hello to Temur, the Eagle of the North," Yulana said. She strode forward without fear and began affectionately stroking the creature's beak. On the ground, Han could see the raptor was practically horse-sized, its feathers ivory speckled with bronze, silver, and gold. It had the head and beak of an eagle, the body and tail of a peacock with two long trailing ribbons, and two sets of falcon's wings. "Didn't I say that all Guardians of Dawn had companion beasts? Temur goes everywhere with me, don't you, my friend?"

"Not that I would dare call Her Highness a liar," Han said, "but I think we would have remembered a giant mythical avian creature following the princess . . ." He trailed off, meeting the bird's sky-blue eyes. With a start, he realized they were the exact same color as those of the raptor he usually saw perched on her shoulder.

Yulana clapped him on the back. "Now you're getting it, Prince Rice Cake."

"Is Temur a . . . a phoenix?" Anyang asked in awed, hushed tones.

"Temur is unique unto herself," she said, patting the creature on the chest. Han blinked as it preened. *Preened.* "I suppose phoenixes in fairy tales are based on her, but as far as I know, there is only one Temur, and she is real."

"Not to interrupt this beautiful moment," Jiyi said. "But the princess hasn't told us exactly how this—this *Temur*—is supposed to solve the problem of us getting to Zhara in time. Not to mention"— she gestured vaguely at the scene of destruction around them— "there is also all . . . *this* to deal with." A bolt of magical lightning split one of the watchtowers along the palace walls, and everyone flinched.

"I thought it was obvious," the princess said. "Han and I will ride Temur up to Mount Zanhei."

"I'll do what, now?" he interjected.

"And what of the rest of us?" Xu asked in a panic. "We need all the magical assistance we can get until Zhara returns and is able to transform them all back. The Bangtan Brothers and"—they glanced up at Sajah—"this, uh, beast won't be able to hold them off forever." Out in the great courtyard, two more people convulsed and jerked before bursting into scales and claws and teeth.

Yulana bit her lip, looking conflicted. "I suppose Han and Temur can go on ahead of us," she said. "I'll stay and help fight—"

"Don't you dare make me ride this hellish creature alone," Han demanded. Temur nipped at his elbow. "Aiyo! Stop that!" The giant bird nipped at him again. "Yah!"

"Apologize to Temur," Yulana said. "And then she'll stop."

The bird stared at him expectantly with one enormous sky-blue eye and bit him again for emphasis.

"Fine," Han yelped. "I'm sorry for calling you a hellish creature. Now can we please get on with it?"

Yulana hesitated. "Temur can carry up to six people, but she'll be a lot faster with fewer."

"Stopping the Chancellor is more important than fighting abominations," Jiyi said. "We need to cut off the head in order to stop the rest."

"Did no one hear what I said?" Han asked, his voice cracking in panic. "I'm supposed to *fly* to Mount Zanhei? And then what? Fight off the Chancellor and whatever demon minions he might have? With what army? And what weapons?"

"Me," Yulana said, in the decisive manner of someone accustomed to making quick decisions on a battlefield. "I'm the weapon. I'm a magician, and the Guardian of Wind. If anyone has a chance to stop a greater demon, it's me."

"Then why do *I* have to go?" Han knew he was whining, but the thought of soaring far above Zanhei on a giant bird's back was making him feel ill.

"Because I need something to slow the demon down while I figure out how to destroy it. Besides," Yulana said with a smirk, "if you survive, Prince Rice Cake, I'm sure Bubbles will reward your courage with a kiss."

"Now is not the time!" he shouted.

"Han." Xu placed their hands on his shoulders. "I know you're scared," he said quietly. "And I'm frightened for you. But time is of the essence. The sooner you go, the better your chances of catching them before they get to Mount Zanhei."

He closed his eyes. He knew his best friend was right. He knew he should leave immediately. But it was more than fear of what awaited him on the slopes of the volcano that terrified him; it was what would happen to Anyang if he couldn't be there to protect him.

He opened his eyes and met his brother's gaze. Anyang was looking at him with such love and trust it made his heart ache.

"I believe in you, gogo," Anyang said softly. "You can believe in me." He held up his hands, fingertips glowing a faint purple as he called on his power. "I can do this. And you can too."

Han's throat tightened as he nodded. "All right," he said hoarsely. "Let's do this."

Yulana instructed him how to climb onto the phoenix's back, where to sit, and how to hold on, which Han tried his best to follow without falling off. His hands trembled so hard as he gripped the bird's feathers that he was afraid he might tear them out.

"I don't suppose Temur wears a saddle or anything," he said weakly.

"Too much weight," Yulana said as she hopped onto the bird's back behind him. "Don't worry, Prince Rice Cake. I've got you." She winked, and she threaded her arms beneath his and around his waist to grab the feathers at the nape of Temur's neck. "Don't worry, she's never dropped anyone." Yulana grinned. "Yet." She shifted her weight behind Han so that he was securely ensconced in her arms. "All right, girl," she said to the bird. "Let's go."

With a great leap, the creature took off, four wings beating hard as she carried them higher and higher into the heavens. Han squeezed his eyes shut as the wind whistled past his ears, praying and holding on for dear life.

"I suppose this is probably not a good time to mention I'm afraid of heeeeeeeeeeeeeeeights?"

41

IT WAS THE OVERWHELMING, OVERPOWERING STENCH OF brimstone that woke Zhara. For a moment she wondered if she had let some eggs boil for too long as she struggled to open her bleary eyes to darkness. Her mouth tasted foul and her head ached, a fierce pounding at the inner corners of her eyes and temples threatening to drown out all reason. Images of a masquerade ball, dancers dressed as fantastical creatures from the otherworld, and fireworks bursting above a golden roof lingered in her mind, remnants of a dream she wanted to keep.

Then she saw Suzhan, bound, gagged, and unconscious beside her.

Panicking, Zhara struggled to get up only to find her own hands and feet bound with chains. "Suzhan!" she cried, choking on her sister's name and the fumes around her. Rolling over onto her stomach, she inched her way along rough gravel and rock to her sister's side. "Suzhan, mimi, wake up," she pleaded, shaking the girl's shoulder. "Please wake up."

Suzhan groaned and stirred under her touch. "Nene?" she said groggily. She tried to crack her eyes open, but they kept rolling to the back of her head, her lashes fluttering shut.

Zhara frantically patted her sister's cheek. "No, no, mimi. Don't fall back asleep. Stay with me. Don't—"

"Leave her be," said a smooth voice behind her. "The dose was quite strong. She'll be under for a while."

She whirled around to find the Chancellor—Lord Chan—standing before her with hands clasped, a serene little smile on his frog-like face. "What did you do to my sister?" she demanded.

"My darling bride will be fine," he said with a wave of his hand.

"The bookseller laced her tea with some sedatives. She'll wake up eventually, none the worse for wear."

But Suzhan was to have left for Jingxi several days past. "The academy," she said quietly. "A lie?"

"Naturally," the Chancellor said. "I needed her to give you up somehow, so I told her whatever she wanted to hear."

Rage flashed through Zhara, power igniting the blood in her veins. The chains about her wrists and ankles glowed white-hot, and she cried out in pain as the metal burned her skin.

"Fascinating," the Chancellor—demon—murmured. "So the Guardian of Fire has indeed awakened."

Tears streamed down Zhara's face as the skin around her wrists and ankles blistered. "Please," she said. "I don't know what it is you want, but I promise I'll be good. Please, please." She thrust her arms out to the Chancellor, sobbing and screaming.

"Sometimes I forget how fragile human bodies are." He sighed.

With a snap of his fingers, the manacles fell from her hands and feet, but the pain did not dissipate. Instead, the agony intensified, and Zhara thought she would lose her mind. The Chancellor bent down and wrapped his fingers around her wrists and then her ankles. Instantly, the fires cooled, as did her magic, which snuffed itself out as though someone had smothered it. When he pulled his hands away, she saw that he had healed the burns into a mottled pattern of scars.

"There," he said. "Now we can talk."

Zhara gulped down a sob, her breaths hitching. "What do you want with us?" she whispered.

"With her?" He glanced at Suzhan, still unconscious. "She's nothing." He turned his bulbous eyes on her. "With you?" The tip of his tongue flicked across his upper lip like a frog catching a fly. "Everything."

Fear swamped her like a wave, but her magic did not respond. It felt thick, sluggish, groggy, as though someone had drugged her powers with a sedative as well. "What did you do to me?" she croaked.

"I'm afraid that my abilities and yours are somewhat diametrically opposed, although similar in their own ways," the Chancellor said.

"Like lodestones that either attract or repel each other, depending on which side faces the other. As a result, when I used my magic to heal you, it left both our powers a bit . . . fatigued. It'll pass."

As her heart rate slowed, Zhara was better able to take in her surroundings. They appeared to be on a rather narrow outcropping at the top of a mountain. In the distance, she could see an enormous lake reflecting a half-moon, and behind her . . .

. . . a bubbling lake of fire.

They were on top of Mount Zanhei.

Zhara gasped and scuttled away from the edge as the caldera belched and burped the stench of brimstone at her. "Why did you bring me here?" she croaked.

"I thought it was obvious," the Chancellor said. "You, my dear girl, are to be a sacrifice. An offering to Tiyok, Mother of Ten Thousand Demons, so that she may enter this world using your body as a vessel."

"A vessel? You mean . . . possession?"

"Nothing so vulgar," he said, waving his plump, bejeweled hand dismissively. "I mean so that she may consume your essence—your soul—and inhabit your body instead."

A chill fell over Zhara despite the searing heat of the volcano's caldera. "Is that what you did to Lord Chan?" she whispered. "Consume his essence? And inhabit his body instead?"

"Ah," the Chancellor grinned, his slimy smile spreading wider. "Not quite. What I'm doing is in fact possession, but as a greater demon, I know how to maintain my host's original shape." He puffed out his chest. "I am the First Lord of Tiyok, the Frog Demon of Poison and Pestilence."

He looked at her as though he expected her to be awed or overwhelmed.

"I knew this already." She sighed. "Master Cao told me."

"Who?" the Chancellor seemed confused.

"The bookseller." Zhara clenched her fists. "The traitor."

"Oh, him," the greater demon said. "The little nut-brown man. Yes, that was his name, wasn't it?"

A sudden misgiving overcame her. "What have you done with him?"

The Chancellor shrugged. "He had served his usefulness, so I dispensed with him."

Fear raised the hairs along the back of Zhara's neck. "Where is he?"

The demon gestured behind her at the lake of fire. Her heart clenched with pity at the little bookseller's fate. He had been so afraid of possession that he had been willing to bargain with a Lord of Tiyok. She stared into the depths of the bubbling caldera, several hundred feet or so below the lip on which they stood.

"Does this feel a bit like a homecoming for you?" the frog demon asked, coming to stand next her. "Mount Zanhei was said to be the resting place of the Guardian of Fire, after all."

Zhara stared into the glowing pit of molten lava. "Not really," she said. "I've only ever been here once before."

"You really don't remember, do you?" The Chancellor gave her a curious look, half pitying, half longing. "You don't have to possess bodies; you're reborn into them."

"They say when the world is out of balance, the souls of the Guardians of Dawn are reborn," she murmured. "Ah, poor Master Cao."

"I must admit, I'm a little jealous," the demon said. "To be fully human as well as the Guardian of Fire, ah, that must be quite a gift. You *are* Jin Zhara. I only wear Chan Gobu's face."

Zhara turned to look at him. "Why did you do it?" she asked. "Possess the Chancellor, I mean."

"Chan Gobu summoned *me*," the demon corrected. "Well, he was actually trying to summon *you*, but it didn't quite go as planned, since you lot can't be summoned."

"Why was he trying to summon the Guardian of Fire?"

"To be fair, he and three of his magician friends were trying to summon all four of you—Fire, Wood, Wind, and Water—but got me and my siblings instead." The Chancellor's features seemed to be growing froggier by the second. "You see, for the past hundred years or so, the balance between order and chaos has once again been tipping in Yan's favor. Happens when there is injustice in this mortal realm. When the wealthy feed on the poor, when those in power stomp on the necks of the powerless, when the people pollute and poison the land that feeds them, chaos reigns. And when chaos reigns, Tiyok grows."

Zhara once again reached for the well of power within her. Almost. Almost. She didn't know what she would do when her magic regained its strength, but at least she would have something to work with.

"Tiyok grows, and so does the presence of demons in the land. Your emperor—not the Warlord, the other one—happened to get possessed by one of my more enterprising lesser siblings. Unfortunately, possession by lesser demons tends to turn humans into abominations."

"And the Warlord put all the realms' magicians to the sword," Zhara sighed. "More chaos."

The Chancellor grinned. "The Warlord has the empire's best interests at heart, really. He just had the source of the problems all wrong. He thought the problem was magic, not injustice."

"And Chan Gobu? What of him?"

"Oh, he and his friends had the source correct, but the means all wrong. When they tried to summon the Guardians of Dawn, they happened to open a portal to Tiyok instead. And so," the demon said happily, "here I am."

A faint tingling began at the base of Zhara's spine. She just needed a little more time. "You said when these four magicians tried to summon the Guardians of Dawn, they summoned you and your siblings. Who are they?"

"The Lords of Tiyok."

"No." She shook her head. "Where are they? And who are they?"

The Frog Demon shrugged. His skin had taken on a bruise-like color, and his bulging eyes had slowly started to migrate to either side of his head. "They're here and there," he said disinterestedly. "Mount Zanhei is not the only portal to Tiyok that has been opened. Chan Gobu and his friends tried to summon all four Guardians, remember, and each one had a different resting place. I don't know what form my siblings took, but I'm sure they're each out there trying to find the best vessel to offer our mother. But mine is the best," he preened. "Because my gift is you."

"Could Tiyok have possessed anyone?" Zhara asked. The tingling beneath her skin had grown to the point where she could almost use her magic again.

"Any magician, yes. But obviously, the more powerful, the better. You see," the demon said, "I had initially intended to use the Second Heir as the vessel. The boy will grow up to be quite a powerful magician, much like his mother. I had tried to use her, as a matter of fact, but she revealed her powers to the Kestrels and got herself executed. Obstinate girl."

The Royal Consort. Poor Han.

"What of the magicians in the caverns below the mountain?" she asked, desperate to keep him talking. "What are they for?"

"Oh, them," the demon waved his hand. Webbing had grown between his fingers now. "Fodder. Fuel. Food. Their magical ki keeps the portal open."

Zhara gathered her magic in her hands, steeling herself to fight. So close.

"Well," the Frog Demon said, glancing up at the stars. "It's almost time. I've never seen my mother in the physical realm before. It will be quite exciting to see what she can do."

"What's going to happen now?" she asked.

He gestured to the lake of fire below. "You'll throw yourself in, of course."

"What makes you think I'll oblige?" A shadow passed over the face of the moon, and Zhara looked up. A pale, sinuous shape winged above, and she thought she could hear the sound of someone screaming.

"Ah, that's where your sister comes in." The demon smiled. His mouth stretched to his ears, revealing several rows of small, yellow teeth. He hauled the still-unconscious Suzhan up by her arm and held her over the edge of the crater. "If you don't throw yourself in, I'll sacrifice your sister instead."

"No—" She started forward, then stopped. "I thought the vessel needed to be a magician."

"It does. But that doesn't mean my mother won't appreciate a little human snack. Non-magical ki isn't quite as filling, but it will do in a pinch."

"What makes you think I'll care if you throw her in? She's not even related to me."

"Oh, please," the demon scoffed. "When I was your sister's fiancé, I could see you would move the earth for her. You love her. I don't understand it, but I suppose that's what comes with being reborn as a human. You get all the soft human feelings as well. And those are incredibly easy to manipulate."

"Why do I have to jump?" she asked. "You could just as easily pick me up and toss me in yourself."

"True," he said. "But it's more fun this way."

The screaming was growing louder now. This time, the Frog Demon looked up as well to see an enormous white bird with four wings headed straight toward them. There was someone on the creature's back, shouting with terror at the top of their lungs.

"Mistress Brandyyyyyyyyyyyyyyyyyyyyyyyyyyyyyyyyyyyy!"

"Han?" she asked in astonishment.

The white bird swooped in close and Han leaped off its back to tackle the Frog Demon to the ground. Zhara leaped forward to catch Suzhan before she fell, rolling them back to safely. Behind her Han and the Frog Demon grappled with each other as the bird circled back up for another pass, a second figure still on its back. Han choked as he wrestled with the demon.

"Yuli!" he said in a strangled voice.

Behind him, the enormous white bird dove straight for the Frog Demon and an arrow whizzed through the air, embedding itself in his shoulder. With a snarl, he turned to face his new attacker—Princess Yulana, reddish hair streaming behind her as she notched another arrow on her bow and let it fly.

This time it lodged deep in the Frog Demon's throat. Growling, he tossed Han aside as though he weighed nothing and ripped the arrow out, thick, black sludge pouring out of the wound where human blood ought to have been. Yuli jumped off the bird's back and landed with a graceful roll, bringing her leg up and across the Frog Demon's head in one smooth, easy motion. He stumbled back a few steps before swinging his arm up to catch her beneath the chin, sending her flying.

"Well, well, well, what do we have here?" the Frog Demon asked, voice distorted and twisted from the wound at his throat. "It seems we have another Guardian on our hands." He grabbed the northern princess by her hair. "Which one are you, Fire Top?" He raised his eyes to the bird circling above. "Wind?"

"Yuli!" Summoning her fire, Zhara rushed the demon, wrapping her burning hands around his neck.

"Is that all you've got?" the Frog Demon laughed, the sound bubbling and gurgling through the torn flesh about his neck. "You haven't even realized the full extent of what you can do, have you, Jin Zhara?"

Faster than the eye could see, he reached out and grabbed Zhara by the throat. Her magic sputtered and died, drowning against the tidal wave of his corruption. Her hands went to his as she struggled to breathe, kicking futilely at his chest.

"The last time I battled you," the Frog Demon snarled, "you shaped the very world to your desires. You put a bit of your fire into all that you touched, transforming the mundane into the magical. You could enchant a blade to cure possession. You could gift an ordinary human with powers and you could take them away from those born with them. You could even change your very shape, like that lion friend who was always with you. But you're not the warrior of old that I remember. You're just a little girl now, aren't you?"

Just then, Han came barreling in from the side, catching the Frog Demon off guard. Zhara coughed as she struggled to draw breath, as she fought off the poison in her magic and in her ears. She tried to summon her magic, that fire he had spoken of, but she didn't know how. She was just a girl. She was not yet the Guardian of Fire.

"Enough of this." The Frog Demon reached out and scooped Suzhan off the ground once more. "Time to end it," he said, and he threw the girl off the edge of the crater.

"No!" Zhara cried, running after her sister without a second thought.

"Mistress Brandy!" Han yelled, reaching for her hand.

But it was too late.

Zhara jumped.

And she was gone.

42

THE FALL WAS LONG.

The air was hot—too hot—and it scorched Zhara's lungs as she tried to breathe. She could feel her magic struggling through the bonds placed upon it by the frog demon, struggling to break free. Zhara tried to call it forth, to use all the power of her fear and desperation to stoke it to life. Mind over magic. She could do it. She could.

But all her attempts failed. Fear was not a motivator; instead it dampened everything, paralyzing her.

Be good, and be true.

I tried, baba, she thought. *I tried to be both good and true, but in the end, it didn't matter.*

There was a sort of peace that came with accepting death. For once, the knowledge that she was powerless was not the end of the world, for the end of her world was already here. And with that peace came clarity. Calm. Control.

Her magic flickered to life.

Hope flooded her meridian pathways, clearing them of the Frog Demon's poison. Zhara closed her eyes and thought of cooling waters, of snowfall, of ice. She thought of the Infinite River that wound its way from the Sweet Sea to the Shining Sea, the Gleaming River of stars in the heavens.

Around her, the furnace began to cool.

Zhara thought of feathers, of clouds, of pillows. She thought of the kitchen, of her pallet before the hearth, of her sister curled up beside her as she read to her before bed. She thought of the softness of Sajah's fur, the slippery-smooth feel of silk beneath her fingers, the tender, tender touch of Han's lips upon hers.

Her descent slowed, cushioned by the slowly thickening air around her.

She thought of the blanket of humidity that covered the Infinite River delta this time of year and imagined it slowly turning into fog. A thin haze surrounded her, growing thicker and thicker until she could no longer tell which direction was up. It was as though she had stopped falling entirely, suspended in a featureless void. A sense of vertigo overcame her, and she was suddenly unsure of where she was. Was she in a dream? Was she dying? Or was this real?

Zhara held her hand before her face. Magic illuminated her skin with its rose-gold glow. He had said the Guardian of Fire could shape the world around them to their desires. She grasped at the void and began shaping it, forming the crude shapes of a stool, a pallet, and a book. Slowly, the forms began to solidify, and the kitchen of her step-mother's apartments came into view.

She looked around at her new surroundings. The details were perfect, from her father's death tablet above the stove to the light dusting of ash on her pallet before the hearth. Zhara wondered whether she ought to be more astonished, but as she was still unsure of whether or not she was dead or dreaming, she allowed herself to adjust to this new reality.

"Now, why did I choose this scene?" she croaked. The pain in her scorched lungs seemed to indicate she was still alive somehow, but she ignored it, exploring the kitchen instead. Her apron hung from its usual place beside the threshold, and when Zhara removed her father's memorial plaque, she found the enameled rosewood box that contained his belongings tucked into its usual hiding place. Beside her pallet was a copy of *The Maiden Who Was Loved by Death*—the second installment, the one she had never gotten around to reading. Picking the book up, she thumbed excitedly through it but was disappointed to find the pages blank.

"You've never read it, that's why it's empty."

She whirled around to find the Second Wife sitting on the low folding stool that was Suzhan's usual seat. Her stepmother was dressed in her elegant but threadbare dressing gown, her hair tied into a loose ponytail at the nape of her neck.

"Your mind can't fill in the pages, even if it can conjure the title," she said, rising from her seat.

"What—" Zhara said hoarsely, backing away. "What is Madame doing here?"

"This is your world, Guardian of Fire," said the Second Wife. "You're the one who shaped it." She looked around the scene with interest. "Humans are strange. Your soft little emotions are so funny. In the moments before death, is this the best your limited little mind can conjure?"

"You're not the Second Wife," Zhara said with dawning realization. "You're . . ." She couldn't finish her thought.

"The Mother of Ten Thousand Demons." The Second Wife—or the primordial demon wearing her face—clasped her hands before her and gave a bow. If Zhara had not known she was dreaming—or dead—then, she would know it now, for her stepmother had never afforded her such respect.

"Am I dead then?" Zhara asked. "Have you consumed my magical essence?"

The Mother of Ten Thousand Demons shook her head. "Not yet."

"Why not?"

Her stepmother's lips thinned. "Well, you see, you've made things rather complicated for me, Guardian of Fire."

"I have?"

"You have," the Second Wife—Zhara couldn't think of her as anything other than the Second Wife—said wryly. "When you transformed the lake of fire into"—she gestured around them—"this, you managed to keep yourself on the physical plane. You stand at the threshold to my realm, and I cannot cross it."

"I don't understand."

Her stepmother sighed. "Sometimes I forget how limited the mortal capacity for comprehending things beyond the material plane can be. Let's just say that you have fallen into the heart of chaos, but you have transformed that chaos into order."

Zhara looked at the familiar, comforting sights and smells of the kitchen—the feel of the packed dirt beneath her feet, the sound of the fire crackling in the hearth, the gentle, musical tinkling of the beads and colored glass she had strung over the windows for the barest bit of beauty. She ran her hands over the splintered surface of the kitchen table, feeling the tips of her fingers snag and catch on the roughened planks. Rapping on the tabletop, she listened to the solid *tok-tok-tok* of her knuckles against wood. It was all so tangible, so *real*. "So I am in Tiyok?" she asked uncertainly.

"Yes," the Second Wife replied. "And no."

"I don't understand," Zhara said again.

Her stepmother made an impatient sound and rose from her seat beside the hearth. "Tiyok is not a *place*. It is an idea. A *state* of existence. Or nonexistence, if you will." She gestured about the kitchen. "Once, this was nothing but chaos. Nothing but void. Yet somehow you've managed to turn nothing into something—what is it you humans say?—*real*."

"Real," Zhara murmured. She ran her fingers over the mottled scars at her wrists, felt the fever beneath her skin, the burns in her lungs. She was here and she was present. "So this isn't a dream."

Well," the Second Wife said. "This isn't *not* a dream. Right now we are in the in-between places, the liminal spaces. We are where order meets chaos, where reason and dreams intermingle."

Zhara glanced at the kitchen threshold, beyond which there was nothing but a vague emptiness. "Can I leave? What's out there?"

"My realm," the Second Wife said. "Out there I would be able to possess you."

"I see." She sat on the stool before the hearth. "So we're stuck here."

"Yes. Well, you are, Guardian of Fire," her stepmother said. "I can come and go as I please, but the moment you set foot outside this place, I will devour your magical essence." The Second Wife looked around the kitchen, eyes lingering on the shabby pallet, the threadbare blankets, the paltry pantry shelves. "Why did you choose this place?" she asked curiously. "Most humans would have probably created some sort of palace or a beautiful retreat or something like that."

Zhara thought of the masquerade ball at the Night of the Sevens, the costumes, the fireworks, the pageantry, the fun. She thought of Wisteria Court, with its polished ebony walkways, the reflecting pond, the lavender blooms floating down and drifting into the water like snow. Then she looked to her father's death tablet, the book at her side, the bowl of fresh water lilies she had gathered from the riverbank, and the play of colored light on the wall opposite the window. "I suppose I created it," she said softly, "because it was home."

"Home." The Second Wife looked surprised. "This place where your stepmother abused you for so long?"

The word *abuse* struck Zhara in tender places she did not know she had. "I wouldn't call it abuse."

"Wouldn't you?" The primordial demon tilted her head as she studied Zhara. "This woman who only ever took advantage of your gentle nature, your desire to be good, your love for your family without giving anything in return? This selfish person who used you for your magic when it was convenient, then discarded you when it wasn't?"

Zhara flinched, her soul scrabbling for the shadows as though it could escape the truth. "She gave me a place to stay," she whispered. "She fed me. She clothed me. She protected me when she could have turned me over to the Kestrels for my magic. She kept me safe because she——" She choked, unable to finish the sentence.

"Loved you?" The Second Wife's voice was unwontedly gentle, and that gentleness was somehow worse than her customary icy contempt, flat indifference, and violent rages put together.

Zhara couldn't answer because she knew the answer. Ever since she was a child, ever since the Kestrels had taken her father away and left her an orphan, she had clung to the one person who had given her shelter. The one person who did not seem frightened by her powers, the one person who did not think she was a monster. But she knew—had always known—that tolerance was not acceptance. It was not love, yet she had starved herself on the barest morsels of approval, afraid of never feasting again. Tears pricked Zhara's eyes, hot and stinging, as she turned to the demon wearing her stepmother's face.

"Why?" she croaked, her voice cracked and pleading. "Why didn't you love me? Why couldn't you love me?"

The Second Wife studied her. "Because," she said quietly. "You're unloveable."

And Zhara broke.

She buried her face in her hands, sobs racking her body as she fell off the stool and onto her knees. Pain radiated throughout her body as she mourned the loss of the loving stepmother who had never been, love and sorrow mingled together, her magic rising up to meet the overwhelming force of emotion that swept through her. But once the grief had passed, there was a sense of calm in its wake. Peace. Acceptance.

"Interesting," the Second Wife said once Zhara's tears had subsided. "That was the last thing you wanted to hear from your stepmother's lips, yet you made me say it anyway."

Zhara looked up in surprise. "*I* made you say it?"

The Mother of Ten Thousand Demons shrugged. "In here, I'm just an idea wearing your stepmother's face. I have no weight, no substance." To prove her point, she tried picking up the copy of *The Maiden Who Was Loved by Death*. Her hand passed through the book like a ghost. "You are the mistress of this small pocket of order within chaos. I am but a visitor here."

Zhara looked to the low stool in the corner. "If I am mistress of this domain," she said quietly. "Then where is my sister?"

The Second Wife nodded toward the pallet, and the unconscious form of Suzhan materialized before the hearth.

"Mimi!" Zhara cried, crawling to her sister's side. "Is she alive?"

"For now."

Suzhan murmured and shifted on the pallet. She gave a choked, gurgling cough, and Zhara turned her onto her side. "Wake up, mimi," she pleaded. "Wake up."

"She won't wake," the Second Wife said. "Her body may be here physically, but the rest of her—her thoughts, her feelings, her ghost—is with me."

"No!" Zhara gathered her sister in her arms and called forth her magic. Suzhan jerked as Zhara's power traversed through the girl's meridian pathways, but there was no corruption to burn away, no magic to resonate with her own.

Her stepmother watched them both with a look almost akin to pity on her face. "The girl's not possessed," she said. "She's lost."

Zhara gently laid Suzhan back down on the pallet, tears running down her face. "What can I do to save her? What can I give you to save her soul?"

The Second Wife shrugged. "I suspect you already know the answer to that."

She did. "You want to possess me," she whispered.

"*Possession* is such a vulgar word, but yes."

Zhara looked down at her sister's body. "If I let you possess me," she said softly, "do you promise to return Suzhan, hale and whole, to the world of order?"

The Second Wife made an impatient gesture. "Yes, yes, of course."

"How do I know you'll keep your word?"

"You don't." The Second Wife tilted her head to one side. "But that's true of anyone, Guardian of Fire, not just the Mother of Ten Thousand Demons. You must go on faith, I suppose."

Faith seemed like such a strange word on the lips of a demon, but it was stranger still coming from her stepmother's mouth. The Second Wife had never relied on faith or prayers; she had always made her own way. She had fought and fought and fought, then railed and railed and railed when matters didn't turn out her way.

"If I am to go on faith," Zhara said, "then you must offer me a gesture of faith in return. Show me Suzhan's soul."

The Second Wife shrugged. "Very well then."

Outside the kitchen, in the blank void outside, a shadowy shape was starting to emerge. Slowly the shape solidified, growing longer and thinner, until it finally coalesced into the silhouette of what seemed like a young girl, waiting outside the kitchen, featureless and vague.

"Mimi?" Zhara got to her feet and approached the threshold.

The silhouette said nothing, but somehow Zhara *knew* it was her sister's ghost. She could sense the familiar frustration, anger, bitterness, resentment, fear, and anxiety churning on the surface, which nearly overpowered the determination, loyalty, and sweetness that lay at her core. Zhara turned to the unconscious figure on the pallet beside the hearth. The body and the spirit were both Suzhan and not somehow, at the same time.

"I don't know why you're so concerned with saving your sister's life," the Second Wife remarked. "After all, once I take your body, I'll take over the mortal realm."

Zhara smoothed down the flyaway strands of her sister's hair. "If she dies once you possess me, then at least her soul will return to the place of beginnings and endings to be born anew." She stroked Suzhan's forehead. "I owe her that much, at least."

"You really are human, aren't you?" The Mother of Demons sounded intrigued. "Even when there is no possibility of a happy ending, you persist in this misguided nobility."

"*In this life or the next, there is no end when there is love,*" Zhara quoted softly. It was her favorite line from *The Maiden Who Was Loved by Death.* "My sister and I will continue fighting. Perhaps in our next lives, we will write our happy ending."

"But there is no next life for you, Jin Zhara." The Second Wife shook her head. "You have no ordinary soul. Your ghost and your body may be human, but unlike other humans, your soul was not born of the place of beginnings and endings. You are the Guardian of Fire. Yours is not a soul to be dissolved and remade in the cauldron of the universe; yours is a soul made to wait in flames until the need rises once more. Only it won't happen this time. I will consume your soul, and never again shall you and the other Guardians of Dawn imprison me beneath the earth." She paused. "Metaphorically speaking."

No rebirth, only oblivion. Zhara thought of the pain she had caused her sister and wondered if that would be enough to atone for her sins. "What will you do?" she asked. "Once you have taken over my body?"

Her stepmother grinned. "Sow chaos, of course. Unlike humans, it is my nature. That is how Yan made me. Once I set foot in the mortal realm, the eternal battle between order and chaos will be over. And chaos will have won."

The end of the world. Zhara wanted to laugh. It sounded so melodramatic, like something the villain in a play put on by the Bangtan Brothers would say. And yet she knew it to be true.

"I see," Zhara said. "So it doesn't matter if you save Suzhan. She may be alive, but life as she knew it will end."

The Second Wife shrugged. "It is what it is."

Zhara closed her eyes and lifted Suzhan's body in her arms. Her sister was taller than her by half a head, but she was thin, and scarcely weighed anything. She made her slow, agonizing way to the kitchen threshold, where her sister's ghost waited patiently outside.

"What are you doing?" the Second Wife asked.

She turned and looked her stepmother directly in the eye, saying the words she had always wished she could say.

"Writing my happy ending."

And then she stepped into the void.

Out in the nothing, Zhara had to fight to keep her body. To remember her physical self, to know that she had eyes and lips and lungs and skin. Even if there was pain. Even if everything hurt. It reminded her she was alive and that the demons could not touch her. Otherwise she would dissolve, dissipate, disappear into oblivion.

The portal, said a voice that was not a voice. It was the idea of a voice, the concept of sound, of words, of meaning, but not the reality. *You need to close it.*

Zhara tried to answer but couldn't remember the notion of a mouth or words or speech. Pulling her self together, literally and figuratively, she forced herself to ask, "Where's the portal?"

All around you, said the voice that was not a voice. *The void is the portal. Turn chaos into order and you seal the portal, nene.*

"Suzhan?"

Her sister's ghost materialized beside her. *I'm here. You must seal the portal to Tiyok. Now.*

"I can't," Zhara said helplessly. She was so, so tired. "I'm just a girl."

You can, said Suzhan. *You are the Guardian of Fire.*

The Guardian of Fire, whose power was transformation. She was both an elemental warrior and Jin Zhara, a girl and a Guardian of Dawn all at once. But try as she might, she couldn't find that spark of flame within her.

Let me help you, nene.

Suzhan wrapped her weightless arms about Zhara. The ghost was an idea of a person, as insubstantial as a thought, but she *felt* her sister's love and wiry strength as a tangible thing. Suzhan possessed her spirit with determination and desire and anger, allowing Zhara to dig deep into the corners of her own soul.

Keeping a grip on her sister's physical form, she reached out into the void and imagined the formless fog collecting, coalescing, cooling into dew. Into raindrops. Into puddles. Into lakes. Beads of water coated her skin.

Yes, nene, yes!

Zhara's concentration wavered, and the water evaporated. She sensed Suzhan holding on tighter to her, infusing her with more strength. Regathering and regrouping her resources, Zhara focused once more on transforming the nothing around her into something. Fog to dew to rain to water. As she concentrated, she could feel the last reserves of her magic draining fast, this enormous act of power draining not only her power, but her life force, her ki.

Nene, Suzhan's ghost whispered in her ear. *Hold on.*

Water coated her hands like a bubble, expanding up her arms, her shoulders, down her chest, her stomach, around Suzhan's body, down her legs. The bubble grew and grew and grew and grew until it enveloped her throat, her mouth, her nose, her eyes, and she was completely submerged.

Don't stop.

She couldn't stop. Beyond the edges of the void, she could feel the shape of the crater into which she had fallen. She was almost there. The taste of blood filled her mouth but she kept pushing and pushing and pushing and pushing until every last bit of nothing was gone, transformed into water at the heart of Mount Zanhei.

The portal to Tiyok was closed.

Zhara collapsed, Suzhan's body floating away from her arms. She reached out and grabbed her sister's hand, straining for the surface. The light of the half-moon was a beacon above her, and she was close, so close—

She burst free with a gasp. Her lungs burned, scalded by the air of the volcano and from the effort of holding her breath for so long. She cast about for a place to rest, but there was none. Just a large, smooth expanse of dark water around her. Zhara was exhausted—physically, mentally, magically—but she closed her eyes and imagined a chair, a bench, a boat. The waters near her began to bubble as the liquid coalesced into a solid, then solidified even further into wood. A raft.

With the last of her failing strength, Zhara heaved Suzhan onto the craft before clambering onto it herself. She collapsed face-first onto the rough wood and closed her eyes. She wanted to lie there forever and never get up again, but she forced herself to crawl to her sister's side, checking her pulse and her breathing. Suzhan was alive—barely. Zhara didn't know what the extent of her injuries were, or if they were even survivable, but for the moment, the fact that her sister wasn't dead was enough. The fact that *she* wasn't dead was enough.

They had survived.

She lay on her back and stared at the heavens. The crater was almost perfectly circular, like a mirror or a plate, and through it she could see the starry skies. The half-moon of the magpie lovers was positioned in the exact middle, and Zhara thought it looked like Mara's symbol—a circle with a dot in the center, the representation of the Seventh Immortal's all-seeing eye. She was not the praying sort, but she understood better what holy folk meant by surrendering one's fate to higher powers. She had done all she could. The rest was up to the gods. She was tired of surviving. She wanted to rest.

As Zhara let her mind drift away, images crowded in on the edges of her vision like shadows. Lanterns sending a river of wishes to the stars. The play of rainbow light against her kitchen wall as the morning sun hit the beads of colored glass. The crisp, clean pages of a newly released romance serial. The twirling ribbons trailing from the sleeves of Bangtan's tumblers performing at the palace.

Zhara blinked. She could see those sinuous shapes before her now, as something large and white spiraled overhead. A bird. A bird with four wings, circling in slow loops, around and around the crater, growing bigger with each pass. As darkness encroached on her thoughts, her mind turned to Han for the last time, imagining his large, round eyes and dimpled smile. She even thought she could see him on the back of this heavenly creature, hand outstretched and reaching for her.

"Mistress Brandy!"

She thought she could even hear his voice as the world faded away, feel the strength of his arms wrapped around her body, that touch that could both stoke and quell the fires within her. A weightlessness suffused her bones, and she felt as though she were floating, the wind ruffling her hair and soothing her skin.

"Zhara," Han's voice came again, and it was close now, whispering in her ear. "I got you. You're safe."

Safe. But she had moved beyond the need for safety. She had faced the Mother of Ten Thousand Demons and lived. If she survived, then she swore that she would live for more. To be true to herself.

"Will she be all right?" Han asked worriedly.

Zhara's lashes fluttered, and she found herself surrounded by endless night spangled by stars. Then a handsome face hove into view. A strong nose, an even stronger jaw, large eyes, and a dimpled smile. A light, bubbling sensation crawled up her throat, and she started giggling.

"Oh, I think she'll be fine," came a different voice. Northern-accented, amused, and wry. Yuli. "She's got the Good-Looking Giggles."

ℰPILOGUE

THE HUMIDITY BROKE THE DAY THEY WERE due to leave Zanhei.

"Are you ready, nene?" Suzhan asked.

Zhara looked around the rooms in Wisteria Court that had been her home for the past six weeks. In some ways, the world had changed utterly since the Night of the Sevens, but in others it remained the same. After she closed the portal to Tiyok in the crater of Mount Zanhei, all the abominations in the city had returned to their human selves with no memory of what had happened. The palace was in shambles and the Morning Realms were on the edge of war, confronted with the open existence of magicians once more. The Kestrels had been expelled from the southern provinces and the alliance between House Wonhu and the emperor had been broken, including Han and Princess Yulana's engagement.

Not that Zhara had been conscious for any of this. After her confrontation with the Mother of Ten Thousand Demons, she had slept for nearly two weeks straight. For a time, Jiyi said, they had all been worried they would lose her entirely. Lose the Guardian of Fire.

The Guardian of Fire.

The Guardians of Dawn even brought in a magical healer from Mingnan, one of the border towns on the outskirts of the outermost west, but he had claimed he could do nothing for her magical ki. The only thing they could do was wait.

So while they waited, they brought the Chancellor to justice—what was left of him, at any rate. The Frog Demon of Poison and Pestilence had disappeared along with the other abominations, leaving behind the torn and tattered body of the magician it had possessed twenty years before. He lived just long enough to say farewell to his child, Xu, before being beheaded for his crimes against the House of Wonhu. The prince ruled Zanhei once more. No more regent. No more hiding from the world in grief.

When at last Zhara awoke, she had opened her eyes to a new reality.

Magic was no longer forbidden in Zanhei, and she was ready to live her life as she truly was.

"Yes," she said softly. "I'm ready." She turned to meet her sister's flickering gaze then turned her eyes to the zither in Suzhan's arms, folded up and tucked away into a beautiful wooden case carved with a cloud and river motif. "Are you, mimi?"

Suzhan shifted on her feet, nervously fingering the case's clasp. "Yes," she whispered. "I think so."

The academy of music in Jingxi accepted Suzhan into their ranks and had agreed to waive the fees after the traveling master for whom she had auditioned advocated for her inclusion. It was the opportunity of a lifetime and the culmination of a long-held secret dream, yet her sister did not seem excited; she seemed scared.

"Cheer up," Zhara said, gently sweeping her sister's hair from her face and tweaking her nose. "Isn't this what you've always wanted?"

Suzhan squirmed. "Well, yes," she admitted. "It's just that I . . ." She trailed off.

"You what, mimi?"

Suzhan looked away. "I never thought it would ever happen. Not after what I did to you."

Silence fell over the sisters as the memory of the Night of the Sevens returned to them. The turning of the key in the lock, the sound of betrayal. Some wounds were still too raw to touch.

"The past is past," Zhara said gently. "We cannot go back, we can only move forward." She ran the tips of her fingers lightly over her sister's cheekbones, hovering by Suzhan's sightless eyes. "I'm sorry for what I did to you all those years ago," she said softly. "And . . . do you want me to heal you? To bring your eyes back to what they once were?"

Suzhan was quiet for a while. "We cannot go back, we can only move forward," she said. She smiled. "Whatever my eyes were before they became this, it was clear that I was going blind regardless." She wrapped her hand around Zhara's. "There is no fixing me. I don't want to be fixed. I am Suzhan. And I am blind."

The girls sat together on the steps outside Wisteria Court as they waited for their respective modes of transportation out of Zanhei. Zhara was headed to the lands of the outermost west, traveling with the Bangtan Brothers and Han in search of Li Er-Shuan and *Songs of Order and Chaos,* while Suzhan was to be escorted to the docks by Meng Kam, one of the Buri matriarch's older great-grandsons, and then taken on a boat upriver to the province of Jingxi.

"I suppose that in the end," Suzhan said softly, "we are following our own truths, aren't we?"

It was hard to speak around the tightness in her throat. "We are," said Zhara hoarsely. "We're each keeping our promise."

"I will miss you, nene."

"I will miss you too, mimi."

So much. So much to be said, and not enough time. So Zhara wrapped her arm about her little sister's shoulders and held her close. Suzhan was so much taller than her now, but she still felt small and slight in her embrace. When Meng Kam came whistling up the road pulling a rickshaw behind him, Zhara let go of her sister.

"I'll write," she said as the Buri boy helped Suzhan into the conveyance.

Suzhan smiled. "Tell me stories, nene."

Zhara smiled back. "I only know love stories, I'm afraid."

"Even better," her sister called back as Meng Kam began heading toward the docks. "As long as all the love stories are yours."

Other goodbyes were both easier and harder to say.

As Zanhei now teemed with magicians young and old—mostly young—in need of instruction and direction, the Guardians of Dawn had been busy setting up schools and scouring the province for students.

Naturally, Jiyi was chosen as a teacher for the institution in the city, and was known to be an especially harsh taskmistress. Despite this, her students adored her, which the former courtesan claimed was unsurprising. Back in her entertainer days, there were several patrons who paid exorbitant amounts of money just for the dubious privilege of being ordered about by her.

"I hate farewells," the courtesan had said that morning before she left for the newly built school along the canals. "So I shall not say goodbye, and will merely bid you a very good *until next time.*"

"And when might that be?" Zhara asked.

Jiyi gave her one of her rare genuine smiles. "Sooner than you think."

Several of the magicians they found were orphans of the Just War, so, in addition to schools, shelter and care needed to be found. Hundreds poured into the city from throughout the Morning Realms, bringing a diverse jumble of accents, flavors, and cultures to the south. Hundreds were arriving, but Zhara was leaving.

"Be careful out there," Jiyi said. "Many of our caravans are being ambushed by bandits on the road claiming to be fighting under the banner of the Four-Winged Dragon."

The Mugung battle banner.

"But I thought all the Mugungs were dead," Zhara said. "The last princess was just a baby when the Warlord razed the imperial palace to the ground. All they found in the smoking ruins was some bones and hair."

"But not the Star of Radiance," Jiyi said in a low voice. "The imperial jewel was never found among the remains."

"Is that significant?" Zhara asked.

"The imperial jewel is the heart and soul of the land, the founding artifact of the Morning Realms," the courtesan said. "Without it, we will never be truly united."

"Why not?"

"The Free Peoples of the West recognize no leader but the Unicorn King, and the Qirin Tulku swears allegiance to whoever wields the Star of Radiance." Jiyi sighed. "But more than that, it is a symbol of our empire."

"I wonder why the Warlord never had another crystal made and claimed that as the Star of Radiance," Zhara said thoughtfully.

The courtesan shrugged. "Supposedly the jewel has a potent ki of its own that is instantly recognizable and cannot be re-created by the hands of mere mortals. I don't know if that's true. Still, one cannot deny the impact of a good story. A mystical gem that defeated the forces of darkness, passed down through generations in the hands of the Mugungs? The Star of Radiance has great power indeed, but only because we, the people, give it significance."

Zhara said nothing. They lived in political times indeed.

"The important thing is *Songs of Order and Chaos*," Teacher Hu said, emerging from inside Wisteria Court. "Don't let all this talk about the Star of Radiance distract you out there. We need to learn more about these Kings of Tiyok, where they might be, and how to banish them from this plane of existence once and for all."

Saying goodbye to Teacher Hu was more or less difficult in other ways.

"Are you sure you can't stay, child?" she asked, wrapping Zhara up in one of her rare hugs.

Zhara's throat closed tight. "You know I can't, auntie," she said. "I am a Guardian of Dawn, in more ways than one. I need to find the others and warn them about the Kings of Tiyok."

"I know." The apothecary sighed. "I just want you to survive."

Zhara's smile was sad. "And I want," she said, "to thrive."

A few hours later, Han arrived at Wisteria Court, having resolved all palace matters before setting out with Zhara and the Bangtan Brothers. He would join them in their journey to the furthermost west in search of *Songs of Order and Chaos* and Li Er-Shuan. For once, Jiyi did him a kindness and looked away from his red-rimmed eyes and splotchy nose, saying nothing about the tears that still streamed down his face after his farewell with Anyang.

"Are you sure you can't stay, gogo?" the Second Heir had asked in a petulant voice. "I don't want you to go."

Han placed his hands on his little brother's shoulders. "I know, didi," he said. "And I don't want to leave you either." He gathered the boy in close. "But I have to go. Uncle Li won't recognize anyone else. Besides," he said, whispering into Anyang's hair, "someone needs to take care of our father while I'm away."

Prince Wonhu had roused himself from his period of mourning after the death of his regent and began to apply himself to the task of governing his province. He was assisted by Xu, who had just begun their new job as a clerk in the Ministry of Internal Affairs.

"I wish I could go with you," Xu said regretfully. "But this new position is taking all my time."

Han had smiled fondly at his best friend. "Responsibility looks good on you," he teased. "Maybe I will appoint you regent once I ascend the throne."

To his horror, this made tears well up in Xu's eyes. "Oh," they quavered. "What will His Grace do without me to make sure he gets to his majority alive?"

"I'm sure I'll manage," Han said. "It's only two months."

"A lot can happen in two months," Xu muttered ominously. Then they threw their arms about Han's neck and squeezed tight. "Come back safe, my prince."

"I will," he promised. "I will. Now you have to let go or I'll die by suffocation before I reach my majority."

At last, they were ready to set off.

The Bangtan Brothers loaded their painted wagon and hitched it to their nag, Cloud, tended to by Alyosha, one of the younger members of the troupe.

"We have a tradition before we get started on our journeys," Junseo said a bit sheepishly. "A chant to lift our spirits. Join us, if you'd like."

So the seven of them, and Han and Zhara, gathered in a circle, their right hands extended to meet in the middle. "Bangtan, Bangtan," they called. "Bang-Bangtan!"

"Farewell," said Yuli with amusement. "You'll see me soon. Well, in spirit, if not in person."

The northern princess had promised to meet with them at least once a week as they journeyed to the lands of the Qirin Tulku while she traveled back to Urghud with her entourage. To share news, but also to enjoy each other's company.

"I'll miss you southern softies." She grinned, ruffling Zhara's hair. "I've grown fond of you."

She smiled back. "We'll miss you too, Yuli." She frowned. "What are you going to tell your grandfather about the marriage being called off?"

Yuli shrugged. "Obaji won't care. But let's just say there are several members of my clan who are pretty upset that their place in line for the Gommun Kang just got pushed back by one." She winked. "Too bad. I think Prince Rice Cake and I could have had a decent go of it."

"What?" Han asked in panic.

Zhara and Yuli laughed together. "You take care of each other," the northern princess said, giving Zhara a hug.

"We will," Zhara said. "What about you? Is there a pretty lady waiting for you back home?"

Yuli's copper eyes looked sad. "There was, once." She shook her head. "But that's not important. Best be getting on the road soon," she said. "You want to reach the next town by nightfall."

Zhara and Han both declined the offer to ride in the Bangtan Brothers' wagon, although Sajah felt no such compulsion to refuse. The cat—the Lion of the South—rode in the back with all of their things, having made a comfortable nest for himself out of Han's bedding. Han was going to have an unpleasant discovery once they made camp.

Around noon, they stopped for their midday meal and Han pulled Zhara away from the others.

"Here," he said, handing her a small clamshell box carved from mother-of-pearl and in the shape of an actual clam. When she opened it, she found a rose quartz bangle, into which seven perfectly teardrop-shaped freshwater pearls had been set. "I wanted to wait until we had a bit more privacy before giving this to you."

Her tears from the night of their first kiss.

"Oh," Zhara said softly, a hiccough caught in her chest. "I—"

"I meant to give it to you on the Night of the Sevens for your birthday," Han said wryly. "Only . . . well. So it's an apology gift instead."

"Apology?" She was surprised. "For what?"

"Two things," he said. "The first, and most important: I'm sorry for having lied to you. About who I was." He took the bracelet from its clamshell box and fastened it about Zhara's wrist. "My intentions might have come from a good place, but I still hurt you, and I am sorry."

She held his gaze, heart too full to speak.

"Second . . . well, I never did give you your own copy of *The Maiden Who Was Loved by Death*."

Zhara laughed, choking a little on her sobs. Throwing her arms around Han's neck, she stood on tiptoe and pressed her lips against his, this kiss sweeter for the bitterness that had come before.

"Oh, look," Han said once they had pulled apart. He held another handful of pearls before her. "Looks like I have some more promises to keep, don't I?"

She giggled as she kissed him again. "You do," she said. "You do."

"Ooh, the Good-Looking Giggles," Han said. "You must really like me."

"I do," she said. "I do."

Ahead of them was nothing but the long, uncertain road, the end of which was unknown. But as Zhara and Han followed behind the Bangtan Brothers' wagon, they walked hand in hand, toward the setting sun, toward tomorrow, and toward the rest of their lives.

IN THE OUTERMOST WEST . . .

THE PRAYERS HAD GONE ON ALL THROUGH the night.

The old soldier Okonwe watched the ceremonies from his post atop the crenellated rooftops of Dzong Castle, arms crossed and expression grim. The Qirin Tulku stood among the people in the town square—or what passed for a town square in these remote parts— chanting and offering libations to the Pillar to purify the land. It was rare to see the shaman-king outside his palace, and rarer still to see him perform old rituals long forgotten. A touch of foreboding feathered down Okonwe's spine, and the old soldier shivered.

"It's all a sham," said a husky voice behind him. "None of that rigamarole will do the slightest bit of good." A slender youth materialized at Okowne's side, watching the proceedings with their arms crossed in a very familiar pose and attitude. The old soldier shook his head to hide his smile. *Children,* he thought wryly. They proved that not all families were wrought in blood.

"Oh?" Okonwe asked softly. "And how could my liege be so sure?"

The youth turned their face toward the east and the light of the rising sun. The dawn illuminated the horrific burn scarring the left side of their face, a relic of a past life. Okonwe knew that the scarring was the reason—one of many—the people called his ward *Beast.* He had tried to put a stop to it once, but Beast had held him back. *Let the people call me whatever they want,* they said. *So long as they do not call me by my true name.*

"Because," Beast said simply, "the Qirin Tulku himself told me so."

The old soldier said nothing, but pressed his thumb to his lips to ward off the spirits of evil. Rumors of demons abounded, and while Okonwe did not necessarily believe them, it did no harm to be cautious.

The youth fixed their mentor with their good eye, recognizing the gesture. "I did not take you for a superstitious man, Okonwe. How unusual."

"These are unusual times, my liege."

Beast uncrossed their arms, looking down at their gloved hand. "They are indeed, my friend," they said. In their palm lay a cursed flower, its stem wrought of a strange, living rock, its blossoms bizarre polyps like open wounds or sores. The sight of these unholy plants had only grown more common in recent days, which made Okonwe's skin crawl. "They are indeed." Beast drew their arm back to toss the flower over the edge of the parapet, and the old soldier caught a glimpse of mottled, black-and-brown scaly skin between the edge of their sleeve and the top of their glove.

"My liege," he hissed, grabbing the youth's wrist. Beast struggled in his grip, but Okonwe had several pounds and several more years of grappling experience on his ward. He carefully pushed Beast's sleeve out of the way to reveal an arm cursed with the same strange blight as the flower. "You promised," Okonwe said, eschewing politeness for parental panic. "You promised you'd tell me if it got worse!"

Beast wrenched their wrist from their mentor's hand. "I have it under control," they said.

Okonwe could hear the tinge of defensiveness in his ward's voice and knew the words for a lie. "Do you?"

They did not reply, which was answer enough.

The sounds of ritual droning and singing faded as the sun crested fully over the horizon, illuminating the village and the valley below them. Okonwe gazed out over the pilgrims who had come from all reaches of the uncharted west to pray, plead, and petition for deliverance. Beyond the city gates lay a ramshackle shantytown, its ragged edges growing with each passing day as more and more refugees poured in from every corner of the Morning Realms, fleeing the Warlord's justice. He could hear the *tok-tok-tok* of their begging bowls rhythmically calling for attention as the pilgrims wended and wound through the streets.

"It's not enough," Beast said quietly.

Okonwe shot them a sharp glance. "What's not enough?"

"Everything." Their eyes glistened in the early morning light. "There's not enough food. Not enough shelter. Not enough." They curled their fists. "I'm not enough."

Sorrow and pride closed their painful fingers around Okonwe's heart. "It is not on you, my child."

"Isn't it?" Beast's gaze hardened.

Okonwe said nothing because he could not say the words weighing on his chest. *You cannot run from your true name and be who you are meant to be at once, beloved.*

Instead he simply rested a dark-skinned hand on his ward's shoulder. "The Qirin Tulku and his clerics will find a way."

Beast watched the sages in their sage-colored robes make their way back up the 888 steps to Dzong Castle. "Will they?" they asked bitterly. "The Hands can't even admit to the people that the Pillar is dying."

Okonwe flinched. Behind them, in the courtyard below, a massively gnarled and weathered tree grew from the stones. The Pillar. The most sacred site in the uncharted west, perhaps in all the lands touched by the rising sun. "The Hands are poring through every book of magic and history in the library," the old soldier said. "I'm sure they will find a cure."

Beast scoffed. "What they need is a book that has been lost for thousands of years." They shook their head. "No, we don't need magic. We need a miracle."

Okonwe looked to the refugee camps surrounding the village. "We need a few more pairs of eyes is what we need." His ward followed his gaze.

"You think we'll find people who can read the Language of Flowers among *them*?" Beast was skeptical. "The Warlord burned more than books; he burned anyone who could read them too."

"My liege never knows."

"You always say that," Beast grumbled. They waved their hand.

"Fine. I'll speak with the Unicorn King about granting access to the library should we find another translator."

The old soldier nodded. Only the ordained and those with special dispensation from Qirin Tulku himself were allowed to set foot on the hallowed grounds of Dzong Castle. "I'll start my search today."

Beast studied the roots of the Pillar. A scaly blight was spreading up from the courtyard, through its trunk, and up to its branches. The black-and-brown mottled bark mirrored the skin of their arm, and they tugged at their sleeve self-consciously.

"Go," they said in a low voice to Okonwe. "Be discreet. And be quick." They fixed their eyes on the single white flower blooming in the shape of a star on one of the uppermost branches of the holy tree. "I fear," they said, removing their glove to study their cursed hand, "that we are running out of time."

ACKNOWLEDGMENTS

Writing acknowledgments is harder than writing a book.

And writing books is really, really hard.

If an author's job is to evoke, capture, or describe the depth and breadth of human experience with words, then I fail every time I sit down to write acknowledgments. Using words is my job, but try as I might, I can never find the right words to convey the intensity and enormity of my gratitude to the people who have been with me through the ups and downs of getting this book to publication. Nevertheless, I shall try my best, and hope the following know that my feelings are magnitudes deeper and larger than I can write down here.

First, to my editor, Eileen Rothschild, and my agent, Katelyn Detweiler. Never have there been champions so stalwart, so gracious, and so *patient*. You have both held my hand through every rough draft and version of *Guardians of Dawn: Zhara,* encouraged me when I needed kindness, and pushed me when I needed a come-to-Jesus talk. You have taken care of my mental well-being, and you gave me space to find the right story, no matter how long it took, and for that, I am forever in your debt.

Many thanks are also owed to Denise Page and Sam Farkas at Jill Grinberg Literary, and Lisa Bonvissuto, Rivka Holler, Meghan Harrington, and Brant Janeway, as well as the entire team at Wednesday Books, for helping turn this book from a story in my mind to a story out in the world.

Second, to Lemon, Renée, and Rosh. There are friendships made for a reason, a season, and a lifetime, and yours are for a lifetime and beyond.

And last, but certainly not least, to my family. To my parents, Sue Mi and Michael, and to my little brother, Taylor, thank you for being my safe place. To Bear, for being my helpmeet, White-Harp's play-mate, and Castor and Pollux's fun parent. I love you.